Praise for *Die for Me*

"I'm obsessed. Lyrical prose, relatably complex characters, a steamy love story with mounting dread that is at once sensual and full of yearning . . . *Die for Me* is utterly unique and still at its core about the most universal of stories: a woman vanquishing fear through love."

—Ali Hazelwood, *New York Times* bestselling author

"*Die for Me* is bold, edgy, and hypnotic. It lures you into its dark and intoxicating world from the very first page. Sean and Julian are a roller-coaster ride that I couldn't predict and never wanted to end, and Obuobi's voice is crystal clear. Stunning."

—Lyla Sage, #1 *New York Times* bestselling author

"*Die For Me* is extraordinarily beautiful and sharply original. Shirlene Obuobi has crafted a story rich with passion, heart, and an emotional intensity that holds nothing back—it kept me up long after midnight and I have zero regrets. Quite simply a stunning read."

—Nalini Singh, *New York Times* bestselling author

"Edgy, sensual, powerful, *Die for Me* proves Obuobi to be an up-and-coming powerhouse. With deft genre bending, Obuobi gives romance and paranormal readers what they're salivating for—and then some."

—Christina Lauren, *New York Times* bestselling author

"A gripping paranormal romance that had me utterly obsessed from the first page to the last. Obuobi's characters are sharply crafted and their chemistry is deliciously addictive—one of my favorite romances of the year."

—Kaylie Smith, #1 *New York Times* bestselling author

"Smart, sexy, and addictive—a paranormal romance that hits every single craving. I *loved* it."

—Abby Jimenez, *New York Times* bestselling author

"This smart, sexy novel by Obuobi . . . is already drawing praise from romance heavyweights . . . Bracing and addictive."

—*Marie Claire*

Praise for *Between Friends & Lovers*

"*Between Friends & Lovers* was an absolute joy to read, with messy, realistic, and deeply lovable characters. . . . Obuobi's perfect balance of humor and wisdom made this one a true standout."

—Emily Henry, #1 *New York Times* bestselling author

"I adored *On Rotation*, so I had high expectations going into this book, but with *Between Friends & Lovers*, Shirlene Obuobi gave me a once-in-a-lifetime reading experience. It's sweet and steamy, perfectly written, overflowing with heart, and it became an instant favorite. . . . Basically: I'll recommend this book for eternity!"

—Ali Hazelwood, *New York Times* bestselling author

"This book is spectacular! It is deft and voicy, sexy and emotionally brilliant. I am honestly obsessed with Shirlene Obuobi's *Between Friends & Lovers* and cannot wait to shout about it to every reader I encounter."

—Christina Lauren, *New York Times* bestselling author

"Meaty, complex, and steamy. Obuobi takes it all on! Add *Between Friends & Lovers* to your TBR; this is an author to watch."

—Abby Jimenez, *New York Times* bestselling author

"Obuobi's emotionally insightful novel explores the tension between friendship and love." —*The Washington Post*

"Shirlene Obuobi's sophomore novel is a beautifully written depiction of being vulnerable enough to love deeply and be loved that same way in return. *Between Friends & Lovers* is sexy and heartfelt, and I still think about Mal and Jo all the time."

—Riss M. Neilson, author of *A Love Like the Sun*

"If you delight in complex, charming love stories, this one's for you."

—*Marie Claire*

"Obuobi tackles the reality of being a medical professional, racial microaggressions, and the meaning of family. *Between Friends & Lovers* is at times heart-wrenching, but, in the end, it is absolutely charming."

—*Booklist* (starred review)

"Obuobi's second novel is a powerful exploration of finding yourself . . . a vulnerable, page-turning tale about trust, mental health, and second chances. Read this book—doctor's orders."

—*Kirkus Reviews* (starred review)

Praise for *On Rotation*

"As a fan of *Grey's Anatomy* (and *Chicago Med*!), I couldn't put down *On Rotation*, and you won't be able to either. Shirlene Obuobi makes you feel as if you're actually right there with the lovable Angie, and I personally couldn't get enough."

—Meg Cabot, *New York Times* bestselling author

"Smart, funny, and utterly swoon-worthy, *On Rotation* is a layered and deeply compassionate novel of navigating life and love in your twenties. Angie Appiah will be your new best friend."

—Grace D. Li, *New York Times* bestselling author of *Portrait of a Thief*

"*On Rotation* is a charming story from start to finish. The ending will melt your heart!"

—Tracey Livesay, award-winning author of *American Royalty*

"*On Rotation* by Shirlene Obuobi is part rom-com, part coming-of-age story—a book so full of life that I badly missed Angie, Obuobi's protagonist, the moment I finished. It's been a rough couple of years for all of us, so scoop up this completely delightful debut for a shot of joy."

—*Marie Claire*

"Obuobi's debut features a winning cast of characters who alternatively help and hinder Angie, whose first-person narration is warm and relatable. . . . Obuobi ably navigates plot twists and emotional turns while addressing millennial angst and issues facing Black women. A funny, emotional page-turner that will have readers rooting for Angie."

—*Booklist* (starred review)

"A genuine delight from start to finish, *On Rotation* will appeal to fans of Rainbow Rowell, Talia Hibbert, and Ali Hazelwood and resonate with any reader who enjoys multicultural, multifaceted, inclusive love stories starring unapologetically strong and complex women."

—*BookPage*

"Fresh, romantic, and hilarious . . . The story of a Ghanian American medical student, *On Rotation* is whip-smart and sharply observed, filled with laugh-out-loud moments while not shying away from heavier issues. With *On Rotation*, Shirlene Obuobi establishes herself as a writer to watch."

—Brenda Janowitz, author of *The Liz Taylor Ring*

"Humor and honesty leap off the pages of this addictive read. A binge-worthy romance with a hilarious and relatable heroine that will steal your heart from the first sentence."

—Jane Igharo, author of *Ties That Tether*

"Narrated by a strong lead with an unforgettable voice, *On Rotation* is an original romance novel bursting with charm, humor, and the most lovable characters. I'm besotted with Angie and her posse!"

—Lizzie Damilola Blackburn, author of *Yinka, Where Is Your Huzband?*

"If you're looking for a swoon-worthy beach read, you've found it."

—*Good Housekeeping*

"Obuobi offers a thoughtful storyline that just about every young person can relate to."

—*POPSUGAR*

"Author Obuobi, a physician and cartoonist, is in her wheelhouse chronicling the hectic, and sometimes solitary, life of a medical student. The often witty footnotes, frequently describing medical jargon or Ghanaian traditions, add an amusing flair to Angie's personality, but the novel's true strength shines in its more serious moments. . . . Guaranteed to make your heart beat faster."

—*Kirkus Reviews*

"This effervescent story is a treat."

—*Publishers Weekly*

Shirlene Obuobi is a Ghanaian American cardiologist, cartoonist, and author who grew up in Chicago, Illinois; Hot Springs, Arkansas; and The Woodlands, Texas. Her novels *On Rotation* and *Between Friends & Lovers* have been featured on multiple national outlets such as *Teen Vogue*, *The Washington Post*, and *Good Morning America*.

ALSO BY THE AUTHOR

Between Friends & Lovers
On Rotation

Die for Me

SHIRLENE OBUOBI

First published in Great Britain in 2026 by

an imprint of Quercus
Part of John Murray Publishing Group

This paperback edition published in 2026

1

A CIP catalogue record for this book is available from the British Library

PB ISBN 978 1 52944 855 9
EBOOK ISBN 978 1 52944 853 5

Typeset by Adobe Garamond Pro

Printed and bound in Great Britain by Clays Ltd, Elcograf S.p.A.

Papers used by Quercus are from well-managed forests and other responsible sources.

Quercus
Carmelite House
50 Victoria Embankment
London EC4Y 0DZ

John Murray Publishing Group
Part of Hodder & Stoughton Limited
An Hachette UK company

The authorised representative in the EEA is Hachette Ireland, 8 Castlecourt Centre, Dublin 15, D15 XTP3, Ireland (email: info@hbgi.ie)

For those who have been told to shrink, to dim their light for others' comfort, or to choose an agreeable status quo over their own dignity and truth. For those who have broken down their carefully structured lives and rebuilt them, brick by brick, on stronger foundations. And finally, for my Black girls who squinted at the pages of the paranormal romances of the early aughts, wishing to see themselves there. *Die for Me* is for everyone, but it's especially for you.

For those who have been told to sacrifice their own light for [illegible] [illegible] [illegible] [illegible] [illegible] [illegible] who have [illegible] [illegible] lives [illegible] their [illegible] [illegible] [illegible] the edges of the [illegible] [illegible] [illegible] [illegible]

Love . . . is a risky business.

Shere Hite, *Women and Love*

Die for Me

One

The Grand Ballroom of the Edison Mansion is a study in gold: gold velvet curtains, gold pillars, gold candelabras from which amber-colored flames flicker and flare. Brandon Pendersen, my colleague and fellow Broadview Hospital lifer, fits right in with a gold satin tie that matches his new wife Leila's golden beach waves. I still remember his first wedding, fifteen years ago, under a sagging drop ceiling in the basement of Chicago's city hall—Brandon in an ill-fitting navy suit, Winona, his ex-wife and my best friend, in a vintage tea-length dress she'd thrifted from Goodwill two weeks earlier. They'd had nothing between them but five hundred thousand dollars in student loans, thirty cumulative hours of sleep that week, and a promise to love each other forevermore . . . which Brandon broke two years ago when he fell in lust-love with the twenty-something-year-old device rep with whom he is currently swaying to Ed Sheeran's "Perfect."

Under the table, I text Winona.

Winny. You sure it's okay for me to be here? It feels wrong.

Winny's response is immediate.

Of course I'm sure. I asked you to go. And besides, Sophie needs an ally out there.

My eyes flicker to Sophie, Winny's twelve-year-old daughter, who is sitting at the head table in a burgundy cap-sleeved dress and examining her black fingernails with the determination of a preteen who can be forced to sit still but not to put on a show.

Well, if it's any comfort, Brandon's hairline looks like someone drew it on with a marker.

I can almost hear Winny's laughter in my ears, more wheeze than sound, like she's choking on a marble.

Oh my god the plugs! You should have seen what they looked like when they were growing in. Like a Christmas tree farm on New Year's Eve. Was hoping they would all fall out for his big day.

Trust me girl, that would've been a blessing. He looks a mess right now.

Like an old man in denial, Winny responds.

I snort, then take a sip of Bordeaux to cover for it.

Brandon invited the entire interventional cardiology subsection to his wedding, but I was still shocked to receive an invitation. On a professional level, he and I were still cool. We covered each other in the cath lab when one of us was running late, traded calls when necessary, jumped in on each other's cases when we needed a first scrub with more experienced hands than our trainees could provide. On a personal level—well, he'd courted and eventually cheated on my best friend right under my nose at our shared place of work. Maybe our many years of calling ourselves a throuple had given him the impression that he could split my allegiance like he had his daughter's custody, but I was Winny's before I was his, and I would be Winny's forevermore. When Brandon betrayed Winona, he'd betrayed me too, spat on the sacred union that was husband, wife, and perpetual third wheel. For all his faults, Brandon should have been smart enough to know that.

And yet he'd still invited me to his wedding.

"I know you hate me right now," Brandon had said as he'd handed me the wax-sealed gold envelope. "But I still consider you my friend, Sean. I really do want you there."

Later that night, I'd asked Winny if she wanted me to burn it.

"I want you to go," she'd said instead. "If only to bear witness."

To the end of their marriage, as I had once its beginning.

The ballroom erupts with applause. I place my drink, and my phone, down on the table, plastering what I hope is a polite smile on my face as Brandon dips Leila into a passionate kiss on the dance floor.

"Gorgeous," Joseph Krause, one of the four other interventional cardiologists at my table, says. He's twenty-five years older than the rest of us and clearly losing his edge in the lab. Despite this, he still sees himself as a steward of the kind of wisdom that requires imparting whenever he senses he's losing the spotlight. Like now. "Second weddings are always much more romantic than firsts, don't you agree? You've learned more about yourself. Know what true love *actually* looks like."

My colleagues, most of whom have had lavish second weddings themselves, laugh. I exchange a queasy look with Haoran, the only man at our table still with his original wife, a lovely woman named Katherine who cuts furiously at her chicken breast and pretends not to care that the rest of the table seems to think she has an expiration date. Her arms are sloped, doughy, and the fine lines on her forehead have never seen Botox or filler, and she'd once confessed to me at a work dinner that she too felt like it was only a "matter of time."

I don't agree. Haoran is dutiful and kindhearted, a family man through and through. He also, however, isn't the confrontational type, which means that while Krause expounds on his idea of true love only being found on the second go-round, he says a whole lot of nothing.

Which means I have to be the bad guy.

"I don't really understand the need to get married again, in that case," I say, tilting my head to the side. "If you don't know yourself well enough to reliably keep a vow, why make another one?"

Once upon a time, seeing Krause shoot daggers at me from across a table might have made me nearly wet myself. Nowadays, it's like watching a baby throw down his rattle.

"You've never been married before, right, Sean?" Krause says, tossing an arm around the back of his (second) wife's chair. She beams up at him, either unaware or unfazed by the fact that she is being used as a prop. "I'm not sure you would understand."

"I'm not particularly interested in tying myself legally to someone, no," I say primly.

"Yes, I'm sure there's a line of suitors just banging down your door," he sneers.

I hold back a snort. Krause doesn't know that I was once engaged—albeit to a horrible man—or that my phone log is full of texts from guys who made it to date three and are begging for a chance at number four. Men like him can't comprehend that they might be the worst thing to happen to a woman. They can only conceive of themselves as a gift, even though most of us consider Krause a very powerful nuisance on his best day.

"I see you've been by my place," I snip. "You can take a ticket, if you'd like."

Krause's scowl thins his lips so much that they disappear behind his Colonel Sanders–esque white mustache.

"Marriage gives you stability. A home to go back to," he says. "Eventually you'll get old and gray, and all those suitors you turned your nose up at will head out for greener pastures. You should settle down before you run out of options."

The laugh that escapes my chest is hoarse with righteous indignation.

"Is that why you cheated on your ex-wife?" I ask. "Because she was getting a little too old and gray for your tastes?"

Krause's wife gasps, someone chokes on their drink, and Katherine gives me an appreciative look. Meanwhile, Krause's hold on his fork tightens like he's thinking about lodging it in my neck.

"Oooookay. Daggers away," Haoran, ever the peacekeeper, says. "I propose a toast—to an open bar on Brandon's tab!"

We raise our glasses, Krause begrudgingly. Then, before our tentative peace can be disrupted, the emcee clinks a glass; it's time for speeches.

For the rest of the program, I keep my attention on the happy couple, who look up at each other with sugary smiles as friends and family exalt them and their relationship. The mood is light and airy, as if the happy couple formed their bond at a run club rather than through clandestine meetings in the cath lab supply closet. The Pendersens are many in number, but I note that Leila's side is eclectic, strikingly young, and only takes up one table. I'd pieced together her backstory through brief conversations we've had since she started working at Broadview: parents who died young, an older brother who followed only a few years later. What family she has now she had to forge on her own—something that I felt had connected us. Before she became my best friend's ex-husband's love interest. Still, for a wedding celebrating such an unseemly union, it's surprisingly mundane. By the time the third speech ends, I'm fighting back yawns.

Then Leila's man of honor steps up to the microphone, and the whole room stills. He's tall, brooding, a storm cloud of a man, crackling with an unmistakable and unteachable magnetism, and racially ambiguous in the sort of way that makes me wonder whether his hair would curl if he grew it out.

My type? Not exactly; I usually like my men to be a little less *pretty*. And older. Considerably older than the twenty-something years this young man has on him. And yet here I am, working half the muscles in my face to keep saliva from oozing out of the corner of my mouth. Questionable choice in current husband/former affair partner aside, Leila sure has some good taste.

"Hello everyone," he says, in a deep, vaguely British-accented voice that is as smooth and sonorous as a cello's hum. "I'm Julian."

"Hi, Julian," the room calls back. He smiles, almost bashful, and every person in the room sits to attention as if someone has turned a crank.

Okay so this is very inappropriate, I text Winona, after I have picked up my jaw. But Leila's man of honor is FOINE.

Really? Winona responds. Omg. You should snatch him up. She steals my husband, my best friend steals HER best friend. It's perfect.

I suck in my inner cheek. Yes, Julian is glorious, but not glorious enough to settle my unease. All of these festivities, all of this money, has gone to celebrate the breakdown of Winona's family. Almost everyone in attendance knows her, but not one person has asked after her, skirting around her existence like she's a Bloody Mary who will appear in the middle of the ballroom if they say her name thrice. Only Sophie seems to serve as a reminder, her cascade of dark curls, sand-colored skin, and bulbous eyes too unlike the Pendersens' Scandinavian features for anyone who greets her to forget their origin. Over an elaborate crystal centerpiece, I catch my goddaughter's eye, then throw her a thumbs-up. Sophie sticks her tongue out at me in response: our shared signs of resistance.

A few feet away, Julian is finishing up his remarks. His speech is pretty standard: cute anecdote about how he met Leila (age fourteen, in her high school cafeteria where he was visiting as an exchange student) and the first time he met Brandon (last year, on the North Avenue Beach volleyball court), well-wishes for the couple. In between staring at him, making faces at Sophie, and texting Winona under the table, I miss most of it.

"And Sophia," Julian says suddenly, turning to the head table just as Sophie uncrosses her eyes. "I know today must be full of conflicting emotions for you. That you might feel like your dad's happiness came at the expense of yours. That by celebrating his new union, we are betraying your old one." He gives her a beatific smile, and she stares back, slack-jawed. "My hope for you is that whatever pain you might feel right now eventually makes room for some joy. Leila might never become another mother to you, but I hope that maybe someday she might become something like a friend."

The tense silence that follows is suffocating, like someone's just dropped a smoke bomb into the room. It's only interrupted by a loud clatter—my phone, sliding off my lap and onto the floor.

At the head table, Brandon tries his best to maintain his composure, but his bride takes it out of his hands.

In a slow, sweeping motion, Leila raises her glass.

"Screw you, Julian," she says, giving him a dazzling smile.

Julian grins.

"Only in your dreams," he says. And then he takes his seat.

Two

Once the lights dimmed for the reception, I excuse myself from the festivities, lingering in the ballroom just long enough to see Brandon's dad spin Sophie onto the dance floor to ABBA's "Take a Chance on Me." My mind shuttles to what feels like a lifetime ago: Winona, Brandon, and I meeting for dinner during residency. Somehow Brandon and I had been placed on the same cardiology rotation, and on a schedule that would allow us to see each other to boot. And so we gathered—Brandon pre-call, me exhausted and post-call, Winona post–proposal defense for her psychology PhD program—around the peeling dining room table we'd garbage-picked three years before, inhaling Taco Bell soft shells between complaints about our micromanaging preceptors. Halfway through her Crunchwrap Supreme, Winny suddenly braced herself against the table, then excused herself into the bathroom. Brandon and I exchanged a concerned look as he raced after her. It took ten minutes for them to emerge, and when they did, they wore identical expressions: shell-shocked but ecstatic.

"Food poisoning?" I asked.

"Worse," Winny said. Then she held out a hand, turning over her fist to reveal a positive pregnancy test. Her eyes welled with tears, and Brandon buried his fingers in her curls to press an adoring kiss to her forehead. "You'll be godmother, obviously. If all goes well."

"Obviously!" I cried, standing up to pull both of them into a hug. Our tears intermixed, three and a half bodies pressed close, nothing between us but love.

And now the "food poisoning" is twelve years old and that love has been snatched away and repackaged for someone else, and here I am, meant to celebrate it all.

At least she hasn't stopped grinning since Julian's speech. I take that as a signal that she's doing well enough that I can afford myself a moment.

I'm wandering around the venue, I text Sophie. Plan to head home at 8?

7:30, Sophie says, ever the negotiator.

Deal, I agree. One hour more. I've burned an hour in worse places than my best friend's ex-husband's wedding, and I know exactly where I want to spend it.

I sweep past the swinging doors that house the kitchen, the pink-wallpapered parlor room, down a short flight of carved cherrywood stairs. Already the sounds of the festivities are behind me, the thrumming of the bass guitar fading to a hum in my feet. Finally I arrive at a closed oak door that I'm sure marks my destination. Looking left and right, I turn the key still stuck in the ornate handle, silently rejoicing at the *click* of its opening. Then, quick as a cat, I slip inside.

The room is large and cluttered; old, wrapped furniture is pushed into a pile on the side opposite a window. I shake out the heavy curtains before throwing them wide open, wincing as golden sunlight spills inside and shrouds my target: a beautiful Steinway and Sons grand piano. I first caught a glimpse of it through this window the night before when I dropped off Sophie at the venue for the rehearsal dinner and thought, *Poor thing. I bet no one touches it.*

I bet correctly. The layer of dust on its lid is thick as a carpet, and when I blow it off, it peels away in tendrils. I lift the fallboard and run my fingers over the keys. To my surprise, it's in tune.

A surge of excitement rushes through me as I pull out the bench. In terms of poor wedding guest etiquette, sneaking away from the reception to play the grand piano tucked away in a hidden room in the venue is probably minor, but it still feels like a thrill. My fingers flex above the keys, and I let them decide what song to play.

They choose Chopin's "Prelude in E Minor." In the still room, each keystroke feels like a stab into the silence. Suddenly I'm no longer in Edison Mansion, a few hundred feet away from a rip-roaring reception, but in a fishbowl-shaped world of my own making. I transition into Lianne La Havas's "Lost & Found," delighting in the responsiveness of the keys, the creak of the pedals underfoot, the sight of the recently disturbed dust still swirling in the orange light of the sunset. I close my eyes, moving by muscle memory, singing its melancholic melody over the music.

Suddenly, an intrusion: an elegant chord progression that harmonizes beautifully with mine. Except I didn't produce it. My body recognizes danger before my mind can grasp it, and my hips reflexively push the bench backward in a bid to escape.

"Sorry to interrupt," the man who has just joined me says, straightening. "I heard you playing, and I couldn't help myself."

As my vision clears, I put him together. A shorn head, bronze skin, long, elegant legs that end in spotless brown leather oxfords, shoulders that seem broader now that they've been freed from their burgundy suit jacket.

Leila's best man, Julian, is looking down at me.

During his speech, I'd been so sure that his eyes were dark brown, but in the light of the setting sun they take on a different hue—amber, maybe even green. His lashes are long and doelike, his features a clash of feminine softness in the lips and masculine angularity in the shape of his face. I think, numbly, that he might be the most beautiful man I've ever seen this close.

"It's okay," I say, adjusting the front of my jumpsuit. Now that I've convinced my body that we were not just in the midst of an assault, I'm embarrassed by my reaction. "I just. Um. Thought I was alone."

Julian settles onto the bench next to me, his shoulders knocking against mine, and I stiffen, bewildered by his presumptuousness. He smells unexpectedly sweet, like vanilla and bourbon.

"Well, you aren't anymore." He lays his right hand gingerly over the keys. "Start again?"

My curiosity gets the better of me. I start the song from the top, and he weaves in his improvisations fluidly.

I can't remember the last time I played like this with another person, making music just for the love of it, feeling them respond to the minute changes in my tempo with their own. I learn more about Julian in one song than I would have in the kind of inoffensive conversation a wedding would require: that he's bold and brash and not afraid to try new things, that he's inventive and creative—and really freaking talented, considering I've probably been playing for longer than he's been alive. When the song is done, we turn to each other, grinning in the resonant silence, strangers no more.

"I liked your speech earlier," I confess.

"Did you?" Julian says, raising an eyebrow. "Didn't think you heard it. You were on your phone the whole time."

My jaw drops, stuck between embarrassment that he'd noticed me and astonishment because, well, *he'd noticed me*.

"You were watching me, huh," I say.

Julian turns to face me, the corners of his eyes crinkling in a smile that ends before it can reach his mouth.

"You're a very beautiful woman who wasn't paying attention to me," he explains plainly. He doesn't give me a second to recover from the first shock before delivering a second. "It's Sean, right?"

I raise an eyebrow.

"How do you know my name?"

The melody Julian plays now is lilting and familiar.

"Maybe I did a little recon," he says. "Maybe I planned for us to meet like this all along." When I give him a blank stare, he grins. "Okay, fine. Brandon's mentioned you."

The reminder of why Julian and I are one degree removed slaps me back into reality. Of course. He's the best man of Brandon's new wife, a player in his new life. I imagine Leila, Brandon, and Julian sharing a drink after their beach volleyball game, Brandon complaining about me *taking sides*, like I'd once overheard him doing with our colleague Shiv in the cath lab reading room.

"Interesting," I say, finally.

"All good things," Julian assures me.

"Not sure I can say the same for him," I mumble under my breath.

Julian laughs again.

"Well, as you might remember, my name's Julian," he says, holding out a hand for me to shake. I take it. It is unexpectedly soft, but its grip is firm. "And I know it's not good to speak ill of the groom, but I don't blame you."

An age-old reflex to defend Brandon springs to my mind, and I bite my tongue and push it down. For so many years, I'd fielded complaints about Brandon's sometimes prickly nature with an "I know he seems like a hardass, but he's actually a good person," comforted the residents who came to me after he'd reamed them out with assurances that he was harmless. Because he was. He cried when his favorite clinic patients died and bought breakfasts for the trainees who worked weekends in the ICU. Kept an eye out for the learners who looked confused but were too scared to voice it and took special care to go over a topic until everyone in the room had absorbed it. Organized a committee of guys to move me out of the apartment my ex and I shared in six hours flat and build my IKEA furniture in my new studio.

He'd been, for the most part, a good man. I'm not sure when that changed. *If* it did, or if, as Krause had said, he'd just gone and found true love in the messiest way possible.

I close my eyes. I'm exhausted. If Sophie and I didn't have an hour-and-a-half-long drive home in front of us, I might have liked another glass of wine.

"Well. This was lovely. But I think I should probably start heading home."

I try to push out the bench to leave, but it's stuck, set firm by Julian's counterweight.

"Did I upset you?" Julian says innocently, as if he isn't intentionally keeping me captive. "I didn't mean to."

"No, I just—" I start.

"Then forget why you're here," Julian interrupts. "And play with me some more."

If there was any doubt in my mind that Julian is hitting on me, it's obliterated by the command in his stare. His eyes are golden now, lupine. From so close, they're a vortex, sucking me in.

"You're pushy," I observe.

"Sometimes you have to be, to get what you want," Julian says, with all the easy confidence of a man who has never been rejected in his life.

"And what you want is . . . ?"

Julian smiles.

"Nothing much," he says. "Just to get a little more time alone with the woman I've been wanting to talk to all night."

I ignore the traitorous thrill in my stomach. *This is a young man,* I remind myself. Somebody's *son*.

"I am thirty-eight years old," I announce, holding my age out in front of me like a shield. "I'm an elder millennial at best. Didn't have a cell phone until college. My goddaughter says I use old lady emojis."

"Yes," Julian says, as if to say, *Your point?*

"And you're, what, twenty-four?"

"Twenty-seven," he corrects.

"Brandon's got some cute cousins your age," I continue. "Did you meet Hannah? Brown hair, bangs? She's lovely, and I'm sure she'd love to meet you. You'd have a lot more to talk about. There's also Bridget; very sharp, very pretty—"

"Just so I understand," Julian says, the corners of his eyes creasing with amusement. "Are you suggesting, based solely on our respective ages, that you and I won't have anything in common whatsoever? That there's no chance that you'll find our conversation riveting? And are you currently offering me to other women in response?"

I cross my arms.

"Be serious, Julian. A riveting conversation is *not* what you're looking for."

Julian's grin becomes a laugh, and his fingers dance over the keys again. I watch the tendons in his hands flex, then look away, annoyed by the hummingbird flutter in my chest. *Pull yourself together, Sean.* Julian's running circles around me, and he knows it. This is probably fun for him. Girls his age have probably gotten boring, but an older, seasoned woman? Better yet, one with an axe to grind, who might consider a night with her best friend's ex's mistress's man of honor a particularly exhilarating form of vengeance? I would be an adventure.

"You're right. I'm greedy. I also want to ask you to dinner," Julian continues. "But for now, yes, a conversation will do."

I narrow my eyes.

"I'm not going to sleep with you, you know."

Julian smiles wickedly.

"Not *yet*, maybe," he teases, and before I can think of a sharp retort, he barrels on. "You were singing when I came in. Why did you stop?"

Heat prickles up my neck. I thought the piano would have drowned me out.

"I'm not much of a singer," I confess.

"Sure you are. You're an alto. You're not hitting any whistle notes anytime soon, but of what I heard, your tone was flawless," he says.

And then he begins to play a song. A few notes in, I recognize it as "Killing Me Softly." He flashes me a smile that is all sugar. "If you're going to deny me the pleasure of a conversation, at least give me another song."

I swallow. I've never sung anywhere I could be heard. It was something I did on my own—in my shower, at the piano in my living room—but never with an audience, and most certainly not with a partner. This is possibly the most intimate thing a stranger has ever asked of me. At any other time, in any other place, I might have feigned humility and changed the subject. But there's something about this room, its glowing flecks of dust, its stacked furniture and floor-to-ceiling French windows, that make it ripe for memory making. My exquisitely handsome companion—whose hand, I've just noticed, spans over an entire octave—is a nice addition to the dreamlike ambience.

"Fine," I say, clearing my throat. *What the heck.* "But maybe you should play 'Smooth Operator' instead."

"I can do you one better," Julian says, and when he starts playing again, I realize it is Sade's "Is It a Crime?"

I throw my head back in delight. Julian has managed to convert a song full of saxophone solos and jazzy undertones into a piano ballad while still remaining recognizable, and I don't know whether to be jealous or impressed.

"Okay, fine, so you know a few good songs," I confess.

"More than a few," he says, and then he settles into the verse and looks to me expectantly.

I'm shy at first, my voice barely a rasp over my piano accompaniment. But after the first verse passes and Julian doesn't burst into laughter, I sing a little louder. By the time we reach the chorus, I've abandoned all apprehension. Julian's shoulders bump into mine as he stretches along the span of the keys, and I find myself leaning into him, thrilled to the point of pleasure when he begins to harmonize with me. His clear baritone adds a haunting, resonant quality to our siren song, and I find myself fixated on the shape of his mouth, watching it stretch and shift around a voice that is clearly trained. He has full, pillowy lips, I realize, the kind that would look fishlike on a less balanced face, and I resist the urge to reach out and touch them. They curve into a slight smile around his open mouth, and my own goes dry.

I shouldn't want to kiss Julian. Shouldn't be wondering how those large hands would feel spanning along my back, that supple mouth opening against mine. He's cocky and handsome and I know exactly the kind of damage his type can wreak, and yet I can't look away. When was the last time I desired someone so immediately, and so intensely?

I don't notice that we've both stopped singing. The final note hangs, suspended, in the air.

"You're staring, Sean," Julian purrs.

"Am I?" I whisper, inching ever closer to my mistake. "How rude. I should definitely know better."

Julian's chuckle is breathless. He shifts his body closer to mine, brushes a thumb against my chin in a caress as bold as it is bracing.

"Don't worry," he says. "I like it."

There is no question that Julian is going to kiss me. More puzzling is my realization that I am going to let him. The sun has shifted away from us, but Julian's eyes still seem to glow, the flecks of gold and green in his irises spreading like moth's wings as his pupils shrink into pinpoints. *Beautiful*, I think distantly, but also *That's wrong, shouldn't they be getting bigger—*

The door jostles open.

"Auntie Sean?" a tinny voice says.

I spring away from Julian in horror . . . and promptly tip off the piano bench. I land on my side hard, downed like a felled tree.

Terror that she is, Sophie bursts into laughter.

"W-What are you doing here? I thought we agreed on leaving at seven thirty?" I stutter, my face burning with humiliation. Julian extends a hand to help me up, but I ignore it, dusting off the seat of my pants.

"It *is* seven thirty." Sophie stuffs her hands into the pockets of her dress, looking wickedly from Julian to me and back again. "You're the homewrecker's best friend. The one who gave the speech."

"*Sophia*," I warn, but Julian bites back a smile.

"Pleased to meet you," he says.

Sophie grunts noncommittally, but even from across the room I can tell that she's blushing. Christ, do my twelve-year-old goddaughter and I have the same taste?

"Okay, enough of that, we're going," I say. I give Julian a brief sidelong glance, as if a part of me knows that looking any longer will suck me back in. "Thank you, Julian. It was lovely playing with you."

"You're not going to give me your number?" Julian asks, a smile in his voice.

"I gave you a song," I say plainly, and then I hold out my hand for Sophie to take. "Ready to hit the road, nugget?"

"Duh, that's why I'm here," Sophie responds, her preteen impertinence contradicting her childlike hold on my hand.

We walk out the door of the music room, out of Edison Mansion, onto the grounds.

I don't look back. Something, a primordial instinct, tells me to keep moving forward.

Three

Two hours later, I pull into the driveway of the monstrosity that is Winona's house. The four-bedroom, three-and-a-half-bath behemoth nestled in the center of Oak Park has all the trappings of new money: a cream brick façade, a manicured front lawn, and a "Secured by ADT" sign peeking out from the holly bushes. It's a home much too big for a two-person household, but despite her complaints about the high property taxes and the neighborhood's draconian homeowner's association, Winona hasn't been able to let it go.

Motion sensor lights click on as we disembark, illuminating the front door just as it swings open.

"Hi, baby," Winona says to Sophie, who folds into her embrace like she needs it. "How was it?"

Sophie shrugs.

"The cake was gross. I don't know whose idea it was to cover it with black fondant but it literally tasted like chalk. Thankfully they had cupcakes, so I had one of those instead. And the chicken was, like, super dry, but Dad let me have some of his brisket and that was pretty good."

Winona's mouth screws up like she isn't sure whether to laugh or reprimand her daughter.

"Well, thanks for being a good sport. I know it was important to your dad that you were there." She looks up at me with shining, haggard eyes. "You got your bag?"

I swing my overnight tote into view.

"Of course," I say, inviting myself inside.

The living room of the former Pendersen-Evans household is sparse. Brandon and Winona purchased the home with the intention of having an interior designer outfit it to both of their tastes, but when Brandon met Leila and his interest in his familial home waned, Winona deferred her refurbishing dreams for the three-bedroom condominium that she is still yet to purchase. What Winona has by way of furniture is a peeling pleather sectional with a matching La-Z-Boy that is in even worse shape and an already aged Persian rug that has made the move from her parents' attic to the grad school apartment she'd shared with me to the one she'd shared with Brandon before finding its home here.

It is on this rug that Winona and I, after sending Sophie to bed, debrief.

"So . . ." Winona says. We've changed into comfortable jersey pajama sets, and the baggy shirt hangs limply over her thin frame.

"So," I say.

We laugh in bitter unison.

"Well, I've heard Sophie's opinions," Winona says. She blows over a mug of Earl Grey. "Where're yours?"

When your best friend asks you what you thought of her ex-husband's second wedding, you have a moral obligation to tell her it was shit.

"For one, I got put at the Boys and Babes table," I start, using our nickname for my interventional cardiology group and their significant others. "Krause was Krause. One of Brandon's cousins kept badgering me about how I look like a woman he once worked with until I reminded him that I was familiar because I was Brandon's ex-wife's maid of honor. And Sophie wasn't kidding about the cake."

Winona hums, satisfied. She stretches across her carpet, dropping her head back until her curtain of black curls brushes against the floor. She is runway pretty, all harsh lines and heavy eyelids. We used to joke that we were aesthetic opposites, her gaunt, Burton-esque features contrasting with my rounded, lush ones.

"What about the fine-ass man of honor?" she says after a moment.

I take a too big gulp of my chamomile tea.

"What about him?" I say.

"You get a closer look?"

Without warning, I am back on the piano bench, Julian's face hovering right before mine. His gaze ticks slowly from my eyes to my lips and back. This memory of him—because that's what this has to be, a memory, though I'm not sure Julian had leaned in so close, so long—seems strangely solid. I can feel the heat of his body radiating close to mine, the final notes of the piano dispersing like smoke. I resist the urge to reach out and touch him, and as if he can hear my thoughts, he smirks, the corner of his mouth turning up in an expression I'm quite sure I haven't seen before.

"So . . . ?" The word forms around Julian's mouth, rounding his lips to an O, but the sound produced isn't his voice or his intonation. *Winona's*, my mind supplies sluggishly, remembering where I am. *She's talking to you.*

I wag my head to shake him away, but Julian lingers, seared into an afterimage on the back of my closed eyelids.

"Oh, she got a real close look," another voice answers for me.

All at once, my vision clears enough to catch my goddaughter peeking through the railings of the stairway. Heat rises to my face. The little snitch.

"I know you know better than to be in grown folks' business," I say.

"And you should know better than to lie," Sophie taunts. "You were about to kiss him. I was there. I saw. Which is really weird because you, like, *just* met him."

Oh, I cannot *wait* to use that line on her in four years or so when she asks her Auntie Sean to cover for her teenage debauchery.

"Bed, Soph," Winona says with some force, and we endure a few minutes of whining ("I'm not a baby, Mom!") before Sophie's bedroom door finally slams shut.

The instant it does, her mother rounds on me.

"You almost *kissed* him?" Winona hisses. When I don't immediately deny it, she smacks me with a throw pillow. "Oh my god, Sean! How could you not lead with that?"

"It felt wrong," I admit, ashamed. "I shouldn't have even entertained him."

Winona might claim that me cavorting with her ex-husband's new wife's best friend would be the perfect revenge, but I know that a dalliance like that could cause distance between us. Julian is Leila's. He'd walked her down the aisle and everything. How could I have let myself forget that, even for a moment?

"We aren't twenty-two anymore," Winona says, interrupting my thoughts. "There aren't rules of engagement like there used to be."

"What do you mean?" I ask.

Winona shrugs.

"You know, that we can't talk to each other's exes or be friends with girls I don't like. All those guidelines we had to follow to demonstrate our loyalty. We're past that. You know as well as I do that life is too short for all that BS." Winny grins.

"You're my soul sister, Sean. And I would very much like for you to have some fun. Even just so I can get the tea later."

"Winny . . ." I start.

Winona holds up a hand.

"I don't want to hear it," she says. "I do, however, want to hear about this guy. And spare me no details. I want to know name, height, build, ethnicity, and how you ended up all snuggled up."

I snicker, then indulge her.

Sleep descends upon me that night. One second I am slipping under a pink paisley comforter in Winny's guest room, and the next I'm immersed in a realm of darkness, trapped in a purgatory of consciousness between wakefulness and slumber. And then suddenly a snap, a room. It is familiar, bustling, the colors oversaturated and blurred like I'm staring at it through tear-filmed eyes. I recognize it as Brews and Beans, the coffee shop at my hospital.

There is a man sitting at a window. He is well-built, tall. His long legs stretch elegantly out under his table, his broad shoulders angled toward the street. I feel a desire, suddenly, for him to perceive me. Want more than anything for his eyes to meet mine and hold. I know what they will look like: amber, burning like hot coals in a sculptural face.

As if he can sense my interest, the man turns and gives me a syrupy smile.

"Dreaming of me, Sean?" Julian says, and I startle awake.

Four

Monday rolls around. I drive to work with circles under my eyes, knowing that I will be desperately needing to stop in at the very coffee shop that haunted me all weekend for my much-needed caffeine fix. I've been sleeping like crap for the last two nights, no thanks to a certain unwelcome visitor who keeps infiltrating my dreams. It seems like every time my eyelids flutter shut, Julian is there behind them, giving me the same infuriating, knowing grin from a table or behind the espresso machine or at my kitchen counter. I jolt awake what feels like every few hours, my body humming with so much frustration that I almost text Dave, the cute but self-impressed law professor who'd bought me a drink a few weeks back, to come over and relieve it.

What is wrong with you? I think as I step into the back of the line at Brews and Beans. *He's just a pretty man you had one sort-of romantic moment with. Get over it.*

My phone buzzes: one of the cath lab nurses, Pamela, sending me a text.

Patient's in preop, Sean. Rolling in five.

Shit. It's the morning rush, and the line for coffee stretches around the corner of the shop. A single beleaguered barista bustles behind the bar while another takes orders in a brusque, businesslike tone. Maybe it's time to cut my latte habit and invest in an office Keurig. I look at the cath lab schedule on my phone: my first patient is a complicated case and will probably take at least an hour. My male colleagues could get away with strolling upstairs late with a cup of coffee, but I learned quickly that the staff and patient families tended to be less forgiving of me. Blowing out my frustration, I step out of line . . . and right into a firm chest.

"Sean?" a voice says.

It's familiar, deep, with a perfect, musical tone, and it takes me a second to realize that it's the same one that's been echoing in my skull for the last two nights. Except now it's here, in the exact coffee shop where I'd last imagined it. Where I'd last imagined *him*.

I sputter. Blink. Bite down hard on my cheek. The pain is like a lance—sharp, bright, *real*. I am, to my relief, most assuredly awake.

"Owww," I say, raising my hand to my face.

Julian looks down at me. He looks confused but pleased and not at all like the smug creature who leers at me in my dreams.

"Sorry about that," he says, holding an arm out to keep me from toppling over. "Didn't mean to startle you."

Without my heels, Julian is a full head taller than me, and I have to tilt my chin up to properly meet his eyes. Even dressed simply in a maroon sweater and jeans, he's stunning, and the simple fact of his beauty is irritating. Even more irritating is the steaming cup of coffee in his hand. My uncaffeinated goblin brain stews with envy.

"What are you doing here?" I say.

"Had some business in the area," he says vaguely. Before I can ask more questions, he grins. "I see I've caught you in your natural habitat."

I grimace. In my OR bonnet, yellow lead-lined radiation goggles, and too-big hospital-issue scrubs, I know that I'm a far cry from the glamorous woman who'd caught his eye at the wedding.

"Yeah, well, only briefly," I grumble. "My first patient's almost on the table and this line is too long. Nice seeing you, but I've got to run."

A hand closes over my upper arm before I can make my escape, and I glance down at it, affronted. I thaw some when I look up to meet Julian's face; his expression is tender.

"Wait," he says. "How do you take your coffee?"

"Either black or loaded with milk foam and flavored syrup, no in between," I answer automatically.

Julian drops my arm, then holds out his cup.

"This is a caramel latte," he says. "Take it."

My jaw drops, and I look from his earnest face down to the proffered coffee.

"No, no, I couldn't do that," I say, shaking my head. "I should have gotten here earlier, I—"

"I haven't drunk from it, and I can always get back in line and grab another," he says. "You, however, should be adequately caffeinated before you go up there and save lives."

"Don't go invoking any emergencies for me today," I grumble, my hand already closing over the cup. It smells divine. "But thank you. I appreciate it."

Julian doesn't let go. Our fingers overlap, the knobs of his joints sliding against my skin, and the touch sends a curious, bracing sensation through me, like I'm being pinched awake by a cold breeze.

"And in exchange," he says, "I'm going to insist on getting your number this time. No running away."

I snort. In my front shirt pocket, my phone chimes; probably another text from Pamela telling me to get a move on.

"You're so persistent," I say, but both of us recognize that it's not a rejection, and I watch the corners of his eyes crease with victory. Out of the light of the setting sun, they are a normal, human brown.

Julian's stare smolders as I type my number into his phone.

"Great," he says, saving my contact. "Try not to be a stranger."

"Yep," I say, already scurrying away.

"I mean it!"

"Okay!" I call back, then make a break for the elevator and try to tell myself that the flush in my cheeks is all exertion.

My patient is not yet prepped when I burst into the cath lab control room.

"Oops," Pamela says. She's dressed like me in scrubs except for a face that looks like it's been given the star treatment in a makeup artist's chair. "Probably could've given you a bit more time. Just didn't want us to leave the patient waiting."

She's right, of course. If she applied that principle more evenly, I probably wouldn't resent her for it, but I know she wouldn't dare call Krause a second before he was needed. Sighing, I collapse onto a chair and log on to a computer, taking a long draw of my ill-gotten coffee.

"Who's on call again today?" I ask. "Because it better not be me."

"Pendersen," she says.

"Brandon?" I repeat, stunned. "Isn't he on his honeymoon?"

Pamela screws up her mouth like she's hiding a secret. Which, well, she probably is. She's a veritable vault of cath lab secrets, if a vault could be reliably cracked opened with two tequila sunrises and five minutes of hopeful nudging.

"He canceled it," she says. "And he signed up for, like, all the moonlighting slots this month. Methinks wife number two is a little *expensive*."

I pull up the schedule, and lo and behold, there he is: B. Pendersen, signed up for half the shifts. Between clinic, his intensive care blocks, and lab days, he's left himself three days off this month.

"He's going to die," I mutter, just as the door to the control room opens and Brandon storms in.

He looks harried. Whatever glow he had in the ballroom of Edison Mansion is gone, replaced by the gray, wan expression he'd worn during much of his divorce proceedings.

"Where is my patient?" he says to Larry, the nurse manning Cath Lab 2. It's a tone that would earn me serious side-eye and a feature in the group chat as the bitch of the week, but Larry looks up at Brandon, nonplussed.

"Still in preop," Larry supplies. "Ten minutes."

"Ten minutes?" Brandon says. He makes a show of looking at the board. "It says up there that this case was supposed to start at seven thirty. It's eight fifteen. What's wrong with the picture here?"

Pamela turns to give me a look, both perfectly shaped eyebrows arched high. There's a loud screech; Larry, scooting back in his chair. He's been working in the cath lab since Brandon first learned his ABCs and is known to take very little shit.

"Things run late sometimes," he drawls, with the patience of a saint. "Don't know what to tell you."

Whatever bluster Brandon had been sporting seconds ago blows out. He scratches the back of his neck, suddenly sheepish.

"Sorry," he says. "It's been a long week."

"I was about to ask whether we needed to go get you a Snickers bar," Larry huffs. "Coming in here like a diva."

"Just trying to see what I can get away with," Brandon quips.

They both laugh, and the cath lab warms back up to its normal temperature. I turn back to my computer screen, pulling up my patient's chart to prepare for my next case. I'm so immersed that I don't notice the presence behind me until I hear someone clear his throat.

"Thanks for making it out Saturday, Sean," Brandon says. He looks a bit hopeful, a bit guarded, and I refrain from rolling my eyes. "And for taking care of Sophie. I really appreciated it."

"Don't mention it," I say. I turn back to my computer screen, scrolling through the results of my patient's last stress test. Behind me, Brandon doesn't budge.

"And for getting her home after," he continues. Then after a pause, "How's, um, Winny doing?"

My fingers still over my keyboard. I want to snatch Winona's name out of his mouth, cut out his tongue like a vengeful medieval king might his impudent subject.

"Why don't you ask her yourself? She's the mother of your child. You talk every week." I push away from my desk and make to stand. I can practically feel Pamela's drama-seeking antennas extend toward us with interest.

"O-Of course," Brandon stammers, and I tamp down the part of me that still sympathizes with him. He's always been like this: capable of feeling shame, but also of blowing through the discomfort of it to get exactly what he wants and then expecting absolution afterward. Maybe if circumstances had been different. If he'd gone about things the proper way—informed Winona that he was developing feelings for someone else, moved out, done the administrative work of filing for divorce—I could have given it to him. As it stands, the most I can offer him is tolerance.

I peek through the window that separates the control room from my cath lab. My patient is ready. Stepping around Brandon, I strap on my lead skirt and apron, then step outside to wash my hands.

Our late start means that I work through lunch, which would be more tolerable if I'd remembered to eat breakfast this morning; I make it through all my morning cases on nothing but Julian's coffee and two of the donut holes Larry brought in from the shop next to his house. I feel like Superwoman. I am also in grave danger of passing out.

Lunch is one of the prepackaged meals I keep in the break room freezer to tide me over for days like this one, when I'm too harried to remember to bring something better. I nuke my cauliflower rice power bowl for the four minutes suggested on the box, then push up my goggles and pull out my phone.

There are seven text messages waiting for me, but I skip those, head for emails first. The cardiology service wants to add on a case for a diagnostic coronary angiogram, and Brandon's schedule is stacked for today, can I do it? I answer ("sure," no punctuation or capitalization because I am an interventionist and efficiency is key), then skim through the rest—the November service schedule, an email from my doggy daycare supplying me with my daily photo of my bully mix, Onix.

It's only then that I open my texts.

Winona: absolute cluster of a morning. Had like three intakes with forty somethings with incurable cancer. This JOB.

Winona: Anyway I just sent you a calendar invite for Sophie's dance recital next month, as I have recently been made aware that she expects you to be there. Let me know if you can make it!

Questionably Literate Bakery Guy: how was ur weekend gorjus?

Pamela: your 1pm patient ate breakfast at 9am, push him to 3 or reschedule for tomorrow?

I'm mid long-suffering sigh when I notice them: two texts from an unknown number that halt my breath halfway down my throat.

(Unsaved number): any chance you appreciate art as much as you do music?

(Unsaved number): [image]

I tap the image, and it expands on my screen, revealing a slickly designed announcement for a gallery opening by Margaret West. *PERPETUITY,* the title reads, in dense, italicized font. Underneath it, a maelstrom of colors: one of Margaret West's pieces. The event starts at nine p.m. this Saturday.

My phone buzzes in my hand.

(Unsaved number): this is Julian Conrad, by the way, and I would very much like you to save my number as such.

I smirk. It's as if Julian can see Questionably Literate Bakery Guy two text threads down from his. I save his name, but respond back: as opposed to . . . ?

Julian's response is prompt: something impersonal, like Handsome Charming Talented Pianist.

I snort. Oh wow. I see you're quite the humble one.

> Humility is so often a farce, don't you think? I'm aware of my charms. They've gotten me this far, after all. Besides, I don't think my pride could take it if you responded to me with a "who's this?"

Sean: You have to earn the contact save. Demonstrate that you're consequential.

Julian: Oh, I can show you consequential.

Julian: But if we're playing that game, I'm going to save you as "songbird."

Sean: How very presumptuous of you, giving me a pet name before a first date.

Julian: If you think bullying me is going to scare me off, I'm afraid you're sorely mistaken. I have a thing for mean women.

Julian: Oh, and if it's not abundantly clear, this is me asking you out.

I'm grinning at my phone and thinking of a good response when the door to the reading room swings open.

It's Leila.

Leila is gut-punch pretty. Her skin is tawny, almost the same color as her hair and only a few shades lighter than her yellow-green catlike eyes. She has an extra-large pink thermos in one hand and a tote bag in the other, and her fitted forest-green scrubs showcase a lithe body.

She is also, to my chagrin, kind of a sweetheart.

It's a naïveté that's gotten her in trouble—Pamela and I once spent a week walking her to her car in the parking garage because one of the security guards mistook her politeness for romantic interest and started following her out of the hospital. The saga only ended when I flashed my stun gun and reported him to his management. He'd gotten fired, something Leila had worried might have been too much, but still appreciated.

"Hi, Sean," she says in a high, bashful voice. "You're in the lab today, right? Do you have any cases you might need me for?"

I should hate her, but I can't. Before she and Brandon began their dalliance, I really liked having her around. She's a bright young woman, thoughtful and whip-smart, and as a device representative for Palette Biotech, she's walked me through some pretty neat new equipment for the lab. And though at twenty-four she is most certainly an adult, she feels less culpable than the forty-year-old father who made her into his second wife.

"I don't think so," I say, giving her a quick smile. "Does Brandon?"

Leila nods, then starts rambling about the complex atherectomy that Brandon is planning for this afternoon. I listen impassively, wolfing down my lunch as quickly as possible. Romantic relationships between proceduralists and members of the interdisciplinary team happen so frequently that I don't think the hospital could stop them from working together even if they wanted to, but it's still curious to me that the smiling couple has come rushing right back to work as soon as possible.

I don't have time to think more about it before my phone screen lights up again on the table. Leila's gaze drops to the screen reflexively before jumping up to me, beaming.

"Oh my god, you're talking to Julian," she says, raising her fists in excitement. "I'm so glad. He hasn't shut up about you since the wedding."

The look I give her could probably cut steel. I'm still formulating my response—because she genuinely sounds pleased for her friend, and I'm realizing that most of my annoyance is because I don't want Pamela to be lurking in the halls and waiting to call me a cougar in the group chat—when the door opens again and Brandon marches inside.

Leila twists to smile up at him and it's as if I've become a part of the furniture. Brandon's hands fall on his wife's sides, and suddenly his shoulders drop and the tense frown lines at the corners of his mouth loosen. I'm reminded of the Brandon I met in medical school, the one whom the residents used to send into patients' rooms after delivering bad news. The one who could charm a snail out of its shell, a person out of their tragedy.

"Hey, kitty," he says gently.

Leila unfurls into him like a curling leaf reaching for the sun. Her lips brush his stubbled chin, and he relaxes like she's just injected life back into him.

My stomach turns. I feel like I'm witnessing something indecent. By the time Brandon notices me, I'm already tossing my empty bowl into the trash.

He releases her. The instant they step apart, a shadow falls over his face once more.

"Sean," he starts.

I don't let him finish.

"All yours," I say, gesturing toward the empty reading room. Then I flee.

The lab gets busy fast. The simple diagnostic coronary angiogram I allowed the floor team to add on to my schedule during lunch turns out to be a nasty lesion that takes me and my fellow, Aaron, an hour and a half to fix up. Then our first patient of the day sits up too early in postop and opens his femoral artery access site, and it takes Aaron almost forty-five minutes of holding pressure to stanch the bleeding.

Miraculously, we make it through the rest of our cases before five thirty. I rip off my gown, tear the shoulder strap off on my lead apron, and am about to step into the control room, home free, when Pamela's voice rings into my headset.

"Keep your lead on, Sullivan," she says. "I think they might need you in the other room."

I peer through my window, across the control room, and into Brandon's. I can't see much around the equipment, but I can see Brandon's movements, frantic and harried, his gown soaked through with blood.

Before I can make sense of the chaos, the side door to the supply room blasts open and Leila and Larry rush out, hands full of unopened gear.

"What's going on?" I ask, following them into Brandon's room, where shit is most definitely hitting the fan.

"RCA dissection," Leila explains, handing a package over to the nurse who is running Brandon's lab. "What's your glove size?"

"Six," I say, and she scrambles to retrieve a set for me as I open up a gown.

"Is that Sean?" Brandon says, from behind the table. "Thank god. I need a hand."

He gets me up to speed as he works—"Proximal RCA CTO, got the wire past the lesion, definitely in the true lumen, dissected to the first acute marginal after we ballooned"—and together we talk through the plan and delegate tasks: "I'll prep a balloon pump." "What do you think? Covered stent?" But as we do, I make a few troubling observations. This case is a two-man job at minimum, but Brandon's fellow is nowhere to be found. The images Brandon flicks through of his attempts to fix the blockage demonstrate that this was a predictably tough case, and yet he appears woefully unprepared. There are no necessary meds on the table, no venous access site, none of the safeguards we lecture our fellows about every other week.

It's unlike him. For all his faults, Brandon is a damned good interventional cardiologist, and a careful one too. Of all my colleagues, he's the one I'd trust the most to work on my mother. This feels . . . reckless for him. Haphazard.

I look to Leila. She stands a few feet away from the table, her hands tucked into the top of her burgundy lead apron, stone-faced, irritated, and colder than I've ever seen her. As if he can't help it, Brandon looks up to meet her gaze. She pulls her own away.

Brandon's movements slow. Even among the chaos, I can sense his despondency behind his mask.

All the while, the patient's blood pressure is plummeting.

"Brandon," I hiss, just as Larry shouts, "Pressure!" into the mic from the control room.

The patient's heart rate drops: within a few beats, I know he's in complete heart block. I curse, grab a needle, jab into the vein in his groin.

"Pads on the chest," I tell the nurse, and then, to Leila, "Get me a pacing wire. *Now.*"

An hour and a half later, we finally leave the lab. The patient, now stable, is transferred to intensive care for monitoring. Complications happen, and this case was high-risk; the patient has known Brandon for many years and is understanding.

But I am pissed.

"Thanks for jumping in," Brandon says, giving me a wolfish grin and a pat on the shoulder. "Just like old times—"

I shrug his hand off.

"It was *not* like old times, because you definitely know better now," I hiss. "Why didn't you have backup access? Where were your meds? Where was your *fellow*?"

There's a beat of silence between us, a moment when I know that I have hooked into a nerve and strummed. But then Brandon's gaze turns glacial.

"I asked for your help, Sean," he says. "Not your judgment."

"I'm trying to understand what happened in there," I say. "I *know* you, Brandon. We all make mistakes, sure, but—"

"Exactly. We all make mistakes. So maybe instead of putting on your typical, self-righteous, 'I'm the only one who actually cares about people' act, you can cut me some slack," Brandon interrupts. There's a warning in his tone, a promise that if I push, he will take us to a place from which we can't return. He holds my gaze for a second that feels like it stretches into eternity, then wipes the sweat from his brow and looks behind him at Leila. "Come on, babe. Let's go."

They walk out. Only Leila looks back at me, eyebrows turned up in a helpless apology.

The instant the door clicks shut, a hand lands on my shoulder. It's Pamela.

"For what it's worth," she says, in a softer tone than I'm accustomed to, "I'm on your side."

I squeeze her hand with one of mine, pull out my phone with the other. I am buzzing with an ugly, roiling sort of adrenaline, and I need a distraction—a mindless cat video, a quick scroll through a social media feed.

I get something better: a text from Julian.

You've left me hanging, Sean. Am I taking you out, or are you turning me down?

I am about to complain when I see the time: eight p.m., a full eight hours after he asked. I bite my lip. *You know what, why the hell not.* Then I respond: All right. I've been convinced. It's a date.

Five

The week before *PERPETUITY*, I dream of Julian Conrad three more times.

In the first dream, we are back in that room in Edison Mansion, except this time Sophie does not interrupt. The last note of our rendition of "Is It a Crime?" rings in my ears as Julian's hands shift from skimming along keys to clutching the sides of my jaw, and when he kisses me it feels like violence. In the next, we are at Brews and Beans, crashing into displays and knocking over kitschy multicolored thermoses and satchels of dark roast in our haste to get at each other's skin. I tug his shirt open, and his buttons scatter.

The final dream is different. Julian sits at my kitchen island, his head propped on the heel of his hand. His stare penetrates, pierces past skin and flesh to probe at whatever lies within, and I find myself frozen, unable to look away. *I need him*, I think. *I need him I love him please don't stop please don't look away from me—*

Something warm and wet slides against my face, and I'm jolted out of my sleep to find Onix hovering over me. Discovering me awake, he rears back in delight, bathing me in dog breath and frantic kisses.

"Onix! Oh my god!" I grab both of his paws, holding him just out of reach. He is not allowed on the bed without permission and is most definitely not allowed to kiss me on the mouth, but, by the relieved wag of his tail, he clearly doesn't regret it.

And if I'm honest, neither do I. Now that I'm awake, I can recognize that what Onix just pulled me out of was a nightmare. My body roils with residual anxiety—my teeth chattering, hands clenching, breaths coming quick and hard. It's not longing I'm feeling, though in my dream my desire for Julian was desperate. It's fear.

Which makes no sense. Because why in the world would I be afraid of Julian Conrad?

Luckily, there are no more random run-ins with Julian in the hospital, and he is yet to materialize inside my house. And while I find him significantly more engaging than, say, Questionably Literate Bakery Guy, my interest in him is measured. I do not spend the days leading up to our gallery date hurriedly searching for an outfit or retightening my locs. When I call Winny, it's to make plans for dinner, not to recount my messages with my newest suitor. Not that there's much to report. The messages with Julian themselves are tame enough in volume, frequency, and content; every other day or so we share songs we think the other will like (to my irritation, he pins down my tastes almost immediately), we discuss our favorite restaurants, and he sends me more details for our upcoming date. He does not text me good morning with an assortment of indecipherable emojis. He does not ask for nudes or hit me up at midnight for a booty call or get annoyed when I take six hours to respond to him because I've been caught up in the lab. He behaves, in general, with more decorum than most men ten years his senior.

On my way, he texts simply, the night of the exhibition. Be there in twenty.

I use those twenty minutes to get ready. The turquoise pantsuit I pull from my closet is low-cut and loose fitting, a look Sophie would describe as "Rich Auntie" and Winona "Tracee Ellis Ross." Next are my earrings, half faces of a woman crafted out of thick gold wire that Sophie bought me from an artisan's fair a few years back. My heels are sensible, the kind worn by a woman for whom maintaining ergonomics is a matter of job security, and my makeup is minimal.

I look good, but I will also be able to eat all the hors d'oeuvres at this gallery without worrying about my bloat.

Julian is waiting outside his car for me when I descend. He's wearing a charcoal peacoat and a gray wool scarf, and his nose is a little pink with cold. When he spots me, his face brightens. And . . . wow. It's a subtle transformation, a shift that takes him from sculpture to real boy, and it rocks me.

"Sean," he says.

"Julian," I manage, inclining my head.

He opens the passenger-side door of his car—a black Audi with a tan interior that smells like new leather—then snaps it closed behind me before walking over to the other side and settling into his seat. The locks click shut.

At the sound, the hairs on my body stand on end and a cool sweat creeps down my back. It takes me a second to realize that what I'm feeling is panic—that, for reasons I can't pinpoint, my body has registered the click of the car lock like the shutting of a trap and is reacting accordingly. But it's immediately assuaged when Julian begins to speak.

"So, what made you change your mind?" he asks, turning a smooth corner.

"About what?"

"About me. I was under the impression that you thought I was a kid, but now here we are, on a date."

"Well, you did rescue me from a terrible caffeine headache," I tease.

"Ah, yes, of course, it was the coffee." He glances at me sidelong, eyes twinkling. "Definitely not my dastardly good looks."

"You're aware of your charms," I say, invoking his earlier words.

Julian laughs. I like the sound of it, hearty, honest.

"I'm guessing if I go fishing for compliments I'm going to come out empty-handed with you, aren't I."

His voice catches just enough for me to realize that he's nervous. I think about what Leila said, that Julian hadn't shut up about me, and soften. This is not the preternaturally perfect apparition who has been slinking around my brain. Julian Conrad is just a guy. A guy who, inexplicably, might have a crush on me.

"I'm curious about you," I say abruptly. "That's why I said yes. Because I think I might just find you interesting."

Julian sucks in a cheek to keep from smiling, and I find that I like that too.

We spend the next ten minutes making bashful, inane conversation before pulling into the parking lot of a small but handsome stucco building just outside the museum district. "Harrison & Conrad Galleries," the decal window sign reads in a curling font. A squat man dressed smartly in all black opens the door.

"Welcome, Mr. Conrad," he says.

In a few paces another man holds out his arms for my and "Mr. Conrad's" coats, and another offers "Mr. Conrad" and me a glass of wine as we head inside, and, dumbfounded, I put two and two together. The smart navy suit Julian reveals under his peacoat is likely not just extremely well tailored, but custom, with emerald cufflinks that gleam not with the crisp, jagged facets of glass but the imperfect glow of the real deal. It appears that my date tonight is *rich*. And not working rich like me, but vacation house in the Hamptons, private musical tutors, "My daddy owns a fucking art gallery" rich.

"Hold on," I manage. "Are *you* the Conrad in Harrison and Conrad?"

The look Julian gives me is sheepish.

"I'm on the board, yes," he offers. "It's mostly a formality, but—"

He pauses, holds up his glass to a woman who is fast approaching us. "Ritika!"

Ritika is dressed like a tempered version of me in a black pantsuit that hints at a muscular chest and arms. She sweeps a lock of curly hair, styled into an asymmetric bob, behind her ear.

"Fashionably late as always, *Mr. Conrad*," she deadpans. Her eyes tick to me, though the glance is not so much hostile as it is curious. She holds out a hand for me to shake, and I take it. "Dr. Sullivan, I presume?"

I reel with confusion that Julian rushes to abate.

"Ritika is my assistant," he supplies.

"As well as his event coordinator, guest wrangler, and occasional house sitter, yes," she says. "Nice to meet you. Love the outfit."

"Likewise," I say. Ritika gives me a stiff smile, then swivels to Julian to get him up to speed: the event is progressing according to schedule but for the DJ, who arrived half an hour late and is just finishing up his set—and Margaret West, the guest of honor, has just asked after his whereabouts.

"We'll find each other," Julian assures her, then gestures for me to enter the hall.

The exhibition space is larger than it looked from the outside, with high white walls and industrial piping above. We're greeted by a biography of the artist, Margaret West, and an introduction to the exhibition. Crisp white downlighting illuminates each of the pieces, which, unlike the colorful image displayed on the website, are composed primarily of rust reds, blues, and gray-brown crusts. Margaret is a master of multiple mediums; even from our position near the entrance, I can see oil and acrylic, watercolor and ballpoint pen, even a sculpture displayed in a raised glass case. Fifty or so guests mill around the space, accepting passed hors d'oeuvres, leaning against the bar, and examining the work as early 2000s hip-hop plays in the background.

Julian gets pulled away by a guest, and so I wander around the gallery alone. Intermixed with the more abstract pieces are more realistic ones: a still life featuring a skull surrounded by rotting fruit, a nude man reaching for the sky as blood pours from his neck. I stop at a particularly strange painting: a woman, dressed in white, is draped dramatically over a table, her arms splayed around her in surrender and eyes squeezed shut in distress as a naked man squats on her stomach. His skin is white pale, and he peers at the observer through a curtain of black hair. The name: *The Recurring Nightmare.*

"It's a recreation of *The Nightmare* by Henry Fuseli." I turn to find that Julian has returned. He cocks his head at the strange skull painting. "That one's referencing a Cézanne. *Still Life with Skull,* I think."

I pull out my phone to look them up and raise my eyebrows, impressed.

"I can't assume a single thing about you," I say. "What exactly do you do for work, Mr. Conrad? Are you a musician? An art historian? An extremely talented nepo baby?"

Julian gives me a lopsided grin like he's just told me a good joke.

"I'm an investor," he says.

I raise an eyebrow. Most of my friends are in healthcare, a side effect of years spent practically living in the hospital, and so he may as well have told me that he wrangles hamsters for a living.

"What does that mean in your day-to-day?" I ask.

"Well, these days, whatever I want it to mean," Julian says, brushing a hand against the back of his shorn head. "I caught a good windfall a few years back. So now, I identify small creators and entrepreneurs with promise and give them backing so that they can have a shot in the market. It's like being a curator. Or even a philanthropist, maybe."

I'd recognized something in Julian, a simmering ambition that suggested that he didn't live in a world where he didn't get what he wanted. Hearing that he's a finance bro doesn't surprise me.

"Does it count as philanthropy if you take a cut?" I ask dryly.

"It's a much smaller one than most," he says. When I snort, he considers me. "I can't tell whether you're impressed or disgusted."

"Neither. You're a dirty capitalist, but aren't we all." I shrug. "Though I have many more questions now."

Julian answers them as we circle the perimeter of the gallery. It was co-founded by his grandfather, Robert Conrad, and his close friend, William Harrison, after they moved to Chicago from England in the 1950s, then converted to a nonprofit when they moved back twenty years later. *That explains your accent*, I say, and he laughs and confesses that it's a bit mangled, a consequence of years of international school and a self-proclaimed addiction to travel. He has no siblings, and like Leila, his parents passed before he could formulate lasting memories of them—"It's how Leila and I got to know each other," he says, and I, who have two elderly parents living out their best lives in a bustling retirement community, am reminded of my good fortune. I learn that Julian's parents left an impressive amount of assets, and much of his time is spent managing them.

"But mostly, I'm a gentleman of leisure," he says. "A collector of beautiful things."

His eyes rove over me as he says it, and I look away and toward the painting before us. It is enormous and, if I'm honest, a little grotesque: orange speckled with splotches of brown and black reminiscent of mildew, tactile chunks of gray-brown arranged like soapsuds along the corners.

"I don't know if I would quite describe this as beautiful," I say.

"You're not supposed to."

I turn toward the voice and find myself face-to-face with an elegant, full-figured elderly woman. She is brown skinned and cat-eyed, a feature she complements with similarly shaped glasses, and her gray hair is cut into a short pixie. Her bone structure is dramatic: high, strong cheekbones leading to a sharply hewn jaw. She's dressed entirely in blue: royal blue wide-leg pants, a textured blue blazer, a cerulean-blue shawl, chunky turquoise jewelry. On her arm is a man who resembles a bulldog, replete with bleary eyes and drooping jowls.

"Margaret!" Julian says, opening his arms to pull her into a hug. Her companion frowns, and Julian turns to him next. "And nice to see you too, Stanley."

Stanley gives a noncommittal grunt, latching himself on to his date. His hostility doesn't shift until Julian introduces me.

"Sean, this is Margaret West, our artist of the hour, and her husband, Stanley," he says. "Margaret, this is Dr. Sean Sullivan, my date tonight."

"Ah, the famed pianist. Such a pleasure to put a face to the name," Margaret says.

I swing around to squint suspiciously at Julian, but he dodges my gaze. I can't tell if I'm flattered or annoyed that he is apparently going around telling everyone who will listen about our clandestine meeting. It feels pushy, like he's trying to make it seem like we mean more to each other than we do.

"It's nice to meet you too. Your work is incredible," I say to Margaret, opting not to feed her curiosity. "Are you an artist as well, Stanley?"

I hope the question is welcome. At cardiology department events, I've always made a point to tend to the non-medical spouses, the (typically) wives of cardiologists and section heads who have grown so accustomed to being treated as their partner's window dressing that they almost tear up when I ask them about their interests.

If Stanley is comforted by my acknowledgment, he doesn't show it. His eyes swivel lazily to me and hold for one contemptuous beat, before he says, in a voice that sounds like it needs a good clearing, "No."

Well fuck you too, I think, but I don't let my smile waver. I bring my attention back to Margaret, who is considerably more pleasant to look at.

"Not every day you get to meet the artist as you appreciate their work," I say. "Would it be irritating if I asked you what this one means?"

The corners of Margaret's lips quirk in an almost smile.

"I'll only tell you if you promise to keep it a secret," she says conspiratorially.

"Of course," I say, intrigued, and she gestures me closer. Her perfume is heavy but pleasant—an overlay of almond tones on tonka bean that envelops me like a warm embrace. She clasps my shoulder to draw me into her, and I tense at the force of her grip, how it triggers an instinct to fold my hands behind my back.

"It's a lobster," she whispers.

She releases me, and I draw back, confused. She laughs, a tinkling sound.

"What?" I say.

"Lobsters don't die unless they're killed. Left to their own devices, they can theoretically live forever. And I found that fascinating. Look at this simple, ugly creature, able to achieve the immortality that humans have been searching for as long as we have existed. Death is something that *could* happen to them, not an inevitability." She pulls back, holds my gaze for a moment. There is a flicker of tension, and for one bizarre second, I wonder if she's going to kiss me. Then she grins. "At least that's what I read on some forum on the internet. It's not true, of course. They get to fifty years or so, then stop molting and suffocate. I should have looked it up. But you know, by the point I thought to do my own research, I was already three pieces deep. So here we are!"

"Oh," I say, discombobulated. I turn back to the painting to reorient myself, and suddenly it becomes abundantly clear what I'm looking at: a macro view of a lobster's shell. "Oh! I see it!"

When I glance back at Margaret, she looks pleased. She lifts a finger to her lips in a coy "shush" motion, then hooks her arm through Stanley's.

"She's lovely, Jules. Excellent catch," she says with a wink, and then, before I can decide whether her assessment of me is complimentary or patronizing, she sweeps away, and her husband stumbles after her.

I watch them cross the room, Stanley's steps lumbering alongside his wife's confident strides.

"How did that happen?" I mutter.

Julian snorts. In the time I've spent chatting to Margaret, he's acquired what appears to be an old-fashioned, and he clicks his glass to mine before beginning a slow amble around the gallery's perimeter.

"She's got a thing for ogres," he says. "You should see some of the guys she dated in the seventies. You'd think she found them under a bridge."

When I ask Julian about how he came to meet Margaret, he regales me with a tale of an artisan's fair in Katy he attended as a teenager, a gigantic kaleidoscope of a canvas that Margaret revealed to be a tortoiseshell.

"Our realities are nothing but perspective, she told me. Something that appears beautiful at first glance can be horrifying when examined up close. Something simple, complicated; something wicked, good. It changed how I thought about, well, everything." He stops, lowering his gaze to me. "Everyone too. It becomes a little bit of a game for me, I think. Meeting people and trying to guess who they are beneath the façade they present."

"Ah, so I'm being actively psychoanalyzed," I say, bemused. "All right. Let's hear what you've come up with. Who do you think I am?"

Julian smiles and takes a small sip from his drink.

"Well, let's start with what's on the surface," he says. "You're a Black woman in a well-respected, male-dominated field that required fifteen years of grueling training to enter. You're thirty-eight, single, and don't have children, and thus the same accolades your male counterparts are praised for cause others to be suspicious and resentful of you. You're rarely respected and regularly undermined, and your attempts at being agreeable have probably historically led to you being taken advantage of, and as a result you've developed a tough, no-nonsense exterior and a sort of . . . deliberateness to your actions that can come across as cold to those who aren't accustomed to it."

I rear back to squint up at him; his assessment is oddly astute, even if it is a little reductive.

"I'm curious," I say. "Do you think it's *just* an exterior? Am I stone all the way through, or all soft and squishy under the surface?"

Julian smirks.

"Oh, definitely the latter," he insists, and I raise a hand to my chest in faux outrage.

"A baseless accusation," I declare. "Take it back."

"I will not," Julian challenges. "You care so much about your friend that you gave up a rare weekend to drive an hour and a half both ways to take her daughter to an event that you would rather have swallowed glass than attend, where you tipped the bartender handsomely and helped wheel one of Brandon's elderly great-aunts to her table before dinner. You checked in regularly with Sophie to ensure she was comfortable and greeted the people you knew from Brandon's side first to ease any potential discomfort around your presence. And then, likely exhausted by the many hours spent taking care of everyone in sight, you sought your solitude."

The air between us shifts, and I feel it again: that charge that sparked between us when we first met in Edison Mansion, tension so electric it shifts across my skin like static. My mouth opens to respond, then clamps shut. Julian has, to my astonishment, succeeded in stunning me into silence.

"You weren't joking about watching me," I manage after a moment. I don't know how I feel, now that I know how closely I was being observed that night, how closely he continues to observe me now.

Julian tucks one of my locs behind my ear, his fingers skimming ever so lightly against my cheek.

"Did you think I was?" he says.

This is the seduction I expected, I think, as I watch his eyes darken, his gaze drag jaggedly down my body. It's a safer space than whatever it was he was attempting before—gushing about me to his friends, introducing me to his colleagues, treating me like I'm anything more than a conquest. *I'm grown*, I want to tell him. *You don't need to pretend to want anything other than fun from me.*

But for the next two hours, Julian continues to pretend, and I continue to play along. He loops my arm through his, sweeps me around the room, talks to me about music and art, and asks me questions about myself that I give simple, half-true answers to. ("Yes, I'm an only child." "You're right, I should try caffeine mints." "Yes, I have a dog, his name is Onix. I tell people it's a reference to a brand of stent we use in the cath lab, but he's actually named after the Pokémon. Don't you see the resemblance?")

As the night goes on, the room fills, the lights dim, and the music transitions from a pleasant hum to booming. A party. The crowd gets younger, and they slap Julian on the shoulder or pull him into hugs and smirk knowingly at me. They get rowdier too, drunk off the open bar and the headiness of community and the DJ's infectious energy. I'm drunk too, or at least more drunk than I've been in a minute, courtesy of the two glasses of red wine I'd sipped while we made the rounds and the blackberry mojito I'd downed, given to me by a cute blond woman who complimented my pantsuit. My hangover will be immense, but at the moment, I can't be bothered. I feel good. Better than I have in a long time. My blazer is draped over my arm, leaving me in a thin camisole that clings to my skin. Julian's respectful hands have gotten daring, and when the song shifts to a slow R & B jam, he pulls me backward into him, wraps his arms around me as we sway. I clutch his forearms, closing my eyes, feeling the beat reverberate through our bodies.

"Having fun?" he asks. I feel the brush of his stubble at the corner of my jaw, and I close my eyes and hum in the affirmative. Most days I enjoy my solitude, my quiet apartment, the full breadth of the bed I sleep in alone. But there are small things that I miss. The heat of a man's chest against my back. The feeling of being wanted, desired. Of being wrapped in strong arms and held tight.

Julian pulls me in closer. My ass tucks into the cradle of his hips, his firm thighs. The song changes to reggaeton, and he tilts his hips in an exquisite suggestion.

I hiss, eyes still shut, and accept his invitation. The last time I threw it back on an almost-stranger at a party, I was twenty-three with knees that didn't click on the way down. But apparently wining is like riding a bike, and it only takes a few beats for me to find a dangerous rhythm.

Julian is clearly not new to this type of dance. He follows my lead with ease, not just along for the ride but an active participant, our bodies rolling together in perfect harmony. It's like we're in the room at Edison Mansion again, but instead of making music we're responding to it, transforming it from sound into movement.

Maybe this is why he's been chasing me so doggedly. Maybe he realized back then what I'm just realizing now, that we're compatible in a primal way, possessing the kind of organic, inescapable chemistry that only comes around every blue moon. Maybe the reason why I keep seeing him in my dreams is because my subconscious knows just how sublime it would feel to take him to bed.

I can't tell the exact moment when our dancing shifts to something else, just that suddenly Julian's breath becomes labored, his grip on my hips becoming a downward press. I swallow a gasp. He's hard against me, and the full extent of what he's working with is simultaneously shocking and enticing. As if he can hear my assessment, he rocks into me, slowly, sensuously, and I drop my head back into his shoulder.

"Jesus," he mutters, and I find myself pleased by the fact that he's losing control too, that I am affecting him as much as he is me.

"'Sean' is just fine," I tease.

I feel his smirk against the side of my face as his hands begin to trail slowly higher and higher, dragging up my rib cage until they stop just under my breasts.

"Do you want to do something crazy?" he croons into my ear.

I don't realize that I'm panting until I try to answer. My body burns with warmth and want and wildness. I feel like an iron thrust into coals, a freshly spun pot glowing hot in a kiln. I feel like I'm about to be transformed or destroyed or both.

"Yes," I manage, and Julian snatches my hand and drags me off the dance floor.

Six

Julian guides me out of the gallery, through its swinging glass doors, and down the amber-lit hallways. His pace is brisk, his hold on my wrist tight, and he barely acknowledges the cries of "What's up, Julian?" and "Hey, Mr. Conrad!" that trail us as we storm past. His back is tight with tension, and though I can't see his face, I imagine that his mouth is taut, his brows furrowed.

It's a single-mindedness that should scare me. A man I barely know is dragging me off a dance floor and into an undeclared, unseen space, and I am going with him not only willingly, but gleefully, like a silly, horny coed in a horror movie headed to her certain doom. But that concern feels irrelevant, now that I've had a taste of him. I don't particularly care where Julian is taking me, as long as it's out of sight.

Eventually we come to a door. Julian pulls a key fob from his pocket and lifts it to the knob. The door is barely open before it's shut again, and I'm pinned against it, Julian's mouth open against mine.

He tastes like scotch and smoke, like breathing deep next to a bonfire, and my body sags at the feel of his against mine. Distantly, I recognize that this is just a kiss, that I've had a thousand before it. But I've never felt a kiss like this, never been so aware of the searing sweetness of a tongue sliding against mine or a body pressed close. Kissing Julian feels like a revelation, like how, as a studious adolescent with an obsession with romance novels, I'd imagined it to feel, and I become greedy, desperate to dig deeper, discover more of him. Mindlessly, I help him shove off his jacket, scrabble at the buttons of his shirt to gain access to the sculpted chest I know is hiding underneath it. His cufflinks clatter to the floor, and I run my lips along a neck that is now properly exposed.

Julian's groan is guttural, and in the next second, he's palming my ass and lifting me into the air. I squeak—I'm heavier than I look—but I wrap my legs around him and let him carry me farther inside.

We're in a conference room, I realize. The long oak table is elegant, the black leather chairs expensive. Julian kicks one away, then lowers me carefully onto the table, and finally, we're looking at each other.

His eyes are smoldering. Like he's about to eat me down to the bone. He hardly seems like the same man who picked me up from my apartment earlier this evening, and I can't tell if it's alcohol that has unleashed this beast or if he's been this way all along. He takes my hand, presses it to his lips. Then, with an aching slowness, he drags it down his chest, over the ridges of his taut stomach, the trail of dark hair, until finally he's cupped in my palm.

Good lord. *Is that even going to fit?*

"Do you want this, Sean?" Julian breathes wildly, hips roving in a steady grind against me. "Do you want me?"

If I'd known that I was going to end the night getting fucked on a conference table, I might have elected to wear a skirt.

"Yes," I say, sighing when Julian lowers himself to kiss me again, when he slides the V of my camisole open to expose my breasts, drags himself down my body to trail kisses down my sternum—

"Oh my," a voice that isn't Julian's says.

I feel like someone has just dunked me into a vat of ice. Reflexively, I tuck myself back into my top, then push against Julian with a firm hand to give me space to sit up and face our intruder.

It's Margaret. I thought she'd left hours ago with the rest of the over-sixty crowd, but here she is now, tapping her chin thoughtfully with one finger as if finding Julian topless and bent over his date is as shocking as happening across a stray cat.

"Not wasting time with this one, are you, Julian," she says with a smirk.

"Have you heard of *knocking*?" Julian says, his voice still husky.

"It's a conference room, dear. Not exactly private."

My face feels hot. Julian doesn't seem mortified by Margaret's interruption, like her insinuation that she regularly catches him in flagrante with his dates has weight.

"Get out, Margaret," he says.

Margaret's eyes glint with amusement.

"Sure, sure," she says. "Have fun, kids."

The door clicks closed, and suddenly we're alone again.

"We got carried away, didn't we," Julian breathes. He drops his head onto my shoulder and laughs, then presses a soft, indulgent kiss onto the damp skin of my neck. "Would you like to take this somewhere more private? I live close by."

His suggestion jolts me back to life. I think about my behavior over the last few hours and wince, because what the hell have I been doing all night? Grinding on the gallery's owner in full view of all his friends and colleagues. Almost letting him have his way with me on a hard table that would have definitely given me bruises, in the middle of a party, with a crowd of guests a stone's throw away. Julian was right about one thing: I am usually very intentional. And tonight? I have been everything but.

I push him gently aside and propel myself off the table, snatching my discarded blazer from the floor.

"I think I've had enough for tonight," I say, pleased to find that my voice doesn't shake.

I don't turn back to look at Julian, but I can hear him scrambling around the room as I slip through the door. Outside, the hallway is empty, the only evidence of the ongoing party a steady thrum of bass from the DJ's soundtracks. My walk of shame, it seems, will be largely unwitnessed. I make for the coat check, pulling my phone from my pocket to call for a ride and pretending not to hear the sharp clack of footsteps echoing behind me. Just my luck—there's a driver right around the corner from the gallery. I make it to the counter and give the attendant a bright smile just as Julian stops beside me. Out of the corner of my eye, I catch the glint of his emerald cufflinks and marvel at how he managed to gather them up and still take chase.

"Sean, wait," he starts.

"Look, Julian," I say, not looking at him as the attendant disappears into the closet. "I had a great night. But that was very out of character for me, and I think that's as good a sign as any that it's time for me to go home."

"It was out of character for me too," Julian says, breathless. "Honest."

I turn to him then, raise an eyebrow. He's a bit flushed, and his shirt is gaping open underneath his blazer. It's the first time I've seen him look even the slightest bit disheveled, and he more than pulls it off.

I'm struck, suddenly, by how little I believe him, and how much that pisses me off. There's nothing in his expression that should make me feel this way—he's damn good at playing at sincerity, all desperate, wide eyes, parted lips, and upturned eyebrows—but I'm not stupid. The man I met in the conference room has had practice, and I wish he'd stop pretending otherwise.

"It doesn't matter to me, you know." I dig in my pocket for cash for a tip, then hand it to the attendant as he gives me my coat. "If you do stuff like this often. We just met. You don't owe me anything."

Julian winces, and I'm not sure what he's wounded by: my insinuation that we are strangers or that he's a bit of a slut.

"You're right. I don't owe you anything. But I think you could be someone special, and I want you to take me seriously. And I think that maybe I got ahead of myself tonight and gave you the wrong impression. I have to apologize for that." His voice softens, and he shifts closer, leaning forward with one arm on the counter. "Sean, please. Look at me."

I do. It's obnoxious, really, how beautiful this man is—even more so when he begs. A weaker woman, a woman I was once, would have bent to a face like that long ago. She would have never left the conference room.

"No need to apologize, really. I had a great time." Right on cue, my phone dings; my ride has arrived. "Have a good night, Julian."

Julian doesn't respond right away, not until my arms are through my coat and I've walked through the gallery's glass doors. I hear his footsteps behind me, one, two, then a final, resigned third; he is letting me go.

"Get home safe," he says.

His voice is thin, but it carries, whisps too loud past my ears and through my skin. I shiver, and not from the chill. I feel like mist, sifting through his fingers.

Outside the gallery, the air is crisp and cool. I tilt my head to the stars, then step into my car.

I don't notice that I've left one of my favorite earrings behind until I make it home.

"You did *what*?" Winona says, hand clapped over her mouth.

On the weekends when Brandon has Sophie, Winona drives into the city after drop-off to hang out with me. Normally, we spend Sundays with our laptops out, catching up on patient messages and clinic notes, but today is different, because I have a development.

I.e.: getting caught with my tits out by a glamorous old lady I met at an art gallery while making out with a trust fund kid eleven years my junior.

Brunch talk.

"I'm not particularly proud of it," I say, stabbing at the slab of fried chicken overlaying a waffle. It's exactly the kind of meal that will land me on my own cath lab table in fifteen years, but damn it if it isn't necessary right now.

"Are you kidding me?" Winona exclaims. "I am! In fact, I'm so proud that I could weep."

I scoff. It's hard to believe that the vixen who'd nearly hooked up with Julian in a conference room not even a full day ago is me. I am boring, work-obsessed Sean Sullivan. I can't remember a time when I might have considered asking a guy if he had a condom on him, because all the sex I've had in the last decade was somewhat premeditated, in a controlled environment, and after careful review of my partner's STD test results.

"So? When are you going to see him again?" Winona asks.

I dab syrup off the corner of my mouth.

"I'm not sure."

There's a sharp clink; Winona has dropped her fork.

"I'm confused," she says. "What's the problem? Has he not reached out?"

"Um, yes. He has." I clear my throat. "Called me, actually."

"And . . . ?" Winona prompts. "What did he say?"

I bite my bottom lip.

"I . . . didn't pick up." Before her jaw can drop, I hold up my hands to defend myself. "I was in the gym!"

"And I'm sure you called him back after." It's not a question, because she already knows the answer.

I swallow. "He left a message."

"Which you haven't answered."

"I don't know how to respond!" I confess.

It's true. When I left the gallery, I'd felt so certain that I'd done the right thing by walking away. An iron wall had fallen in front of my heart, reverberating as it slammed shut—because I knew, with certainty, that Julian Conrad was too good to be true.

But he's since brought a battering ram to my defenses, and I'm starting to feel them shake. Most of what I've assumed about Julian is based on his superficial attributes—his youth, his looks. What if I'm judging him too harshly, failing to see him beyond his façade, as he'd attempted to see beyond mine? What if he wasn't lying through his teeth when he said that he wanted me to take him seriously?

My cheeks warm in a familiar, upsetting way, and across from me, Winona freezes.

"You like him," she whispers. Then, louder, her eyes sparkling with mirth, "Oh my god, you *actually like* him!"

A group of women sitting at a table a few feet away snicker along with her, and I lean back, crossing my arms in defiance.

"Volume, Winny," I mutter, waiting for her to gather her wits.

"I'm sorry," she says, dabbing her eyes with a napkin. "It's just . . . it's been so long since I've seen a besotted Sean. I forgot how completely *useless* she could be."

"Now you're just being mean," I say, but my ears are burning and my stomach is leaping and I know that she's right: I am indeed crushing on Julian, and admitting it to myself, even if just the tiniest bit, feels like participating in the Polar Plunge. Exhilarating, maybe, but supremely stupid too. I might die of hypothermia.

"In my defense," I say, "he's almost impossible *not* to like. Even his voice is sexy."

"Can I listen?" Winny says, holding out an expectant hand for my phone. I navigate to my voicemail, and she lifts it to her ear. I know when it starts by how her eyes widen, and I know what she's hearing, because I've listened to it a thousand times: Julian's voice, pitched low into a growl that is clearly not for public consumption. His tongue curling around the syllables of my name like an incantation.

Sean Sullivan, the message begins. *You seem to enjoy running from me. Unfortunately for you, I'm quite tenacious, and I'm not above using petty tactics. I'll be seeing you soon.*

Winny lowers my phone. Sighs. Takes a swig of her water.

"What, and pardon me saying," she says, "the hell was that?"

"I know," I lament.

"I *felt* something, and that wasn't even meant for me."

"I *know.*"

We look at each other, then squeal in unison.

"Okay, now I need to see what this man looks like," she says. "I need to know what face goes with that voice."

I'm already scrolling through my phone to find the pictures from Brandon and Leila's wedding.

"He isn't on social media," I say as I search. "Trust me, I've looked. No Instagram, TikTok, not even a LinkedIn."

"Rich *and* private," she coos. I hold up my phone to the one picture I have of him, snuck at the end of his speech. It's in profile and a bit out of focus, but it still gets the point across.

Winona moans around a bite of French toast, so loudly that a waiter squeezing behind her barely muffles his laughter.

"That is absurd," she says. "No way that man is flesh and blood. He looks like AI."

"Oh, he's flesh and blood all right."

Winona wags her eyebrows suggestively, and this makes us laugh even louder. When we recover, smacking our chests and downing our water to clear our throats, Winny taps a finger against the table.

"And the petty tactics?" Winona asks.

"He's holding my earring hostage," I explain, biting back the enormous grin that threatens to bloom across my face. I show her another picture, this one of my wire-face earring held up by its hook next to a torn piece of paper with the date. Under it, a text: if you ever want to see her again, you know how to find me. I wait as she scrolls maniacally through the rest of the thread.

Sean: wow. are you resorting to extortion now?

Sean: fine, I'll hear you out. What do you want.

Julian: You know what I want, Sean. The question is, do you love your precious little face earring thing enough to give it to me?

Sean: You're a very nasty man, to do this. You know Sophie gave those to me, right? My goddaughter?

Julian: Nasty? You're the nasty one. I'm not asking for anything improper. I'm just trying to get a second date.

"That's it, I'm officially jealous," Winny says, handing back my phone with a pout. "This just gave me necessary inspiration. It's high time I put myself out there too. Find some strapping young cutie to help me get my groove back."

She says it as a joke, but I know there's truth to it. Winona is an objectively beautiful woman, but she's also a working mom who has been cast aside by her ex-husband for a pretty little thing who doesn't have her C-section scars or her smile lines. There's only so far positive self-talk can go in restoring her self-esteem. What she needs is cold, hard evidence. Emphasis on the *hard*.

"I agree," I say. "You've been through it, Winny, and it's time. Go get wined and dined like you deserve."

"Wined and dined sounds lovely," Winny says wistfully. She sighs. "I can't even remember the last time I had a . . . little romance, you know? I feel sexless down there. Like a Barbie doll."

"I get that," I say distractedly. "There's only so much healing you can do on your own. You have to put yourself out there, learn to trust your judgment again."

The moment the words leave my lips, the mood shifts. Winona puts down her fork, folds her hands on the table, and stares at her French toast like she half expects it to walk off her plate.

"I'm happy for you, you know," she says. "You haven't been this excited about a guy since, well . . ."

Acid rises to my throat, and I dab my napkin to my lips to push past it. I know what she means, but the young woman who had once been caught in my ex-fiancé Eric's web doesn't exist. I cast her in a fire alongside our engagement photos and watched her burn.

A hand covers mine, and when I meet Winona's gaze again, she's giving me the look. The one that means that she is ceding the floor to me, reminding me that no matter how many times I've recounted this particular trauma with her, she's here to listen again. It's the same regard that she gives to her cancer patients who are grappling with the question of their mortality alongside side effects from chemo, providing a safe space for them to scream and mourn in ways they can't with their families. The depth of her compassion is what makes her clinic routinely run late, but also what probably makes her the most beloved psychologist in her practice. And without a doubt, an incredible friend.

"I'm sorry," Winona says, when I don't fill the silence she's provided. "I shouldn't have brought him up in this context."

I shrug.

"Yes, well, he's unfortunately a very relevant part of my story," I say. "Besides. You're probably right."

And I hate that she is, because I hate what it bodes for me. Sean in love is not a reasonable woman. She abandoned herself for a man who held her in an ever-tightening grip, who abandoned her in turn as she bled out on the carpet. She accepted disrespect and even rage and made herself compact, and I cannot ever go back to being her. Not for anyone. Ever again.

"For what it's worth, I think this is a good thing," Winny says. She squeezes my hand. "Even if you aren't totally sure what you want out of this. You're healing, Sulley."

I smile and squeeze back.

"Healing, and having fun doing it." My smile becomes wicked. "Which, if I'm honest, I'm not sure you're capable of having. You care too much."

Winny crosses her arms, affronted.

"I am capable of fun!" she insists. "Besides, when will I have *time* to foster a relationship? Sophie has dance, Science Olympiad, and violin practice, and between mom duties, work, and grant application deadlines, I can barely find the time to cook. Whoever I meet will have to be fine with a little 'wham bam thank you ma'am' every other weekend."

"Oh, you'll definitely be able to find *that*," I say, and we snicker as I guide Winona through my assortment of dating apps—"LMT is my favorite—it's professionals only, so you don't have to swipe through bums"—when a text lights up my screen.

It's from Julian—another picture, this time of my beloved earring dangling over what appears to be the Chicago River. I'm running out of patience, Sean. And Ms. Face is running out of time.

Winona lets out a laugh.

"I swear to god if you don't text that poor man back, I will," she declares. Then she props her head up on her chin. "In the meantime, please teach me your ways."

I do not teach Winona much of anything, on account of having zero game and acquiring the affections of a baddie purely through chance and despite objectively poor behavior. We do create an account for her on LMT, though, and for the next week she sends me photographs of eligible bachelors (Darren, forty-two, engineer, "Proud dad of 2, Go Astros"; Manny, thirty-two, financial planner, "high-value man, first three dates won't be dinner"; Lawrence, twenty-six, project manager, "My secret talent is getting back my hoodies after you steal them.")

I respond to approximately half of them. Not out of lack of interest, but because I can hardly muster the energy to get through my clinic day, let alone sufficiently roast some of the creatures she is sending my way (though in the case of Lawrence—whose potbelly and male pattern baldness suggest that he's either the very rough twenty-six he's claiming or a still-struggling forty-seven—the jokes write themselves). Since Monday, I've been hit with a sudden, deep-seated exhaustion. It feels like I've got the flu, though all the rapid tests I've snuck from urgent care keep coming up negative. If I hadn't spent the last five years regularly placing stents into patients on a cumulative two hours of fitful sleep, I probably would have collapsed at the cath lab table.

When I tell Winny, she gets concerned.

"Your flu tests have been negative? COVID too? Had your iron levels checked recently?" she asks, then flips through a laundry list of symptoms—*Body aches? Fevers? Chills?* I'm exhibiting none of them. I understand why she's worried; so many of her young female patients showed up first with fatigue before being found to be riddled with cancer. "Keep a symptom journal. And maybe call out and rest?"

The last thing I want to do is call out, and so I ignore her second suggestion but take the first. Every morning before work I scrawl a line into one of my hundred brightly colored notebooks, always the same: *Feel like death. Managed to walk Onix before daycare but only went a block. No shortness of breath, no congestion, no pain, tired.* Just the act of recording seems helpful in its own right.

As it is, I stay standing, everyone stays alive, and I make it through Friday morning clinic without having to cancel anyone's long-awaited appointments.

"Dr. Sullivan," my medical assistant says, popping her head into my office as I finish up clinic notes. "Um . . . there's someone here for you."

I push my chair back from the table and give her a weary look.

"What time was their appointment?" I ask, rubbing circles into my temples. It's a moot question; we both know that I'll see them anyway.

"They . . . aren't a patient," she says. She looks outright delighted, and I squint with suspicion, which only mounts when she follows me out to the front desk.

I see Julian's admirers before I see him—a room full of brightened cheeks and shyly averting eyes. He looks out of place in our standard-issue clinic chairs, like a grown man sitting in a plastic playhouse seat. My body's reaction is instant, a sudden wash of delight, like I'm thirteen again and my crush has just shown up at my volleyball game.

Julian stands to greet me.

"What are you doing here?" I whisper, aghast.

"I'm returning your earring," Julian says, pulling out the gold wire face from his pocket as if that is explanation enough. He's wearing a white shirt under an olive-green cable knit sweater, and the getup makes him look like someone's sexy professor. In contrast, I look like I've been hit by a truck.

"Ah yes, and that's a totally normal reason to show up at my place of work," I mutter. It's the kind of boundary-breaking behavior that I know I shouldn't tolerate, that's cute now but might get worse. But I'm also self-aware enough to admit that I kind of like it.

If Julian is bothered by my lack of enthusiasm, he doesn't show it. Instead, he gives me an inscrutable smile, like he knows something I don't.

"Well, to be fair, I'm not here just for you. I was in the area for a meeting, so I figured I'd stop by, see if you were too."

The burning humiliation in my cheeks I expect. The despondent drop in my stomach at the realization that Julian is just here by coincidence and not because he has been chasing me down I do not. *Get yourself together, Sean*, I tell myself, willing the misery away.

"Oh," I say, hoping to sound casual. "Well, you know what they say about assumptions."

Julian's expression softens.

"You didn't make assumptions," he says. Then he bends to pull something out from under his chair: a crisp, large white paper shopping bag with golden rope handles. "For you."

Curious, I take it. My shoulder drops with the weight; it's heavier than I expected.

"What for?" I ask, mollified. If Winny could see me now, she would laugh; I'm soft for surprise gifts.

"Bargaining didn't work, so I'm trying for bribery instead," Julian says. He looks left, then right, as if suddenly remembering that we are in a public place. "When are you done with clinic?"

"I just finished," I say softly. "But I still have to make a few phone calls, and then after that I pick up Onix from doggy daycare, but—"

"Dinner tonight?" Julian interrupts.

I look down at the bag in my hands to hide my surprise.

"Am I so lame that I look like I don't have any plans on a Friday night?" I say. "Wait. Don't answer that. I am lame. And fine, I'll take dinner. No need to pick me up. I'll make my way there. Just tell me where to go."

There is a tittering of giggles around us, and behind me, I hear a triumphant *"Woop!"* from my medical assistant, who's been spying on us from the clinic door.

Julian grins like he's the one who's been handed a prize.

"Great," he says. "I'll text you the details. See you at seven."

And then he squeezes my hand, turns on his heel, and leaves, picking up a fallen cane for an elderly man as he passes him. The ghost of his warmth lingers on my skin for minutes after he's gone.

It takes me minutes more to realize that he's taken my exhaustion with him.

Seven

Julian has bought me not one, but *two* espresso machines, as a text from Pamela confirms (OMG this super hot guy just dropped off an ESPRESSO MACHINE at the reading room and said it was from you! Thank you thank you thank you Sean! Don't tell Haoran but this is why you're my favorite!), one for the clinic, and another for the cath lab upstairs. They're not just any espresso machines, either, but ones that cost six hundred dollars (I checked) and come with a milk frother. In the small card he enclosed inside the bag, he writes: *You're someone who I think could be special to me. Sorry for behaving in a way that might have made that hard to believe. In exchange, a way to ensure that you never start your days uncaffeinated again.*

This is too much, I text back. I'm already bewildered enough by the fact that I seem to have been cured of the malady that's been ailing me for the last week, but Julian's generosity pushes me right over the edge. I don't like not knowing what's waiting for me down below.

It's nothing, he responds. See you tonight.

I meet Julian at the Gundis, a Kurdish restaurant in Lakeview: one of his favorites, he says. It's cozier than I expected, the kind of place that you'd only know about through word of mouth and cavorting with locals. I spot him from the window, speaking enthusiastically to his waiter, who laughs as he places down rolled cutlery. When I open the door, it takes me a moment to realize they are not speaking English.

I settle into the seat across from him, cross my hands on the lacquered table.

"Are you Kurdish?" I ask.

Julian gives me an inscrutable smile.

"Lovely to see you again too, Sean, I had a wonderful rest of my day, thanks for asking," he says.

"I've just been wondering where you're from," I ask. "I can't place you. Ethnically, I mean."

"Why do you have to?" Julian asks, a twinkle in his eye.

Because I don't understand you at all, I want to say, *and I think a little cultural guidance could point me in the right direction*.

"I'm just curious," I say instead. "I want to know why this place, of all the spots in the city, gets into your top slots. And why you can speak the language."

Julian takes a hesitant sip of his water.

"I'm neither Kurdish, nor was I speaking it. That was Turkish, which Devram, our waiter, is, and which I only speak conversationally, because I studied abroad in Istanbul a while back." He clears his throat. "And I like this restaurant because it reminds me of a café in Beşiktaş I used to frequent. There's a lot of overlap between Kurdish and Turkish cuisine, and it's nostalgic."

Every time Julian opens his mouth, he reveals a piece of history that makes putting him in a box even more impossible. A wealthy orphan with a vaguely British accent whose short twenty-seven years on the globe have taken him across continents and helped him amass more wealth and experience than people twice his age? Nothing about his story feels quite real, like he's been plucked out of a fan fiction written by an overenthusiastic horny fandom queen crafting her ideal leading man. I ask him a few more questions and learn that Turkish is actually his *eighth* language; he's also fluent in French, Spanish, Portuguese, Bengali, and Arabic and apparently can get around in Bengali and Tagalog too.

"I'm so confused," I say out loud. I know that Julian wants me to be impressed, and I am; I know just enough Spanish to get through a clinic visit with a native speaker, but the moment someone asks me about my hobbies, I draw a blank. "You're so young. How did you learn so many languages?"

Julian smirks.

"I have a natural talent for it, and so I've indulged in it some," he says. "And I've had great teachers. Tutors. International schools. Travel."

"Okay. Well, please don't get offended—"

"Great place to start," Julian interrupts.

"But *what* are you then?" I press on. "White?"

Julian grins, wolfish.

"Do I look white?"

I squint at him. I've never met a person more impossible to categorize. I've seen Italian men who look like Julian, but I also have light-skinned Black cousins who resemble him too. Middle Eastern, mestizo, all would be plausible. I could even see Southeast Asian; he'd probably look right at home in the middle of a salu-salo. It doesn't escape my notice that the languages he names are all predominantly spoken by groups of people he could conceivably resemble.

"Maybe?" I say. "I don't know. There might be a little seasoning in there. I just don't know if it's sumac, garam masala, or Cajun."

This makes him laugh.

"I'm a bit of everything," he says cryptically, regarding me through long, thick lashes. *Sultry*, I realize his eyes are. A little sleepy, like he's just been roused from bed. "And given my whole family is dead, I don't have much in the way of a detailed history for you."

Right. Tragic backstory.

"Since we're playing this game, Sean Sullivan," Julian asks, "what are *you*?"

"Black," I say with a laugh. When he gestures for me to elaborate, I do. "Hyde Park, born and bred. My momma's house is thirty minutes away, down Lake Shore. But her parents are from down south."

His smile is restrained, an almost smug tilt of his lips.

"You mean you've been in the city all this time, and I'm just finding you now?"

"Well," I say. "Have you spent much time south of the Loop?"

"You say that like you already think you have an answer to that," he drawls.

"It's a fair judgment, I think," I say. "You feel very North Side."

The sound Julian makes is half bark and so unlike him that I almost laugh too.

"What could possibly make you say that?" he says, shaking his head in disbelief.

I gesture in his general direction.

"How you dress, for one," I say.

Julian looks down at himself as if he can't quite remember what he's wearing. He's ditched this afternoon's sweater, and his current outfit, consisting of a white shirt and navy trousers, is so finance-bro adjacent that he'd stick out anywhere south of Thirty-Fifth. If it weren't for his inscrutable *ethnic-ness*, I'd write him off as the kind of guy who thought Hyde Park was full of bullet holes instead of bumbling university students.

"That's not fair," he complains. "I had a meeting today with the board of trustees at your hospital. I couldn't exactly come in streetwear."

The image of Julian dressed in the bold, unstructured styles that are in vogue among his peers almost makes me crack up. Instead, I pick up the piece of information that he dropped for me and ask, "Why were you meeting with the board of trustees? Are you working with them?"

Julian makes a gesture that is half nod, half shrug.

"Kind of," he says. "It turns out that when you give an institution a lot of money, they like to keep you involved so that you consider giving more."

I raise an eyebrow.

"Oh? Your aforementioned philanthropy at work!" I exclaim. "Is there going to be a wing named after you? Will I be headed into work next month at the newly christened Conrad Catheterization Lab?"

Julian gives me a wry smile.

"Didn't give quite that much," he confesses. "But next time you go in, search among the plaques on the walls outside your cafeteria. Who knows. You might find me there."

His manner of speaking, cocky but matter-of-fact, tells me that he isn't bragging, exactly. Having wealth so unconscionable that he can give enough away to put a dent in a hospital's funding goals is simply a fact of his life.

"You've got to be the youngest person in that room," I muse.

Julian shrugs.

"Not always," he says. "There are some lawyers. And the young old-money socialites whose only job is to be the face of their family's charity work."

"You say that with derision," I observe. "You don't relate?"

"I don't," he says. "Most of them are the family misfits. As long as they show up every few months, wear a suit, and smile for pictures, they can spend the rest of their lives snorting lines and going to forest raves."

"Sounds like they're *also* people of leisure," I taunt, calling back to how he'd described himself only a week before.

The irreverence is gone from Julian's expression now; his gaze turns razor-sharp. I feel pinned by it, like it's diving through my sweater and nailing me to my chair.

"What are you insinuating, Dr. Sullivan?" he says.

"I'm not insinuating anything," I say innocently. "You clearly want to differentiate yourself from your peers, and I just want to understand why."

Winona would call what I'm doing now "self-sabotage." I'm taking a needle to his defenses, jabbing at the soft parts to see what makes him flinch, and it's unkind, and maybe even rude, but I can't help it. I want to know who Julian Conrad becomes when he feels disrespected, whether he raises his voice or demeans or belittles, if his indelible charm is actually conditional. I want to know if my sneaking suspicion that he's a fraud has any validity or if I'm just cynical and hypervigilant. And it's working. Bit by bit, Julian's veil—the one he wears to convince me that he is toothless, that he is a cub with a crush and not a wolf on the hunt—is falling, and I am ravenous to see who he is underneath.

More interesting still, I can see that he *likes* this. Brandon might think I am self-righteous, but Julian is hooked into me, staring me down with a lethal mixture of disdain and interest that reminds me of the version of him I briefly met in the conference room of his gallery. The one who looked like he might just swallow me whole.

"I identify innovation," Julian says. "I take risks on people with big ideas and help them turn them into reality. I take money and turn some of it into more money and convert the rest into art and homes and resources. Those people," he takes a vicious swig of his water, gulps, places down his glass firmly, "are not my peers."

"But you share the same spaces. You're often in the same rooms, which is why you know what they get up to when they're not in them."

Julian doesn't wince, exactly, but he does go still, and it's his sudden rapt attention that gives me the confidence to let my thoughts continue to flow, unfiltered, from brain to mouth.

"I'm just saying," I continue. "I don't think I have to look through your portfolio to know that you're probably putting your money where everyone else is. Broadview Hospital is in one of the richest neighborhoods in the city. They will never be short of funding. Margaret? She's talented, of course, but an easy pick. Your friend, and already famous in her own right. She's been showing in galleries for thirty years, doesn't even need a day job. And I've looked up some of your other exhibitors—rising stars from all over the world, but none from your own backyard.

"There are a hundred Margaret Wests in Ingleside who are trying to have their work seen and won't get the opportunity because people with money in this city don't even think to look anywhere outside their spheres of influence." I cross my arms. "You would never have found me, Julian. The places where I existed . . . you probably would never have thought to look."

There's music playing in this restaurant, but I can't hear it over the roaring in my ears. I mean what I say, every word of it, and there's a power in speaking it out loud and looking at this man who has probably been able to use his money to get into the few places his face might deny him and telling him that I don't find him that impressive.

"Careful," Julian croons in that same low tone he'd purred into my voicemail earlier this week. "I might think you're calling me uninspired."

"Maybe I am," I say with a shrug. "But I notice that you aren't calling me *wrong*."

Julian opens his mouth to counter, but he's saved by Devram, who sweeps up to us with a barely suppressed grin that tells me he can sense the tension emanating from our table and is enjoying every second of it.

"Are you ready to order?" he asks.

Julian doesn't let me get a word in, just launches into an exchange in rapid, syllabic Turkish, only pausing to ask if I have any dietary restrictions. Devram laughs as he writes down the order, gives me a quick glance like he's in on some joke that I'm left out of, then spirits away.

"That was presumptuous," I say when Devram is out of earshot.

"I was getting hungry, and you've been too busy lecturing me to look at the menu even once," Julian notes.

"You could've prompted me."

"You were distracted," he says. He throws a languid arm over the empty chair next to him and smirks, well aware of the pretty picture he makes. "Understandably."

I roll my eyes. "You're so full of yourself."

"As I should be," he says. He blinks those sleepy eyes, gives me a smug smile. "As you should be too."

I pause, unsure how to respond to the unexpected compliment amidst our barbs. Devram returns with two tulip-shaped glasses and makes a show of filling them with streams of steaming hot, fragrant tea before offering them to us off his silver tray. Julian waits for him to step away before lifting one to his lips.

"I assumed you might have decision fatigue," he explains, his gaze softening. "I asked you to meet me tonight, after you've spent an entire day making hard choices for other people, and so I thought that making this one for yourself might feel overwhelming. That you might not know where to start, because you aren't familiar with the cuisine. I took it off your hands."

My stomach is growling, but my few furtive glances at the extensive menu have only made my head hurt. I don't know how he saw this, but of all the things Julian has said tonight, this is the first I can't find a response for. *Thank you* doesn't seem quite right, because ordering for your date is absolutely a faux pas, but for a woman like me who is so accustomed to doing everything for herself, it feels like he's lifted the tiniest burden off my shoulders.

I'm still busy trying to figure out whether I'm a bad feminist when Julian leans forward and surprises me again.

"Also," he says. "You're right."

They're just two words, but they almost make me spill hot tea down my front.

"Sorry?" I say stupidly.

"I said you're right. I've been myopic. I pride myself in investing in my community, but there are many pockets of the city that I've left unexplored." When he turns to me, the solemnity in his expression feels like an olive branch. "Our director wants to start discussing exhibits for next spring soon. Do you have any South or West Side Chicago–based artists you would recommend?"

It occurs to me, suddenly, that I'm about to change somebody's life. About half a dozen names come to mind: the sculptor whose work I first saw exhibited in Hyde Park Art Center, the multimedia artist who created stunning works by tying and manipulating durags and bonnets, the self-taught seamstress who poured weeks of labor into a striking embroidered portrait that I'd purchased after seeing her posts on Instagram.

"Yes," I say. "Yes, actually. There are quite a few."

"Tell me about them," Julian says.

The tone shift after that is abrupt. Julian pours my tea, offers me food from his plate, and I offer him some of mine. We pore over the profiles of local artists, and Julian keeps note of the names of the ones he finds notable and makes me promise to visit their exhibits with him. Our conversation transitions naturally to our first shared love, music, and here his knowledge is diverse and deeper than mine: Julian can tell me about the history of New Orleans bounce and South Korean trot but also adds about four new composer/pianists to my Spotify account. And as we talk, his words come back to me. That he sees me as someone who could be special to him. That he wants me to take him "seriously." It had seemed like a game before, a meaningless declaration from a seasoned playboy picking his best path into my pants. But I think I understand him now. Maybe I'm just feeling what he felt right away two weeks late. Like I'm safe to be my truest self, to reveal my thoughts without window dressing or placation or explanation. Like, for the first time in a long time, I'm speaking to my equal.

Which is concerning in its own way, because "serious" might mean something to him that I can't provide.

"What did you mean, in your note?" I ask, when we've all but cleared our plates. "About me being someone who could potentially be special to you."

Julian dabs his lips elegantly with his napkin, then says, "You say that like it was a threat."

"I just don't want to waste your time," I insist, holding up my hands. "Because depending on what you mean, I might not be able to be that."

To my chagrin, he looks only more intrigued.

"And why not?" he asks.

I answer his question with one of my own.

"How many people have you dated, Julian?" When Julian's grin broadens, I roll my eyes. "How many have *meant* something?"

Julian's smile falters, and his expression grows morose. Suddenly, I'm jettisoned into a memory: me, just a few years older than Julian is now. Gripping Eric's phone in my hand as he slept soundly in my bed, incriminating screenshots saved and sent to my email, my heart sitting pulverized in my chest. I'd been young, true, with many more potential loves in my future, but that didn't stop my pain from being world ending.

"One," Julian finally says, just when I think he's going to avoid the question.

"One," I repeat, after a moment, feeling the enormity of his response. My answer, I know, is the same.

I realize then that I'm once again doing Julian a disservice. I don't know him or what he's been through. I don't know who has hurt him too. The narrative I keep trying to craft for him has never quite fit, and yet I keep trying to force it to, like if I can predict who he is, I can protect myself from what he is capable of.

We are silent for a moment. Devram sweeps by our table to bring us more tea, but we don't look away from each other, trying to decipher something in the other's eyes.

I'm the one to break the silence.

"I don't want to get married," I start. Even though I've rehearsed this spiel a hundred times, I'm nervous to give it. I feel, every time, like I'm providing the prelude to my own disappointment. "I don't want children. I'm not sure I even want to share a home with anyone, let alone a bed. I would like a life partner. Someone I choose every day, who chooses me, not because of a legal document or a mortgage, but because we want to be together."

Like Oprah and Stedman, I used to tell potential partners. They'd all nod their heads and feign understanding, claim to be progressive, cosmopolitan men who would happily accept an arrangement that absolved them of financial responsibility over me. Until the fire burned out and they realized just how many benefits they were missing out on. A live-in cook, maid, housekeeper, sexbot. Someone who couldn't run from them once they tired of providing romance, because they provided shackles instead.

Julian is rubbing his chin in thought.

"I could have sworn you were about to ask me to join a sex cult," he says after a moment.

"Julian," I deadpan, and he laughs.

"Seriously," he says. "You're an established woman. I expect you to know what you want. And who knows, maybe I want that too."

"It's not a life most twenty-seven-year-olds would want—or know they want, yet," I say.

"I'm not most twenty-seven-year-olds."

"I'll concede that," I allow.

"And I don't need you to tell me what is or isn't good for me. That I get to decide for myself," Julian continues. "What you do need to do . . . is be honest with me and yourself."

I sit back in my seat, both ruffled and a little impressed by his forthrightness.

"Fighting words," I say.

"Are they? Admit it, Sean. You *want* to be special to me. That's why you're having dinner with me right now. It's why you came out to talk to me this morning at your clinic instead of sending me away and blocking my number. It's why you ran away from me after the gallery, after Margaret walked in on us. Because you find most everyone just a bit boring, but me? I, at the very least, intrigue you." He leans in closer, his voice deepening, and for a split second, his eyes seem to flash. "Or am I wrong? Is it something simpler than that?"

I suck in a breath. Our conversation thus far has been cerebral, a friendly fencing match between two people who are too smart and too smug about it for their own good, but he's shifted to seduction and I am completely unprepared. An image flashes to mind: Julian hovering over me, shadows playing in the dips of his clavicle and the divot of his heaving chest, the hot, hard curve of him pulsing under my hand—

"What are you saying," I manage, but my voice cracks and it comes out less cool and more breathless, and I see the triumph flash across Julian's face, like he knows exactly what he's caused me to remember.

"What do you think?" he croons. "It's fine, you know. I'll be a bit disappointed, I admit. But I'm not that pure a man. If you're just having dinner with me because you're hoping for something to happen after, I won't complain."

My ears are hot and my tongue is tied, and by the look on his face, he knows he's won.

"You're so . . ." I search for the word, stunned by his audacity. "*Arrogant*."

"But I'm not wrong." His voice drops almost to a whisper. "Don't think I forgot how ready you were for me at the gallery. You act so very prim and proper, but if we hadn't been interrupted, you would have let me fuck you right there on that table—"

I practically leap across the table to clap a hand over his mouth just as footsteps still in front of us.

"Shall I come back?" Devram says, holding the dessert menus to his chest like a shield against our indecency.

"No, it's fine—*ah!*"

I snatch my hand back and drop back into my seat.

Because Julian has just *sucked it.*

My face is hot as Devram goes over our dessert options, and I turn my hand over on my lap, staring at the pulp of palm that has just been in Julian's mouth. My mind replays the moment over and over again, scrabbling to recall the exact look in his eyes when he did it, if there had been teeth—

"Anything for you, ma'am?" Devram asks, thrusting me right back into reality.

"Yes, Sean, anything for you?" Julian asks, not even bothering to hide his amusement.

"No thank you," I say, wearing my most genial smile. "Just the check."

Twenty minutes later, we're making out in Julian's car.

I don't know exactly how it happens. The last thing I remember is putting on my coat and preparing to call an Uber, formulating plans about calling Winona to give her a recap, and stepping out into the cool September evening. What follows afterward is a blur—I vaguely recall Julian convincing me to let him drop me off, walking one block to his car, and piling inside. I don't remember if we drive to my apartment first or just go at it right there in the street. I have no clue who makes the first move. I don't even remember how we end up in the back seat.

What I do know is that touching Julian feels like an original sin. That we snap together like magnets, my arms around his neck, his wound tight around my waist, the space between us molecules thick. His desire feels avaricious, his mouth molding, molten, to mine, hands exploring my every square inch. He trails them up my back, finds my bra, unlatches it, and I hike his sweater up to expose his chest, wanting to feel the heat of his skin against mine. Distantly, I wonder what the car looks like from the outside, if the soft glow of streetlights is enough to illuminate us for all to see, if the contrast between the heat of our bodies and the chill of the outside autumn air is enough to layer our windows with suggestive condensation. But I don't care enough to look. I'm much too preoccupied by the feeling of those full lips trailing down my neck, those broad hands cupping my breasts under my shirt. I've devolved, I think, regressed to some more primitive life form that wants to fuck first and ask questions later.

Julian seems determined to get me there. The bulge in his pants hits me just right, sending alarming bolts of pleasure through the seat of my thin leggings as we kiss. His hands drop to cup my ass, guiding my frantic motions, arching his hips the way I'm sure he would if he were inside me. I'm climbing higher, higher, our movements becoming so urgent that I'm certain we're shaking the car, and am I really about to come from rutting on this man like a repressed teenager—

Yes, yes I am.

"Oh god," a voice cries out, mine. Layered under it, Julian's low, satisfied groan.

Seconds pass. Our breaths gust between us.

What the ever-loving fuck.

There's post-nut clarity, and then there's post-nut enlightenment, and I am tragically experiencing the latter. My mind reels with updated information like a phone turned on after a flight: yes, Julian did in fact drive me home. No, he did not make the first move; that was me, leaning over the center console after spending the entire fifteen-minute ride staring at his mouth. As for how we got to the back seat—well, clumsily, and yes, I will feel that in the morning.

"Hey," Julian says, looking up at me through half-lidded eyes. He pulls me to him by the nape of my neck, kisses me slow, and the combination of shame and panic churning in my stomach abates somewhat. "You're freaking out. Don't."

I bow my head against his and squeeze my eyes shut.

"How can I not freak out?" I manage. Then, because I'm clearly still woozy, I confess, "I can't think straight around you."

"Sean, I am about to have an exceedingly uncomfortable drive home because I couldn't keep my hands off you," Julian deadpans. "Believe me, you're not alone."

Logically, I know his words should be comforting, but they aren't. Because what I'm trying to tell him is that I've been floating in and out of consciousness, and this time I haven't drunk a lick of alcohol to explain it.

What if he drugged you?

The question spears me, and I consider all the possibilities: the glasses of water already laid out on the table before my arrival, the brief seconds when I'd turned away to smile up at Devram during which Julian could have theoretically reached across the table and sprinkled something onto my food. Even as I'm thinking it, I know it must be ludicrous. What drug clears out of your system immediately post-orgasm?

"I . . ." I start. Julian's sweater is still riding high, and I swallow at the sight of his shadowed, toned torso. Then, gingerly, I clamber off him. "Good night."

Before I can open the door to let myself out, an arm loops around and encircles me. I land gracelessly, half on his thigh, half on the seat, and Julian turns my face to his by my chin.

"When do I see you next?" he says.

It's dark out, but his eyes seem to have found a source of light. They glint and glisten as he waits for my response.

My pulse hastens. It's not lust I feel under his scrutiny now, but trepidation. Like I've just heard my name whispered in an empty room.

"I don't know," I say softly.

"It doesn't have to get physical next time," Julian whispers back. "We have another exhibition to catch, remember? We can behave."

For the first time in a long time, I don't know exactly what I'm feeling. I can't isolate why I'm hesitant to respond with anything other than a resounding yes. It doesn't make sense, this disquiet, the way I both want to drag Julian close and run away screaming. I squeeze my eyes shut, interrogating myself. Is it fear that I might choose wrong again? That his insistence that he wants me to be *special* to him is just a ploy to draw me in, and that I will allow myself to be pursued only to be discarded or mistreated once he's caught me in his grasp? Or is it my own anxiety about the realities of modern dating, the fact that while my pool of eligible bachelors is the size of a puddle, my hot, wealthy, charismatic counterpart's is composed of every person with a pulse and an attraction to men? I imagine the next several months "dating" Julian, my enjoyment of our connection tempered by the awareness that at any given moment, a hot new bombshell could burst into his life: someone younger than me, easier to love, and willing to idolize and prioritize him in ways I never can.

My jaw clenches at the thought. As confused as I am right now, I am now certain of one thing: if we decide to do this, I do not intend to share.

"You have to be with just me," I say abruptly. "I mean it. I'm too grown for will-they-won't-they. If you're taking me out, if we're doing *this*," I point at him, then me, "then I do not consent to being on a roster."

Julian's chuckle rumbles through me, and I shiver at the feel of it.

"Who else could compare," he says. Then he seals the deal with another kiss, and it takes me another thirty minutes to make it upstairs.

Eight

When I walk into the control room of the cath lab that Monday, Pamela's jaw drops.

"Excuse me for saying this," she says. "But *damn*, Sullivan. You look *good*."

"Umm, thanks," I say, making my way to my computer to pull up my cases for the day. Pamela continues to ogle as I scroll through the cath films for my first patient, a gentleman who has traveled from southern Illinois to have a particularly crunchy blockage in his left circumflex artery addressed. It's a case I'll need a Palette representative for, and what do you know, Leila is on today.

"Did you get a facial?" Pamela continues, ever curious. "Score the world's best concealer match?"

"No?" I say, a little self-consciously.

"Well, you're glowing," she says. Then wickedly, "Did you get laid?"

My ears burn, but I've gotten too good at controlling my face over the years to let my embarrassment slip.

"Is this sexual harassment, Pamela?" I deadpan. I take a sip of my espresso, made using Julian's machine. It's delicious, makes Brews and Beans taste like sludge.

"Oh you're no fun," Pamela whines.

She isn't wrong that I look good. The woman I've been catching in the mirror for the last two days isn't drastically different from the one I've gotten used to, not particularly older or younger or freer of crow's feet, but she looks like an alternate version of me, one who doesn't have a years-long sleep debt or worries like *Will I kill a patient today*? I'm looking less like a beleaguered interventionist and more like the pampered trophy wife of a hedge fund manager who spends her days doing juice cleanses and chemical peels and whose only worry is whether her housekeeper did a good enough job cleaning the baseboards.

Brandon, on the other hand, looks a mess. Since his wedding, he has only grown more haggard. There are frown lines bracketing his mouth that I don't remember being there before, dark circles under his eyes, and a patchy five o'clock shadow now omnipresent on his normally clean-shaven face. He's quieter than usual too, almost glum. Brandon isn't the most boisterous of our colleagues—that honor goes firmly to Shiv—but he is generally loquacious, and the cath lab feels sterile without the background droning of his friendly chatter.

Pamela tells me that he's signed up to moonlight in other hospitals.

"He's overworking himself," Pamela says, as we both watch him trudge into his lab for his next case, responding to all Larry's questions with grunts of affirmation. "He needs to slow down."

I respond with a noncommittal "Hmph" that I hope communicates my lack of interest. Ever since the dissection incident, I've been determined to mind my business. I'll help Brandon if he asks, jump in if I'm needed, but he's made it clear that my opinions aren't welcome. We work, as we have for the last couple of weeks, not together but in parallel. But I do watch him and wonder what's changed and if Sophie has noticed it. Winona says her daughter has become oddly mum about her trips to her father's West Loop loft, and I hope that the coldness he's displaying here doesn't persist—or worse, turn to hot anger—when he's home with her.

I pull out my phone and send my goddaughter a quick text: checking in on you, nugget. We're overdue for a girls' date.

Sophie responds immediately, even though I'm pretty sure she's in the middle of class. Let's get sushi. Or ramen. Or both. You're coming to my recital, right? Did you watch the video I sent?

Wouldn't miss it, watched the video, we can go somewhere that serves both, pay attention in class, I type back with one hand.

The door from Brandon's lab into the control room bangs open, and I jolt, tucking my phone back into my pocket like I've been caught looking at something questionable. But it's only Shiv, beaming down at us with his hands on his hips and a plan he clearly intends to execute.

"You guys coming to SCAI next month?" he says. "And more importantly, you coming out Saturday night for the after-party?"

SCAI, or Society for Cardiovascular Angiography and Interventions, is an organization for interventional cardiologists and industry representatives that hosts an annual conference to share new innovations. This year, it's being held in Chicago, which means that many of my colleagues in the city will be leading the sessions and planning the after-hours events. A few of my fellows will be presenting their research, so I intended to go to support them anyway, but I know that my attendance is as good as mandatory. Fewer than 5 percent of interventional cardiologists are women and an infinitesimally smaller percentage also Black, which means that my institution will be sure to parade me around the exhibition halls as a singular symbol of their progress. I've already gotten three insistent emails from Krause double-checking that I'll be present for the Broadview SCAI photo, where I will be positioned in the center, as I have for the last four years.

"The after-party?" Brandon says glumly from his side of the room. The sound of his voice alarms me; I realize that it's because it's been some time since I last heard it.

Shiv waves him off.

"I already got confirmation from your better half, so you're handled," he says. He turns hopefully to me. "Sean? You in?"

I wince. I enjoy SCAI—interventional cardiology is a small world, so I'll get the chance to meet up with some old friends—but the after-parties are another story: too much alcohol, too many hot pharma reps in designer clothing, too much potential for mess. Last year, a very married interventionist from Tennessee, emboldened by two Long Island iced teas and the egging-on of his coworkers-turned-regressed-frat-boys, spent the better part of an hour trying to convince me to go back to his hotel. Leila had been the one to rescue me, with the excuse that my colleagues were taking a group picture.

"I'll think about it," I say.

Unfortunately for me, Shiv refuses to accept defeat.

"Aw, come on, Sullivan, I'm smart enough to know when I'm being let down easy," he says.

"I'm a hermit, Shiv, remember?" I remind him.

"Well, come out of your shell," he insists. He gives me a pleading smile. "Just make an appearance. Twenty minutes! I'll buy you a drink. And you can even bring a plus-one!"

The words have barely left his mouth before the door to the control room swings open again and Leila springs inside, throwing her hair into a neat bun as she crosses the room. She lifts her head, grinning when she sees Shiv.

"Are you being bullied into going to Shiv's after-party?" she asks.

Shiv huffs, affronted.

"I'm not bullying anyone—" he insists.

"You should come," Leila says to me. Then, brightly, "You can bring Jules! He'll be an excellent meat shield."

Brandon and Shiv exchange a glance, and I'm not sure if their confusion stems from learning that I might actually have a plus-one to bring, recognizing that Leila is referring to her man of honor, or wondering what Leila means by a "meat shield." Either way, my stomach drops at the mention of Julian's name. There is nothing technically off-color about our relationship, but I'm not quite ready to bring the rest of the world into it yet. Maybe because it's so new. Maybe because he's so young, and the curious stares we have occasionally gotten in public are more bothersome than I'd like to admit. Maybe because the voice note he left me this morning reflecting on my opinions on his investments and suggesting a trip to the Hyde Park Art Center to view their recurring *New Art* ground-floor exhibition left more stirrings in my belly than the searing kisses he'd given me in his back seat.

Or maybe it's because I can sense that I'm catching feelings and don't want to throw our fledgling dalliance off course by suggesting something so intense as *meeting my entire professional network*.

As if she can hear my thoughts, Leila adds, softly, "He would probably really like it if you asked."

I narrow my eyes in her direction.

"Does he already know it's happening?" I ask.

Leila's cheeks pink, and she makes a show of tying on her surgeon's cap to avoid meeting my eyes.

I am about to bury myself under the tile when Pamela, of all people, comes to my rescue.

"Woop, your patient's here, Sullivan," she says. She hops out of her chair and all but hoists me out of mine. "Enough chitchat. Time to suit up."

"Thanks for the save," I whisper as she ties my gown five minutes later.

I can't see her face, but I can hear the shit-eating grin in her voice.

"I didn't do it out of the goodness of my heart," she says. "I'm going to need you to spill the deets about this 'Jules' guy later."

Behind my mask, I bite my cheek, but I don't dare to protest.

Over the next two weeks I see Julian more than I have seen any one person since graduating from medical school. He melds into my life seamlessly, inviting me for impromptu meals at restaurants around the city, joining me at the gym during my evening workouts, and even occasionally misusing his hospital visitor pass to drop off lunch for the entire cath lab. To my relief, he never surprises me on days when Brandon or Leila are in the lab, and my colleagues who'd attended their wedding don't look at him for long enough to register where they've seen him before. Thus, our entanglement remains something of an open secret.

Which is how I like it. It's been years since my last real relationship, and I'm clearly out of practice, because I've totally forgotten how to pace myself. I'm like a little girl again, simpering and kicking my feet over the boy I tell my friends I "*like* like." The truth is: Julian's world is a brighter, kinder place than I'm used to, and it's hard to not want to move into it. When we go out to dinner, we get placed at the best tables, the ones by the window with a city street view. He makes one self-deprecating joke and suddenly the waiter is laughing and the manager is too and we end up with a dessert, a drink, an appetizer on the house. When we walk down the street the crowds part like the Red Sea around us, and no one bumps my shoulders or steps on my toes. Everyone smiles and is pleasant and understanding and just a bit more beautiful, like he is drawing the best out of them.

And as much as the "Julian effect" amuses me, I understand it. I'm just as bewitched as everyone else, though less by his beauty than the brain behind it. Julian seems to know a little bit about everything, a natural consequence of his voracious curiosity, and what he doesn't know, he learns. He's like me, in the sense that no topic is too niche for exploration; he understands how I can simultaneously dive deep into music and design and medicine because he dives deep into everything himself. Thankfully, he seems just as fascinated by me as I am by him. Our conversations never quite end, starting in person before transitioning to voice notes, video chats snuck into stolen moments between my cases and his clients, phone calls that only end as we both nod off to sleep.

Even then, I find him in my dreams, no longer a leering trespasser, now a welcome companion. The night a pregnant twenty-four-year-old woman dies on my table from a massive pulmonary embolism after my attempt at an aspiration thrombectomy fails to turn her around, Julian stays on the phone with me for hours, lending a listening ear. Long after we hang up, I relive twisted versions of her death in a nightmare, and he returns to me in my subconscious to hold me through the horror. When I wake up in the morning to a cool, empty bed, I feel, for the first time in a long time, bereft.

"Love looks good on you, Sulley," Winona observes over a video call.

"I am not in *love*," I insist. I'm getting ready to meet Julian; as we're both free for the full day, we're finally making good on his request to visit the Hyde Park Art Center. He saw an advertisement for a farmer's market while looking into the area, and so we plan to start our day there. It's one of the last outdoor markets before the weather officially turns, and I've tried on about seventeen outfits for Winona's approval. When I show her the last option—a calf-length sweater dress with heeled booties—in my floor length mirror, she whistles. Onix, sitting at my feet, huffs in agreement.

"Absolutely yes, that one is definitely getting you laid tonight," Winona declares. "Which . . . why hasn't that happened yet? This is all really fun and sweet, don't get me wrong, but I'm supposed to be living vicariously through you, and you're being real old-school right now."

I prop my phone up on my vanity, stepping away from the camera so that Winny can't see the look on my face. Truthfully, there have been opportunities. Nights when it would have been so easy to invite him up to my apartment or accept his implicit invitation to come up to his. But I haven't followed through because I'm scared. I want to attribute our attraction to chemistry, or to the fact that I haven't had sex worth writing home about in years, but I can't shake the fact that there's something more. Because when Julian kisses me, I lose all reason. I become irresponsible. In my symptom journal, which lately has become just a journal, I write, *I don't think I could survive anything more.*

But if I tell Winona that I'm holding back from sleeping with my paramour because I'm worried it'll be a bit *too* good, she'll either roll her eyes and tell me to stop bragging or give me the "look" and ask if I think I don't deserve it.

"It doesn't have to be vicarious, Winny. You can go get yours too," I say simply. "And I don't know. Right now, it feels good to go a little slow. Figure out if we actually like each other's company, or if it's just pheromones, you know?"

Winona hums and I silently rejoice; she's accepted my answer.

"You inspired me, Sean," she says. "I set my minimum age lower on LMT this morning. I didn't think the dating pool could get worse after our twenties, but it's turned into a swamp! Like, check this guy out—"

She sends me a profile of a somewhat attractive man in his forties whose bio reads: "Five ten and twelve inches, loves hot meals, photography, and nude art, if we hit it off, I'll draw you 🎨."

I make a retching noise and start my makeup as Winona regales me with tales of botched profiles and disastrous conversations. I've just put on the finishing touches when a text drops down from my screen.

Julian: Here.

"Winny, I've got to go," I say. "But! Don't forget! I'm borrowing my goddaughter next week, so please take advantage of your day off and get someone to take you out! Please!"

"Oh yes, please go," Winona pleads. "And I will try! But you have to promise to get some tonight! And then tell me all about it after."

"Ha!" I bark, then blow her a kiss and hang up.

Julian is waiting for me downstairs when I arrive, and god does he look delectable. His beard is shaved down to stubble, and he's wearing the hell out of a charcoal sweater and camel trench. A watch glints on his wrist; a Patek Philippe, he told me once, one of many vintage timepieces he's collected over the last couple of years. *That's why you like me*, I'd joked. *You're an old man at heart.* He brushes a kiss against my lips that makes me feel champagne-bubble fizzy, and

I brush my hand against his cheek. Something catches the light in his chin: a single silver hair.

"You have grays," I observe, surprised. Now that I look closer, there are a few more, scattered in his stubble and across his temples.

Displeasure flashes across Julian's face, and I see that I've touched a sore spot.

"Yeah, well," he mutters thornily, like I've just told him his breath smells. "Happens, I guess."

"Come on now, it's not that bad. I started getting them in my twenties too." I gesture to my own head, which has started a steady salt and pepper transition from black at the tips to graying at the roots. "And you don't seem to mind them on me."

This seems to bring Julian back. He grins, squeezes my hand where it rests against his cheek.

"I *like* your grays," he says. "You otherwise look quite young, and the contrast is kind of . . . mystical."

"Mystical," I repeat, amused. "I've genuinely never heard that one before. Is that another way of saying I look old and wise? Like a wizard?"

Julian rolls his eyes.

"Ethereal, then," he revises. "You know, the first time I saw you, I thought you looked like a fairy."

"A fairy?" I repeat, chuckling.

"Yeah. You know. These wide-set eyes on your heart-shaped face." He drags a finger down the side of my face, bumping past my prominent cheekbones, the hollows beneath them, ending at the point of my chin. "And this bone structure. Both delicate and dramatic."

He is appreciating me the way an artist might, breaking down my features as if he intends to commit them to memory and then to canvas. I'm almost sucked into his spell when he adds, playfully, "Also, you're quite short."

I scrunch my nose in faux indignation, then twist out of his reach and head for the door.

"You do know shorter people live longer, right?" I say over my shoulder. "Remember that the next time you want to look down on me."

Julian laughs a little too hard for the joke, then quips, "I'm always looking down on you," and I bite back a smile that he can't see as I push open the door and step out into the cool air.

The farmer's market is in full swing by the time we arrive, and even having walked this street a thousand times before, I'm still struck by how much Hyde Park has changed since I left it. Where there had once been mom and pop restaurants there are now Sweetgreens and Nando's, and the elegant brownstones are now accompanied by looming glass and steel apartment complexes. We wander down rows of tents of people selling their wares: fresh produce from community gardens and local farmers, the occasional artisan selling skin-care products and beaded bracelets. A man I've only ever known as the "bread guy" but haven't seen in years greets me like an old friend and convinces us to try his pecan sticky buns, and we wait for far too long in line at a coffee shop that serves us uniquely flavored lattes (rose cardamom for me, black sesame for Julian). Julian stops at a boutique perfumery, charms the woman who mans the booth, and walks out with three bottles for the price of two. I'm almost annoyed until I watch him tuck a hundred-dollar bill into her tip jar.

"How do you do that?" I ask him when we are out of earshot.

Julian reaches down, grasps my hand in his.

"Do what?"

"Make people feel so at ease." I tuck a loc behind my ear, a little self-conscious. "Make them, I don't know, *like* you."

I expect Julian to laugh me off, not to turn pensive like he does. His hand slips out of mine and into his pocket as he looks out into the crowded street. A dozen people look back, turning to him like blossoms to the morning sun.

"They don't like me," he says eventually. "They don't know me enough to like me."

"But they might want to," I say.

Julian shrugs.

"No, they don't," he says. "They want me to be who they think I am, and I indulge them. They like the performance."

What I'm feeling isn't empathy, exactly. I'm precisely the kind of woman that most people *don't* like: too prickly, too unaccommodating, too much the career-obsessed harpy that every early 2000s rom-com sought to fix with the power of love. But I get it. On the occasion when being liked has been necessary, the box I've had to fold myself into has always felt constricting.

"Then stop performing," I say, matter-of-fact. "Just be you."

The look that Julian gives me is half exasperation, half affection. He opens his mouth to respond when a hand taps him on the shoulder from behind.

Julian turns, and I have to school myself not to gape.

The young woman standing behind him is movie star striking, with feathered bangs and a perfect smoky eye. She looks chic in an ankle-length duster, unbuttoned to reveal a slender figure that turns her simple black shirt and jeans into a statement.

"Hi. Sorry to interrupt," she says, acknowledging me with a brief glance. "But is that vintage Burberry?"

Julian straightens and gives her an answer, and I shrink as blood rushes to my face. A woman is flirting with my date, and he is flirting back. Well, okay, flirting might be an exaggeration, but he is engaged in a conversation about his coat, the small signs in the stitching that the beautiful woman ("Alicia," she says) used to verify it as the real deal. The only time I've ever commented on Julian's distinctively posh style has been to poke fun at it, but Alicia appreciates it, can pick out the value of his pieces on sight. They look good together, like they would be paired for a magazine photo shoot or cast opposite each other in a romantic comedy. Anyone passing by would assume that they were a couple, and I just an awkward bystander struck still by their beauty.

I realize, suddenly, that what I am feeling is *insecurity*, and the twist in my stomach that comes soon after is *shame.*

"Where did you get it? I've been hunting for one forever," Alicia asks. She reaches for his lapel, trails a finger down it in a caress. "Maybe you can show me your favorite thrifting haunts?"

Julian takes a full step out of her reach. The rejection is anything but subtle, and Alicia and I simultaneously flinch.

"Please don't touch me," he says with a smile so tight with disgust that I wilt with secondhand embarrassment.

Alicia rears back as if she's been slapped.

"S-Sorry," she stammers. "Sorry, I just . . . I didn't think . . ."

Julian nods patiently, like he's pretending to understand a babbling toddler.

"Right," he says. Then he turns his smile to me, and his expression softens. "I should get back to my date. Good luck with your search."

"Ah," Alicia says. Her eyes drift to me, tick up from my sensible DSW boots to my polyester blend TJ Maxx dress and linger on my fading roots. "Sorry, ma'am. Didn't realize he was your man."

I bite down hard on my tongue to keep from saying something I regret—but I don't have to. Because Julian tugs me tight into his side.

"You didn't?" he says warmly, lifting my chin toward his face. "But we look so good together."

The way he's looking at me, I'm surprised I don't burst into flames. Alicia clears her throat, then excuses herself with a muttered *Have a good day*.

Once she's shuffled out of sight, Julian lowers his hand, and my stomach somersaults back into place.

"That was kind of mean," I mumble, fixed somewhere between pity, because that poor girl will be replaying that interaction in her head for the rest of her life, and schadenfreude, because calling me "ma'am" was absolutely unnecessary and so maybe she deserved it.

"Well, you did just tell me to stop performing. Maybe being 'kind of mean' is my natural state." He smirks. "So? What do you think? Do you like me a little less?"

The truth is that I like him a little more, but admitting that out loud feels like a disservice to poor Alicia. So instead I tell him through touch, lace my fingers through his and bite my cheek when he squeezes them.

"I think we're done here," I say. "Next stop?"

"As you wish," Julian says.

The *New Art* exhibition at Hyde Park Art Center is larger than I expected. Every medium possible is represented on the large white walls and concrete gray floors: rich, colorful textiles next to pieces that look like textiles but are exquisitely molded clay, TV screens with grotesque but arresting imagery and inscrutable titles like *Leishmaniasis*. Julian wanders the floor ahead of me, assessing the pieces with a curator's focus, hands clasped behind his back.

He stops at one, then looks over his shoulder for me.

"What do you think of this one?"

I jog to catch up. The piece he wants to show me is an oil painting. It's small, not much bigger than the sixteen by twenty posters I have on my gallery wall in my apartment, but I can understand why it stopped him in his tracks. A woman, rendered in black and white, huddles in a blanket that consumes the entirety of the canvas, like she's wrapping herself in the empty space. One eye stares out from under the fold overhead, and it captures me head-on, both fearful and defiant. It's the look of a cornered animal that has chosen fight instead of flight, one who is ready to lay her life down in defense of it. I don't have Julian's eye for fine art, but I know that this makes me feel something, and that means it's good.

"It's . . ." I search for the word. "Striking."

"Thank you!" a voice says from behind us. "It's one of mine, actually."

Julian and I whip around. A young man with a head full of ringlets stands behind us, and I have to swallow back a sudden rush of emotion. *Because I know this man.* His heavy brow and long, diamond-shaped face. A body that, eight years ago, was lanky with youth and has become svelte in adulthood. Eyes that are a pretty brown to his brother's hazel, but skin that is his same dappled ochre.

My heart is a battering ram against my ribs. Blood drains out of my head and rushes downward, and I slip my arm through Julian's, holding on to him like a pillar as stars dance in front of my eyes. When Eric and I first broke up, the fear of running into his family or friends haunted me every day. But with time, the fear faded, so much so that I forgot that this particular nightmare could become reality.

Jared, Eric's youngest brother, and I regard each other for a second, and his brows squeeze together in confusion.

Then he grins, and the shock of his delight almost offsets the churning in my stomach.

"Oh my god, Sean!" he says, launching himself into my arms.

The last time I saw Jared, he was seventeen and desperately hunting down a gold tuxedo for prom that we'd eventually found in the back storeroom of a vintage thrift store in Milwaukee. He'd always been a sweetheart: good-natured, quick-witted, and one of the few members of Eric's family I genuinely missed after our split. It doesn't come as a surprise that he's pursuing art as a career, and yet seeing him here, holding him, feels surreal.

"Sean. Who is this?"

I draw back from Jared's hug to meet Julian's stony expression.

"Oh," I say dumbly. "Um, this is . . . Jared."

Jared snickers knowingly.

"Don't worry, sir, there's about zero chance of me trying to steal your girl. Don't take this personally; she's a very beautiful woman. Just, erm, not my type." He drops his wrist to demonstrate who is, then laughs. "Sean's my favorite of my brother's exes."

The way he says it, so blasé, causes my body to stiffen. I've always wondered what Eric told his family about how we ended, if he claimed that we'd just drifted apart or manufactured a tired tale of me as the stuck-up doctor girlfriend who didn't make time for him. He has certainly not told them the truth, or Jared might not be so familiar.

"It's nice to see you again," I say, half meaning it. My mouth manages to be both dry and tacky with saliva, and I swallow, praying that my nerves don't show. "This is your work?"

Luckily for me, Jared is as chatty as I remember, and at my invitation happily tells us all about his journey as an artist, pulling out his phone to show us his portfolio. His pieces are impressive, simple enough that they could hang comfortably in homes while still having gallery appeal, and the longer we speak, the more relaxed I become. Jared isn't his brother and never has been, and even if the resemblance is uncanny, they could not be more different.

"You finished training, right? Are you finally a badass rich cardiologist who can afford one of my pieces?" Jared asks, waggling his brows. Then his eyes flicker up to Julian, and his grin turns coy. "Or will Mr. Tall, Brooding, and Beautiful be my customer?"

Behind me, Julian has been mostly quiet, trailing behind us like a ghoul. At Jared's invocation, though, he reaches into his wallet and hands him a business card.

Jared looks down at the card, his eyes going wide.

"Harrison and Conrad Galleries?" He looks from me to Julian, realization dawning on his face. "Holy shit, Sean. You're dating a *Conrad*? Way to level up!"

"You're very talented," Julian says in a brusque, businesslike tone. "That email goes to my assistant, Ritika. We'd love to showcase your work, but we also have connections with some national galleries that might be interested in you as well."

"Yes, of course." Jared's joviality is gone, and I'm worried that he might start bowing at any moment. "Thank you, Mr. Conrad. This is such a great honor." He pulls out a couple of business cards of his own. One goes to Julian. He scrawls something onto the back of the second: his number. "And Sean. It was so good to see you. Don't be a stranger! I would love to get coffee and catch up!"

Numbly, I take the card. I can't tell this very darling boy-turned-man that I'll never use it, that I can't stomach forty-five minutes across from him in a coffee shop because looking at his face reminds me of the darkest era of my life. I should thank him, give him an empty platitude ("Sure, definitely!") but the words are gravel on my tongue, impossible to spit out or swallow down.

Julian's voice slices through the muddle of my thoughts.

"Hope you have a good rest of your day, Jared," he says. He wields his dismissal like a sword, and Jared jumps back in understanding.

"I will!" he assures us, scurrying away. "You too!"

The hall is sparsely attended, a small showing on the exhibit's last week, and another guest, having eavesdropped on our conversation, pulls Jared into another. He nods and beams and shows them his phone as well, and even with the spectrum of emotions clashing in my chest, I recognize a warm undercurrent of pride.

A hand on the small of my back guides me out of the main hall and into a quiet corridor.

"You're not okay," Julian says. It's an observation, not a question, and my vision blurs with tears.

"No," I confess.

Julian doesn't ask me why. He doesn't probe me on why seeing my ex's little brother has left me shaking when I am so generally unshakable. Instead, he sighs and pulls me into his chest.

It's just a hug. A chin on the top of my head, arms wound around my shoulders. But when he holds me like this it's hard to stop the tears from coming. I stand in his embrace for a long time, and I realize, numbly, that this experience is new. I am so completely used to crying alone.

"God, this is embarrassing," I confess when my breathing finally slows. I sniff, pull back to make sure I haven't left part of my face behind on his Burberry trench coat, and wince when I see a smudge of foundation. "Sorry. I can pay for dry cleaning—"

"Absolutely not," Julian says. He reaches into his pocket, produces a handkerchief, and dabs my cheek. The gesture is so tender, so oddly paternal, that it almost makes me cry again.

Voices echo around the corner, other art center guests leaving the exhibit. Julian pulls me in to shield me from view and waits until they pass. In the huddle of his arms, I feel completely encapsulated. Warm. Small. Safe.

"Where do you want to go?" he whispers when they leave.

"Anywhere," I say.

And so Julian takes me home.

Nine

Don't ever let a man show any signs of violence around you," my daddy told me when I came back home during winter break my freshman year of college and confessed that I'd finally acquired my first boyfriend. "Not even as a joke. He uses his fists to solve a problem his mind should be able to handle, you leave him, and you don't look back, 'cause one day, he might decide you're the problem. And your daddy doesn't want to get locked away for murder, you understand?"

My father never hit my mother, but he showed his contempt in other ways: birthdays, anniversaries, and holidays during which he expected to be celebrated but routinely neglected her, temper tantrums thrown about her *disrespect* when she didn't jump to attend to his every need. For him, the line was clear: he would never raise a hand against her. As long as he did that, he was a good man, and my mother agreed.

I thought that Eric was a good man. On the surface, he had all the markers of one: an educational background that promised financial stability, a close-knit family, the kind of homegrown chivalry that dictated that he bring flowers to a first date. My father thought he was a good man too. The first time I came crying to him—because

Eric had called me *selfish* and threatened to leave me for considering an offer to attend my dream training program—my father warned me that my ambitions, while nice, would limit my romantic options and that good men like my boyfriend, who would be fine with my stubborn insistence against "continuing his legacy" with children and my constant need for schooling, were hard to come by. When I caught Eric flirting with one of his female coworkers over text and he claimed to feel *neglected*, my father insisted that, well, men were weak to sins of the flesh, and it was my job to keep him satisfied or be content to watch him stray.

It was all bullshit. A part of me knew that even then, but I buried those voices down deep and did what I was told: trusted and believed. Eric was too stressed by his postdoc to cook, so I made sure to meal prep for two and keep the fridge stocked on the weeks when I was on service in the intensive care unit. Eric wanted a woman who prioritized him, so I neglected my friendships in favor of his and ended our relationship with a circle significantly smaller than the one with which I'd entered it. Eric hated when I cried, claimed that my tears were *manipulative*, and so when I couldn't hold back my frustration and hurt I cloistered myself in the bathroom, gripped the edges of the sink, and waited for my sobs to subside. I didn't question if I deserved comfort, only why I was so weak as to want it.

Which was probably why I felt so tense, receiving it from Julian now.

"How're you feeling?" Julian asks when we pull into his building's garage.

I lean back against the headrest and close my eyes.

"Like I need a stiff drink and a day-long nap," I say.

"Lucky for you, I make a pretty good whiskey sour," Julian says. He snaps the locks open. "You want to try one?"

I do. I follow him through his heated garage and into the mirrored elevator. Julian's apartment is on the twenty-fourth floor, and the first thing I notice when he swings the door open is its dazzling view of the city.

"Wow," I say as I step inside. The Chicago skyline glitters outside his window, the lake a dark expanse just beyond it. I imagine the view in the daytime is just as breathtaking. "You wake up to this every day?"

Julian snorts as he helps me out of my coat. I wander farther in, marveling at the beauty of this space. It's not a sparse bachelor pad, nor is it outfitted in the typical neutral palette favored by most young professionals. Instead, the walls are a rich, dark navy blue, the decor a mixture of golds, greens, and burnt oranges. A healthy fiddle-leaf fig tree sits in a carved concrete pot by the window, and a patchwork throw is tossed artfully over the back of a plush couch. And then there's the bookcase, cherrywood, floor to ceiling, and filled to the brim.

It's the home of an established man who has clear and distinct tastes. Difficult to form at his age, and yet he's managed.

At his kitchen island, Julian is assembling supplies to make our drinks.

"Make yourself at home," he instructs.

I slip off my boots, arrange them carefully by the door.

"Your place is beautiful," I say. It's the truth. Julian's apartment is imbued with so much personality that I feel like I know him better just by standing in it. I bend to examine a small polished wooden sculpture that resembles a fertility goddess, listening to the steady clink of glasses hitting granite, the slosh of his shaker. There is art hidden throughout his living room: a painting in the undercarriage of his coffee table, a bronze figure tucked under the lamp on a walnut buffet. Prints and pieces in eclectic frames, sizes, and subjects cover the wall across from the television.

My gaze snaps to one, a medium-sized canvas adorned by an ornate gold frame. It's a different style than the rest, impressionistic and dreamily depicted. The label tells me that it was painted by one Ifeoma Nwagwu in oil, and the title is *Together*. It features four teenagers, two girls and two boys. The first girl, sharp featured and brown skinned with thick wavy hair that skims past her hips, grins knowingly at her companions: a laughing woman with thick golden waves; a pale, slight man with a face like an angel and shoulder-length black hair; and a man with dark springy curls and smiling eyes. Their clothes are light and airy, white linen shirts and dresses that shroud them in innocence and meld into a sky bleached by a noonday sun.

It takes me a moment to realize why they look familiar.

"Is this you?" I ask, pointing to one of the figures.

Julian moves so silently that I don't realize he is right next to me until I feel the coolness of a glass being pressed into my hand.

"Yes," he says.

"That's Leila," I realize, looking at the blonde. "And these ones . . ."

"Old friends. This is Rose," Julian says softly, pointing to the other woman. His finger drifts, then lingers on the man. "Alphonse."

"*Together*," I read the title out loud.

"I commissioned it a few years back," Julian says. "The artist has this exceptional ability to capture personality and movement. She had an exhibit at the Whitney Museum in New York last year."

I marvel at the effort he's taken. It's clear these people are important to Julian, and that makes me want to know them.

"Tell me about them," I say.

Julian sips his drink, and I echo him, lifting my glass to my lips. His whiskey sour is sweet, tangy, and concerningly drinkable.

He gestures first to the woman with long black hair.

"Rose is an artist," he explains. "A brilliant one. Has shows all over the world. You've probably seen her work before—she submits a lot of it anonymously."

I squint at her.

"Can you give me a hint on which ones?" I try.

"Not a chance. I keep my friends' secrets," Julian says in a tone that is teasing but firm.

"You're no fun," I say. My finger trails to the other man. Even in this rendition, his features are delicate. "How about Alphonse? Where is he now?"

Julian hums, like he's suddenly remembered something.

"Alphonse . . ." he says softly, "is no longer with us."

My heart seizes. There is pain in his tone, yes, but also acceptance. This is an old wound, scabbed over but still raw under the surface.

"Oh," I say, stunned into stupidity. I'm astonished. I look at the boy closer. Alphonse's arms are crossed, his expression more tempered than the others'. I imagine him as the source of reason in the group, the one who kept them out of trouble. I wonder how it would feel to lose Winona and I have to exhale out the horror that the thought brings.

"When did he—?"

"A long time ago," Julian interrupts. I understand it for the gentle reprimand it is—that I shouldn't pry further. For a moment, I regret asking anything at all, and then change my mind. There has to be a reason why this painting is displayed so prominently. He must want people to ask. To keep Alphonse alive, in this small and mighty way.

"He was so young," I say, eventually.

"He made good use of the time he had," Julian says.

Sadness suddenly floods me. What Julian has in the way of art, he lacks in mementos of family. The only child of only children, he is the last remaining member of his line, cut off from tradition, heritage, from a history that I have taken for granted. What family he has now he has had to build.

I turn and meet his stare.

"What are you thinking?" Julian asks.

I'm thinking a lot of things. That despite his veneer of perfection, Julian's life has been filled with endless loss. That the caricature I built of him as this rich, erudite, arrogant playboy seems silly now. The real Julian Conrad is unmoored and searching for his anchor.

"That you're a bit too good to be true," I say instead.

Julian snickers.

"I'm being serious," I say. "I'm half convinced that you just rented out a model apartment to impress your dates with."

"A fascinating theory," Julian says. "So, the commissioned painting of me and my friends . . . ?"

"An add-on to the package, to lend to the illusion," I explain. "A broke art student in a basement whips one out for you in three to five business days. Comes complete with a tragic backstory."

The corner of Julian's mouth twitches upward with mirth.

"Ah, yes, the dead friend trick," he says. "Gets all the ladies going."

"Sorry," I say, wincing. "I shouldn't have joked about that. I'm not sure if you've noticed, but I put my foot in my mouth a lot."

Julian tilts his head to regard me more closely.

"Don't apologize," he says. "You say what you mean. It's refreshing."

"Yeah, well, you won't get a performance from me," I say. "Just awkward, radical honesty."

His eyes brighten with affection. Then, "In the spirit of radical honesty, are we going to talk about what happened out there today? With Jared."

A chill goes down my spine, the same iron walls that Julian has been lifting humming with the desire to lock up tight. It's been eight years, but telling men about Eric always feels like handing them an instruction manual on exactly how to break me. I drift away from the painting and toward the floor-to-ceiling windows, watch the city spill out at my feet.

"I . . ." The words get caught, and my next breath comes in a gasp. "I don't know where to start." At the beginning, when I first met Eric in the econ library, bent in half over a textbook? Or at the end, bleeding out on my bedroom floor as my calls went to his voicemail over and over?

"Somewhere easy," Julian offers. His voice is a rumble against my back, and I feel it as much as I hear it. "How you're feeling right now? In this moment?"

I let his question hang in the air unanswered for a moment as I process. *Warm*, I think. *But also terrified. Like I'm most of the way across a tightrope with no harness, and I've just made the mistake of looking down.*

"You first," I say.

Julian laughs. His reflection in the windows is translucent, ghostly, and when I look up at it, I can almost convince myself that he's not actually here with me. That the man behind me is the one who appears in my dreams.

"Helpless, I think," he says. "I don't like seeing you cry. I'm a person who fixes things, and I can't fix this."

"Is that what you want?" I ask. "To fix me, I mean."

"No," Julian says. "I want to *know* you."

Warmth rushes fast to my cheeks, and I swallow against the squeeze of my throat. It feels natural to lean back against him, and Julian accepts my embrace, resting a hand on my hip.

"God that's romantic," I mutter. "Like, I don't even know what to say to that."

"I don't know," he says, his hand dragging slowly up to the nip of my waist. "Maybe that you want me to know you too?"

I close my eyes, letting myself exist in this moment. I'm surrounded by him so fully that I feel like I've crawled under his ribs to breathe for him, to fuel his body with my hummingbird heart.

"It's not that I don't want to talk about it," I confess. "I just . . . don't know how. You have this idea of me as this tough woman who takes no shit, and . . . I guess I don't want to disrupt that."

People don't like tough women, but they do respect them. They don't fuck with them without a posse and a plan, and I like being unfuck-with-able. It's so much better than being the frightened, fragile thing I was before. That I fear I might still be.

I can almost hear the gears in Julian's head shifting.

"I want to show you something," he says abruptly.

I drop my head back to give him a quizzical look, but he's already stepping back, taking my hand before guiding me down the darkened hallway that bisects his apartment. I wonder, for a second, if we're heading to his bedroom, but then he stops at a set of double doors and swings them open.

This room looks considerably more lived-in than his artfully cluttered living room. Mounted records line the walls, and even more sit in stacks on the floor, in the bookshelf. Three guitars, two acoustic and one electric, hang from the wall above a worn denim couch. Two enormous amps double as side tables, and the walls are padded with what I realize is soundproofing material.

And in the center of the room, taking up most of the floor space, the prize: a sleek black baby grand piano. I can't help it; I gape.

"Are you serious? A Bösendorfer?" I say, zipping to the bench. "I've never seen one of these in real life!"

Julian's lips quirk in a smile.

"You're an unusual woman," he observes. "The quickest way to your heart seems to be through fancy pianos."

I wrinkle my nose at him, almost annoyed by how rapidly he's set me at ease. I lift the fallboard to run my fingers along the keys, and the sounds make me want to melt into the seat.

"Ugh, I'm so jealous. I have a console at home. Can't fit a baby grand in my apartment."

"As you can see, I can barely fit this one either," Julian says, settling next to me. His piano bench is smaller than the first one we shared once, and so we're wedged close, our arms welded together. "It takes up most of the space in here. Not exactly our room in Edison Mansion."

"*Our* room, was it?" I tease.

Julian starts to play. I recognize the song within a few notes as "Gymnopédie No. 1."

"I like to think of it that way," he says. "Don't you?"

I nod, biting back a smile. *I like the sound of that too much*, I think.

After Julian assures me that his downstairs neighbors won't be disturbed, I reach for the keys, playing out the treble notes of Debussy's "La Fille aux Cheveux de Lin" with my right hand. Julian takes over the bass, and we finish the short piece together, letting the final notes ring out into the night. It's only when they have finally faded away that Julian begins to speak.

"Remember when you asked me if anyone had ever been serious for me, and I told you there had been one?" he asks. I am about to turn to him when he abruptly begins a Chopin piece, and I realize why he brought us here. When we are both playing, we can't look at each other. It makes it easier to speak freely.

"Her name was Claire," Julian says. "She was an incredible pianist. Taught music at an elementary school, but she made extra money playing at lounges. That's how we met. I walked in for a business meeting and botched it completely. I couldn't focus. There was just . . . something about her, you know. The biggest hair I've ever seen. Skin shining in the dim light. Making the most beautiful music."

I'm floored by the emotion in his voice, how it goes so quiet that I have to strain my ears to listen even from right next to him.

"I was just an okay pianist then. I wanted to be close to her, and so I hired her to tutor me. And, well. You can guess what happened next."

"Sweet, hot love against the keys?" I guess, and out of the corner of my eye I can see him smile.

"Eventually," he says. "Took a while. She was very serious about teaching me. Wouldn't even let me take her out on a date until I mastered 'Clair de Lune.'"

"Sounds like my kind of girl," I say, and Julian bumps me playfully with his shoulder.

"You're a lot alike, actually. I'm not sure if I would have ever wanted you in the same room. Who knows what sort of torment you would come up with together." He straightens as if he's just realized something. "I have a type, don't I."

I surprise myself by laughing out loud.

"Well, not to sound full of myself, but she sounds pretty amazing to me. Why'd you break up?" Next to me, Julian tenses, and I realize that I have once again broached sensitive territory. "Sorry. Didn't mean to pry. You don't have to tell me—"

"You aren't prying. I'm telling you," Julian interrupts. His voice is suddenly hoarse, like he's using it for the first time in days, and he clears his throat. "We, erm, never broke up."

It takes me a moment to process what he's just told me. My first instinct is outrage, because why is he seeing me if he never ended things with her, then confusion, because maybe they were never really together. It takes me a few more seconds to put together the context clues. The heaviness in his tone. The fact that all this time, he's been speaking about her in past tense.

"She was an incredible person," Julian continues, and I hear it now: his raw, raging grief. "Tenacious. Fierce. She dreamed so big and so loud, and she deserved so much better than what she got."

"You loved her," I whisper.

"So much," he confirms.

"What happened?" I turn to him, try to learn him by the expression he wears, but his face is tucked down toward the keys.

"An accident," he says. "She's gone now."

"Oh." All of a sudden Julian is transformed in my eyes, not just orphan but widower, his youth eclipsed by the depth of the pain I now know he holds. I cup his cheek in my hand and find it quivering. "Oh, Jules. I'm so sorry."

Julian nods.

"Your turn," he says.

My tale of woe seems so small now. One terrible ex-fiancé from eight years back, and I still have panic attacks after seeing his brother. It feels like an inadequate offering in the face of what Julian has shared tonight.

But he's let me know him. And I know what Winny would say: that I should let him know me too.

"Do you know 'Passacaglia'?" I start. "I don't remember who it's by. Starts with an H—"

"Handel and Halvorsen," Julian supplies. "Yes."

Our start is about as clumsy as my words. But I still get them out.

"I met Jared's older brother my first year of medical school," I say. "I used to sneak off to the econ library to study, and he lived there. No matter how early I got there, he'd always seem to beat me to my favorite desk. By the time I struck up the courage to ask him for coffee, I think I was already smitten."

All these years later, I can still see him. Thinner than he was in our last years together, one hand always clutching an ear like he wanted to tear it off as he pored over his books. The sweet twenty-two-year-old girl who used to giggle to Winona about the cute guy she'd discovered in the bowels of a library across campus seems so unlike me that I see her in third person: marked white Air Force 1s, DIY crochet braids, an open, hopeful heart that she wore on her sleeve.

"He was sweet at first, you know. Did all the right things to woo a girl: bought me flowers, took me to nice restaurants. Told me he liked me for my ambition, liked that I planned to hold my own. I told him I didn't want to get married or have kids, and he would go on these long diatribes about how 'marriage is the stupidest financial decision you could ever make' and how glad he was that I was *enlightened* enough to not want it." I snort to cover my misery. "It's so funny. The red flags are always so obvious in retrospect."

Julian hums but doesn't interrupt. Instead, he flips the page of the book of sheet music to a song I don't know, and I squint at the notes, trying to decipher them as I do my memories.

"Still, I can't pinpoint when things changed. Maybe when I graduated? He was in his postdoc, I was in residency, and life got hard. And I thought it was just that we were both stressed, not our best selves. That maybe I wasn't paying enough attention to him, and that's why things went south."

Arguments started over things that I didn't understand—my taking calls from work was "disrespectful," hanging out with Winona after work was "not prioritizing him." He'd punish me by leaving our home, turning off his phone, only to return days later and pretend that nothing had happened. Physical altercations that seemed like they could be accidents—shoves that could be explained as him "moving my body," pinches at my side so hard they made me yelp that he claimed were "playful."

"It was always something. At some point, I started catching him talking to other girls—nothing too crazy at first, because he was smart enough to never completely cross the line, you know? They were just friends, they were bonding over video games I didn't play, couldn't he have a social network, et cetera. He'd tell me, *Don't you trust me?* And that would turn into this whole thing about how I was a terrible partner for *not* trusting him, and I would sit and wonder. Like maybe he was right, and I was the problem? I felt . . . crazy. Everything was upside down and inside out and nothing I could do was right. I was so sure he was going to leave me. So scared he'd decide that I was too insecure or controlling or whatever the issue was that day and finally dip. But instead, one day, we went to his family's barbecue and he pulled out a *ring*."

Julian stops playing; it takes me a second to realize that I have stopped too. This memory plays back too crisp and too loud, the sounds discombobulating to the point of distraction. The crunch of dry grass under Eric's knee as he knelt before me, the rattle of his emotionally incestuous mother's envious gasp, the sizzle of the noonday summer sun on my exposed shoulders. The distant, foghorn sound of his question: *Will you marry me?*

"He proposed? After all that?" Julian asks, his tone lethally flat.

I laugh mirthlessly.

"Yeah," I say. "And you want to know the worst part?"

"What?"

"I said yes."

I laugh harder, but Julian doesn't join me. He is stone silent as I finish, as the words rush out of me like they're pressurized. This isn't the first time I've told this story, but telling Julian feels like a different sort of release. I am showing him my belly, stripping away more than just clothes, and there is something freeing about this. Suddenly, I don't care if Julian respects me less. What matters most is that he *sees* me, for more than the hard-shelled, soft-inside woman he thought he knew at Margaret's exhibition. What matters is that he doesn't look away.

"I thought it would fix everything," I continue. "That Eric changing was my fault, that I gave him too little, demanded too much, and that by saying yes I was proving my commitment to him. That he'd just been stressed, just suffering, just struggling. And that his proposal was evidence that he loved me and was just looking for reassurance that, even after all the ways I'd let him down, I loved him back. I thought, well, things will get better now, he'll *feel* better, now that he knows what I'm willing to compromise for us."

I pause. We are riding the crescendo of this story, about to reach a deafening climax, and I need my fingers to be busy again.

"We need a new song," I say.

Julian bends to grab a binder with a label that, in better circumstances, would have made me crack a smile: *Film scores, most certainly stolen.* We sift through the printed, well-loved pages, taking a brief intermission, and then settle on a theme from *Gladiator.*

"What happened then, Sean?" Julian's voice is soft.

"Then I got pregnant," I say. The notes shiver on the page. I hit a treble A instead of an F that makes us both flinch but we carry on. I don't search for his reaction, because I know that if I do I'll lose momentum. "Who knows how. We used two forms of birth control. That psychopath probably microwaved my pills. Only found out because I had a miscarriage. Ended up in the ICU. My fiancé was nowhere to be found, of course, because a couple of days earlier he decided we were done and skipped town to be with his new girl. Just, you know, forgot to break up with me first."

It's the most concise manner in which I've ever told this story because I leave out the details. How I'd had no time to reconcile with the reality that I was pregnant before I abruptly was not, how despite having no desire for motherhood, there had been no relief alongside my horror. I should have gone to the emergency room, should have sought immediate care, but I was still an interventional cardiology fellow, the first woman my program had matched in fifteen years, and so I bled through three sets of scrubs, stole bulky hospital-issue pads from the supply closets, stuffed my underwear with toilet paper, and cried in bathrooms between cases as I waited for the nightmare to end. But it didn't. I remember waking up a few days later, feverish, disoriented, *wet*. In the dim light of dawn, the blood had stained my sheets black. And there was so much of it, more than I thought my body could hold.

Silence rings in my ears; it takes me a second to realize that we have once again stopped mid-song. Suddenly I am self-conscious. I hate how recounting this memory makes me feel small and simple-minded, hate the urge to reach back into my past, grab my old self by the shoulders, and scream at her to demand better for herself before it's too late.

"You almost died," Julian says. "He almost killed you."

My stomach clenches.

"I was stupid," I say softly. "I know what they say: *Hindsight is twenty-twenty, I was only operating with the knowledge that I had*, et cetera, but it doesn't change the fact that he treated me like trash for years before the end. If I'd just seen the signs, had more self-respect, none of that would've happened—"

"You were not stupid," Julian retorts. We're wedged so close that when he turns to face me, he's blurred and out of focus. Everything but his eyes, which are creased with rage that soothes rather than unsettles. "You promised to love someone. To give them grace. That level of trust, that capacity for forgiveness, is a gift that people spend entire lifetimes seeking in others. It isn't your fault that your ex was so shortsighted and weak-minded as to exploit that."

Oh god. I am going to cry again. I bite back tears, turning away so that he can't see them.

"Thank you for saying that," I manage. I don't know whether he knows how deep his words reach. For so long, I've felt ashamed of this anguish. Like I should have gotten over it years ago. Like the hollow I still feel in the pit of my belly is power that Eric still has over me. I've never heard anyone call that love I'd given, so selfless, so self-abandoning, a *gift*.

"Thank *you*," Julian says. "I know what it must have meant for you to tell me this. I don't take it for granted."

My exhale comes out in a shudder.

"You're good at this, you know," I say, smiling weakly at him.

"At what?" Julian asks.

"At cracking me open," I say. "I feel, I don't know. Safe with you."

Julian's eyelids flutter, and I see something shift in his gaze. He sits back, swallows, and tilts his head up to the ceiling.

"Safe," he chokes, like the word is a baton against his chest. I'm trying to make sense of his reaction as he lifts my hand from the keys, turns it palm up, then presses a kiss oh so gently to the juncture of my wrist. "Should you? Feel safe, I mean."

"Should I not?" I ask. My pulse pounds against his lips, and I feel the soft gust of his breath blowing against it.

"I don't know," Julian confesses. "I'm not a normal man. I'm greedy. I want everything life has to give to me, and I want to imbibe it. To gulp it down, as fast as I can." He cradles his cheek against my hand, nuzzles into it. "That includes you, Sean."

His words feel dangerous. As if we've been coasting along a straight road, and he's just made a sharp turn that's left me reaching for the grab handle. I can't look away from him, caught in his web, unable to do more than try to calm my breath.

"I want all of you," Julian continues, confesses. "All of your secrets and more of your memories. I want to know the things that make you laugh and cry, what you're proud of and what you'd rather keep close. I want to catalog every kiss"—he kisses my palm—"every touch"—he sucks the meat of it between his teeth—"just so I can return to it in my dreams." He smiles as he looks at me, a slow, sultry thing. "Does that scare you?"

My heart is a jackhammer in my ears, drowning me out. Julian's right. His intensity *should* frighten me. But it doesn't. Instead it feels like I'm being seen for the first time in a long time. Like he has just held up a mirror to the version of me I've tried to squirrel away, the one whose love was boundless and unabashed and *too much*, and given her permission to exist.

"No," I whisper.

Julian's eyes flash; his laugh is no mirth and all warning.

"No?" he says, and suddenly his voice is different, now husk and echo, and his grip becomes iron tight. More the man I see in my dreams than the one who held me to his chest in a quiet corridor just hours before. "I've just told you that I might be just a little obsessed with you, Sean Sullivan, and you aren't running away screaming? What does that say about you?"

"That I'm the same, probably," I confess, breathless, and he shifts closer, hanging on to my every word. "I think you're *fascinating*, and I want to know you too. I don't think I've ever wanted to know anyone the way I want to know you." I swallow, bewitched by the gentle parting of Julian's lips, his steady unraveling. "I . . . I dream of you too—"

The sound Julian makes is half snarl, and in one smooth movement, he kicks back the piano bench, and suddenly I'm in the air, lofted into his arms with my legs wound around his waist.

We're doing this, I think as he pushes the door to the music room open and takes me down the hall. *We're actually doing this*. My body is all too eager, every part of me straining for him, and I nuzzle into his neck and inhale. Good lord this man always smells so good. I want to sneak into his cabinet and douse myself in his cologne. Julian shivers.

"Careful, Sean," he warns.

I'm tired of being careful, I think. *Tired of being afraid*. I fold his skin between my lips and tug, kiss my way up to his ear, and delight in the shuddering sigh I earn in response. Julian boosts me up in his arms until we are face-to-face and backs me into the hallway wall. The feeling of him hard against me as his mouth crashes into mine whets my most primitive appetite. I want to touch him properly this time. Want him in my mouth, his fist in my hair. Want to watch his eyes roll back as he succumbs to me, to show him just what I'm capable of making *him* feel for once—

A grating beep interrupts my thoughts.

"What is— Oh shit."

It's like I've been dropped into a dunk tank; I am instantly sober. I pat Julian on the shoulder and, obediently, he lets me down.

My pager forwards to my phone, which is currently in my purse on the kitchen island, and I pad, barefoot, toward it. My stomach churns with uncertainty—I'm not on call, so either some unfortunate intern has accidentally paged the incorrect interventional cardiologist at the most inopportune time, or something is greatly amiss.

As is my luck, it turns out to be the latter.

"I'm so sorry to do this to you, Dr. Sullivan," one of the cardiology fellows, Nasreen, says. "But we have a STEMI, and we can't reach Dr. Pendersen. Can you come in?"

Ten

The thing about emergencies is that they care very little about convenience. The fifty-nine-year-old gentleman about whom I have been called was jolted out of a deep sleep by crushing chest pain after a long shift at the auto shop and was rushed in by ambulance. I am being dragged from my date possibly minutes before getting ravished in order to fix him. Neither I nor my patient is particularly thrilled by the interruption, but we're both here because this situation is quite literally as serious as a heart attack.

Julian drives me to the hospital. The electrocardiogram that Nasreen forwarded to me looks foul.

"I'm so sorry," I say to Julian for the thousandth time.

"It's fine. You're saving someone's life," Julian says.

He doesn't look fine. His grip on the steering wheel is perfectly set at ten and two, and he's barely spoken to me since I got off the phone with Nasreen. He's disappointed, and I don't blame him, because I am too. I just don't quite understand why it's led him to this sullenness when we can just pick up where we left off the next time we see each other.

"This doesn't usually happen," I say. *It never happens*, I almost amend. Brandon is the one on call, but he didn't respond to the page and isn't picking up his calls or answering his texts. But to quote every interventional cardiologist ever, *Time is myocardium*, and I am not about to sit by and let someone die because I'm caught in my own romance. Still, Brandon Pendersen better be lying in a ditch right now to justify ruining my night.

"It's fine," Julian repeats, but when we pull up in front of the hospital, he doesn't lean forward to kiss me good night. He is so many miles away from the man who sat with me on the bench just minutes before, telling me he wants to gulp me down.

"It's clearly not," I say as I gather my things.

Julian sighs, but his gaze doesn't lift from the wheel.

"Maybe," he says slowly, "we should hold off on going to each other's places for a little while."

The whiplash almost strains my neck.

"Wait, what?" I blurt out, bewildered. "Sorry, but why?"

Julian gives me a plaintive, puppy-dog look, the same one I get from Onix when I catch him going through the trash.

"Because we get carried away," he says. "We should be taking things slow. Getting to know each other properly. It's hard to do that, with what we get up to whenever we're alone."

I almost retort that I think I know him plenty well enough already, and that being within the public eye has so far not stopped us from getting handsy with each other, but I can't afford to entertain his contradictions. I have to go and *now*.

"Let's finish this conversation later," I tell him, throwing the car door open. "Call me? Tomorrow?"

Julian nods, but his mouth is still set tight.

"Hope it goes well," he says.

I try not to let his chilliness bother me. Men being intrigued by my career in theory but spooked by it in practice is par for the course. Knowing that neither stops the twinge of disappointment from turning my stomach nor the panic from squeezing my chest—Did I tell him too much tonight? Overwhelm him with details? Does Julian suddenly want to take things slow because now that he's had a minute to process my baggage, he's realized he doesn't actually want to carry it?

The thoughts plague me as I rush into the hospital, change into my scrubs, and throw on my lead. The case is straightforward but deadly—a blockage in the left anterior descending artery that pops open with the first inflation of our small balloon. We get a stent in quick, and my annoyance at being interrupted fades as my patient goes from sweating through his gown and cursing us all out to comfortable and apologetic in just under half an hour. There's peace and purpose in the catheterization lab, a regimented process that involves minute, fine movements. It feels like art, twirling micron-thick wires into millimeter-wide arteries, calmly directing my fellow to adjust the X-ray arms, pull the table, flush the sheath.

I take a Lyft home afterward. Onix is sleeping when I make it, and I hear him shaking awake as I turn the key in my apartment. He plods wearily to the door, nudging it open with his snout, then gives me a scathing look like a parent who has just caught their delinquent daughter sneaking back into the house after curfew.

"I would have been back early enough tomorrow to take you out," I assure him. He releases a long-suffering sigh, like he pays rent, then hobbles back into my room and flops onto his mattress at the foot of my bed.

It's late, and the drastic swing of emotions from anticipation and excitement to dread and careful concentration has left me drained. I send Julian a quick text letting him know I made it home as I brush my teeth, then collapse gracelessly into bed. My descent into sleep is precipitous; one second I am staring up at my ceiling, and the next I have slipped into darkness.

When I wake up the next morning, I feel like death warmed over.

I spend all the next day in bed. Onix is thankfully gracious about his delayed, abbreviated walks, and in return I let him lie next to me under the covers, shivering against his body heat. I take five flu and COVID tests and they all come back negative. In my symptom journal, I write: *Jittery. Nauseous. Extreme fatigue. Body aches.*

When I tell Winona that my symptoms are back, she forces me to reach out to my primary care doctor, Dr. Steinbeck. He orders a few tests: blood counts to see if I have an infection, inflammatory markers to assess whether my body is attacking itself, a chemistry panel to check my organs and electrolytes, a respiratory viral panel to make sure we aren't missing a strain that wouldn't show up on my home tests.

Everything comes back normal. I am, by Dr. Steinbeck's estimations, the picture of health.

"Maybe it's just a really bad cold," he tells me over the phone.

But it doesn't feel like a cold. It feels like being hit by a monster truck. I suspect, glumly, that I may just be suffering from a contused heart, because days after we swapped traumas over the keys of his ostentatiously fancy piano, Julian still hasn't called. Worse, my check-in text, the totally neutral, definitely even-keeled request for him to let me know if he still wanted to talk, has been left unanswered, but because his read receipts are on, not unseen. Surely, I think, the rapid oscillations in my heart rate and blood pressure whenever my phone dings with a text from someone who is inevitably not him can't be good for me.

Regardless, no positive tests and no clear infection means that I have to go in to work.

"Don't be a pussy, Sullivan," Krause, who is officially the head of the cath lab and unofficially the king of unpunished Title IX violations, says, when I ask him if he or any of our other interventional cardiologists can cover my day in the lab. "Just wear an N95 and do your job like the rest of us."

I try each of my colleagues directly to see if any of them are willing to cover me, but they're all either on vacation, out of town giving talks, or, in Haoran's case, on after-school pickup duty this week.

Brandon is insufficiently apologetic.

"I promise I'll pay you back," he says. "It just might take a while. I've picked up some extra shifts, so the schedule is pretty outrageous right now. Sorry you aren't feeling well."

Sorry that you're useless, I want to say, but I have neither the energy nor the desire for another fruitless confrontation with yet another man who destroyed my belief in love and loyalty. So I drag myself in and manage to get myself through my cases without passing out into my sterile field.

In some ways, I am happy for the work. It distracts me from perseverating 24/7 on the fact that Julian still hasn't reached out. It's hard to sink into despair when someone else's life is on the line, to dwell on the tragic coincidence that his disappearance coincides with my decision to confide in him about the fallout of my last relationship. In the lab, I am the cool, precise Dr. Sullivan, jamming to my playlist of nineties R & B while I give my patients their second leases on life. The moment I step outside it, I collapse into a pathetic pile of achy goo who can't go longer than five minutes without checking her phone for a missive from a man who, at this point, has made it abundantly clear that he wants nothing to do with me.

It doesn't help that I still see him every night. He's different in my dreams too, distant—a passerby in a crowd, a stranger standing opposite me on a darkened train platform. When I call his name, he averts his eyes, and in this space in which my hold on my emotions is tenuous at best, his dismissal feels like torture.

Through the force of sheer will alone, I make it to my girls' date with Sophie. I'm about 99.99 percent sure that I'm not contagious, but my appetite is shot and I don't want to get my goddaughter sick, so I wear a mask, push the menu at our favorite ramen spot to her, and tell her to go hog wild.

Go wild she does. Sophie orders a pork tonkotsu ramen with all the fixings, karaage, and a green tea red bean crepe for dessert. She nibbles through her feast like a mouse sampling its way through a pantry all while regaling me with the latest in middle school drama—Peter Rindell, the boy most of the seventh-grade girls have a crush on, was apparently caught with a strawberry-kiwi vape behind the bleachers and gave all the tween girls the ick. I listen to her chatter with amusement. Kids her age are a clash of contradictions; Sophie still ties a remnant of her blankie around the arm of her backpack, is scared of the dark, and crawls into her mom's bed during thunderstorms. But she can also have a surprisingly coherent discussion about gender ("It's weird that they don't like him because they think strawberry-kiwi is a girly flavor instead of because being addicted to nicotine at thirteen is lame"), her future job prospects ("I hate when people ask me what I want to be when I grow up when no one pays enough to live anymore"), and the ethics of brachycephalic dog breeds ("How do people think pug snorts are cute? You're literally hearing the sound of them suffocating with every breath"). I'm glad to see her in good spirits. I almost don't want to bring up her dad, but I know from my own days as an occasionally troubled preteen that kids Sophie's age can be remarkably good at normalizing the abnormal. I'm thinking through ways to start the conversation: *So, how are you liking spending time with Leila, how was last weekend at your dad's, how are you doing with the split,* when Sophie jumps in for me.

"Don't tell Mom," she says around a mouthful of chicken, "but Dad's been acting really weird lately."

With the mask covering my mouth, the only part of my face I have to control are my eyebrows.

"How so?" I say, feigning surprise.

Sophie shrugs.

"He's tired all the time," she complains. "He spends, like, the entire day on the couch watching TV. He doesn't really even talk to me or Leila unless we talk to him first. It's like he's a robot."

"Huh." I search for what to say next. "So if he doesn't talk to you and sits on the couch all day, what do you even do when you're there?"

Sophie slurps her noodles so aggressively that her broth splashes onto the table.

"I'm almost thirteen, Auntie. I can keep myself busy," she says. Then she pauses, like she's about to confess something shameful. "And besides, Leila and I hang out."

This I did not expect. My left eye twitches, and then I clear my throat.

"Oh?" I say. "What do you do?"

"All sorts of things," Sophie says. "We bake, sometimes. Last week we made a pumpkin roll, and before that we made a cheesecake from scratch. Also we watch a *lot* of music videos. She's a dancer too, so she's been helping me out with my routine. She's really nice to me."

She pauses, her eyes downcast. "I don't think Dad is going to come to my recital Sunday. I told him about it like three times, and every time he acts like he's never heard of it. Leila said that she wants to be there, but it might be awkward with Mom."

My heart aches for Winona. There's no doubt in my mind that she'll be happy that her daughter feels at home with her new stepmother, but I also know that learning that Sophie is making memories that Winona often doesn't have the time to provide would sting. She's already lost her husband to Leila; I can't imagine she'll be excited about sharing her daughter too.

"Do you want Leila to come to your recital?" I ask Sophie.

Sophie lowers her chopsticks. She has her mother's protuberant eyes, but hers are framed all around with thick, doll-like lashes. When she was born, I stared at her for minutes, stunned that my best friend could make such a perfect being.

"Yes?" she asks hopefully. "Can you ask Mom if it's okay?"

I bite my lip. I imagine Leila dressed in a sleek Lululemon athletic set, helping guide Sophie through her choreography. The pride that will shine on Sophie's face when she gets through her routine onstage and looks into the crowd to see Leila beaming up at her.

"I can ask," I say, reluctantly.

An hour and a half later, I keep my promise. Sophie hugs me good night and springs inside her house to take a shower before bed, and I linger in her mother's foyer, leaning against the wall to keep myself upright. After a full week of work and several nights of subpar sleep, I feel like I'm going to pass out, but I figure I can't until I deliver this message.

Winona responds just as expected.

"She wants Leila to come? Why?" she snips. Her mouth is pressed thin, and the crease between her furrowed brows deepens. Then she sighs. "What am I thinking? Of course Leila can come if Sophie wants her there. I should be grateful that she's treating her well. Her father on the other hand . . ."

"Yeah," I mutter. Navigating being Brandon's coworker and Winona's best friend has required delicacy; we have a general understanding that I don't bring up what goes on at work. But this feels important. "He's been strange in the hospital too. Sloppier with his cases. And he missed a STEMI Saturday. I had to come in for it."

Winona gapes at me.

"Wait. You mean last Saturday? Isn't that when you were out with Julian?"

I wince. Hearing Julian's name stings like my upper lip after a wax.

"Yeah, well." I sigh, then change the subject. "Look, Sophie is genuinely concerned that Brandon won't show up for the recital, and I know for a *fact* that he's not on call or on service that day. Just . . . wanted to let you know."

Winona is all fire and brimstone.

"That is unacceptable," she hisses. "I'm going to talk to him. Thank you for letting me know."

"Of course," I say, creeping for the door. I have a forty-minute drive and a minimum twenty-minute walk with a cooped-up Onix ahead of me, and I don't think I can manage an additional second on my feet. It's not fatigue that plagues me so much as a bones-deep weakness, like it takes all the energy I have left to hold myself up. "I'm, um, going to head out."

Winona nods, then reaches for me to give me a hug. I step just out of her reach, then point up to my mask.

"Still not sure what I've got," I remind her.

"You can't still be contagious," Winona complains, but she doesn't try again; most of her patients are immunocompromised and I know she takes keeping herself healthy seriously. "Stay safe on your drive back tonight. There's apparently a blizzard coming; don't want you getting caught up in it."

In my desperation to make it from one day to the next, I have neglected to keep up with the weather. I pull out my phone, swallow my despondence, when I notice that there are still no new texts waiting for me, check the radar—and there it is, an ominous, swirling cloud of purple and white sweeping toward the city.

"Then I really have to go," I say. "Good night."

Winona squeezes my shoulder, like she can't help but express her gratitude through touch.

"Thanks again, Sulley. For everything. And no pressure to come Sunday; you need to rest, and I know Sophie would understand."

"And miss out on her sick moves?" I laugh. "No way. See you then; save me a seat."

Eleven

As foretold, a blizzard descends upon the city. I avoid the worst of it by the skin of my teeth, turning into my building's garage just minutes after the first fat, wet snowflakes land on my windshield. Onix, who is thirteen years old, arthritic, and doesn't have any time for this shit, is greatly displeased by the change in the weather. Ten minutes into our squinting hobble down the street and he's done, employing all seventy pounds of his bulk to drag me back home.

The next morning the snow turns to hail and then to sleet. I spend the morning in my office slouched in my chair, fending off sleep, watching my clinic appointments disappear from my schedule and googling inane things like "why did he ghost me" and "getting over a crush in your thirties." I'm halfway through a video by a self-proclaimed feminist dating coach advising me to "teach myself to be disgusted by his disrespect" when my assigned medical assistant pops open the door. I hurriedly silence my phone and place it face down on my desk like a guilty kid, but luckily, he doesn't seem to notice.

"Your eleven forty no-showed, so I'm heading to lunch early," he informs me.

"That's fine," I say, my words swallowed by a yawn. "I'm going to take a nap. Tell whoever's covering you to wake me up if someone shows up."

He nods and closes the door, and I'm alone again. The exhaustion I've been fighting to get through my clinic day suddenly weighs heavy on my shoulders, and I slump forward onto my desk, nestling my head in the dark space made by my folded arms. My eyes flutter closed, and between one second and the next, I'm gone from the world—

—and waking, abruptly, to a new one. It's all white: endless white walls, white sheets only distinguishable by the shadows in their folds under a gossamer white canopy. I look down at my body and see white silk and delicate lace: a robe that might have once been worn by a 1940s starlet on her way to seduce her producer.

"I've missed you," a voice says.

I snap toward it, my heart leaping as adrenaline surges within me. I shouldn't be surprised to find Julian here, now that he's established himself as a recurring player in my dreams, but I *am* surprised to hear him speak. He looks different today. Otherworldly in a way that makes me fight not to avert my gaze. His eyes glow amber, like they had in the music room in Edison Mansion so many weeks ago, and his bronze skin seems burnished gold, a demigod stepping foot on Mount Olympus and becoming divine. He tilts his head as he regards me, and I get the distinct feeling that I'm trapped, a fawn caught in a bear trap.

"Whose fault is that?" In this space, I don't bother to hide my irritation. "You're the one who ghosted me."

Julian tilts his head. He looks pleased, and that annoys me even more.

"Does that mean you've missed me too?" he asks. His gaze drops to my chest, lingering on the nipples that peek through the thin white fabric of my robe. This is a dream, I have no reason to be shy, but I still cross my arms to hide them from view. Julian smirks. "Certainly seems like it."

"Asshole," I whisper.

Julian laughs. The sound echoes off unseen walls.

"Asshole, am I?" he says. "I've simply stopped performing, just as you suggested."

I scoff, turning away. The motion makes my head swim, and I realize, with some horror, that this is the first time that my symptoms haven't dissipated in my dreams.

The canopy over my head shudders, and suddenly my back is flat against plush pillows and Julian is crouching over me, his knees squeezing my hips between them, arms trapping me in a cage. I'm very sure he'd been wearing a shirt a few seconds ago, but it's gone now, leaving just a gleaming chest that I ball my fists into the sheets to keep from reaching out to touch. As if he can hear my thoughts, he snatches my hand, places it on his abs, and tenses. The muscles ripple under my palm, and the space between my legs throbs like he's touched me there.

"I can make you all better, you know," Julian promises. His voice is a low, sultry whisper. "Either here and now, or later, out there. Anywhere you want. Any way you want too. You just have to ask."

"I . . ." I squeeze my eyes shut. "I don't want that from you right now."

Julian quirks an eyebrow, then lowers his hips into me, presses close until I can feel every inch of him against me, every ridge. I suck in a breath to keep from crying out and squeeze my eyes shut, enduring.

"Are you sure?" he teases.

The heat emanating from Julian's body is both oppressive and soothing, like sitting too close to a hearth, and it turns my mind liquid. The truth is that I'm *not* sure. Why shouldn't I let Julian have his way with me here, insulated from reality? It would be harmless, I think. And by the way it already feels now, even with thin layers of clothing still separating us, transcendent. My hips rise to meet his, and he presses me closer, flattening me against him and dragging a sigh out of my throat. I feel his groan at the nape of my neck, throaty with triumph.

"That's right," he says. "Give yourself to me."

His voice is resonant, like there are five of him in the room, all speaking in haunting unison. The words themselves are less seduction, more command, but I don't have time to consider the strangeness of them, because suddenly his hands are everywhere. Gripping my chin to open my mouth to him, tugging open my robe to roll my nipples between eager fingers. He sucks at the skin at the base of my neck, draws the flesh into his mouth, bites down. The pinch of his teeth makes me gasp, and desire drips down my body like slow-poured honey.

Suddenly, a voice, echoing in the distance.

"Sean?"

A sensation like ice water trickles down my back.

I know this voice. I hear it multiple times a week. It asks me about new cath lab equipment and always tips the baristas 20 percent at Brews and Beans and giggled through her vows at an ornate floral altar a few weeks ago.

Leila.

I am at work, I remember suddenly. *I am taking a nap in the clinic right now.*

I push Julian away with two hands against his chest.

"Wait," I say.

Julian pulls back ever so slightly.

"Wait?" he repeats, and for a second, the air around us falls still.

Then, without warning, the bed bursts into flame.

The heat is instant and overwhelming. I understand, implicitly, that I am on fire. But this is a different kind of burn, an overstimulation that leaps past pleasure and into agony. The flames lap at the erogenous zones behind my thighs, arms, under my breasts like so many tongues, leaving sizzling trails of humming skin in their wake. The rush of sensation is so staggering that I squeeze my eyes shut to stem the sensory overload.

"Tell me to wait again," Julian croons. His voice comes from everywhere, a whisper in my ear, an echo in my skull. "Tell me you don't want me right now."

"I—" I try, but I can't find the words. My body is twisting, writhing, both darting away from and arching into my own immolation. I feel so good that a part of me, irrational but deafening, thinks that I will not survive this. That the human mind is not meant to comprehend pleasure so all-consuming, that my brain cannot possibly translate the signals that my every minuscule nerve ending is currently sending. Julian's hands pry my thighs apart like a clamshell, his palms so hot I can see the red imprints of them behind my closed eyelids, and when he blows a gust of steam over my core, I finally wrench my eyes open.

The creature between my legs is obviously Julian. It has Julian's balanced bone structure, his full lips and dark, curling lashes, his broad shoulders and large, veined hands. But the Julian I know doesn't glow from the inside out like a hot coal. His eyes are a warm, inviting brown, not the slit-pupiled amber that spear me like a flailing fish now. And his tongue is a normal, human length, not this terrifying, alluring appendage that slinks out of his mouth and splits me down the middle.

"Say it," this Julian monster says, in between languorous laps that sand at my sanity. "Say that you're mine."

The words he wants bounce around in my head, ring in my ears like they are the only ones I know. *I'm yours I'm yours I'm yours*, "I'm—"

"Dr. Sullivan!"

A bolt of recognition jolts me back into reality. I snatch back my legs so quickly that I almost kick the creature in the face. Within the next instant, Julian is human colored again, and he sits up to watch, stunned, as the scene around us falls away like a straw house in a maelstrom, white walls peeling in ribbons to give way to the drab gray cabinetry of my office. Just before he disappears, he turns back to me, nostrils flared, eyes dark, and I'm not sure whether it's lust or rage that I see on his face.

There is a hand on my shoulder, shaking me, and then the world I had with Julian is gone, blown away like a candle flame.

"Sean?" Leila repeats, her tone high with rising concern.

I blink up at her, disoriented, my ears still ringing and skin still buzzing. For a second, I see the creature again, its unblinking stare, the way my mind went blissfully blank in its grasp.

But it's just Leila, and she's stifling a laugh.

"Must have been a good nap," she says from behind a parted hand. Her diamond glimmers on her finger, and an old, hateful part of me tenses at the sight of it.

"I'm tired, what's new," I say grouchily. "What are you doing here? I've never seen you in clinic."

Leila holds up a rolled-up set of hospital-issue scrubs.

"Brandon used all his scrub machine credits and said he had an extra set here. I'm just running them up before his next case," she informs me.

Instantly, my hackles lower, and I feel the burn of embarrassment. *No more monster smut for you*, I think, because did I really just have a sex dream about a long-tongued lava man in the middle of the work day? A terrifying thought occurs to me: *God, what if I made . . . sounds?*

"Sorry," I say, stretching to cover for my grimace. "I'm a bit of a grump when I first wake up."

Leila assures me that there is "nothing to worry about, I'm the same too," and I comfort myself with the knowledge that her grin would be a bit more knowing if she'd caught me moaning in my sleep. I'm getting ready to shake my computer awake to check my schedule when Leila lays a gentle hand on my shoulder.

"I heard about the missed STEMI," she says. "I'm so, so sorry about that."

Julian's expression crosses my mind, more sheepish than I'd ever seen him look: *We should be taking things slow.*

"Yeah, well," I grumble, last week's bitterness returning. "Things happen."

Leila's expression darkens.

"But they shouldn't, and it wasn't okay," she says. "Don't worry. I've talked to him about it."

I'm not sure if I've ever heard Leila sound so . . . irritated. Trouble in paradise already?

"Thank you?" I say.

"No, thank *you* for covering him," Leila says. "Oh! And for asking Winona about the recital. I know Sophie was nervous about inviting me, and she told me you helped convince her."

At this, I stiffen. I can't help but feel like Leila is bragging, though I can't conceive why. Maybe it's the insinuation that Winona had put up any sort of resistance to having her there, or the overdone, puppy-dog pout she's giving me now. She's always felt genuine to me, but right now, I can't help but feel taunted.

"It didn't take any convincing," I insist. "We share an interest in making the kid happy, after all."

"Of course," Leila says sagely. Then her grip tightens. "Have you heard from Julian lately?"

I tense.

"No, I haven't, and I'd rather not discuss it." I sound snippy, but as a woman scorned I think I'm allowed it.

"Oh, well, I was going to tell you that I'm worried about him," Leila says. "He ghosted me for dinner last week, and he wasn't answering, like, any of my texts and calls, so I got worried and reached out to Ritika. Apparently, he's not well. She had to cancel all his meetings this week—which, like, never happens by the way, that man would work through a hurricane—but he's refusing to go to the hospital."

Oh.

I can't remember the last time I felt this embarrassed; maybe when I said someone's residency potluck dish looked like compost and turned to find the cook standing behind me.

"He's sick?" I repeat.

Leila nods, chewing on a thumbnail, and I wonder whether the haughtiness I'd felt from her was actually nerves.

"He does this. Pushes himself past his limits. Putting himself in danger like this is so unnecessary—" Her voice cracks, and she gives me an apologetic shrug. "Sorry. I just . . . He's like a big brother to me, and I just wish he would treat himself with a bit more care."

I remember, abruptly, that Leila's actual big brother is no longer with us—that there's perhaps a reason why she's visiting me now that goes beyond socializing.

"I've been wanting to stop by his place to check on him, but I have to drive to Evanston a bunch this week to prepare a demonstration I'll be doing with one of the interventionists there for SCAI," Leila says, confirming my suspicions in the next breath. "And honestly, Brandon doesn't like the idea of me going over to another man's house alone, and I'm trying to respect his wishes. So . . . I was hoping to ask a favor. Since, you know, Jules is important to both of us."

The concern that I have for Brandon being maybe a bit more controlling than I like is only trumped by my horror at the image of Julian sprawled out, half dead, on his couch.

"You want me to go check on him," I say.

"Please," Leila says.

It's a no-brainer, even if it ties my stomach into twists. Despite everything, my traitorous heart beats faster.

"Of course," I say.

Twelve

Leila gives me the code to Julian's apartment and calls his concierge to request I be placed on a guest list. It feels a bit wrong, getting permission from a second party, but when I try to call Julian again and it goes to voicemail, I reason with myself that I'm only breaking and entering in his best interests. I go home, take Onix out, then putter around my house grabbing supplies. I find my stethoscope, a blood pressure cuff, a pulse oximeter, Tylenol, and ibuprofen, and throw them all into a tote bag. I bring a bottle of water too, pop a couple ibuprofen for good measure, and wash them down. Then, because I can't be bothered to hunt down parking around Julian's downtown apartment, I call for a ride, jittery with nerves.

The last time I visited Julian's place, we entered through the parking garage, which, while neat, had been concrete and unremarkable. The lobby itself is opulent, gilded, with a doorman dressed in a crisp navy uniform under a smart black coat who steps out into the cold to open my passenger-side door.

"Are you here for Mr. Conrad?" he asks. When I confirm, he directs me to the elevator. "Hope he's doing okay."

I nod, though behind my mask, my mouth has set into a line. I'm not sure whether it relieves or concerns me that someone else picked up that something is amiss with Julian. The anxiety doesn't abate as I step onto the elevator, go up to the twenty-fourth floor—only heightens when I find his apartment, 2401, and knock.

"Julian?" I call out after a moment.

There's no answer. I stand there, feeling uncertain and a bit foolish. There's a nonzero chance that Julian has just been intentionally ignoring me and hoping that I'll get the point. That I'll burst into his apartment and find him not in it, somewhere across the city at another board of trustees meeting, or worse, tangled up in another woman's embrace. And then there are further questions: What if he's too out of it to answer the door? Should I have just asked his doorman to accompany me for a wellness check? Should I have called emergency services instead of imposing myself—no, he would be pissed if I did that, honestly he might be pissed that I'm here at all—

Just when I'm about to turn tail and head back down twenty-four floors to ask for help, I hear him.

"Hello?" Julian says, in a voice that sounds like he's using all his energy to project.

"Julian," I call back. "It's Sean. I'm coming in."

He doesn't respond, and I figure that's as close to permission as I will get.

Hesitantly, I tap in the code, wait for the lock to click open, and turn the doorknob.

Julian's place is different in the daytime. Even with the blinds drawn, it's flooded in light, and the colors that seemed so rich at night are muted and warm now. It's not as spotless as it had been previously; errant mugs are on every surface, and I nearly step onto what I realize is likely one half of a fleece pajama set as I walk inside.

From the entryway, I can make out dishes in the sink and a knocked over box of Wheat Thins on the kitchen island.

And in the center of the living room, sprawled out on a couch under a mound of blankets, is the owner.

"Who?" he calls out weakly.

I hang my jacket on the coat rack, unwind my scarf, slip off my boots.

"Sean," I repeat awkwardly. Even from the door, I can tell that Julian is in a bad way. His face is slick with sweat, and his gaze when he looks at me is distant and unfocused. Dark circles hang under his eyes; I wonder when he last had a good night's rest. "Sorry for breaking and entering. Leila gave me the code, and—"

Julian groans, squeezing his eyes shut.

"Why would she *do* that?" he grumbles, and even though I know it is an appropriate reaction, I grimace.

"You're clearly very sick, and I am a doctor," I say, approaching him slowly. "She wanted to check up on you herself but had . . . some obligations. So she asked me to come instead."

But Julian is already shaking his head.

"No. *No*," he mutters. "No, you don't understand. I don't . . ." He searches for the words. "You can't see me like this."

The awareness that it is vanity that keeps Julian from wanting me here and not lack of interest eases my nerves somewhat. I close the distance between us.

"I assure you that you're still devastatingly handsome, even like this," I say. "I assume this is why you haven't texted me? Called me back?" I don't wait for him to answer. "Say ah."

Julian's hand reaches from behind the blanket, so quick that I'm caught off guard, grasps my wrist, and grips tight. I look up, stunned, as he sits up. The blankets fall off his shoulders and pool at his waist, and I swallow against a throat that is suddenly parched.

I am going to hell. Because I should not be objectifying him right now. But it's hard not to. I've never seen his naked body in broad daylight, and it is exquisite, all rolling shoulders and glistening pectorals and abs that shift in and out of view as he breathes in big, heaving gusts. It's a body crafted by a female gaze, both functional and aesthetically arresting.

He's not well, I remind myself. *And neither are you.*

"Julian," I say slowly, rolling the syllables on my tongue as I drag my gaze reluctantly back to his eyes. "Please let go."

In response, he tugs me closer. I stumble into the space between his knees, catching myself on the back of his couch, and his knees tighten, trapping my hips between them. Heat comes off his body in oppressive waves, and I'm reminded of the creature from this afternoon's dream, his fire iron glow.

"You shouldn't be here," he murmurs, as if he's speaking to himself. "I can't . . . I can't be around you right now. It's dangerous."

"Well, good thing I'm sick too," I say. "Not really sure which of us is patient zero, but I think it's too late to worry about spreading it to each other."

Julian's laugh is hoarse with disuse, and when he presses his forehead to mine, he's hot to the point of discomfort.

"You're so difficult," he says. Then, "Is that really what you think I mean?"

The gravel in his voice is enticing, but I feel an edge of fear too, a rush of adrenaline that makes my body tense to flee.

"Let go of me, Jules," I repeat. It's a command this time, the growl before the bite. I trust Julian not to hurt me, but he's still a man with several inches of height and many more pounds of bulk on me who is too sick to know his strength.

This time, he listens. Julian drops my wrist, and I bend back down to dig through my bag. I can feel him watching me, and I duck away from his stare, which has suddenly gone from dazed to hyperfocused. When I find his face again, his smile is gone. It's as if a breeze has blown through the room and taken part of him with it, and I still, intrigued and unsettled by the abruptness of his shift.

"You're actually afraid of me," he croons, so softly that I have to read his lips to make out the words. "*Fascinating*."

The breath I've been holding comes out in a huff.

"Yeah, well, you kind of freaked me out just then," I say, finding the thermometer. I hold it to his mouth. "Say ah, you big weirdo."

Julian obeys, opens his mouth wide, and takes the thermometer like I've just fed him something sumptuous. His eyes don't leave mine until I tear them away to wrap the blood pressure cuff around his upper arm and run it. They result at the same time: 110/74 (normal), 103.6 degrees Fahrenheit (decidedly not).

"You're burning up," I mutter. I'm a bit relieved to find that his odd behavior can be attributed to a fever-induced delirium. "Hold up, where's my stethoscope—"

Before I can bend back down for my bag, Julian reaches for me again, but this time his touch is gentle. I hold still as fingertips skim past my cheek, soft as butterfly wings.

"Can you look at me?" he whispers. "Please?"

I still, then oblige. Julian's focus can be intense on most days, but today it's different. He stares at me like a man who has lived in darkness might at his first glimpse of the moon. Like I am wondrous and luminous and terrifying all at once. Moving slowly, he tugs my mask off my ears, then cradles my face in his hand.

"I just don't understand. You're here because you want to help me. You came of your own free will."

I'm even more confused than before.

"Um, yeah," I confirm. "Lean forward, Julian. Let me listen to your lungs. It's no chest X-ray, but if I hear something, we're definitely going to the hospital."

It's like he can't hear me. His thumb drags along my bottom lip, and he watches the flesh fold with great interest, his tongue trailing absent-mindedly along the points of his upper teeth.

The gesture is absolutely mind breaking. Suddenly I'm flooded with heat, the space between my legs clenching with arousal that comes so quick that I have to hold back a gasp. I can *feel* my pupils dilate, watch the world go out of focus and then recalibrate. It's true that Julian is ill—I haven't seen a temperature that high in an adult in a minute—but he also oozes sensuality so dense I can taste it. It's copper sharp, like the air after a lightning strike.

"That's more like it," Julian says, still fixated on my mouth. "I was beginning to think I'd lost my touch."

"Still arrogant as ever," I mutter, even as my heart races.

Julian's gaze drops to the throbbing pulse in my neck and stays there, transfixed. Even pressed so close, he seems so far away.

"You don't make sense, you know," he whispers. "You refuse to bend to me even one inch. And yet here you are, coming to my aid because you *want to*."

I swallow.

"I don't really know what you mean by bend," I say, hesitantly. "But . . . yes? I do want to?"

Julian leans in until his face becomes a blur, until the tip of his nose brushes mine, until his eyes merge and fill my entire field of vision. They flicker in the shifting light: brown, green, amber. Pupils pinprick small.

"Fascinating," he repeats. His voice is frayed, more wind than sound, and I inhale it in. He shouldn't smell so good, *taste* so good, right now—should be stale and sickly instead of smoky and sweet—and yet he does. I want to be immersed in him. To burrow under his skin and make a home.

"Why," I ask, as he wraps his arms around my waist to tug me closer, "do you keep saying that?"

Julian smiles like he's just told a joke that I'm not privy to. And then he slides his hand to the nape of my neck, pulls his body up to meet mine, and kisses me.

I thought I'd gotten used to kissing Julian, to the way I turn punch-drunk and liquid in his arms. But though the mechanics fit—his mouth clashing hot against mine, hand weaving into my hair to keep me locked in place—what Julian is doing to me should not be described as a kiss. This is conquest. This is his body staking claim to mine, a flag lodged into my lands, an invasion that goes deeper than a plundering of mouths. Julian nips and pulls and sucks and I unravel, the spool of my thoughts spinning loose and free around a center that is him, always him.

"I just want," he says, dragging his lips down my neck, "a little taste."

I feel his words ring through my chest like a gong, echoing. All my thoughts, of his sickness and mine, the despair I felt over the last several days in his absence, vanish. I'm empty, and I want him to fill me, to merge us together until I don't know where he starts and I begin. This taste he wants, I want to give it to him. I smooth my hands over his shoulders, drag them down his chest, reach behind for his back and revel in the solid ripples of muscle that greet me.

"Please," I gasp.

Julian's answering groan is guttural, and suddenly everything burns, and my world goes dark.

It is four in the afternoon, but my kitchen is flooded with early morning light. Seated at one of the barstools of my island is Julian. He's dressed comically in a white undershirt and my favorite leopard print robe, with sleeves that only reach halfway down his forearms, and is blowing over coffee in my favorite "Boss Bitch" mug. His getup tells me that we have been sleeping together for long enough for him to feel comfortable borrowing my clothes, but not so long that he's earned a drawer in my dresser. Strange as the sight is, it feels familiar and comforting in its banality.

Except he should not be familiar, because Julian has never been inside my apartment.

"Interesting," he says, lowering his mug to the counter. "You've got the real thing out there right now, but you're still in here with me."

"What?" I ask, discombobulated, and Julian smirks.

"I'm just saying that I was right," he says. "You *do* like me more."

I'm still looking at him with confusion when suddenly my vision tips, and I find myself slipping into darkness. But this is not the bottomless darkness of sleep, but something more dynamic, with shifting light and heightened awareness. It takes me one heartbeat to realize that it's because my eyes are squeezed shut, and then another to realize that I'm not at home at all.

The instant I do, I'm wracked with a thousand sensations at once—shuddering, electrifying aftershocks, the feeling of being catapulted out of my own body, pleasure that pulses through me in waves. I'm *coming*, I realize, though I've never come like this, all at once with no clear buildup. The rasping cry that pierces the air is from my throat. My arms are wrapped around a strong neck, holding on for dear life as my knees buckle underneath me, and searing, soothing kisses are raining down the side of my face.

"Shh," Julian says. "It's okay. I got you."

There's a sloppy, slurping sound, and with it, an absence. Julian's fingers, withdrawing from where they'd been. Inside me. He brings them to his mouth and sucks.

"Oh god," I say, stuck somewhere between pleasure and consternation. Hazily, the memories return, patchy and disjointed; I went to Julian's apartment . . . to check on him? To yell at him for ignoring my texts?

The rest is a blur. The surface behind my back is unyielding, not plush, and we are upright—a door? Julian crowds my vision, his body blocking my view of the space, but I can tell by the furniture that it's likely his bedroom. He's still mostly dressed, as am I; my panties are still on, just shoved to the side, and my leggings are halfway down my thighs.

Another memory returns to me, one that makes my face turn even hotter. Julian asking me if I *want this*, me answering by dragging him back to my mouth. Pushing *him* against the door, only to be flipped back against it myself after Julian decided he was done being manhandled.

"What are you *doing* to me?" I gasp, still catching my breath. Julian smells intoxicating, a mixture of soap, sweat, and sex that, despite everything, I want to wrap myself in.

"I could ask you the same thing," he says. He reaches behind him, unlatches my hand from its vise grip around his neck, and lowers it to his bare chest. Under my palm, his heart is galloping.

"That's . . ." He bends to kiss my neck, and I bite down on my cheek, trying to maintain focus. "That's not what I mean."

Julian hums, only half interested in helping me reach the epiphany I seek.

"What do you mean, then?"

I try to divert my focus from his overwhelming presence to the lightness of my limbs, the fact that my head no longer throbs and my body no longer aches. I know better than anyone that healing is a slow process, done over days to weeks to months, not instantaneous. But this isn't the first time this has happened, is it? It feels like something out of a fairy tale: Julian touches me, and I become whole again.

"I mean that I feel good," I manage, clumsily converting my jumbled thoughts into speech. "Why do I feel good?"

Julian chuckles, then brushes his lips over mine in a caress.

"Should I be insulted?" he whispers.

"No, no," I say, shaking my head. Julian gives me an indulgent smile, then, unceremoniously, drops to his knees and drags my underwear over my hips. "No, I don't mean it like . . . *oh*."

Julian presses his face into the valley between my legs, and I reflexively tilt my hips forward to give him better access. He rolls the pearl of my clit around his tongue before probing deeper, and whatever ideas I'd been formulating are gone to the wind, chased away by a desperate need to stay standing amidst this siege. And that's what it feels like—like he's waiting me out, unbuilding me brick by brick. When he pushes his fingers inside me again, my body welcomes his intrusion as much as it pines for more. They curl, find a spot that makes my toes clench.

It seems impossible that I could be having a second orgasm on the heels of the last, but Julian is relentless, employing mouth and nose and hands to drag me, caveman style, to the cliff edge. When he throws me over, I have to bite down on my tongue to keep from crying out. It doesn't work—the moans escape my throat like they've been sucked out, filling the quiet evening air with illicit song. I become boneless, my teeth chattering, knees buckling, and Julian tightens his hold to keep me from crumpling to the floor.

What could be seconds or minutes or hours later, I finally stop shaking. Julian places a reverent kiss on my mons. He rests his head against my thighs and sighs, kneading my ass like a sculptor working clay, and the waft of his breath against my still sensitized skin sends shock waves skittering down my legs.

I drop my head backward against the door, chasing down the breath that he's stolen.

"This is so unfair," I groan through gritted teeth. "Do you have a *manual* or something?"

It's supposed to be a joke, but Julian doesn't laugh.

"I've wanted this for so long," he says, in lieu of an answer. His voice is unexpectedly ragged.

"It's been maybe two months," I tease.

"Two months too long." Julian unfurls himself to his full height, then twines our fingers together. "If I'd had my way, I would've been on my knees for you right there at that piano at the mansion. Figuring out what other sort of music you could make."

My god. My mind has liquefied into soup, the thoughts I'd tried so hard to hold on to floating out of my grasp. Julian guides me to his bed, and I hobble after him, knock-kneed, my movements restricted by my half-doffed clothes. He sits on the edge, runs his hands up and down my sides, his eyes weighed down by a question I am already answering in my head: *Yes, please, now.*

Our clothes come off in a frenzy. I peel off my shirt, nearly tip over dragging my leggings off my remaining ankle, and Julian mirrors me, standing to drop his pants in an unceremonious swoop. My eyes snag on the tent in his boxers. I've seen him hard through his clothes before, grinded against him until I was quivering in his arms, but this is different. More immediate. He lowers his boxers and my eyes widen into saucers.

"Oh," I say.

"Oh?" Julian repeats. He wraps a hand around the generous base, strokes up and down his length as if to further demonstrate his virility.

"I just . . ." I whisper, trying to keep the trepidation out of my voice because *good lord I am far too out of practice for this.* "I understand where you get your confidence."

Julian laughs breathlessly, but his eyes are almost black with desire. He reaches for his nightstand, pulls a condom from his drawer, and makes a show of pulling it on.

"Come here," he growls. Before I can oblige, he's grabbed me by the back of the thighs and lifted me bodily onto his lap. We hiss as he slides through my folds, his tip settling at my entrance.

It occurs to me, suddenly, that this is it. That in a matter of seconds, the very memory-wiping dick I've been half running from is going to be pounding into me, and that, by the buzzing hollowness that has been ringing inside me since the second I laid eyes on it, I'm going to like it. I'm going to like it too much.

But Julian doesn't realize my fantasies right away. Instead he chases down a nipple, sucks it into his mouth. Rocks against me. Without layers of clothing, the sensation is exquisite. I wrap my arms around his neck, content to let him take the lead, to lose myself in the warmth of his embrace, the easy, mounting pleasure of our rhythm. He kisses me, deep and slow and tender, and the anxiety that surrounds me like a shell casing cracks.

"I want to fuck you," Julian whispers, the salaciousness of his words belying his gentle tone. "Tell me you want me to."

In this moment, I don't think I've ever wanted anything more. Not my medical degree, not my beautiful downtown apartment, not the job I've spent my life working for. Just Julian, fucking me, *now*.

I raise my hips, tilt him so that we are aligned, and lower myself onto him.

Oh.

My general consensus on sex is that it is nice, lovely even, but not necessary or even desirable outside of the occasional treat, like indulging in a cheesecake or a warm bread pudding. I have gone years without much more than the occasional craving quickly sated by an efficient rendezvous with a battery-powered friend.

But Julian isn't even fully inside before I know that this is different. My body adjusts around him and I think that this is what a person must feel after the line of cocaine that makes them lose control. That they're experiencing the last moment of awareness before the addiction takes hold, when they find themselves awash with euphoria and realize that all the small joys of their life will forever pale in comparison, that they will spend eternity chasing this same high.

Julian moves slowly. I've become boneless, rendered useless by pleasure, and so he does all the work, rocking into me in a steady, shallow rhythm that sends electric currents into my core. His kiss, in contrast, is vicious, a clash of tongue and teeth that leaves my lips stinging and my lungs straining for breath.

"Shit, Sean," he groans into my mouth, and I want to laugh, because I understand. Because nothing legal should ever feel this good.

Suddenly, a flicker, and the room becomes bright. I'm back in my apartment, but it can't be my apartment, because there's a king-sized bed in the middle of my living room, and someone is having sex in it.

I see a man's rippling back, shining with sweat, two brown legs curled tight around his waist, two brown arms holding on for dear life around his neck. A woman lies underneath him, her body arched, her head tilted back, desperate, keening sounds dragging from her mouth.

"Julian," she cries, in a voice that is mine, from lips that are mine.

I don't have time to fully process what is going on before another set of arms wraps around me from behind.

"Do you like seeing yourself like this?" a voice croons into my ear. A hand raises, cups my breast through the thin silk pajamas I only wear when I have company, and squeezes. "Does it turn you on?"

The Sean on the bed seizes. This is her third orgasm of the night and her hardest one yet, something she wasn't sure was possible after the last. She scrabbles for purchase on her partner's back, and he swallows what I'm sure would have been a scream down his throat. I watch her spasm underneath him, her stare upward and glazed with pleasure. She doesn't have time to recover before he pulls out, flips her onto her stomach, and drives into her again. He's rougher now, his pace relentless, one hand pushing her shoulder into the bed, the other delving between her legs.

The space between mine pulses. I tear my eyes away from the scene before me to the one behind. Dream Julian grins down at me. He's still dressed in my leopard-print robe. Over his shoulder on my kitchen counter I see his mug, still steaming, like no time has passed at all.

He grabs my chin, directs my attention back to the bed.

"Don't run away from it," he says. "Let go."

"I'm not . . ." I start, but I'm silenced by Dream Julian's fingers, prodding my lips for entry that I reflexively grant. He groans into my neck before withdrawing his fingers and sliding them down my body until they dive past the band of my shorts.

"You're perfect," he pants, working a pace that that makes me grasp onto his arm to keep from collapsing. "So perfect. I can't wait for you to lose yourself to me. It won't be so bad, I promise. I'll make sure of it."

The Other Sean is going to come again. I can tell because I am her, because I can feel the same dick that is grinding against my ass pummeling inside me, because I can see the way her teeth clench and fingers curl into the sheets and feel the strain on my cheeks and tightness across my knuckles. Because Julian and I not only feel good together but look good, my brown skin against his golden, his hard lines against my lush ones. Because this is the sexiest thing I've ever done or seen in my brief and careful life, even as it is the most frightening too.

"Say it, Sean," Dream Julian says, the pad of his finger worrying my clit in circles that get tighter and faster. "Tell me you're mine."

I'm so close that it's agony. So close that I almost don't notice that Real Julian said the words too, that their mouths moved at the same time, that they are both looking to their corresponding me (us) with ravenous anticipation. I bend forward, grab hold of the footboard of the bed, and Julian follows me down, dogged in his pursuit of my answer.

"I'm yours." It comes out in a gasp, but the words fill the room, echo against the walls like I've shouted them. "I'm yours, Julian, oh god, please—"

The lights flicker, and suddenly I'm back in Julian's bedroom, his hot skin sticking to mine, hot breath wafting against my neck. His hands grip my hips hard enough to bruise, and when he pulls back to meet my eyes, there is something helpless in his gaze. Like he has let go of the reins and allowed his body to pull him asunder.

"Oh Sean," he whimpers, and it's a prayer, an invocation to the divine, and the moment my name leaves his lips I am overcome. The heat between us mounts, overwhelming. I'm being remade, I think, reforged, a phoenix forming in a bed of ash. I remember a distant dream, a room on fire, an echo in my skull: *Give yourself to me.*

And then I recall nothing else, because nothing else matters—just this, just us, just now, just this towering tidal wave of molten pleasure that crashes into me and turns me into sea-foam.

Thirteen

I wake to an alarm I don't remember setting in a room I don't remember falling asleep in, in a bed I was sure I shared with someone else. But I'm alone, and the sheets next to me are cool.

Before the panic can set in, I take a deep breath and activate Emergency Sean. Emergency Sean does not freak out because her patient's blood pressure is tanking or the guy she (finally) slept with has left her alone in a strange bed. Emergency Sean catalogs facts and figures out what she needs to do next.

I find my phone plugged in on the nightstand. According to the home screen, it is still Thursday, and it is seven thirty in the evening, which means that I've been out for about two and a half hours. I also know that, despite getting somewhere in the vicinity of an hour of sleep last night, I feel better rested than I have in days.

There is also the where. This one is easy, even if it sets my cheeks to burning—I am in Julian Conrad's bedroom, in Julian Conrad's bed. As far as *what* happened in it . . . beyond the most rudimentary terms, I am not exactly sure. On one hand, I've just had what was easily the best sex of my life. On the other hand, I appear to have intermittently passed out several times over the course of the act, judging by the presence and, erm, *participation* of the Julian I encounter in my dreams. Which . . . wow. I must be sicker than I thought, in all senses of the word.

There's a robe hanging from the door. I hop out of bed, slip it on, and tiptoe down the hall.

I find Julian sitting at his dining table, a pair of thick-rimmed glasses balanced on the bridge of his nose, staring down at his laptop screen with rapt concentration that's only broken when I speak.

"I didn't know you wore glasses," I say.

Julian starts, whipping the glasses off his face as he rushes to my side.

"I don't usually. I've been staring at a lot of screens lately; these supposedly help with the eye strain," he says distractedly. He cups my face in his hand, studying it from under a brow furrowed with concern. "You crashed pretty hard. How are you feeling?"

"I'm good," I say, blushing under his close attention. It's hard to look directly at him, so soon after he wrought rapturous havoc on me, and so I turn toward his computer instead. "What are you working on?"

There is a brief moment when I see Julian hesitate, sense that he might press me for more. But then his hand falls from my face and he settles back into his seat. I collapse across from him.

"I invested in a company based in Delhi that's developing small solar-powered kitchen appliances, with an emphasis on stoves," he says. "They've been running into some issues with their manufacturer and the NGO that was supposed to help with distribution just lost their grant, so I've been helping to put out fires."

"Solar-powered stoves," I say, curious. "Who would those be for? Campers?"

Julian rests his chin on steepled hands.

"Delhi has some of the worst air pollution in the world," he says. "Almost two million people live in the slums surrounding the city, a lot of them in poorly ventilated quarters. They do a lot of their cooking with makeshift earthen stoves, and the initial idea was that these would replace those. They're a good team, very mission driven, but I think they're missing their target as far as consumers."

He goes on to explain the clear barriers to adoption—many of the foods cooked by the entrepreneurs' community require open flames for charring rather than induction ovens, and the team of engineers, composed entirely of men who have never cooked a day in their lives, arrived at a solution to a perceived problem without seeking the opinions of their actual potential users first. Besides, their proposed consumers are unlikely to have the resources to help them reap a profit. A noble mission, Julian emphasizes, but misguided.

"The actual technology has so much promise," he states. "I personally want them to pivot. There are so many other devices they could apply this to that can still help address their goal of decreasing emissions and making renewable energy attainable at a consumer level, but—" He freezes. "I'm boring you."

"You aren't," I say. I mean it. When we first met, I'd poked fun at his description of his work as philanthropy, but a dig through Reddit forums reveal that he wasn't kidding about only taking a meager cut. Getting sponsored by the Conrads is apparently the equivalent of acquiring a fairy godmother; his firm functions as both an accelerator and an investor, providing significant mentorship in addition to funding in exchange for considerably less equity than his competitors. His passion is both obvious and infectious, and, if I'm honest, attractive too. "I think it's cool that you're so involved."

"I have an incentive to see them succeed. Not just financially. This is about advancement," Julian says. "I see this happen all the time—brilliant people with good ideas who are just asking the wrong questions. Part of my job is leading them to the right ones. They do this properly, and they could change the world."

He wags his head, then snaps his laptop shut and reaches for my hand, brushing a thumb across my knuckles.

"But enough of that. I've missed you."

I roll my eyes. "Ha! Whose fault is that?"

The moment I say it, I freeze. A second realization has dawned on me: Julian ghosted me, and for over a week. So how did I end up here, in his apartment, in his bed? My memory is hazy, like I've drunk four too many margaritas at happy hour and shuttled forward in time. I consider the series of events that could have led me to Julian's dining room table, and it takes them a moment to crystallize: falling asleep in morning clinic, running into Leila, her voice cracking as she declares *Jules is important to both of us* . . . "Wait, weren't you just on the brink of death?"

It's probably my hypervigilance talking. Probably a relic from the way I used to search Eric's face for the slightest shift in mood to govern what would be safe to say next and what might send him into a rage. But I could swear that right before Julian laughs, his eyes widen with shock.

"I was sick for a while," he explains. "And then when I finally started feeling better, I was so behind on work that I've been pulling all-nighters trying to catch up. And what with my most active team being halfway across the world . . . I think my body finally gave out." He grimaces. "I realize I never responded to your messages. I'm sorry. I kept meaning to, and then I'd get stuck putting out another fire."

I frown, my annoyance flaring when he confirms that he did, in fact, ignore me.

"You realize I'm not the best girl to use the 'I'm busy' excuse on, right?" I say. "It would've taken two seconds for you to text me back."

"I know, I'm sorry. It won't happen again," Julian says. He drapes himself onto the table, looking up at me with pitiable brown puppy eyes. "And if it does, you should break up with me immediately. I'll deserve it."

"Break up with you?" I scoff. "Didn't realize it was that serious."

Julian straightens, affronted, and I realize that he was neither joking nor using a figure of speech.

"It isn't? But we *are* only dating each other, right?" he asks, gesturing between us. Another revelation falls over his face, and it folds into an expression that is one part horror, one part hurt. "Wait. I've been calling you my girlfriend. What have you been calling me?"

"Hold on," I say. "You're joking, right?"

"Why would I be joking?"

Julian crosses his arms and leans back in his chair, and the look he's giving me is accusatory, as if I'm the one in the wrong. And hell if I'm going to allow him to put me under the spotlight right now.

"Um, maybe because you took me on a date, brought me home, and then didn't talk to me for a week?" *And after what we'd discussed*, I almost add, but I feel too raw to let him that close again. "That's not exactly how you treat a girlfriend. If Leila hadn't asked me to check on you, I would've assumed that was a message in and of itself and blocked you."

I tug my robe closed and turn toward the twinkling Chicago skyline. I'm not sure where my accumulated hurt went in the last several hours, but it's back now, squeezing my chest so tight that it's hard to breathe deep and even harder to face him. With it comes anger. Anger at myself, because how could I still sleep with him after he treated me so poorly? Why haven't I walked away? Anger at him too, for making me question my own carefully rebuilt self-worth. And anger at the universe, for bringing a person into my life whose soul seems to resonate so beautifully with mine, but in the form of such a *boy*.

There's a creak and groan: Julian pushing his chair back and making to stand. I listen to his footsteps as he circles the table, curl my fists tighter when his torso enters my peripheral vision.

"Sean," he pleads. When I don't budge, he drops to his knees in front of my chair.

I'm too shocked by the gesture to notice that he's succeeded in regaining my attention until it's too late.

"I'm sorry. It was wrong of me not to respond to you," Julian says. He peels my hands off the table and closes them between his. "I reasoned that the next time we spoke, it should be about, well, us. And I didn't feel like I was in the physical or mental space to have that conversation, and so I avoided it altogether. And with every day that went by, it felt even more impossible, because I didn't know what I wanted to say. I, erm, never really know what to say to you."

His honesty stuns me temporarily into silence.

"Yes you do," I say. "You always say the right things." *Practiced*, I'd thought, when we first met.

But Julian is shaking his head.

"No, I don't," he insists. "I genuinely don't like people. But I like you. And that makes me skittish, and foolish, because I want to do things the *right* way with you, but I don't know what the right way is." He pauses, chuckles nervously. "What we got up to tonight probably wasn't it, though."

"I have no complaints about anything we did tonight," I interject. I don't add what I'm thinking: that if he gave me one inkling that he's down for a second round, I would drag him back to his bedroom myself.

The light comes back into Julian's eyes.

"You've already forgiven me, haven't you," he says, just a little wickedly.

I pout and look away, but after his little admission, it's taking genuine effort to stay upset. The online dating gurus were clear as day about situations like this: *Don't let a man show you he doesn't want you more than once.* But none of them have beheld Julian's face, felt his grip dimple their thighs. They might allow him a couple more tries if they did.

Recognizing victory, Julian grins, bracing himself on the arms of my chair to place a kiss on the corner of my mouth, my cheek, my forehead. When I scrunch my nose, he goes for the kill, grabbing my face between his hands to rain a torrent of noisy kisses on my face as I squeal and twist out of his grasp.

"You're a terror," I whine in between giggles.

"And you have a horrible savior complex, turning up with a whole medicine bag even though I'd just done you wrong," he says, ending his offensive by pulling me into an embrace.

I twine my arms around his neck, let him rest his head on my bosom, and breathe him in.

"You can't just charm your way out of this, you know," I say, knowing damn well that he already has.

Julian's quiet laughter rumbles through my chest.

"Ah, I see," he says. "What is the best way to properly show my penance, then?"

I think about it.

"I want one of those giant grocery store teddy bears," I say. "The ones carrying those huge plush hearts that say something obnoxious, like 'Be mine.'"

Julian nods sagely.

"Noted," he says. "Man-sized teddy bear."

"And a card," I add. "With a checkbox on the inside saying, 'Do you forgive me? Check yes or no.' And I'm going to check whatever I want, and you'll have to deal with it."

Julian draws back just enough to pinch my cheek.

"So vicious, you are," he says. "All right. It will be done."

We sit like this for a minute, holding each other, until Julian's phone alarm goes off and he peels away to disable it.

"We should get back to Onix. It's past his walk time," he says. "You took an Uber here, right?"

I am so distracted that it takes me several seconds to realize that, one, Julian remembers that my elderly dog needs regular walks to prevent accidents despite me mentioning it offhand to him once a couple of weeks ago, and two, that he said "we."

"Are you . . . trying to come home with me?" I ask, a little bewildered. My apartment hasn't been visited by a gentleman caller in months, and I nearly go cross-eyed trying to imagine the state it must be in: clothes on the floor, coffee grounds on the counter, Onix's toys strewn across the carpet.

"Is that okay?" Julian asks, sensing my hesitation. "I don't have to come up, but I really have missed you."

He sounds so earnest that I fold immediately.

"Okay," I say, adjusting my robe. Then, more softly, "Yes. That would be nice."

"And tomorrow?" he presses on. "You have clinic on Fridays, right? Could I borrow you after that?"

My *Yes, why not* is on the tip of my tongue before I remember that I will not be in clinic at all, because tomorrow is the first day of SCAI.

"I'm going to be at a conference," I confess.

We lob back and forth availabilities. Julian is traveling to Austin Monday to meet with some shareholders, and I'm covering service in the intensive care unit for Shiv for a few days when he gets back. Between our schedules, it'll be over a week before we'll be able to see each other again.

The thought sends me into a tizzy. The last week without Julian has been dim and painful, and even though I don't fully understand why, my body recoils at the thought of spending so much time apart again. I mentally scan through my schedule, then bite my lip when I think of it. Because there's one event that I *could* invite Julian to attend: the SCAI after-party on Saturday night.

I twist my fingers together. It's a big step. Maybe not to Julian, who brought me to his close friend's gallery opening for a first date. But it is for me. The idea of fully merging our worlds, of letting Julian be known to mine, terrifies me.

The thought of being without him, though?

"Actually," I find myself saying, "are you free Saturday night?"

Fourteen

The after-party that Shiv and his organizing committee have planned is exactly as I expected: loud, lavish, and bordering on the edge of ostentatious. The lounge they reserved for the event is an homage to the Roaring Twenties, with gold geometric outlines in the ceiling, huge peacock feather centerpieces, and large, bedazzled posters of the burlesque performers who grace the center stage on most nights. In lieu of that today, we have a live band, a buffet selection of heavy appetizers, and a significant fraction of the world's interventional cardiologists gathered into one room.

"They really went all out," I mutter.

"I know, right?" a voice responds.

I jump, but it's just Leila, looking pretty and professional in a well-tailored pencil skirt, her hair up in a neat chignon. Just a few hours before, she'd led a live video demonstration of a new Palette device with one of the interventional teams in a hospital in the north suburbs. I'd watched not only to offer my support but also because she's a genuinely good teacher.

"Oh hey!" I say. "Congrats on the demo, by the way. You did great. Are you already heading out?"

"Thank you, and yes," she says. "Brandon's not feeling well, so I figured I would say hi to the crew and head back home."

My displeasure is definitely showing on my face, because Leila's smile wavers some. Brandon looked his usual sullen self sulking around the conference today; not at his best, but certainly not ill enough to drag his wife home to play nurse. It bothers me, that on the evening when our section will most certainly want to celebrate Leila's achievement, she's leaving to take care of him. There's a part of me that should feel some schadenfreude—some part of Leila must have felt like she'd won when she stole Brandon away from his wife and child—but I see too much of my old self in her right now, too much of Eric in him, to let this slide without comment.

"You're aware that he's a grown man, right?" I grumble. "He can take care of himself for one night."

In the dim room, Leila's eyes gleam like polished stone.

"It's fine," she says. Her grin is back, big, bright, and brave. "I'll see you Monday."

She squeezes my arm, then prances toward the exit. I catch at least one double take from people closer to her age as she goes, and the quiet simmer that I feel whenever I see her and Brandon together, the one that wants to shake him for siphoning this beautiful young woman's youth, bubbles to a boil.

My phone lights up in my hand. It's a text from Julian: I'm here. Near the stage.

I deflate. My hypocrisy isn't lost on me, for as much as I can claim that Julian is peculiarly precocious, he is still half a generation my junior. Anyone who looks at us together could easily cast the same judgments upon me that I am casting upon Brandon. Today will be the first time I'll be leaving myself open for them. In a just world, I would have nothing to worry about—after all, most of my colleagues have brought their partners, and a quick survey of the room shows that Julian will not be the youngest of them.

He does, however, shine the brightest. It's how I'm able to eventually find him in the crowded, dimly lit room; all I have to do is follow the paths of cheek-biting smiles and half averted eyes to see that he's settled himself against a pillar near the stage. I raise my hand to catch his attention just as a pretty woman with silken auburn hair approaches him.

Poor thing, I think. I can't hear the exchange between Julian and this woman, but after how he'd dismissed Alicia at the farmer's market, I have no doubt it will be painful. As predicted, Julian turns a glacially indifferent glance to her before turning away in a physical rejection of her presence. The woman whips away like she's just been slapped, and I take on a brisk stride to close the distance between us before someone else can attempt to occupy it.

It's been just under forty-eight hours since I saw Julian last, during our cold, nighttime dog walk around my neighborhood, but my mind has counted down every second until this moment. It's like he's broken something inside me; I can hardly blink without being transported back to Thursday night, to the things he'd made me feel. When he catches sight of me, his eyes darken, and I'm certain that he's remembering too.

"Hi," I say, a little shy. "Hope you haven't been waiting long. Got caught in a session."

"I haven't," Julian says. His hand drops to the nip of my waist, and in the dimly lit room, his eyes are almost black. They tick down my body. "Is this what you wore to the conference?"

I look down at myself. I'm wearing a simple sheath dress: form-fitting, sure, but with the blazer that's currently put away at coat check obscuring my shape for most of the day, hardly scandalous.

"Yes?" I confirm, and his hand squeezes. "Is there a problem?"

"No. Well," Julian draws me just a little closer, bending to my ear. "yes, but I understand it's completely unreasonable. It's not like you can leave this body at home."

I'm still trying to regain my composure when I hear someone call my name.

"Sean!" a voice says. "Get in here!"

It's Shiv, beckoning me from across the bar. The Broadview interventional cardiology crew is all here: Pamela, dressed to the nines in an iridescent sequin dress with the boldest blue eyeshadow I've seen her sport yet, Krause, Larry, even Haoran, who like me hardly makes it out for our section's extra-clinical activities. They're gathering for a photo. Only Brandon and Leila are noticeably absent.

"One second," I tell Julian, pulling out of his grasp and jogging to my team.

Shiv raises an arm to bring me in, but not before spotting Julian a few paces away and doing a double take.

"So you did bring a date!" he exclaims. Then, "Hold on. Don't I know you?"

"Say cheese!" the camerawoman, Shiv's wife, Olivia, says. I freeze, putting on a rictus of a smile, until the flash goes off and Shiv whips back to Julian.

"Yes, that's right," he says. "You were at Brandon and Leila's wedding. You gave a speech."

Julian quirks a brow in amusement, then offers a hand to Shiv to shake.

"Yes, that's correct," Julian says. "Nice to meet you. Julian."

Shiv scans the room in bewilderment as if to say *Do you guys see this?* before finally taking Julian's hand.

"Shiv. I work with Sean." While Julian introduces himself to the rest of my colleagues, Shiv turns his attention back to me and throws his arm around my shoulders. "So you decided to try out the cougar life, huh? Good for you."

I stiffen, then gently disengage from under his arm.

"How old is Olivia again?" I ask, knowing for a fact that she was twenty-three to Shiv's thirty-six when they first met.

Shiv holds up both hands in a gesture of surrender.

"I didn't say it was a bad thing," he says, but the grin on his face is anything but apologetic.

His comment, spoken quietly, still has the effect of an airhorn. By addressing the elephant in the room—the scandalous fact that Julian appears to be at least a few years younger than me—Shiv has ripped the bandage off a taboo topic and made it fair game. The looks Julian gets change, going from curious or admiring to smug or dismissive, and I become a deviant. It doesn't help that the night has progressed, and everyone is one too many glasses in. One woman, whom I recognize as an executive from one of the device companies, makes a comment about Julian's obvious *stamina*. An interventionist I've worked on papers with from a different Chicago institution refers to him as my *boytoy* as if he isn't standing right there. It's ugly and intrusive, how suddenly the entirety of our relationship gets reduced to the sex that we've only really had once, how I can practically see people imagining the mechanics of our coupling when they greet us.

The double standard infuriates me. Of course I'd noticed how often women like Olivia and Leila are reduced to being their partner's accessories instead of autonomous individuals with depth of their own, but there's a level of acceptance for their relationships that isn't afforded to Julian and me, despite our smaller age gap and similar stages in life. A beautiful young woman is the just reward for a successful older man. A beautiful young man with a successful older woman? Clearly a perversion.

Julian takes the barbs with thinly veiled amusement. I tilt my head and tell the device executive outright that asking about my boyfriend's prowess is deeply inappropriate, and she turns scarlet, blathers on about "just being curious" and how "things haven't been the same since my divorce" before fleeing the scene. When, annoyed, I inform the interventionist that my *boytoy* is actually an extremely successful angel investor, Julian interjects with a question about a biotech company that is developing a new design for percutaneous valve replacement that makes him raise his eyebrows, impressed.

"He's a smart one," Doug, the interventionist in question, tells me when their conversation winds down. Then to Julian, "What are you, one of those Silicon Valley wunderkinds?"

"He's a genius, yes," I say snippily. "Speaks over six languages, creates grants and opportunities for local creatives, invests in and mentors up-and-coming entrepreneurs on a global scale. He does what we all hope to do, which is make the world a better and more interesting place simply by being in it."

"Must be why he's with you." Doug is slurring, giving Julian what appears to be an attempt at a conspiratorial wink. "I always preferred an older woman myself. More established. Cuts you a little more slack about the time you're spending building yourself. And they're so much more grateful, if you know what I mean." In case we didn't, he adds, "Absolutely crazy in the sack too. I've got some stories from when I was younger—"

"So sorry, Doug, but I just realized that my date is empty-handed," Julian interrupts, attempting to soothe my ire with a gentle press to the small of my back.

Doug laughs, the drink in his hand—far from his first, I'm sure—tilting precariously. He doesn't seem to notice, or take offense to, Julian's clear dismissal or my mounting indignation.

"Can't have that!" he says good-naturedly, waving us away.

Julian trails behind me as I stomp toward the bar, his pace leisurely.

"I'm sorry about that," I tell him, still fuming. "Unfortunately folks in my field aren't known for their tact."

Julian tilts his head to regard me as if he might find something new to observe from this angle.

"I've noticed," he admits. "But it's fine. I'm having a good time."

"Really?" I ask, incredulous. "You enjoy getting increasingly more invasive questions about our sex life?"

"I enjoy learning about your work," Julian counters. "Seeing you in your element. Watching other young women approach you to express the ways that you've inspired them. I've gotten to know you some, but this was one piece of your life that I hadn't yet seen." He winds an arm around my waist and draws me close. "Also, I get to dance with you again."

In my fury, I haven't noticed that we've wandered onto the small, crowded dance floor. The live band is playing Luther Vandross's "Never Too Much," and while half of the guests are standing and milling around, a few are rocking to the music. Julian draws my arms around his neck and guides me into a sway, and my worries melt like day-old snow under a noontime sun.

"We have to keep it PG, Jules," I warn him, my cheeks warming as I recall what happened the last time we shared a dance floor.

In response, Julian spins me away, then pulls me in so that my back is to his front.

"What, are you worried I might teach your colleagues a little thing or two?" he says into my ear before spinning me, giggling, back around.

We dance chastely but with abandon, without regard for skill or thought about the audience, laughing, working up a sweat. The band has chosen a repertoire of mostly eighties jams, and we sing along out loud and intentionally out of tune, barely a drop of alcohol between us to drive our energy. It spreads, infectious, until soon the whole floor is full of interventional cardiologists and industry professionals ripping off their blazers and loosening their ties to make merry. Across the floor, I spot an ecstatic Shiv fist-pumping into the air; he flashes me a thumbs-up.

Five songs later, I'm sweaty, parched, and desperate to pee. I bounce to my tiptoes to give Julian a quick kiss.

"I've got to go to the ladies'," I tell him.

"I'll get us water," he says. "Don't get lost out there."

The bathroom is tucked away behind the stage, and I twist between dancing couples and high tables laden with forgotten plates and stacked glasses until I reach it. I catch my reflection in the mirror above the sink. I've always conceived of myself as looking younger than I am: my brown skin, shining with sweat, only wrinkles when I smile, and the fine lines at the corners of my eyes are barely perceivable up close. My grays are the biggest giveaway; they course halfway down my locs, denser at the root than at my black tips. Julian is undeniably a young man, but I wonder if dyeing my hair would lessen the visible age gap. Maybe a little Botox could help too, some filler under the hollows of my eyes . . .

Someone behind me giggles. I look over my shoulder to find a pretty woman standing against the wall behind me, looking down at her phone. Our eyes meet in the mirror; she gives me a grin that feels like it's at my expense.

I dry off my hands, perturbed. I'm being paranoid, probably. Definitely imagining things. Because for a second, I could almost swear that she'd just taken a *picture*.

I'm wandering the floor looking for Julian again when I hear it again; the unmistakable sound of a camera shutter, a flash of light, followed by a torrent of giggles.

"I can't believe *that's* his type," a woman's voice says.

I pivot. Three women stand behind me, crowding around a phone. I recognize the one in the middle: she's the auburn-haired woman who approached Julian earlier. I read her immediately: she's pretty and knows it, the kind of woman who believes that the combination of her slender build, youth, and white race should make her every man's Helen of Troy. I wonder what company she works for; either way, she must have missed the "don't alienate your clientele" lesson during orientation.

"Did you just take a picture of me?" I ask coolly.

The women titter among themselves.

"Why would we take a picture of *you*?" the ringleader says. "Have you never taken a selfie with your friends before?" To demonstrate, she gets into position with her girls and throws up a peace sign.

"The flash was toward me," I say. "Please delete it."

She lowers her camera, and though the smile doesn't leave her face, her eyes are now cutting.

"I said we didn't take a picture of you," she says. Then to her girls, "I'm telling you, these Gen Xers are *so delusional* these days—"

Even understanding what's happening—that this girl is reacting out of envy and nothing else, that she's dealing with rejection the only way she knows how, by taking it out on the other woman like the villainous cheerleader in a teen rom-com—the words cut. It's like she heard all the insecurities I recited to myself in the mirror minutes earlier and is repeating them to me out loud, and instead of a sharp retort, all I find is helplessness.

I'm about to walk away, find some place to lick my wounds, when suddenly the woman freezes, catching sight of someone over my shoulder.

It's Julian. He approaches us in a brisk, confident stride, his hands tucked into his pockets, and the world seems to slow and darken with his approach. I swivel to watch as he sweeps past me in a swirl of long legs and stops in front of the woman. He leans in close, brushes a thumb ever so lightly over the apple of her cheek. My face spasms with a strange, alien rage just as hers blooms with color.

"That wasn't very nice, was it, Melody," he says, in a voice that sounds like it should be crooning sweet nothings instead. I feel arrested by it; I can't move. His palm settles fully on her neck, and she releases a breath that sounds like a whine. I hold mine. It occurs to me that Julian is speaking softly, that I shouldn't be able to hear much of what he says at all over the band. But the words sound like they're being whispered into my ear, like I could close my eyes and he would be standing right behind me.

"People like you always overestimate your value. I'll have you know that there's a beauty queen with bad highlights waving from the float of a county fair in every town in Middle America who looks just like you and is of about equal import, and that in about twenty short years, the wickedness inside her heart will become visible outside it. When her beauty and youth have faded, she'll realize how completely she relied on it, how she made no effort to be resourceful or kind or interesting as well. Her town, her people, they abandon her. Her husband's eyes skate past her. Her kids don't call. She becomes invisible at best, a burden at worst. And you can almost pity her, except she once wielded her beauty like a weapon, and so her misery seems more like justice than tragedy. That's your future, and it's one I want no part of. The only one delusional here," Julian pats her neck lovingly, like he would a family pet, "is you."

Melody—I'm not sure when Julian learned her name—exhales in a rattle, her eyes wide and unblinking. Behind her, her friends look on in horror. I can see in their expressions that the shift in power dynamics will be seismic after this; their leader has been deposed.

Julian steps back, holds out his hand. "Give me your phone."

Melody hands it over obediently, and he scrolls through it, finds the photographs, and deletes them one by one. Then he hands it back.

"Good," he says. "Now apologize."

"I'm sorry," Melody says tonelessly.

"Be specific," Julian continues. "Who are you apologizing to, and for what?"

Melody's eyes meet mine from across Julian's shoulder. I expect them to look panicked, terrified even, but instead they are stricken with guilt, like a child caught breaking their parent's favorite vase.

"I-I don't know her name," she blubbers.

"Dr. Sullivan," Julian supplies, and behind her, Melody's friends' eyes widen as they realize their critical error: they'd failed to consider that one of the few Black women in their midst might be one of the interventional cardiologists they were meant to spend this conference wooing.

"I-I'm sorry f-for taking pictures of you without your c-consent, Dr. Sullivan." Melody stumbles through the words like they're a script she's barely read.

Julian looks back at me. His eyes glint and glimmer, reflecting more light than exists in this dimly lit room.

"That work for you?" he asks.

Numbly, I nod. Julian smiles beatifically at Melody and suddenly the air shifts like a cold front and the grayed-out dance floor returns to its electric pink hue. He gestures in front of us just as Melody begins to blink.

"Let's go," he tells me, reaching for my arm like we're fleeing the scene of a crime.

But I can't move. My feet are rooted to the sticky tile floor, because what I just witnessed, what Julian just *did*, is something I can't quite wrap my head around. Sure, Julian is handsome, and sure, he could probably charm the spines off a porcupine, but what just happened couldn't just be explained by charisma. This was a ventriloquist working his dummy, tugging on invisible strings to force her mouth open and the words out. Even now, Melody stares after Julian like an automaton awaiting her next command, the contempt that had distorted her beautiful face replaced by an inhuman placidity that makes my skin crawl.

Suddenly my stomach clenches, threatening to empty its meager contents, and my vision blots and blurs at the edges. I know this sensation, have experienced it a few times after standing too long on a hot day or once when, during fellowship, I accidentally stuck myself with a needle.

I'm going to pass out. *Shit.*

"Julian," I gasp, a warning. "I—"

I don't quite remember falling, just the impact of my knee against tile, the ache of my wrist as it buckles under my body's weight, a bystander's horrified gasp.

Then there is nothing, just an abrupt, blissful quiet.

Fifteen

"Good news, Sean," the emergency room doctor, a plucky young man with a full blond beard who insists I call him Barry instead of Dr. Liederman, says, nine hours later. "Your head CT came back normal. I think you're right, and you just had a vasovagal episode."

"Great," I grumble. "Does that mean I'm free to go?"

"You're free to go," Barry says. "Just remember to stay hydrated and keep wearing those compression stockings."

"*And* rest," Julian chimes in from the chair by my bed. He sits with his elbows propped on his knees, the picture of the concerned, attentive partner. The nurses keep referring to him as my husband, and he doesn't bother to correct them. In fairness to him, neither do I. Julian has spent the entire night sitting dutifully at my side in an emergency room, sneaking ginger ales from the nutrition cupboards and charming the nurses into bringing me warm blankets. It would seem petty to clarify our relationship to well-meaning strangers when he's all but acting the part.

"Definitely do that too," Barry says with a laugh. "Get well soon. Deb should be back soon with your discharge papers."

Then he sweeps out of the room, off to tend to his ever-growing list of much sicker patients.

I release a slow groan. My annoyance at being stuck in an emergency room aside, I'm relieved to learn that I am not dying. As much as I'd suspected that I'd just fainted the normal way, in the split second before I lost consciousness, I'd feared the worst: a ruptured aneurysm, a brain bleed that would take away my mobility and send me into an early retirement. But they'd found nothing.

Julian stands, yawns, stretches. The white tee he'd been wearing under his button-down rides up to reveal a strip of taut tan skin, an arc of a hip, a dark, sparse trail of hair that thickens before dipping beneath the waistband of black boxers. I follow the path of it hungrily, then whip away, mortified, because *how can I possibly be thinking of that right now?* In the copious downtime since we arrived in the emergency room, I've tried to reconcile my memory of our face-off with Melody with the reality of the man who tends to me now. The way the dance floor seemed to drain of color the moment he stepped onto it, how every blood vessel in my body had hardened into steel when he touched Melody's face. His whispered commands, words that skimmed past my skin like feathers, our collective compulsion to obey.

A few years ago, Winny and I saw a magician live. He'd invited a guest onstage to demonstrate his skills at hypnotism, a prim middle-aged woman who went from skeptical to barking on all fours after a few choice words. I'd always thought it was bullshit. Now I'm not so sure.

You're overthinking again. It's much less likely that Julian is secretly capable of mind control and much more likely that he is simply very hot, and hot people tend to get what they want.

"Thanks for staying with me," I tell him.

The look that Julian gives me is one of pure misery.

"This is my fault," he says. "You were sick on Thursday. Instead of resting, you showed up to look after me, and I've been taking advantage ever since."

I give him a rueful look and turn over my arm to examine the IV in the crook of my elbow. I've been pumped full of electrolytes and fluids and feel remarkably better.

"Way to take away my agency," I say grimly. "I've felt pretty good since Thursday night, and I've definitely worked through worse days."

"Just because you have doesn't mean you *should*," he says. "Promise me you'll take it easy today. Stay in bed."

I'm about to concede but remember that I have one more very important obligation.

"Sophie's dance recital is tonight," I say. "I have to be there."

Julian turns abruptly to look at me head-on.

"Tonight?" he repeats. "What time?"

"It starts at six," I say. It's seven a.m. right now; the recital is barely eleven hours away. "I'll get a nap in before I drive over—"

"No," Julian says plainly.

I recoil, stunned. I'm not sure whether it's out of annoyance at his presumption or if I'm the tiniest bit into the command in his tone.

"What do you mean, no?" I sputter.

"I mean, no, you're not driving. You just *passed out*, Sean. Don't tell me you think a forty-minute drive both ways is at all wise." Julian crosses his arms. "I'll take you."

"There's no need," I say. "You heard Barry. It was hot in that room, I was dehydrated, and I probably vagaled. You're traveling tomorrow, and you've been up all night. You should pack and—"

Julian narrows his eyes.

"I just want some time alone," I emphasize. "I spent all yesterday talking to people, and last night was . . ." *Strange.* "Exhausting."

It's an excuse that would make most people back off, but Julian is not most people.

"You'll be alone starting tomorrow," he says. "It seems like right after you get discharged from an emergency room isn't the best time to seek solitude. You're not a dying bird, Sean."

"No, I'm a very much alive and fully autonomous human woman," I insist. "And while I appreciate your help today, I don't have to accept your charity just because you're offering it, Julian."

"Charity?" Julian repeats, gobsmacked. "This isn't charity, Sean. This is me trying to feel a little less useless than I did all night. I'm being selfish, and right now what I want is to take care of you a little. So just let me do that."

He sounds dejected, like a puppy denied a belly rub, and I feel my hackles lower.

"Why is this such a big deal to you, Julian?" I ask softly. "Why does it matter so much?"

Color rises to Julian's cheeks instantly. It's subtle under his golden undertones—a bronze shift—but so abrupt that it makes me blush too.

Oh. *Oh.*

He raises a hand to cover his mouth as if to hide what his face has already revealed.

"You are so much crueler than you look," he mumbles.

My head is buzzing. I feel like I've just downed my fourth cup of coffee and am reaching for the fifth. I want, no, *need* Julian to say what he is implying out loud. Need it more than the air I breathe. Except I've stopped doing that too. Catching myself, I inhale in a gasp, and Julian's brow furrows in concern.

"See? You aren't well," he says. "I'm being serious, Sean. Please. Promise me you'll take it easy today."

Distantly, I know that I'm still being chastised. But from this close, Julian is too overwhelming, and I can't react with the contrition he expects.

"What will happen if I don't?" I say. "Will you tie me down, Mr. Conrad?"

The shift in the mood is instant. Once the suggestion is spoken, I can't shake the image of Julian's hands around my wrists, holding them above my head, of ties and cuffs and ropes that keep me immobile and at his mercy. It's not something I've ever wanted before, if anything found a little distressing, but with this man? My thighs clench, trying to scratch an itch I shouldn't reach.

Julian's eyes flicker to my lap, catching the movement, and then his hand snakes behind my neck, quick as a viper strike, and grips just hard enough to tilt my head back.

"You'd like that, wouldn't you?" he whispers, his mouth hovering so close above mine that I can feel the words form.

I'm not quite sure what sound I make, if it is an affirmative hum or a plaintive sigh, but what I do know is that the second I do, Julian rushes to indulge me. There's an inelegance to this kiss, a clash of tongues that makes me feel like I am being consumed, and my world narrows to the scratch of his stubble against my chin, the iron, inescapable press of his fist in my hair. He isn't touching me, not really, there's too much in the way, IV lines and side rails, but the surging heat of his body courses the short distance between us and floods me with warmth. His free hand shifts to my jaw, *squeezes*, and I pop open to his command like a burst plum.

This man, I know, will be the death of me. Under his grasp, I forget everything—that I might be getting him sick again, that we are in an emergency room with nothing but curtains for privacy, that we could be interrupted at any moment. It's the duality of his control, I think, how quickly he vacillates from a restrained Dr. Jekyll to a ravenous Mr. Hyde, that carries me beyond reason. When he moans into my mouth, my sole thought is how I can get him closer, how I can maneuver my body around in this narrow gurney to press it against his. I don't wonder about whether the neighboring patient will hear us. I certainly don't ask myself why that succession of beeps is getting louder—

"Is everything okay in—oh, come *on*, guys."

Mortified, I tear away from Julian and turn to find Deb, my nurse, looking disapprovingly down at us. My ears pop, and suddenly the beeping that had seemed distant is blaring loud; it takes me a second to realize it is my monitor, reporting to everyone in the emergency department that my heart is hammering away at a hundred and twenty beats per minute.

I've been on the other end of this exact situation before—running in to rescue a patient from a suspiciously elevated heart rate that turns out to be a much needed, erm, release. Those stories always make the rounds in a unit, and I know the one Julian and I just made will be juicy: a local cardiologist getting frisky in the emergency department with her hot young thing.

Julian, for his part, seems unbothered. He unfurls himself slowly, then wipes his mouth with the back of his hand.

"Sorry," he says casually, as if he'd been caught poking around the supply closet and not making out with her patient.

"Well, I guess that's as good a sign as any that you're ready for discharge," Deb says. Then she jabs a thumb over her shoulder. "All right, Romeo. Out."

She watches Julian like a hawk as he grabs his blazer from where it's draped across his chair, tosses it over his shoulder, and ambles out of the room. The second he's out of sight, Deb's mouth screws up in amusement.

"Now, I know you know that wasn't appropriate," she says. "But I can't say I wouldn't do the same."

The laughter that bursts from my chest is mostly relief. Deb is the kind of old-school nurse who reminds me of my aunties, steady and stern and commanding respect, and I'm glad that I haven't disappointed her. When she rounds my bed to remove my IV, I hoist myself up until my legs dangle off the edge.

"Yeah . . ." I say. "I, um, don't normally do things like that. Sorry."

Deb waves me off with one hand and peels away my bandage with the other.

"You don't feel well," she says. "Sometimes a little nooky is just the thing to get your mind off the fact that life is throwing you a curveball. And besides," she adds with a wink, "if *my* husband looked like that, I wouldn't keep my hands off him either."

"I know," I say with a snort. "It's obscene." *And annoying*, I want to add, remembering the howling rage I'd felt when he'd touched Melody, how a part of me had wanted to tear her face off. *Does weird things to your brain.*

"But you know, it's not just the looks. Those don't matter much, in the grand scheme of things," Deb continues. "What does matter is that he seems very attentive. Kind of pushy, if I'm honest."

I don't know what to say to that last part, so I settle for a nervous laugh and a bewildered, "Really?"

"You should have seen him. Badgering poor Dr. Liederman into writing you a work note and stalking all of us for more warm blankets." When I wince, she pats my arm affectionately. "It's a good thing, you know. It's hard to find someone who truly values you." She turns off the pump that has delivered two liters of saline into my vein, then smiles at me. "All right, you're all set. Now get dressed and get out of my ED before you all get up to anything else."

I thank her, take my discharge papers, and prepare myself for what the day has left to offer. With my newfound energy, I'm able to change into my clothes in record time. When I push open the curtain, Julian is on the other side leaning against the nurse's station, eyes closed and arms folded. His eyes open slowly, like he's waking from sleep, before zeroing in on me.

I swallow against a dry throat.

"Fine," I say. "You can drive me to the recital tonight. And I'll stay in bed all day before."

By the smug expression on his face, this is a battle that he knew he would win.

"Can I also walk Onix? Maybe even make you a little chicken noodle soup? Hand feed you grapes while you convalesce?" he ribs.

I nudge him in the side as I zip up my coat.

"Don't push it."

Sixteen

True to his promise, Julian spends the next several hours entirely at my service. We take a ride home to my apartment, and after making sure I am in bed and not on my laptop, he gets an oddly compliant Onix dressed for the cold and takes him for a walk. I sleep the rest of the day away, and Julian leaves me at peace, stocking my fridge with dinner before heading back to his apartment for a shower and change of clothes. When I wake up several hours later for the recital, I feel more refreshed than I have in weeks.

Julian drops me off at the front of Sophie's school while he finds parking, and I wait for him at the entrance, clutching the bouquet we got for Sophie as young families trickle in past me. I watch him approach through the glass doors. He walks like a model, with a devil-may-care stride, one hand tucked into the pocket of crisp pleated trousers, the other held purposefully at his side like there might be a camera trained on him at any moment. It's a quiet confidence that's hard to master, attractive even at a distance.

This, I realize, is my *boyfriend*. Who could be anywhere on a Sunday night but is at a suburban middle school for a dance recital, all because he wants to take care of me. He meets my stare just as he pushes through the double doors, smirks, then with one finger, lifts my jaw closed.

The audacity of the move makes it drop again.

"You . . . what . . ." I start, my heart stammering with a confusing combination of mortification and arousal.

"Don't be embarrassed. Happens all the time." Before I can finish rolling my eyes, he leans in close, tugs at the waistband of my yoga pants, and adds, "Keep wearing these around me, and you'll catch me doing worse."

"Yeah?" I say, blinking away the bright bokeh lights that are dancing before my eyes.

"Yeah," he confirms, like a pledge. His nose skims so close past my cheek that I feel the tiny hairs reaching for him, straining like leaves toward the sun. I think he's going to kiss me again, even though we're in a middle school atrium, surrounded by children in baggy cargo pants and leotards and parents rushing toward seats. Even after Deb's warning, I think I'll let him.

But instead Julian pulls away, and I feel his withdrawal like a gust of chill.

"You must be Winona," he says abruptly.

He's right. It is Winny. She's dressed impeccably in tailored bootcut jeans and a stylish beige blazer, and her makeup is just a touch too heavy-handed for a children's dance recital. It's clear that she's come for battle, and that looking fabulous is her armor.

"And you must be Julian," Winny says, extending a hand. She gives him an appraising look. "It seems you found your phone."

Oops. Hell hath no fury like a woman defending her best friend's honor. In the mess that has been the last few days, I've neglected to let her know that Julian was back in contact and in our good graces.

Julian takes Winny's hand, affecting an expression that is just the right amount of contrite.

"It's nice to meet you, Winona, and I definitely deserved that," he says.

"I know," Winona says. Then she turns a curious glance to me. "I can't say that I expected us to meet today."

I wince. I probably, no, *definitely* should've asked before bringing a date to her kid's dance recital. I was supposed to be Winona's plus-one. Now I've turned her into a third wheel. It's an oversight I never could've seen myself making a few months ago.

"I'm so sorry. I didn't even think to ask if he could come," I confess. "But he drove me all the way, and . . ."

Winona cuts me off.

"I don't mind that. I'm more concerned about why you are here when you should be bundled up in bed right now, high off NyQuil and bingeing *Vampire Diaries*."

I make a point not to look at Julian, who I imagine is giving me a knowing look. If Winona knew that I'd spent last night in the emergency room, she'd probably drop-kick me back into my downtown apartment.

"I'm all better, actually," I say. To prove it, I do a little jog in place that earns me a smirk from a passing attendee. "See? Fit as a fiddle. Even made it to SCAI last night. Besides, I promised Sophie."

Winona glances down at the bouquet in my hands, then releases the world's most dramatic sigh, complete with heaving shoulders and a three-hundred-and-sixty-degree eye roll.

"You spoil her," she says. Then, with a small smile, she adds, "You're glowing. I just assumed it was from fever. I see it must be from something else."

Julian and I exchange a conspiratorial glance: his smug, mine guilty. Luckily, Winona doesn't catch it. She's too busy eyeing the doors of the auditorium.

"Well, no point in pretending not to be relieved. Leila's here. I don't exactly want to make small talk, so I'm pretending to need to use the bathroom—" She blanches, realizing too late that she's speaking to the best man of the woman whom she's currently avoiding. "Not that she isn't lovely, of course . . ."

Julian waves her off.

"No worries," he says. "Happy to be a buffer."

It's a testament to how out of sorts I still feel that it only occurs to me that someone else should be taking on that role when we're walking down the aisle of the auditorium.

"Is Brandon not here?" I ask.

From behind, Winona's body stiffens.

"Nope," she says in a deceptively pleasant tone, and then we stop at a row of seats close to the stage and she holds her arms out in a polite *After you*.

We find Leila at the end of the aisle. When she sees Julian, she raises both eyebrows in an expression that could almost be mistaken for disdain before it turns quickly to delight.

"Oh my gosh, what are you doing here?"

She throws herself into his arms. It's the familiar embrace of two people whose comfort in each other has built over years, who have seen each other in sweats and smelled each other's stinky socks and know what toppings the other likes on their pizza. Objectively, I know that there's nothing romantic about it.

And yet I want to tear her small, man-stealing arms from around his waist.

Which is wrong. I know it's wrong. The feeling is alien; even as it rushes through me, I know that it doesn't fit, like a too-small bra found at the bottom of my drawer. Hating a woman for a man's disloyalty has never been my style; I'm much less likely to get jealous and far more likely to get lost. Still, a more vicious voice rings louder: *Was Brandon not enough, you whore?*

Winona places a hand on my thigh.

"You sure you're okay?" she whispers. "You're . . . staring."

The moment she says it, I realize my eyes are so wide that the distant gust of air from the auditorium heaters scratches like sandpaper against my corneas.

"Fine," I say, blinking away just as Leila leans forward in her seat to greet me.

"Hi, Sean!" she says brightly.

"Nice to see you, Leila," I say. "Brandon feeling any better today?"

"Yup," she says cryptically. She gestures toward Julian. "Oh, and thanks for going to check in on Julian. Even if it was a false alarm."

Julian stiffens.

"You shouldn't have sent her," he says coolly to Leila. "Who knows what she could've walked into."

"Sean can take care of herself," Leila says.

"You don't know that," he says frostily, and I squint up at him, not sure what I've missed.

"*You've* never seen her in the lab," Leila retorts. "She gets the jugular on the first stick."

She jabs an unseen needle into the air to demonstrate my prowess, and the grin she gives me is sharp-fanged and wild-eyed and so out of character that I recoil.

Julian must sense my discomfort, because he squeezes my knee. Before he can speak, though, the lights dim, and a man in stylishly baggy clothes walks to the mic to start the show. Next to me, Winona is throwing furtive glances to the now closed auditorium door, and my heart breaks for her. Brandon has been letting her down for a long time, but letting Sophie down is different. She's been working up to this recital for months, and we both know that she'll note her dad's absence.

But the door doesn't open, and we sit together, an almost ragtag crew, and watch the recital without him. It's about as riveting as expected. With the exception of a few standouts, identifiable by their perfectly slicked-back ponytails and the dance moms crowding the aisles to record their performances, most of the kids have more enthusiasm than talent. Sophie is no exception, but she's still satisfying to watch, her thick eyebrows furrowing in concentration as she bounces through the choreography.

They're about halfway through the song when a door bangs open at the other side of the hall. A collective gasp fills the auditorium, a frozen moment when everyone in attendance peers at the source and decides if they need to run. A few of the dancers miss their cues, distracted, but not even their instructor notices, because his and all of our attention is trained stage right.

A tall, thin figure stalls at the door. Light pours into the auditorium behind him, and his shadow casts ghoulishly along the floor. A teacher rushes to him and ushers him inside, closing the door, and our focus drifts back to the stage. When I look back at Sophie, her mouth is set into a frown. She stumbles. I wince.

"Shit," Winona says next to me. "I think that's Brandon."

It's too dark to know for sure, but I think it's him too. Praying he'll stay where he is, I loop my arm through Winona's and she grasps it tight. We focus on the dance for another song, clap as the girls take their position for the next. Here or not, we will not let Brandon ruin—

"I don't know what you think this is," a gravelly voice says, just loud enough to be heard over the music. "But that's my wife you're next to, and my daughter on that stage. So if you don't get your ass out of this seat right now, I'll be putting on a different show."

Sure enough, it is Brandon—and he's in Julian's face, a fist curled into the collar of his sweater.

"Brandon," Winona hisses. "What are you *doing*?"

He doesn't turn, doesn't twitch, doesn't make any indication that he's heard his ex-wife speak. His eyes are trained on Julian and they are filled with fury.

"Move, asshole," he snarls, "or I'll make you move."

To his credit, Julian treats being physically accosted by a crazed man spitting flecks of saliva in his face with aplomb.

"Leila," he says in an exasperated drawl. "Can you please take care of this so that I don't have to?"

I can't see Leila over the two men. I don't know if she is watching the scene unfold before her in dismay or delight.

But I do hear her voice. It carries, melodic and resonant, like a whisper in the wind, and a reptilian part of my brain tells me to sit still and listen.

"Brandon, baby," she says. "Just sit on the floor."

Brandon obeys instantly. The room is dark, but I watch his face slacken, see his fingers loosen their grip on Julian's sweater before dropping away altogether. Obediently, he shuffles backward out of the row and drops, like a chastised dog, on the dirty auditorium aisle next to Leila.

The whole ordeal can't have lasted more than thirty seconds, but it feels like a bomb has just gone off in our row. I hear people chittering around us, but my gaze is fixed on the stage, on Sophie, whose smile has been replaced with a look of fierce determination. She hits every beat. When I turn to look at Winona, her expression mirrors her daughter's. It's as if they have both come to the same conclusion at once: *We don't need him. We'll be fine on our own.*

When the performance is over, Brandon is the first to stand. He slaps his hands together haphazardly, and the sloppy claps echo alone in the theater before they are joined by a round of applause. From afar, he probably looks like a proud, if overenthusiastic, father, but from up close he looks eerie, like someone has taken over his body and is still figuring out the controls.

My gaze drifts, almost reflexively, to Julian. As if he can feel me looking, he turns and gives me a small, inscrutable smile. I can't even consider what it might mean before Winona suddenly crashes into me.

"Oh my gosh, Sophie!"

Sophie giggles wickedly, having snuck up on her mom from behind. Her hair is falling out of its ponytail, but I'm relieved to find her looking so happy after the debacle that was her father's interruption.

"You didn't hear me coming at all!" she declares, delighted with herself. She gives her mom a hug, and Winona pulls her in close. They hold each other for one beautiful moment until Sophie bursts free and turns to me.

"Are those for me?" she asks, greedily reaching for the flowers. I hand them over, and she pulls them to her nose. "They smell so fresh! Thanks, Auntie."

"Of course, nugget," I start, but Sophie is already distracted, having noticed who is standing beside me.

"It's you," she says, aghast. "From the wedding."

"Nice to see you again, Sophia," Julian says, and I can tell he's holding back laughter. Sophie turns a smug look to me, cocking a hip to the side.

"I knew it," she said. "I can't believe you didn't tell me he was your *boyfriend*, Auntie Sean!"

I almost tell her that I didn't know he was my boyfriend myself until a few days ago, but Julian has already turned on his charm for her.

"You were fantastic up there," he says. "Congratulations."

Sophie's expression flickers with knowing. It confirms what I've been asking myself: if she saw what happened between Julian and her father from the stage. It saddens me some when she doesn't address it. It's the surest sign that Winona's baby girl is growing up: she has learned artifice.

When Sophie squeezes past us to greet her dad and stepmom at the end of the row, Julian pulls me into him.

"She's a great kid," he says softly, watching Sophie's three parents put aside their personal enmities to celebrate their daughter. He sounds almost wistful, and I study his face in profile. Anxiety tickles my throat. I can never give him this, and he knows that. *He has to know that.*

"Is that what you want?" I say softly.

Julian turns to me. The amber auditorium lights shroud him in a halo. He swallows, and I follow the course of his Adam's apple like a ball drop.

"I don't think I'd make a very good parent. And that's okay. Family doesn't have to look one way," he says. He tucks a loc behind my ear, and the tenderness of the motion assures me more than his words. "I might like something like what you have with Sophie. Being an impactful adult in a child's life. It looks nice."

"It is," I confess. "Getting to watch her grow up, figure out her passions, form thoughts and ideas . . . it's been rewarding."

Julian nods, pensive. I'm about to ask him if he's considered mentoring youth alongside his entrepreneurs when he freezes, his fingers stilling on my face.

"What?" I ask, watching his brows furrow with concern.

"Your hair," he whispers.

I squint up at him in confusion, but Leila's voice cuts through the din before I can respond.

"Julian!" she says, waving. "We're heading out!"

Julian twitches back to life.

"One moment," he says to me. To Leila, in a voice like thunder, "Wait. We need to talk."

My gaze swings reflexively to Brandon, whose attention has already locked on to Julian. Leila gives them both a beatific smile, then tells her husband, "Why don't you wait right here, honey. Spend a little more time with Sophie."

Brandon doesn't look pleased with being grounded, but he steps aside and lets them go.

And then there were four.

When Winona, Sophie, and I hang out, it always feels natural. But after Brandon's infidelity came to light, adding him into the mix has always made me feel like I'm imposing. I shuffle just slightly outside their circle as Sophie demands her parents' opinion and tries to make a case for Applebee's. When ten minutes pass and Leila and Julian are still nowhere to be found, the panic begins. It comes in a rush: sweat beading on my forehead, my stomach twisting into knots, the sort of nauseating anticipation triggered by receiving a phone call from an ex or walking onto a stage for a big presentation. I imagine Julian and Leila tangled together in bathroom stalls and darkened corridors, stealing away to sneak passionate kisses behind one of the theater's heavy metal doors. The feeling doesn't feel quite my own, and the images are improbable to the level of absurdity—Leila and

Julian interact more like siblings than friends, with a mixture of affection and contempt—but they linger in a way I can't shake.

I turn and catch Brandon's eye, the anxiety breeding behind it. I suspect that he feels the same way, and that the only reason why he hasn't already given chase is because his beloved told him to wait.

"I'm going to the bathroom," I announce as Sophie changes her mind and suggests a trip to Steak 'n Shake instead.

When I break out into the hall, the crowds have already thinned. A movement catches the corner of my eye: two figures, one tall and broad, the other small and slight, turning into a dark alcove labeled "Exit."

I know I shouldn't follow them. Two close friends wanting to have their tiff in private isn't anything out of the ordinary, and if I can't trust Julian alone with Leila I shouldn't be messing with him at all. But something in my body wants to come between them, and without thinking about it, I follow them.

The alcove leads to a stairwell, all concrete and rusting iron that looks nothing at all like the cheerily painted walls of the atrium. I slip inside.

I hear them before I see them, furious whispers echoing against the concrete walls. I can tell they are a floor or two below, out of sight but just barely. Quietly, I settle into a squat, straining to listen.

"What the fuck do you think you're doing, Julian?"

That is Leila's voice, all right, but it sounds different—higher, harsher, and ringing with a level of fury I didn't know she was capable of.

"I don't know what you're talking about," Julian says.

"Oh, save it, asshole. I have *eyes*. And a brain. I know you. You're pulling the exact same shit as last time. Maybe even worse."

"Don't . . . I . . ." I don't think I've ever heard Julian sound so completely lost for words. He clears his throat, says more firmly, "I've got this under control, Leila."

Leila laughs out loud, a sharp, singular hyena's bark that bounces against the concrete like a scream.

"Do you," she says mockingly. "Because I don't think there's any controlling that one, and I think you get off on that."

I freeze. There it is, a veer in their conversation that makes me feel like there's a red honing laser burning between my brows.

The sound Julian makes is curiously close to a growl.

"You're being a hypocrite," he says. "It's quite clear that you don't have much of a handle on your business either."

Leila doesn't respond right away, and when she does, she sounds agitated.

"I don't know what's wrong. It wasn't supposed to happen this fast." She pauses. "This is your fault."

"*My* fault?" Julian whispers, incredulous. "Now how did you figure that?"

"You're *eating out of my bowl.*" Her voice is vicious. "And if you'd been quick about it, I might have let it go. But I'm telling you now that it's getting in my way. So clean up your shit, or I will."

My body seizes at her words. It occurs to me, suddenly, that the *one* who can't be controlled, that the *shit* Julian needs to clean up, might be me, and that what I've just heard is a threat. My brain screams back denials, tells me my reaction is overreaching and overdramatic—*Be serious, Sean, they could be talking about anyone*—but it's too late. My instincts scream danger, and for once, I listen. I stand up abruptly, poised to run.

Then my phone slips out of my pocket and clatters to the floor.

The stairwell goes deathly silent. There is a shift in the air, like a subtle breeze. The lights flicker. For one torturous second, my body locks, and I am held captive.

And then, suddenly, release.

There is no time to think, no time to breathe. I bend to grab my phone and sprint through the open door.

Back out in the atrium, I feel like I've reentered the real world, one bustling with warmth and color. I stand, disoriented, as smiling families course past me, discussing where they're going for dinner or what piece they'll be practicing next. I can feel the residual effects of my fear, jittering teeth and pinpricks of sweat on my brow, but it all feels silly and unfounded now. And yet. I can't ignore it anymore, can't convince myself that the danger I'd felt in that stairwell was imagined. I squeeze my eyes shut, and burning ones stare back.

Someone touches my arm, and I almost flail away.

"Whoa," Winona says. "I was just going to tell you we were leaving—"

"Can I come home with you?" The question comes out in a rush.

Winona blinks owlishly at me. I know she wants to ask me why I'm not going back with Julian, but I'm grateful that she doesn't.

"Of course," she says.

We are in her car and on the way five minutes later. Sophie sits in the back seat, jabbering happily about a song she's going to suggest to her instructor for the next recital, while I try to figure out what the hell just happened. Then I remember what Julian said, the frown that had crossed his face.

Your hair.

My hand dives into my locs. I'd just had them retwisted before the conference—yet my fingers don't slide against exposed scalp, but into dense, compacted curls.

My stomach leaps. Swallowing, I reach for the car visor and sweep open the mirror.

The woman staring back at me looks hollow and shell-shocked. Her mouth is drawn tight, and her catlike eyes widen in horror the longer I stare. It is most certainly my face, but it is not the one I'm used to. That Sean's roots are tight and laced with gray.

This one's are grown in and stark white.

Seventeen

My scream almost runs Winona off the road.

"What the *fuck*, Sean!" Winona shouts, regaining control of the steering wheel.

"Language, Mom," Sophie says, snickering.

"Not the time, Sophie," Winona says. She makes a hard right into the Steak 'n Shake parking lot, then slides smoothly into a spot, hands her daughter a twenty-dollar bill, and points to the door. "Go get yourself something."

Not one to look a gift horse in the mouth, Sophie snatches the cash and leaps out of the car, running inside to get her treat. The moment she's gone, Winny rounds on me.

"Okay, so I wasn't going to ask until we got home, but you're kinda freaking me out," she says. "What's going on with you?"

I'm still shaking. It takes effort to tear my eyes from my reflection to meet Winona's.

"Winny," I say slowly. "Do you . . . notice anything different about me?"

Winona squints, looking at me carefully from top to bottom.

"Aside from the random psychotic break you had just now?" she quips. "No. Not really."

"Really?" I say. I grab ahold of my hair and bend my head until she's looking at the crown of my head. "Are you *sure*?"

There's a heartbeat of silence, and when I peer back at Winona, she looks confused.

"It's . . ." She pauses. "White?"

"Exactly," I say.

"I thought you liked your grays."

"I do," I say, frustrated. She's right—I've always loved them, even more so after my own brush with death, after I started seeing patients my age and younger appear on my cath lab table. Each hair a sign of life, of the years I had been gifted and not guaranteed. But all that's beside the point. "But they're not gray, they're *white*. And they weren't white yesterday."

"Overnight, Sulley, really?" she asks.

I'm stunned by the mildness of her response.

"I'm not crazy, Winny."

The look Winona gives me can only be described as indulgent.

"I'm not saying you're crazy," she says. "You've just had a hard week. Hard month, honestly. Is it possible that you—"

My phone dings, and I dig it out of my back pocket before Winny can complete her dismissal. It's a text from Julian. I read it, and the fear that I'd felt in the stairwell resurges.

Where did you go? it says. I've been looking everywhere for you.

The dance floor at the SCAI conference, drained of its strobe light color. Melody's face, slack and wan, her eyes darting to his in search of approval. His hand splayed on her neck, the slow, sensual hiss of his words, improbably loud against the booming music. Leila's voice echoing against concrete, *I don't think there's any controlling that one—*

That's what she'd said, right? Under Winny's worried eyes, I feel less certain. Maybe I am going crazy. Maybe I've been so sick and sleep-deprived for the last two weeks that my brain is jumping to find supernatural answers to mundane questions. I did go to a new loctician for my retightening; maybe she just did a bad job and my new hair is unraveling. Maybe I'm looking at my roots more closely now because I've been more self-conscious after the conference.

A hand squeezes my thigh.

"Is everything okay?" Winona asks. Concern is etched into every one of her features, and I deflate and squeeze her hand back.

"I followed Julian and Leila, after they left the hall," I admit. "They were talking, and they said some things that sort of freaked me out. And I don't know, I'm probably being paranoid, but . . ."

"What did you hear?" Winona probes.

I tell her. I feel more and more foolish as I speak, because I realize that I've made a hundred logical leaps. They never mentioned me; if I'm honest, they didn't mention a person at all so much as a situation. These two have been friends since childhood; there are a thousand grievances they probably share—a deal gone wrong, a mutual relationship gone awry, money into the wrong hands. Julian's new girlfriend, whom Leila not only approved of but practically helped orchestrate, is probably the least of their worries.

By Winona's pitying expression, she agrees.

"I'm losing it, aren't I," I say when I'm done.

Winona nods, eyebrows up and lips screwed as if she's holding back laughter.

"Yeah, kinda," she says.

We both snicker, and the tension that has made my chest tight since I woke up in Julian's bed a few days ago eases like air out of a balloon.

"I don't know what's wrong with me," I say. "It's like I don't know what's up or down sometimes these days."

Winona turns to face me bodily. She opens her mouth like she's about to say something, thinks better of it, then swallows and tries again.

"You actually like Julian, and he seems to be pretty serious about you," she starts. "It's been a long time since you've let anyone this far in . . ."

Oh bother. I know where this is going.

"You think I'm traumatized," I finish.

"I think you're understandably cautious, and that healing is a process, not a destination," Winona amends. "You've probably done all the work you can as a single woman. But it looks different in the context of a relationship. A lot of your fears that Julian might not be who he says he is, the distrust, might not have anything to really do with *him*." She silences my oncoming objection with a finger. "I just want to encourage you to assess him for *his* actions. No one else's." Her gaze becomes fierce. "Especially not Eric's."

My blood chills when she says his name, but I know why she does, and know that she's right. In trying to protect myself, I've painted Julian with a broad brush, one that overlays all his behavior with ill intent, and it's not the first time I've been guilty of that with him.

"Okay, Dr. Evans," I groan.

Winona rolls her eyes at me affectionately.

"Keep playing around, and I'll run you a bill," she teases.

The door to Steak 'n Shake bursts open, and Sophie walks out with a large milkshake in one hand and a bag of spoils in the other.

"You're right," I say as Sophie skips up to the car.

Winona unlocks the door and gives me a wink.

"I usually am."

It takes me too long to fall asleep in Winona's guest room.

A hand brushes past my temples. It is too dark to see, but I know who it belongs to.

"You ran off on me," Julian whispers. "Why?"

I try to move, but my body is glued to the bed. I am hyperaware of the heaviness of my arms at my sides, the weight of my head on Winona's down pillow, but oddly, I'm not afraid. This dream feels different from the others, like Julian has slid into a layer of my subconscious and is making pleasant conversation rather than pulling me into a new reality.

"You scare me sometimes," I confess. I'm not sure if my mouth moves or if I am just thinking it, but either way, Julian hums in understanding.

"Is it strange that I find that exhilarating?"

"Absolutely," I insist. "I would argue that *strange* is a gross understatement. Fucking terrifying is more like it."

It shouldn't be funny, but we laugh, and when we are done, I feel the mattress lift; he's standing.

"You're brilliant, Sean," he says. "And perceptive. It's one of the things I like most about you."

"See?" I mutter. "That cryptic shit right there? Freaky."

His chuckle fades into the darkness.

"Good night, songbird," Julian whispers. And then he is gone, and so am I, drifting into sleep so peaceful that it feels like a small death.

Eighteen

When I get to clinic early the next morning, my assigned medical assistant greets me at my office with a Cheshire cat smile so bright that I squint at the sight of it. She's young, fresh off her twenty-first birthday, and vaguely unprofessional in a way that is both refreshing and disorienting. It's not yet eight in the morning and my head already hurts; I'm pretty sure the surprise she has in store for me is going to make it worse.

"You have a visitor," she sings.

"A patient?" I ask. I glance at my schedule; my first patient isn't due for another hour, and I'm not even sure the clinic secretaries are at their desks yet.

"God, I hope not," she says. "That would be *super* awkward, considering."

I am back on my feet before my brain can tell me to stand. It's this strange gut response my body has acquired, like just the thought of Julian is enough to spur me to flee, though I'm not sure whether it is toward him or away. My mind is no better, flickering between memories of his body driving pleasure into mine and that moment in the stairwell, the other on the dance floor.

I'd responded to Julian's text asking about my whereabouts this morning with a quick and uncharacteristically dishonest so sorry, thought I'd sent this! Wasn't feeling well so ended up going back with Winny, which I'd hoped would waylay any questions. Because, if I'm being honest, I'm not exactly sure *how* to approach my next conversation with Julian. Winona's advice that I focus on his behavior is running headlong into my trust in my intuition. I don't know how to detangle that contradiction . . . and I thought I'd have more time to figure it out. *He was supposed to be traveling to Austin today,* I think. *Why is he still here?* His spontaneity both thrills and terrifies—*He wants me that bad, huh?* but also *He knows where I work, when I work, how to get to me.*

My medical assistant is looking at me with concern.

"Should I tell him to leave?" she asks.

Sending him away would probably spell the end of our brief relationship, and as I'm not yet convinced that I'm not losing my mind, I shake my head.

"No, no, it's fine," I say. "Bring him back here."

She whisks away and less than a minute later, there's a knock on my door.

"Come in."

A mass of brown fur fills my doorway. Brown legs, brown arms, a huge red bow around its neck. It takes me a second to realize what I'm looking at: a gigantic teddy bear.

It's like someone has snapped their fingers and told my anxiety *Begone.* Julian peeks around the side of the teddy bear's colossal head, and I start to laugh so hard that I almost choke.

"You're joking," I wheeze.

"I take it this means I did good," Julian says, walking into my office and gently kicking the door shut behind him.

"It means you're a fool." I slap my chest, trying to catch my breath. Julian bends to set the teddy bear down on the chair. Even sitting, it's human sized, and I circle my desk, so completely overcome with delight that I can't really remember why I'd felt so unsettled before.

"A fool indeed," Julian says sheepishly. "I'm sorry about Sunday. I made all that noise about you resting, and then instead of getting you home right away, I got caught up talking with Leila."

Guilt gnaws at my stomach as I remember my white lie; Julian had already been beating himself up for not being considerate enough of my health.

"O-Oh," I stammer. "It's okay."

He gives me an apologetic smile, and I'm deciding whether I should fess up when he reaches into his back pocket.

"Also, since you failed to tell your goddaughter about us, I wanted to get your commitment in writing."

He hands me an envelope, and I scrunch my nose as I tear it open, already suspecting what's inside. I still laugh when I flip the card open.

Do you, Sean Sullivan, want to be my, Julian Conrad's, girlfriend? Check yes or no. At the bottom, two signature lines: one already filled by Julian's looping cursive, the other empty and for me.

Teenage me is screaming like she's just seen her favorite boy band live. Adult me is about two seconds away from closing my blinds, locking my office door, putting my hair up in a ponytail and dropping to my knees. I close the distance between us to make good on my heart's wish, but Julian stills me with a hand on my hip.

"Nope," he says. "We're doing this right this time."

He takes a step back and hands me a pen with the gravity of a judge signing a decree.

I snatch it out of his hands and scrawl my signature so aggressively that he would never imagine that just minutes before, I'd thought I might have to escape him. And how could I ever have thought that? My mind might occasionally try to turn Julian into a bogeyman, but in real life, he is this: teasing, sweet, and totally capable of making me laugh until my belly aches. He's hurt me once, yes, but he's spent every second since attempting to make up for it—never made me do anything I didn't want to, always stops the second I say no. A man who lights up in my presence the way Onix does when I get home from work, who seems to derive joy from learning me.

When he curls his fingers into the belt loops of my slacks to tug me close, I almost sigh with the relief of being back in his arms.

"Aren't you supposed to be in Austin?" I ask.

"I will be," Julian supplies. "Flight leaves in the afternoon. I figured I could sneak in a visit."

I hum, kissing the corner of his mouth, then the center.

"And while it is very appreciated, you need to stop showing up at my work unannounced," I chide. "One day I'm going to just leave you in the waiting room."

Julian looks down at me from below his eyelashes.

"Do you want me to text you before?" he asks.

"Please," I say. I run my hand over his shoulder, down the solid curve of his triceps until I'm cradling his elbow in my palm. "The surprises are nice. But I would prefer that, yes."

"Noted," he says. I wait for the excuse, for him to argue that this way is more romantic or *just his way of showing affection*, but he doesn't give that. Instead he drops his forehead to mine.

"My team is meeting with Jared soon," he tells me. "He sent me an email, you know. Not long after we ran into him at the art center. It was full of praise for you."

The mention of my ex's brother throws me for a bit of a loop, and I blink away, hoping the knot in my chest loosens.

"Was it?" I say.

I can feel Julian's gaze on the side of my face. He nudges me back to his eyes, and I meet them.

"Yes," Julian says. "You're an incredible woman, and you make an impact on others. It was just nice to see evidence of that."

I snatch my gaze back. I feel like a live wire, exposed and poised to spark. I don't think anyone has ever looked at me the way that he does, with such naked adulation that it makes me squirm. It's a reverence reserved for miracles and gods. I'm too small, too human, I think, to be regarded with such worship.

"Yeah, you have to leave," I say.

I feel Julian smirk. He presses a final kiss to my lips, then reaches around me for the card on my desk.

"Remember that you signed this," he says. "So you're going to have to get used to me. I'll be much harder to get rid of."

His declaration gives me pause because it sounds more like an admission. Like he's telling me that he's been holding back and that I should prepare myself for who he may become now that he isn't.

Chill, Sean, a voice suspiciously like Winny's warns me.

"Sure, sure, but I'm getting rid of you right now. I have patients to see, I can't be in here *simpering*." I make a show of pushing his back toward the door. He laughs, then grabs my hand for a final kiss.

"Call me tonight?" he asks.

"Yes," I say, throwing open the door. "Now scram."

Nineteen

The thing about being properly loved for the first time is it exposes all the ways in which you weren't before. I'd spent the last eight years of my life fearing relationships, my apprehension only affirmed after watching Winona and countless other women in my circle shrink under the weight of partners who were thoughtless at best, patriarchal at minimum, and, in the worst cases, life-threateningly dangerous. Love, I'd decided, was mostly myth, a fairy tale sold to young girls to con them into signing on to their own servitude.

But Julian spends the next three months challenging this long-held paradigm. His affection and consideration is consistent to a degree that I wouldn't have thought possible. I end many a long day in the cath lab with a text asking when I think I'll be making it home followed by a hot dinner waiting for me in my apartment lobby perfectly timed to my arrival, and I start many more to Julian waking up bright and early to catch me for my morning walk with Onix, with my favorite overly sweet latte in hand. The romance has ramped up too: long gone is the Sean of my twenties, who used to beg for flowers and coo over nuggets of affection. Julian delights in spoiling me; I once mentioned that I liked the look of an Anima Iris bag I'd seen on a red carpet only for him to present it to me two weeks later. But it's the smaller, thoughtful trinkets that get me the most: a planter shaped like a pit bull for my small apartment garden, vanilla beans from his short trip to Costa Rica, reminders that no matter where he is, he's thinking of me.

Being Julian's is quiet. It's soft. I don't have to demand to be seen because he pays attention, understands that Onix is aging and comes to my apartment whenever he can, recognizes when I've had a tiring day at work or when one of my patients passes away and gives me the space to cry or vent or both. His busy schedule never seems to manifest as an excuse not to pour into me; we spend many evenings sitting across from each other at my dining table working in tandem, and many nights curled in each other's arms, exchanging stories about his clients, my colleagues, the books we're reading, the state of the world, before drifting off sweetly to sleep.

What we are not doing, however, is fucking.

"Wait, seriously?" Winona says in shock during our biweekly brunch debrief. "You haven't slept together since then? Not one time?"

"No, Winny, not one time," I hiss. Someone bumps my chair and I glower at them before rushing to fix my face; all my pent-up frustration is turning me feral. Winona covers her mouth to muffle her laughter, and I scowl back. "Don't laugh! This is serious!"

"I know, I know," Winona says, even as she dabs at her eyes. "Sorry, this is just . . . wasn't this the same guy who had you in all sorts of compromising positions back in the day?"

It *is* the same man, and that's the problem. I love my relationship with Julian. He's reliable, and brilliant, and so tooth-achingly sweet. But gone are the days of splaying me out on conference tables, bouncing me on his lap in back seats, and eating me out against slammed doors. Celibacy was easy when I had limited access to men I found attractive. But now that there's a strapping young man who I *know* has A-one stroke game making a habit of walking around my apartment shirtless, wrestling with my dog, and anticipating (*almost*) all my needs, I feel like I'm about to burst.

"He won't even really make out with me anymore," I lament. "It's giving . . . church kisses. Giving 'leave room for Jesus.'"

I tell her about our recent trip to the Red River Gorge in Kentucky, the glorious Wednesday we'd spent hiking the quiet trail and learning about each other that ended in a king-sized four-poster bed in our boutique hotel. A kiss so hungry that it seemed destined for more, hands that had finally started to wander from their respectable homes at my hips. I'd reached for the hem of his shirt—

"And this man had the audacity to grab my wrist and tell me that *actually, he was too tired*," I say, my cheeks red-hot at the memory.

Thankfully, Winona doesn't laugh at this.

"Wow," she says. Then, matter-of-factly, "You think he's cheating?"

The thought has crossed my mind. I've heard of cheaters who behave the way Julian is now, ramping up romance to assuage their guilt. But in our case, it doesn't really make sense for him to.

"He's the one who wanted to put a label on it," I say, then, biting my cheek, "And . . . I don't know. I just really don't think he is."

Maybe because the tension is still there. Even if we aren't acting on it, I can feel it in his lingering looks, how his pupils dilate as I change into my (increasingly skimpier) pajamas before bed, the desperation in his hold, how it sometimes feels like he thinks I'm going to fly out of his arms. I remember that evening when Brandon missed the STEMI, what now feels like a lifetime ago, the queasy expression on his face as he told me that he just wanted to *take things slow*. Of course, he'd flipped me like an omelet just a week later, so I'd assumed that particular bit of insanity had passed. But it feels, strangely, like Julian is afraid of being intimate with me again. Like he's running from it.

"Box was too fire," Winona says solemnly, and that makes me crack a grin. It immediately falls from my face at her next question. "So . . . have you talked to him about it?"

"Oh god, no." When Winona raises her eyebrows in a silent but heard *Really, bitch*? I pout back. "Come on, Winny. You know I would rather die than beg a man for dick. I've still got some pride."

"Pride won't get your back cracked," Winona notes. "But also, you're right. I do know you. You are so incredibly direct, and the only time I've ever seen you hold back is when you're scared. So what are you scared of? That he'll call you desperate? He's *obsessed* with you."

My wince is as good an answer as any. Leave it to my best friend, the therapist, to see right through me. The truth is, even though I want to believe that Julian's desire for me is undeniable, there are moments when I'm not so sure. It doesn't escape my notice that he went from clawing at his enclosure to get to me to slamming the brakes immediately after seeing me fully naked for the first time. Most mornings when I look in the mirror after a shower, I like what I see. But my body isn't the same as it was at twenty-two. It's grown-woman juicy now, with cornbread-fed hips and divots and slightly uneven tits. I look good, but no one will be asking me to be on the cover of *Sports Illustrated*. Compared to Julian, who looks like he was carved from marble by a particularly libidinous Grecian sculptor, my beauty feels . . . mundane. And then there's the matter of my hair. Initially hardly noticeable, the band of new growth is now so stark white that Pamela asked if I'd purposely bleached my roots. Every now and then, I catch Julian staring at the crown of my head, as if he's traversing the chasm of the eleven years between us.

I tell Winona as much.

"He knew how old you were when you met," Winona reminds me.

"Yes, but things were less serious then," I say. "We're thirty-eight and twenty-seven now, but someday we'll be forty and twenty-nine, fifty and thirty-nine . . ." As Winny raises her brow, it occurs to me that I'm thinking of the distant future with Julian, and I drop my face in my hands, defeated. "God, I do just need to talk to him, don't I."

Winona cuts a piece of her berry French toast, dips it into its condensed milk topping, and holds out a bite for me to eat.

"You do," she insists. "Now say 'ah.'"

There in ten, Julian says. Though I admit to being very, very curious about what lies in wait for me. I brought Pepcid just in case.

Don't be a jerk, I respond. See you soon.

Julian has every right to be suspicious. The cookware that has been hanging from the ceiling above my kitchen island for the last several years still gleams silver, and I once spent five minutes rooting around my cupboards while he was over in search of a cutting board. In Julian's eyes, I am not a woman who cooks. And thus, he has made the critical error of assuming I *cannot*.

Which is silly. I was raised to be a good Southern woman who can throw down in the kitchen, and my earliest lesson was that the quickest way to a man's pants (okay, maybe it was heart) is through his belly. I've watched Julian devour a plate of overpriced, soupy mac and cheese knowing that my grandmama's recipe would put it to shame. I spend far too long puttering about my kitchen, tossing together a Caesar salad and pan searing lamb chops while dinner rolls bake in the oven, then even longer cleaning up the disaster I make of my kitchen. Even Onix is confused, padding after me and licking up the scraps as they hit the floor. If only Winona could see me now. *Sean Ernestine Sullivan*, she would say. *I said talk to him, not cosplay as a tradwife.*

By the time Julian has arrived, the scene is set. Lights dimmed to medium low. Food waiting on warm in the oven. Bikini line trimmed, underarms shaved, and entire body exfoliated and then clad in a little black velvet dress, a white apron, and cheap sheer tights that I desperately hope he rips off.

Onix knows Julian is here before I do. He plods to the door and sits, releasing a slow expectant whine seconds before I hear him knock.

"He likes you more than me," I say in lieu of a greeting when I throw open the door.

Julian always looks good to me, but today, he looks particularly delectable. He's been hearing pitches from aspiring entrepreneurs all day, and so he's dressed for business in a well-fitted suit and a crisp white shirt that only helps emphasize the taper of his waist. Only his tie is doffed, probably tossed into the passenger seat on his way over to mine. I have a ridiculous image of him calling out, "Honey, I'm home!" and dropping his briefcase onto the floor before wandering in and asking me what's for dinner.

Me, I would say.

By the way his eyelids flutter as he looks me up and down, Julian would probably respond to that by tying a bib around his neck and saying, "Bon appétit."

"Wow," he says, clearly caught off guard. "You look—"

Onix lunges between us, somehow regaining enough grease in his joints to leap onto Julian's legs, and he falls out of my trap. I watch as Julian drops into a squat right at the door to lavish him with pets and coos, and I find myself a little jealous and not a bit ashamed of it. I give Onix a look that says, *You are definitely going in the crate for dinner.* He gives me a look back that must mean *Ha! Got your man.*

Julian seems to notice the tension between woman and woman's best frenemy, because when he finally stands and steps inside, he pulls me in by the waist.

"Good," he finishes. "I meant to say you look good."

I throw my arms around his neck, glowing in self-satisfaction when his gaze drops to my glossed lips.

"Just good?" I ask, and Julian smirks as his free hand trails up my neck.

"*Distractingly* good," he says. He pulls on the strap of my suspiciously clean apron. "I'm not sure I ever thought I'd see you in one of these. Very domestic of you."

"Do you want me to take it off?" I say. "I look even better underneath."

"I'm sure you do," Julian says, drawing me into him. His kiss starts the way it always has, with a gentle, breathtaking press that is salacious in its suggestion but not its technique. It's the anticipation that gets me, the subtle tensing of his hand at the small of my back, the closing of distance between our bodies. I groan into it, draw myself onto my tiptoes to offer myself more to him . . .

He pulls back and steps bodily away from me.

"I'm eating crow already. It smells amazing in here," he says, whipping off his jacket and arranging it carefully over the back of my chair. He folds up his sleeves, revealing his strong, threaded forearms, and reaches into his pocket. "Got something for you."

Of course you do, I think. When he pulls a Tiffany blue box out, I have to fix my face into one of appropriate gratitude. I take it from him and pop it open to reveal a pair of small diamond-studded hoop earrings. Between the luxury branding and the stones, I know that this gift, one of many just this month, costs more than the engagement ring that was once a permanent fixture on my finger.

"Thank you. They're beautiful," I say. It's not a lie; they're exactly my taste, the sort of jewelry only a man who pays attention could choose for a woman. "Though you know you didn't have to."

"I know. And I like spoiling you in part because you don't demand it."

I scoff, reaching to take out the studs I already have in, but Julian steps up. "I've got it."

He stands close as he works, and every hair on my body strains for him. He's switched colognes to something sweeter, warmer, with caramel and smoke, and I resent how much he smells like home. Resent his gentle reverence as he pops out my earrings one after the other and stows them in the new box, then affixes the new set with the same care. Resent the pride in his eyes when he leans back to regard me, and the way, afterward, he so easily breezes past me to grab a corkscrew for the wine.

The food I've prepared is heavy, meant to be consumed after an energy-draining romp or two. Already my plan to seduce my boyfriend is falling apart, and I'm struggling to hide my frustration. When I take off my apron to reveal the deep V of my dress and the breasts that sit pretty behind it, Julian's gaze only drifts down once before spending the rest of dinner affixed respectfully on my eyes. He fills my petulant silence with compliments on the meal, updates about the breakthroughs the companies he's backing in Malaysia have made, the recent extensions of his odd hours to take meetings, the possibility of him supporting an artist residency in Woodlawn, topics I would normally find interesting but today exhaust me. When he asks me questions, my answers are clipped.

We have just gone through our fourth tense silence when Julian finally sets his cutlery down.

"What's wrong?" he asks.

"Nothing's wrong," I say, even as I stab into a cluster of lettuce.

Julian sighs.

"Sean, you've spent the last five minutes trying to murder your salad for a crime I'm sure it didn't commit," he says. "So why don't you tell me what's going on, so we can discuss it?"

It's a measured, mature, and altogether reasonable response, but I'm no longer a reasonable woman. I'm all fire and brimstone, red wine fanning at the flames of my humiliation. I push my chair back and stand.

"You're a smart man, Julian, I think you can figure it out."

I reach for his empty plate to take it to the sink, but Julian stills me with a hand over my wrist.

"Not smart enough to read minds," he implores. "Please, Sean. Talk to me."

There's an earnestness to his tone that makes something in me crack. I've rehearsed this conversation in my head a hundred times. But the words that finally find their way out aren't the controlled, composed, structured dialogue I've prepared. They're raw, and angry, and my throat closes around them as I speak.

"Are you not attracted to me?" I ask.

Julian's eyes widen with shock, and his hand falls away.

"What?" he says. "Of course I am. How could you even ask that?"

"Oh, I don't know," I say. "Maybe because we've had sex once three months ago, and you seem to have no interest in doing it again."

And there it is, my grievance laid bare. It feels like I've just dragged the elephant in the room onto center stage, and that he's taken a shit on the floor.

Seconds pass, maybe a minute, with no response. My face burns with mortification and I wish, more than anything, that I could start today from the beginning. I wouldn't invite Julian over. Would certainly not have spent the morning pushing my cart around the local Jewel for ingredients for tonight's dinner. I would have been comfortable in sweats and slippers, not battling acid reflux and a nip slip in this too tight velvet number—

Suddenly, I am being propelled roughly forward. It takes me a second to realize that it's Julian, tugging me into the space between his legs by the fabric at my hips. I tumble into him, my hands grabbing hold of his shoulders for purchase and my knees knocking against the edge of his seat, but he doesn't apologize, just watches me with a stare so intense that I feel the pressure of it against my skull.

"Do you think I don't *want* to sleep with you?" he says. His voice is strained. The way it used to get before, like he is one temptation away from eating me alive.

"What else am I supposed to think? I—"

The rest of my words are swallowed in a gasp; Julian tugs the skirt of my dress up and over my hips. The cool air hits my stockinged thighs, and I don't even have a chance to shiver before his warm hands cup my ass. Julian sighs, then rests his head on my chest as his hands wander higher. They find the waistband of my tights, tug at them like he's trying to decide whether to roll them down or tear them apart.

"You don't have to worry about if I want to sleep with you," he says, deciding on the former. I step out of my heels as he rolls the tights down over my hips, pausing to caress the exposed skin as he reveals it. "You should worry more about whether I'll be able to find the strength to stop."

There it is again, hesitation that has no reason to exist. I hook my hands around his jaw, tilt his head back so that he can see the conviction in my eyes.

"Let me make this even more abundantly clear," I say, watching his lips part, his eyes darken. "I don't want you to stop."

I can almost see the moment when the final thread of Julian's tenuous control snaps. He makes a sound that is half growl, half groan, and suddenly I'm being lifted into the air and deposited onto the cool granite of my kitchen island, one leg of my tights hanging helplessly between us. He snatches the rest of it off, tosses it to the ground with a finality that makes my thighs quiver.

"You are something else," he whispers, his mouth hovering so close above mine that I can feel the words form. His other hand wanders between my legs, and I hiss, the familiar friction so welcome that I could almost cry. "So wet already."

"Yes," I whimper. "Always, when I'm with you."

Julian finds my clit through my panties, nestles it between two firm fingers. I'm not sure what sound I make, whether it is a moan or a cry or even his name, just that his jaw tenses with satisfaction and his mouth meets mine. He's rough, but he rides the line between inflicting pain and pleasure as perfectly as if he lives in my head, feels what I feel.

It is everything I have dreamed of, everything that I have wanted. I am hungry for him, my fingers scrabbling at the buttons of his shirt as he searches for the back zipper of my dress. When our bare chests collide we groan in gratified unison, and I mourn all the hours we have spent not pressed skin to skin, not exchanging heat like we do now. My body remembers him, recalls his shape and stretch and rhythm, and this time when I unbuckle his belt and close my hand around him he doesn't pull away, only gasps my name.

"You're so hard," I observe stupidly, stroking this object of my affection.

Julian's eyelids flutter, his chest expanding in a stammering inhale.

"Always, when I'm with you," he repeats, and before I can retort, he takes my chin in a gentle bite, lavishes my neck and clavicle with open-mouthed kisses until he finally reaches my breasts. I push them together with my upper arms, presenting them to him like a gift. My nipples, already pebbled, throb under his gaze, and he jerks, a live, wild thing, in my hands.

Julian's first touch is tentative, a feather-light course of his tongue around my areola that leaves it damp and singing for him. His second is ravenous, a suck of my nipple into his mouth that makes me hiss in pleasure. He wets his fingers, rolls the other between them, and it's like he's flipped a switch, taken me from panting with need to writhing with it.

"Please, Jules," I cry, delirious. I scoot to the edge of the counter, direct him to where I want him. He slides against the seat of my thong, which is still on, *why is it still on*, and my eyes nearly cross. "*Please.*"

Julian's moan rips out of him helplessly, and he ruts against me harder, pushing against my entrance through the fabric.

"I want to, Sean," he says, voice shaking. "I want to so bad—"

I arch against him, demonstrating how badly I want him too.

"Then stop thinking so hard," I whisper against his ear. "Fuck me. I want you to."

Julian's sigh is one of defeat. He breathes into my neck, a slow, almost doleful exhale. Then, finally, he drags my panties to the side, and with a firm, declarative thrust, gives me exactly what I've been begging for.

My world flashes white. *White satin fabric, white walls, amber eyes, pleasure so all-consuming I think it might kill me.* My grip on the back of Julian's shirt is vise tight and my throat feels raw from breathing or crying out or both. There's no gentleness in what he's doing to me right now, no finesse, just an animalistic drive to pound me into the granite. I hold on for dear life, let myself become undone. He feels so good, like every part of him, from these soft lips to those strong hands to the dick that ravages me now, was made just for me, just for this.

"Tell me you're mine," a voice says in my ear.

Julian's voice, but not from Julian's mouth. That one is busy and full of my tongue. Behind my closed eyes, my world flashes white again, and he comes into focus: Dream Julian, with his burnished bronze skin and eyes like hot coals. His fingers twist my nipples as Real Julian's grip my hips, his teeth tug my earlobe while Real Julian's worry my bottom lip, but they're both inside me. I feel them both, like shadows of the other, their rhythm synced *just so*, so that I am always filled. It's sin personified, so debauched that just the thought of it drags me to the edge.

"Tell me, songbird," Dream Julian says again. "I want to hear it."

The temperature we generate rises to boiling, not just the heat of two bodies clasped together, but something else, something that floods me from the center of my chest to the tips of my fingers, pleasure that leaves my nerves shivering in their sheaths. I remember this. I balked at it last time, but now it seems like there's nothing to fear. I embrace it. I want it. *Give it to me*, I think. *Let me burn*.

"Yes," I sigh. "Yes, baby, please, I'm y—"

Julian pulls out of me suddenly, and it feels like someone has just turned on their brights.

"Shit," he says. He yanks up his pants, tucks himself away, and has already started on the buttons on his shirt before I wake up enough from my daze to realize what has just happened. I watch, stunned, exposed, and only half fucked, until he reaches for his jacket.

"What are you doing?" I say in disbelief. "Are you . . . leaving?"

Julian refuses to look at me. His cheeks are still flushed with passion, but his expression is stony. He snatches one of the cloth napkins that I only pull out for special occasions off the table and wipes the sweat from his brow, and that gesture is the one that finally breaks me. I slide off the counter, pull my dress back up over my chest and down over my ass, and grab him by the front of his shirt.

"Are you serious right now, Julian?" I say. "Are you actually about to walk out, just like that, right in the middle—"

Julian pries my hand away, and the callousness of the gesture feels like a slap across my face.

"I have to go, Sean," Julian says, not looking at me. "Sorry."

If this were a movie, I would have snatched the earrings out of my lobes and thrown them at his feet, then grabbed a plate to aim at his head for good measure. But it isn't. I am quite sure I will get a good price on Tiffany on resale and I don't want to go to jail for assault, and so instead I follow him to the door.

"What just happened? What's going on?" I'm shouting nonsense now, letting my thoughts flow freely from my brain to my mouth to his fleeing back. "Am I missing something? Did something happen? Is there—is there someone else?"

This gets his attention.

"Stop," Julian says.

He sounds so cold, like he had with Melody, like Alicia before her. His chill freezes me in place. We stare at each other, chests heaving, but otherwise suspended in this vat of hostility that has no reason to be here.

Julian is the one to finally break the silence.

"You were right. We're in different life stages. We want different things. I was naïve to ignore those differences, but I can't anymore."

This, I think, has to be a nightmare.

"What do you mean?" I whisper.

"I'm twenty-seven years old," he says. "I should be staying out until three a.m., going to forest raves, making mistakes. I thought I could grow up with you, but the reality is: you're right. I don't know what I want yet, but it might include the things you don't. Marriage. Kids. The fucking picket fence. Someone who isn't so in love with their job that I don't figure out they know how to do more than boil water for the five months that I know them. I want that. Not whatever *this*"—he waves in my general direction—"is supposed to be."

I wince. In a matter of seconds, he's managed to take this magical, special thing we had together and turn it tawdry, wave his hand and turn me from his lover into his fool.

"That was mean," I say, stunned.

Julian shrugs.

"Radical honesty," he reminds me, and I am almost sick right there at his feet.

"Okay." I swallow my nausea and cross my arms, lift my head high. "Sounds like this is it, and you want out. We're done. Is that right?"

I hate that he is still so beautiful to me. That when he finally looks at me, I can search for the sadness in his eyes and find it.

"Yeah," Julian says. "We're done."

I open the door for him.

There is no fanfare. Julian doesn't apologize, or tell me good night, or offer platitudes wishing me well. He walks out and closes the door, and with the suddenness of a flash bomb, it is over. From his crate in my bedroom, Onix begins to whine.

The last time I got dumped, I was thirty years old. I had been with my fiancé for eight years, only two of which could be called happy. He lied to me, made me feel like every little thing wrong in his world was my fault, cheated on me, got me pregnant. The day I bled out in the cath lab bathroom, he ignored my first twelve calls. On the thirteenth, he told me never to call him again, and I had never felt more useless and unlovable in my life.

This doesn't hurt like that did. But it comes too damn close for comfort.

Twenty

I don't cry until I call Winona, but the second I hear her voice I lose mine. It's replaced by tears that pour militantly down my cheeks, sobs that shock me with their force. It's just a breakup, I recognize, with a guy I dated for less than five months and with whom I should have known it would never work. But it still feels like my world is ending.

Brandon has Sophie this weekend, and so Winona comes over. We eat my leftovers and top it off with vanilla ice cream from the pint and put on old slasher movies rife with blood and gore and no romance subplots.

"I feel so s-stupid," I stammer, as Winona rubs circles into my back. My head buzzes from the whiplash; I can't believe that tonight is real. That it could contain so many contradictions. I replay the events in my mind, trying to figure out where it all went wrong. How Julian could go from picking out jewelry for me to ejecting himself from my life in under two hours.

"You're not stupid, he's stupid," Winona declares. Furious Winona is a rare but fearsome sight. Woe betide Julian if he runs across her in the street; she's not above a public beatdown. "What did you tell me, when Brandon asked for the divorce? That we are not taking responsibility for men's shitty behavior. That we aren't internalizing their mess."

I look up at her in wonder, my misery temporarily replaced by admiration. The heartbreak I am enduring now will fade. Julian and I have no earthly attachments to each other, and so he will eventually disappear from my life, like Eric once did. I won't know whom he dates next, which companies he'll invest in, or what he thinks about Frank Ocean's next album when it finally drops. But Winona is forever linked to Brandon. They share a child, and they may someday share grandchildren. They'll have to take pictures at Sophie's graduation ceremonies, negotiate holidays, shake hands with each other's partners. And through all of this, Winona has to set her head high and do what is right for her child, even if that means putting aside the mortal hurt Sophie's father dealt her.

"How did you get over it?" It's the first time I've ever asked. *I* haven't gotten over it, and Brandon and I had an entirely platonic relationship, one based on trust that he callously defiled.

Winona turns to give me a wry smile, then flips our blanket over our shoulders and nuzzles into my side.

"Who said I got over it?" When my eyes widen, she laughs. "My husband cheated on me with a twenty-two-year-old white girl. That's not something you just get over. Some days I still wake up feeling like the old hag he probably thinks I've become."

"The finest hag on this side of Chicago!" I declare, aghast. "Winny. You're gorgeous. You know that. I could probably walk outside right now and put together an impromptu barbershop quartet to sing for your heart."

"Oh, I'm aware," Winona says, coyly. "I recruit an outside opinion every now and then to confirm it."

The way she says it makes me sit up straighter.

"Hold on," I say. "Are you seeing someone?"

"Maybe," Winona says. "Maybe multiple someones."

I squeal so loudly that Onix lifts his head to glare at me.

"Why didn't you tell me?" I ask. "This is an *enormous* development, Winny, how could I not be updated—"

"I don't know, because telling my best friend that I'm getting dicked down every other week would be a little insensitive while she's enduring several months of involuntary celibacy," she says. "And, before you ask, no, none of it is serious. I'm dating like a man. Swiping for hotness and proximity."

This makes me laugh out loud, and I drop my head onto her shoulder. I know that I am still in the numb phase of a breakup and that it will take a few days for the true agony to hit, but right now, sitting on my couch with my best friend at my side and my dog dozing at my feet, I almost feel okay.

"You know what?" I say. "Hell yeah."

We laugh, and though I desperately want details, I don't know if I can take them tonight, and Winny doesn't burden me with them.

Three slashers later, we crawl into bed together, just like old times. She falls asleep what feels like hours before I do. I watch the city's lights sift through my curtains, listen to the distant sirens fire from fifteen floors down.

When I finally close my eyes, they open again to white.

"Forgive me," a voice says.

I swivel to find its source. Julian sits on the floor in front of me, but he's not quite the Julian I know; the squareness of his jaw softened, his skin smooth and unshadowed like it hasn't yet met a razor. He's barefoot and dressed all in white: a loose linen shirt, linen pants. He hides his eyes behind a curtain of thick, dark curls.

I recognize this version of him. He's the boy from the painting in Julian's living room, the one who had yet to know loss.

"Oh, fuck you," I hiss.

The curse makes his head rear back, and his wide, sad eyes are Julian's brilliant brown. His lips twist, quiver, and for a second I wonder if he's going to cry.

"You have to understand," he says. "I did it for you. To protect you."

My laughter pierces the air and lingers like a thrummed chord.

"To protect me?" I repeat, incredulous. "You hurt me, Julian. Even though you swore you wouldn't. And now you can't even face me as yourself. You've got to put on this weird *paragon of innocence* costume instead, like the selfish, manipulative bastard you are—"

He slides forward on his knees until he's almost sitting between mine. When he raises his head, he's my Julian again, fully grown and filled out. He wraps his arms around my legs, prostrating himself to me, and I hate myself for not finding the fortitude to shove him away.

"Yes. I'm a selfish bastard," he confesses. "Greedy too. I just wanted to be with you. To love you—"

I recoil. Even for my subconscious, this is cruel.

"Don't," I start.

"To love you," he repeats firmly. "I wanted to love you. And god, Sean, I did. I *do*."

They're words he's never used in real life, and hearing them from this apparition cements me as the pitiable, foolish woman I feared I'd become. I can hardly believe myself, that I could so desperately want to hear that Julian loved me that I would settle for recreating this encounter in my mind, one in which he begs on his hands and knees for me when in reality he'd walked out my door without looking back.

"Julian, please," I say, clenching my teeth to keep from devolving into sobs.

His hands scrabble up my legs until they reach my hips, more beseeching than amorous, his head bent low over my lap in worship. His tears fall, heavy as heartbeats, onto the thin white silk covering my thighs.

"I love you," he says. "In a way that I never thought myself capable. More than I've ever loved anyone. That's why I had to walk away."

"Stop." My breaths are coming hard and fast; any minute now, I will break. "Go away. Let me *sleep*, Julian, please. I'm so tired."

Julian goes still. I don't turn away, breathing in, out, anything to keep from shattering in front of him. I am a bubble about to burst, and he waits me out for what could be minutes but feels like an eternity.

Eventually, as I knew he would, he gives up. I feel his grip slacken, his hands smooth down the path they followed until they hang limply on his lap.

"Okay," he says. Then, more firmly, "Okay. But promise me something."

I owe him nothing, but I am curious enough to hear his request.

"What?" I ask.

"Promise," he says, "to forget me."

I don't answer him, but we both know that I will be doing no such thing.

I don't dream of Julian again after that.

It's disorienting, at first. I didn't realize how accustomed I'd gotten to his company in my subconscious until he longer occupied it, until my dreams went back to being improbable reenactments of my memories and thoughts rather than the coherent visions I'd had when

I was with him. He disappears out of my life with the abruptness of a thunderclap and leaves no wake behind: no social media accounts to stalk, no selfies together to moon over.

Work has always been a gas, capable of filling the entire space of my life if I let it, and so I do. I pick the most complex cases off the add-on board and sign up for every research project, come home late, eat like shit, play with Onix, shed tears onto the keys of my piano. Whenever I use Palette's devices, I look out for Leila, but she's apparently away for "training," and they send a plucky new guy in her stead.

To make matters worse, I get sick again. My head hurts all the time and I sweat through my pajamas every night. Everything turns my stomach; just the smell of Larry's daily egg and bacon bagel leaves me retching. I feel like I'm crawling out of my skin. *I feel*, I write in my symptoms journal, *like I'm going to die*.

"Is everything okay?" Pamela asks me one evening, after we've finished the day's cases and everyone has cleared out to go home. Her frown tells me she's asking out of genuine concern, not just because she wants the tea. "You've been . . . off lately."

The look I give her must be acerbic, because she holds up two hands in defense.

"I don't mean in the lab!" she explains. "You're actually more efficient in there, somehow. Which is freaky, because you *look* tore up."

She's not wrong, but I still grimace.

"Thanks, Pamela."

"I'm not saying it to be a jerk," Pamela says. "I'm saying that something is clearly wrong, and that you should think about going to get checked out."

I think of my symptom journal, of my primary care doctor's already million-dollar workup, my recent trip to the emergency room. There is nothing wrong with me.

Still, I head to his office one more time.

Dr. Steinbeck is kind but seems a bit exasperated as he comes through the door. He's accompanied by a young woman with the roundest, most globular eyes I've ever seen, whom he introduces as Helen, his medical student. When he tells her that I'm one of Broadview's interventional cardiologists, she manages to look even more alarmed.

"Do you mind if Helen listens in?" Dr. Steinbeck asks.

"Sure," I say, with a shrug.

I tell him my symptoms. They're the same I've had before. Nausea, fatigue, body aches, sweats. All nonspecific, B symptoms.

Dr. Steinbeck nods. He's giving me the active-listening doctor face, eyebrows turned up, lips pursed, head cocked as if to say, *I hear you*. Then he turns to Helen, rattles off the battery of tests that we've already conducted, and asks, "What's on your differential?"

All the color rushes out of Helen's pale cheeks. She looks around the room like she would like to escape it. Her fingers wind together.

"Um . . ." she says quietly. "Well, honestly, it sounds like the symptoms of opioid withdrawal."

The genial smile drops off Dr. Steinbeck's face.

"Well, um, wow," he blubbers, scrambling to find a way to salvage this visit from the enormous accusation Helen has inadvertently lobbed. "I'm so sorry, Dr. Sullivan—give us a moment, I'll be back—"

"No," I say suddenly. The blood rushing in my ears sounds like a coursing river. I think of that first time with Julian in the back of his car, how I'd shuttled forward in time and wondered if he'd put something in my food. The night when I woke up in his bed with no clear memory of how I ended up in it. "No, Helen, you've got a point. Thank you." Then, to Dr. Steinbeck, "Test me."

I make Dr. Steinbeck order a drug test with an expanded panel. It comes back negative, but I'm a dog on the hunt now and I have picked up a trail. I flip through my symptom journal. The first entry is dated not long after *PERPETUITY*, and I write that I am inexplicably *tired*. I feel better a few days later, after Julian gives me the espresso machine. Then there's the second time, after I covered for Brandon's STEMI. I'm completely destroyed for a week after that, but the day after seeing Julian again I'd felt incredible, as light as air.

The body doesn't lie, I remember. During the last few years of my relationship with Eric, I'd been hit with a laundry list of maladies: headaches, back pain, indigestion that I went to doctors for and attempted to treat, to no avail. It was only a few months after he left that I realized I'd miraculously been healed of all my ailments. They had simply been my body telling me to run.

This pattern is equally unmistakable. Just as Helen said, I'm following a pattern of withdrawal, and my symptoms are getting worse.

Except my drug of choice isn't heroin, it's a *man*.

"Maybe it's stress," Dr. Steinbeck suggests on his phone call to me after my results come in. "You have a difficult job. Take some days off."

He sends me a work note, and I send it straight to our office manager and CC Krause.

"I'm sick," I tell him, when he calls me to complain. "I'm taking a week off."

"You can't. We're short—" he starts, but I cut him off. This kind of guilt trip might have worked on me a few months ago, but I have no more patience in me for entitled, manipulative men.

"I have a note from my PCP. Coming in while I'm unwell puts our patients at risk, masks or not. I don't want to make a mistake." He hears my implication: *And if you try to stop me, I'm taking this over your head, and we wouldn't want that, now would we?*

It takes me seventy-two more hours to sweat Julian out. It gets worse before it gets better, but I stick it out, arming myself with electrolyte water and soups, calling my dog walker to take Onix out instead of pushing through.

It works. On the fourth day, I emerge from my apartment with my strength back in full force. The winter air is icicle sharp with cold but the sun shines bright, and even Onix seems to get a boost in energy, chasing squirrels all over the park as if his hips aren't arthritic. It's a new year, a fresh start, and I mark it the way I best know how.

"You want me to cut them off?" the stylist says, shifting through my chin-length locs in shock. "Are you sure? They're gorgeous. We can just dye your roots black, maybe do a rinse to tackle the grays . . ."

"Yes, I'm sure," I say. My reflection rages back at me from the stylist's seat, ferocious with determination. My locs have carried me through so much. Medical residency. Bleeding out on my bedroom floor. And now this. There are memories and moments and traumas entwined in the strands. They hold too much, and by the state of my new growth, my body agrees.

My stylist begins her work. I watch my locs fall away one by one, dropping to the floor with soft thuds like lost appendages.

When I return to the cath lab the next week, Pamela is the only one there. She gasps as I walk in.

"Oh my god," she says. "Sullivan! This look!"

I run a hand along my shorn head. My hair is short, silver, and I've kept up a consistent brushing regimen that sets my waves glistening. The effect is striking and more feminine than I could have imagined, and, paradoxically, makes me look younger. Even my stylist was shocked. *Oh honey, you were born to be bald-headed.*

"I know, right?" I say. It feels right, like I've reclaimed what the loss of pigment snatched from me. Looking at myself in the mirror is the only thing that seems to bring me any real joy these days.

"You look magical," Pamela continues.

Ethereal, Julian's voice croons in my ear.

I shake the memory from my head and work out a thank-you, then add on a more genuine one for encouraging me to go to the doctor. At this, she drops back into her chair and sighs melodramatically.

"Almost wish I hadn't done that, if I'm honest. Last week was a shit show without you."

The stab of guilt makes me stand up straight.

"Really?" I ask. "What happened?"

Pamela looks left and right as if to check that we are the only ones in the lab, then whispers, "Well, Brandon was on. And Friday, we had this case, young guy, diagnostic. And he . . ."

The lab suddenly fills with light; someone has entered behind us. Pamela's mouth clamps shut, and I turn to face the newcomers. There are two large, bald men in matching black polo shirts and a smaller gray-haired man in a suit who leans against the table in front of my preferred computer with crossed arms. He looks up at me and gives me a small, tight smile.

It's the chair of medicine, Dr. Alan Agarwhal. Our boss's boss's boss. He's an endocrinologist by trade and I've never seen him outside of a conference room. I can't conceive of a reason why he's made his way to the catheterization lab.

"Hi, Alan," I say hesitantly. "What brings you here?"

Alan shoves a hand through his hair. He's a delicate man, fine featured in a patrician way, and he wears his worry with the melodramatic flair of a Shakespearean actor.

"Nothing good, I'm afraid," he says.

Just then, the door opens again, and Brandon walks in, and I have to fight to keep my jaw from dropping.

It's only been a week or so since I last saw him, but he looks like he's aged ten years. The skin I thought looked weathered at Sophie's recital is outright slack now, his eyes weighted by two sets of layered bags and mouth bracketed by new jowls. His movements are shuffling, Parkinsonian. If I didn't know any better, I'd think I was looking at his eighty-year-old father.

Brandon doesn't seem to notice us as he hobbles into the room, even though all eyes have swiveled to him. He nods to Pamela, then makes a show of adjusting his surgeon's cap. He turns to the screen above his head and frowns.

"Where are all my cases?" he says, lifting a shaking finger to his empty schedule. "Pamela, what is the meaning of this—"

"Brandon," Alan says.

Brandon jerks toward Alan like he's just noticed he's there. His eyes dart to the two men flanking him, to me, to Pamela, before finally settling back on his boss.

"Alan," he says. A gray tongue flicks out to lick lips that somehow remain dry.

"Did you receive my email?" Alan asks. When Brandon doesn't answer, Alan sighs. "Come on, Brandon. You know we don't want to have to do this. This is for you as much as it is us."

"Bullshit," Brandon sputters. Alan doesn't flinch. "Bullshit. You guys are trying to drag me out. That's why you've got security here with you. That's why you're—"

Alan huffs, a sound that comes from deep within.

"You're not being dragged out, you're being put on leave during the course of the investigation. The security is just protocol." His mouth twists with something between sympathy and disgust. "It's done, Brandon. I'm sorry. Go home."

I have never known what it meant to watch a person wilt before my eyes, and the part of me that once had affection for Brandon wants to comfort him. Our friendship may have fallen apart in the last few years, but this was an area where we shared an understanding. Taking away Brandon's access to the catheterization lab is like stripping him of his identity. Of who he has wanted to be for the last thirty years, what he has worked tirelessly toward for over twenty. And not just that. It's that Brandon is clearly unwell, and Alan either doesn't notice or doesn't care.

The door to the lab bursts open again. This time it's Haoran, looking a bit frazzled with his scrubs half tucked into his waistband.

"Sorry I'm late, I was on drop-off duty today," he announces. Then he notices Brandon. I watch in real time as he takes in our colleague's appearance. "Oh. Hey. I thought you wouldn't be in today . . ."

Brandon's face crumples and he pushes past Haoran and out the door. I take a quick glance into my room—no patient on the table, no expectant trainee waiting for me—then go after him.

It's easy to catch up. Despite having several inches of height on me, he's slow. I step around him, cut him off.

"Brandon," I say.

The look he gives me is vicious, and I wince.

"Come to laugh at me, have you?" he spits.

"No, of course not." I approach him like he's a wounded animal—slowly, shoulders hunched, hands up. "I just want to know if you're okay. You look like you've been . . . struggling."

I don't realize how much of an understatement it is until I say it out loud. And not just physically—although his appearance now is alarming—but mentally too. The Brandon Pendersen I know is a cocky asshole, sure, but what interventionist isn't? He's also kind, charismatic, and occasionally sweet. All that is gone now. The man in front of me is his husk.

Brandon seems to realize this too. He looks down at his hands, stares at the thin skin, the liver spots, the blue veins like he's seeing them for the first time.

"I don't know what happened," he croaks. "It was a routine diagnostic angiogram. Big artery. Easy target. It's like I was locked in place, but my needle just kept going." He drops his face into his hands, and I don't realize he's sobbing until fat tears begin to leak between his fingers. "I almost killed him, Sean. And I don't understand how it happened."

My stomach drops with horror, and I clap a hand over my mouth as I put two and two together. Why Brandon is on leave. Why Alan Agarwhal showed up in person to enforce it.

Danger is a hazard of our job. Most of the time we save people, but a misplaced wire, a needle stuck too deep, a valve deployed in just the wrong spot—they can be life altering or ending for our patients. But we can usually gauge the risk and offer our patients guidance for their expectations. Things happen, and we don't have time to dwell on them, because the next patient will be on the table in fifteen minutes.

But there are "never events," mistakes that even our least experienced trainees cannot afford to make. This was clearly one of them.

"Brandon," I say quietly. "You're not well. You need to get help. Go see a doctor, figure out what is going on."

Brandon's right eye widens more than his left.

"I know," he says. "I know, I know, I know, but. I can't. I can't—"

I step closer, reach for him.

"What do you mean, you can't?" I ask slowly. "Why can't you?"

The next half second passes in slow motion. It starts with his shoulders, their steady slouch, and the rest of his body follows, chin dropping into chest, lips dropping into chin. His eyes are the last to go, rolling back in a tight swivel.

I move before I can think. Brandon's weight is full and dead and sends me crumpling to the floor. I land hard, but I barely feel the impact; my fingers scrabble on his carotid for a pulse before my brain can fully process what is happening.

And then it does, and I begin to scream.

"Help!" Under my fingertips, I feel the steady thrum of his pulse: slow, thready, but there. I roll Brandon onto his back and the horror overcomes me. It's like I'm looking at his corpse.

Pamela is the first around the corner.

"What's going on, Sean— Holy shit."

I don't have time to wonder whether she, too, is seeing what I see now—that Brandon has probably been far gone for a while and that we just didn't notice.

"Get the crash cart and have someone call a code," I instruct, and Pamela, a consummate professional, puts aside her horror to comply.

Twenty-One

By the afternoon, Brandon has been admitted to the hospital. The MRI of his brain shows a tumor. It's on the left side, the part that gets exposed to the most radiation, and is infiltrating his frontal lobe. It could explain his recent personality changes, the neurologist tells Winona over the phone.

Brandon Pendersen has fucking brain cancer, and I—we all—assumed he had just become an incompetent jerk. We'd watched him decay before our eyes and said nothing. Now there's another patient in a different ICU fighting for his life because none of his colleagues had the foresight to investigate whether his erratic behavior was actually pathological.

"Left-sided brain cancer," Brandon mutters when I visit him after my cases. He looks oddly at peace. When he smiles the right side goes up higher than the left. I'd thought he was sneering this whole time, but it was actually a neurological deficit. "What am I? A textbook?"

I laugh. All our radiation training modules have emphasized the same thing—that proceduralists who use fluoroscopy are more prone to this particular kind of disease because our left sides get the brunt of radiation exposure. We wear lead-lined caps and goggles to minimize the damage, but we're still significantly more likely to get it. But Brandon is young, having just scratched forty, and shouldn't yet have been at high risk.

"I should bring our fellows down here," I joke. "Show them the scans. Strike some fear in their hearts."

"Especially Paul. Might get him to wear his thyroid shield," Brandon quips. Then he closes his eyes. "Has anyone been able to get Leila?"

I swallow.

"No," I say gently. Not for lack of trying. Between me, the neurologist, and Brandon himself, we've probably called and texted Leila twenty times. Her phone goes straight to voicemail. When I call her coworker to ask after her, he says that she's doing three mitral clip procedures in a hospital forty miles away today and might be tough to reach.

It's an odd excuse. We've worked with Leila in the lab; we know she can access her phone. Winona, who has a full panel of clinic patients today, has managed to answer our calls, arrange alternate pickup plans for Sophie, and is driving in as we speak.

Brandon looks, for the first time, like he's in pain.

"You think I'm pathetic," he says quietly.

I freeze.

"I don't know what you mean," I say.

Brandon's grin is wry.

"Sure you do," he says. "You've thought it from the beginning. That I was a stereotype, leaving my wife and kid for this young woman. Thinking with my *dick*. I'm not wrong, am I?" When I don't respond, he nods, accepting my silence as confirmation. "But it wasn't that simple, Sean. I . . . needed her. In a way that I can't describe. She was the girl of my dreams. She was *in my dreams*. I could never . . . not think of her."

Brandon's monitor beeps in the background, but it's overtaken by the ringing in my ears. Brandon dreamt of Leila. He left Winona because he dreamt of her, maybe the way I once dreamt of Julian. And now he is lying in a hospital bed, impossibly old, impossibly sick. And my hair is white.

My mind takes in this information and draws the parallels, but when it tries to settle on the obvious conclusion, it grinds to a halt. *Occam's razor*, I remind myself again. *The simplest explanation is often the best one.* But the simplest explanation—Julian and Leila are the cause of our rapid aging—is nonsensical.

But no more nonsensical than what's happening to us. Because here we sit, Brandon forty going on eighty-three with a left-sided brain cancer he shouldn't have developed for many more years, me with hair that turned silver-white overnight. My heart is off to the races, and I clutch the side rail of Brandon's hospital bed, trying to keep myself upright. I can't deny what I see with my eyes, feel with my hands, what the CT scans and MRI see in Brandon's brain. *Oh god.* Was this . . . intentional? Were we prey all along?

I've been silent for too long, because Brandon clears his throat.

"I'm tired," he says. "Thanks for checking in, Sean."

It's far from the only thing he needs to thank me for, but I interpret it as the dismissal that it is, steel myself, and stand.

"Don't die," I tell him from his hospital room door.

He cracks a small smile and tosses me a weak thumbs-up.

"I'll try my best."

I barely notice that I've made it home until I slide into my spot in my apartment's parking garage. My body has gone through the motions, automatically taking me down the right streets and dodging pedestrians so that my mind can focus. The evening is eerily quiet, and I sit in my car so long that the automatic light turns out and I am shrouded in darkness. I can't stop thinking about Brandon's wizened face. Wrinkles deep as crevasses, blue eyes bleary and ringed with white. *She was in my dreams*, he said.

Onix greets me at the door and joins me on the couch. I pet him with one hand and with the other pull out my phone and open my photo gallery. I scroll back three years, to the last time Brandon and I were on good terms. The man looking back at me nearly knocks the breath out of my chest. I've never been attracted to Brandon, but it's obvious that he was a handsome man. Vain too. Looking at him here I remember how he'd spent three months testing different types of pomade to induce the best front swoop, how tenacious he'd been about applying sunscreen so that he wouldn't be the "only one aging" between the three of us.

I keep scrolling. Past birthday parties and nights out, past conferences during which I'd still throw my arm around his waist for pictures.

And then I land on one.

It's the Palette company dinner. Leila had just taken over for the last device representative assigned to our cath lab, and she stands, beaming, next to Brandon in a baby-pink minidress. Brandon looks to the camera, but I note what I failed to that night—that his hand is low on her hip and his grip is tight. Two weeks later, I'd walk into the supply room to find them making out behind the balloon pumps.

I zoom in on Brandon's face. Study it closely. It's his hairline that catches my attention first, and I scroll up a picture, taken just two weeks before. I'm not mistaken. Where there had once been a full, straight line, there is suddenly a widow's peak.

I call Winona. She's driving from the suburbs during rush hour and picks up immediately.

"I have to tell you something," I say to her. "You're going to think I'm losing it, but please, hear me out."

"One second, Sean," Winona responds. "I'm in the car with Leila. We're heading back to the hospital."

My blood runs cold as ice.

"Hi, Sean," Leila says, in a small, sweet voice. "It's been a while."

Twenty-Two

It's strange, hearing Leila's voice again, after what I've decided she's capable of. Her voice sounds ragged, like she's been crying, and the things she's saying are perfectly appropriate and not at all sinister: *I left my phone in the car this morning, I can't believe this is happening, I told him to go to the doctor.*

"I-I'm just so grateful to you both," Leila says. "Winny told me what happened. That you were the one who called for help. I don't know what would've happened if you hadn't been there."

Her familiarity with my best friend grates. *Stop calling her that*, I almost snap. Instead, I say, "I'm so sorry this is happening," even as my heart beats out of my chest. I remember the fear in Brandon's eyes just before he collapsed, and this little woman's tinny voice is causing it to surge in me. I hate that a part of me wants to ask her about Julian. "Does Sophie know yet?"

"I'll tell her tonight," Winona says. I can hear the weariness in her voice. "Maybe I'll keep her out of school next week? I don't know."

I feel silly all of a sudden, calling Winona to spout accusations that will most certainly sound like conspiracy theories while she is contending with telling her child that her daddy is terribly, horribly sick. For the last twenty years, I have told my best friend my every unfiltered thought. But this, I decide, is mine to bear. At least until I know for sure.

Winona texts me when she and Leila get to the hospital. She lost both of her parents on a hospital floor, she explains. Didn't want to go alone.

The excuse doesn't quite make sense to me. Leila works in hospitals. True, the cath lab is far removed from the inpatient floors, but she's surrounded by potential triggers all day, every day. But Winny's kindness is abundant, and so even though she could've told her ex-husband's new wife to catch an Uber and suck it up, she took her hand and walked into the hospital with her.

Onix places a heavy paw on my chest. His sigh is soul deep, like he too is toiling over impossible questions.

"What do you think is going on, baby?" I ask him. He blinks at me mournfully, and for a moment I'm struck by how old he looks. The snout on his fur is turning white. When I adopted him he'd already been fully grown, seventy pounds of scary dog privilege for a woman who was still afraid of her own shadow and needed a big friend with even bigger teeth. "Do you think it's drugs? Are Julian and Leila drugging us? Are they slipping things into our drinks? Or . . ." I pause, thinking of how Julian's touches always seem to leave me punch-drunk. "Is it skin to skin contact?"

My search history will probably land me on an FBI watchlist. It's an endless hunt for hallucinogens, sedatives, and synthetics that can affect memory, cause strange dreams, and maybe accelerate aging. I run into the usual suspects, of course—a few people have written about the effects of amphetamines on the brain and skin, but I'm pretty sure I haven't been force-fed meth—but nothing that quite encapsulates what Brandon and I are experiencing, which is not surprising because whatever is happening to us is so out of the ordinary that it can't be a well-known substance. Maybe they have a chemist, someone to synthesize it for them directly. Julian certainly has the funds for one.

I begin the deep dive on Julian that perhaps I should have done from the start. It's only been a few weeks since he left me, but I'm already starting to forget what he looks like, and the internet does not give me a reminder. For his social standing, as I remember, Julian has an oddly scant online presence. There are no interviews featuring the young mogul, no LinkedIn account or features on Forbes.

The paucity of information almost spurs me forward; I am not a woman who easily accepts a no. I search for Leila instead but only find her profile on the Palette website. A search for Margaret West unveils forty years of an illustrious art career, and I pause, finding myself clicking through photographs of her from the eighties, sporting a crown of Jheri curls and leaning over an enormous half-finished canvas. There's no mention of her friendship with my ex, no photos together, just the link to the *PERPETUITY* show that should have been shut down after the event. I click it without enthusiasm; I've been here before and know it's a bare-bones events page. I try not to react as I click through the site and my heart pangs to find that a few of the West and South Side artists I recommended have upcoming exhibitions. When I click back to the *PERPETUITY* page and scroll, I notice that it has been updated with a new link: *Photo gallery.*

I follow it.

There's not much there, just a three-by-two grid of photographs of a small selection of pieces from Margaret's show. I recognize the lobster shell macro painting, one of the sculptures. The weird skull and rotted fruit painting is there too, as is the one with the man crouching on the woman's flank. There's a note under it: *Acquired for the Harrison & Conrad special collections.*

I click that one, and it zooms in. Now that I'm looking again, there's something oddly erotic about the woman's expression, pinched somewhere between pain, fear, and rapture. Her dress is white and gossamer thin, the same stuff the female leads on the covers of old romance novels wear.

And then there's the strange man. He's crouching *on* her, his body curved and tucked impishly, but there's no denying that he's beautiful. More beautiful than the woman, perhaps; Margaret has been careful to render the silken black hair that hangs down his back and before one eye, has paid close attention to his plush pink lips and straight nose. Even through the screen, I feel the impact of his stare. Its directness reminds me of the subject of Jared's painting, though in this one, I don't feel like I'm looking at a cornered animal gearing to fight. This one looks like a predator.

Julian once told me that *The Recurring Nightmare* is a recreation. I don't remember the name of the original, but a quick search and there it is: Henry Fuseli's *The Nightmare.*

"What the hell," I mutter, opening the image for a closer look.

The paintings are nearly identical in theme and composition, except Margaret has excluded the stunned horse head, and the apelike creature squatting on the woman's flank in the original is everything but beautiful. He's horrible, barely human, and his stare, while just as confrontational, is less alluring than hostile. Still, there is the woman, arms flailing in rapture. It's grotesque, and strange, and according to the article that I skim on it, audiences at the time thought the same and reveled in it. I read further, my brows knitting with concentration until I snag on one word, the name of the creature: *incubus*.

I don't know what that is, but luckily the article links to an explanation, and I leap further down the rabbit hole.

incubus:

1 : an evil spirit that lies on persons in their sleep;

especially: one that has sexual intercourse with women while they are sleeping

→ compare SUCCUBUS

2 : NIGHTMARE 2

3 : one that oppresses or burdens like a nightmare

My heart leaps in my throat, but I ignore it, clicking link after link to read further information. In some descriptions, the incubus is hideous, an imp or goblin who holds their victims down and assaults them. In others, they are beautiful demons, targeting women at night to impregnate them with their supernatural spawn. I read a literature review on erotomania, a psychological delusion in which a person believes they have been assaulted by an imaginary figure, which leads me to incubus syndrome, in which they believe they have been touched by a ghostly lover.

There are countless descriptions of them across cultures: the Chilean Trauco, a hideous footless monster with irresistible sexual allure responsible for fathering the children of single women. The Brazilian boto encantado, a music-loving dolphin who emerges from rivers as a handsome man and bewitches unsuspecting women with its charm and joviality before escaping back into the watery depths of its home. There are the lilu, one of whom begat Gilgamesh, a Sumerian demigod, and the wizard Merlin, born of the union between his human mother and incubus father.

I remember the first time I met Julian. Sitting with him on the piano bench. I'd told him I wouldn't sleep with him and he'd smirked and said, "Not yet." Not even forty-eight hours later I'd dreamt about tearing his clothes off.

My left hand, balled into a fist, seizes, and I shake out the cramp. It's one thing to think that Julian might have been drugging me, but to think he is a supernatural creature? Outlandish. Ridiculous. I might be desperate to find answers, but I'm not so far gone that I would accept that my ex is a *demon*.

"Fuck!" I say, and as if on cue, my phone begins to buzz its way across my coffee table.

The screen flashes with a picture of my favorite toothy-grinned preteen, and I am slapped back into cruel reality, where both my best friend and her daughter are grappling with tragedy. I scramble to answer before it goes to voicemail.

"Hey, nugget," I say.

The voice on the other end is muffled and throaty.

"Auntie Sean," Sophie manages, "can I come over?"

"Of course," I say automatically, then look at the time. It's after nine p.m.; I will not put my baby girl in an Uber, nor will I allow her mom to drive in and out of the city for a third time to bring her here. "Have you asked your mom?"

"She'll say yes," Sophie says. "So you should too."

I suck in my bottom lip, pulling my phone away from my ear for long enough to open a text thread with Winona. My question is half typed before I pause; as horrible as this might be for Sophie, I also don't want my best friend to be home alone tonight. Most times, being the fun aunt is a delightful job, and one that Winona is glad I take on. But there are moments like this one, where Sophie puts me between a rock and a hard place, between being something of her friend and all of her mother's.

"Can you ask her?" I ask. "Please."

Sophie is silent for a moment, and I know that she wants to resist. She's twelve now, no longer the scared little girl calling me in the middle of the night to tell me that she'd just seen her dad kissing a strange woman in the kitchen and worrying that I'll be more upset that she'd been downstairs sneaking cookies past her bedtime. She understands betrayal, understands heartbreak, understands the permanence of death enough to know that the father she knew may never come back.

"Fine," she eventually huffs.

She doesn't mute me. I hear stomping feet and the creak of a door opening, Winona's weary voice. They talk for a minute, and when I next hear a clear sentence, it's from Winona.

"It's fine," she says. "She can go to yours."

"Are you okay?" I ask.

Winona laughs. It's the only appropriate answer to my completely asinine question, and the moment I ask, I wish I could snatch it back. With her kid in the room, she can't afford to break down, which, it occurs to me, might be precisely what she needs to do. She's not giving me permission; she's calling in a favor.

"I'll be there in half an hour," I say. "Ask her if she wants me to bring Onix."

"Yes please," I hear Sophie answer in the background.

I'm on my feet and hunting for Onix's harness as soon as I get their assent. As if he heard it too, Onix hobbles to his feet.

"Come on boy," I say. "Let's go get your baby."

Twenty-Three

Sophie is quiet on the ride to my downtown apartment. She greets me with a "Thanks, Auntie" and scoots into the back seat with Onix, who immediately rests his heavy head on her lap. She strokes him mindlessly, and they both fall asleep. When we get inside, she waits until my door is closed before she asks me the question that has been weighing heavy on her spirit.

"Mom says Dad will be okay," she says. "Is that a lie?"

Typical Sophie, to come out of the gate swinging. I busy myself helping Onix out of his harness, and when I straighten, she's still staring me down.

"We're being optimistic," I say.

"It's brain cancer," Sophie deadpans. "Isn't it dumb to be optimistic?"

I fight back a grimace. Both Winona and Brandon are brilliant people; it should come as no surprise that their daughter is as well. I hold out a hand for her coat, then stuff the pink puffer jacket into my closet as Sophie stands behind me, waiting for my response. When Sophie first started asking questions—endlessly, at the tender age of three—she'd been impatient for answers, demanding and irritated when they didn't come immediately. Now I've learned that she appreciates thoughtfulness and truth over speed.

"Hope is never dumb, nugget," I say.

It's the right thing to say, because her doll eyes well with tears.

"Okay," she says, nodding vigorously, as the tears begin to pour out. "If you say so."

I pull her into my arms as her body shakes. Her mother is probably crying like this too, alone in her bedroom, and I ache. Brandon will never mean to me what he means to them, but I know him in a different way. He's never been my lover or my parent, but he has been my colleague and friend. I have seen how he manages exhaustion, how he comports himself when his body is pushed to the limit. He *will* survive this.

I just have to figure out what exactly he's surviving.

When I tuck Sophie in to sleep—in my bed, with Onix, who relishes the opportunity to snuggle with his second favorite person—I begin to research. I've been considering supernatural explanations rather than scientific ones, but what if the culprit is biological? Science, after all, is magic to the uninformed; I imagine that if I went backward in time and showed the people of eras past a device that could not only communicate with anyone across the globe but also record perfect images of them in motion, they would brand me a witch and keep hold of my phone as a cursed relic. What if it's something that sits latently in Leila's and Julian's bodies but can reanimate in the people they touch? What if they have the effect of *Toxoplasma gondii*, the bacteria that removes fear from prey animals and leads them to deliver themselves to their predators, or the rabies virus, which creates a hysterical fear of water and an insatiable need for violence in its victims before killing them? I think about Brandon's obsessiveness over his wife, how he rushed to obey her commands—

What if it's caused by an autoimmune disease, like an encephalitis? I've read books on miraculous recoveries from diseases thought to be entirely psychological; if there is a component of this in Brandon's condition, it would do us good to find it.

I stay up too late going down rabbit holes with strange dead ends, wake up early, make Sophie a big breakfast. She's in better spirits after blueberry pancakes and a good night's rest, and on the drive to Oak Park she's back to her chatterbox self, switching between her favorite K-pop songs and giving me the lowdown on the latest of her dance troupe drama. I half listen, my mind coursing over what it learned last night. I can't stop thinking about *The Recurring Nightmare.* Most of Margaret West's work is abstract, and this piece, the sole work chosen to remain at Harrison & Conrad, is a stylistic departure. Did Julian select it himself?

"How was she?" Winona whispers when her daughter flies back into her house.

"The bravest little soldier," I say truthfully.

So brave that she makes me want to be brave too.

If I want answers, I'll have to do the one thing I've been avoiding so far: going to the source. I need to find Julian.

I put aside my pride and try the simplest strategies first, but when I call his phone number, the line doesn't work, and trying from my alternate numbers reveals that it's less likely that I am blocked than it is he changed his number entirely. His emails bounce back regardless of sender. I draw the line at going to his apartment, but I wouldn't be surprised if I talked to his doorman and found he's moved too. Julian clearly doesn't want to be found.

At least not by me.

The gallery, I think. It's a long shot, but it's also tangible—his family name is engraved into the brick. And though I know his involvement is limited to occasional appearances for exhibit openings and the ability to refer or recommend artists, I also know that it'll be harder to abandon. If there is anywhere I might get clues to track him down, it'll be there.

The door to Winona's house closes, and I set my GPS to the Harrison & Conrad Galleries.

The gallery looks completely different in the daytime. It's smaller than I remember, and without the effect of amber uplighting on the walls and the haunting creep of shadows from the nearby trees, almost quaint. The dead brown remnants of last summer's ivy creep up the crevices in its concrete back, draping over the stucco facade like cobwebs. Its grounds are the most impressive thing about it, a sprawling green lawn that's hard to come by in the city, but they've wilted in the winter chill, the once glorious hedges reduced to well-pruned carcasses.

I walk through the main entrance, lowering my beanie over my ears and huddling into my jacket. They'd clearly dimmed the lights in the lobby during Margaret's exhibition event because the room I walk into is bright white and gleaming, with chrome overlay around digital screens and placards on the wall introducing new exhibits. For all its gleaming glamor, I am its sole guest.

I head toward the concrete counter that sits in front of an extra-large screen that I realize had previously served as the coat check. A young man with an eyebrow piercing smiles hopefully at me from behind the desk. He straightens as I approach. His name tag identifies him as Matt.

"Welcome to Harrison and Conrad Galleries," Matt says. "Is this your first time here?"

"Yes," I lie. "But I've been wanting to visit for a while now. Can you tell me a little bit about this place?"

"Of course," he starts excitedly. "We've got a lot of great artists in here, a few Basquiats, a Warhol, but I would really suggest the Wadsworth Jarrell exhibit on the third floor—"

"I'm actually really interested in the founders," I interrupt, and he nods animatedly, launching into a spiel about the gallery's beginnings. William Harrison and Robert Conrad were wealthy English hoteliers who landed in Chicago by way of London and took the social scene by storm. The gallery was once a small-scale bread factory, he tells me, but sat abandoned after the Great Depression until they acquired and restored it. Avid appreciators of the arts, they opened their eponymous gallery in 1960, filling the first two floors with contributions from their personal collections. As a thank-you to their newfound homeland, the collectors prioritized work by American artists, and their tradition of supporting up-and-coming talent through artist residencies and scholarships was continued by their successors; Julian's penchant for art appreciation is apparently genetic. It is all both interesting and so unhelpful to my mission that I wonder if I should turn back, but then I remember that this is the only lead I have.

So I try a new angle.

"I hear you house some of their personal collections here," I say. "I would love to see them."

Matt grins wide. His enthusiasm is so palpable that I smile back, even through my nerves.

"I love their personal collections, but unfortunately they were closed to the public last week," he says. "Which is a pity, because they contain some of my favorite works. Like, recently we had Margaret West, and she has this stunning recreation of *The Nightmare* that we got to keep."

"Oh my gosh, I love that piece!" I say, hoping my expression gives easy, breezy, and not at all ravenous for more. "But it's so different from Margaret's typical work. I wonder why they chose that one."

"They seem to prefer more allegorical or figurative paintings," Matt supplies. "You know, big moral scenes, people, character. High drama, I like to say. The collection is pretty eclectic otherwise, but that's the common thread."

"That's so cool. I wish I could see it," I say, even as my heart races. I reach into my purse for my wallet to pay the gallery's twenty-dollar entrance fee, and when he accepts my card, I hold on. He gives me a quizzical look, and I return it with a smile that I know is both sultry and conspiratorial. "I mean . . . maybe I could. Maybe you could sneak me in."

Matt gives me a squeamish look, but his eyes brighten, and I know already that I will get a yes. It's true that I'm not great at getting people to like me, but I do have a decent handle on my feminine wiles. It's the combination of a direct stare, an inviting smile and a dash of charm that does it every time.

"Well," Matt says, "I probably shouldn't, but . . ."

"There's no one else here, Matt," I say. "And this is your fault. You got me all excited for it. Besides," I release my card and lean forward on the counter, balancing my chin on my hands, "I won't tell if you don't."

He bites back a grin. So do I. *Still got it.*

"Fine, but we have to be quick," he says in a stage whisper. "And if we get caught, you told me that you're a professor of art history from Northwestern, you have permission to look at our special collections, and I had no reason to think that you were lying, okay?"

"Got it," I say.

We sneak up three flights of stairs and stop at a locked white door with the label "Special Collections." Matt pulls a key ring from his hip, searches the area for any onlookers, then unlocks the door.

"Everything is bolted down and alarmed," he warns me. "So if you're secretly a burglar, you'll have a really bad day."

"I promise not to start my life of crime today," I tell him. I squeeze his shoulder. "Thank you, Matt."

Matt shrugs, and I can tell he already regrets his moment of insubordination.

"In and out," he warns me, and then he hustles back down the stairs and I am alone.

The pieces in this room are eclectic in style, medium, period, and place of origin: pastel-toned Impressionist paintings set next to hyperrealistic works next to black and white photographs next to Japanese ukiyo-e woodblock prints. Even their presentation lacks cohesion: some of the pieces are mounted in elaborate gold frames, others plain wood, more than a few in glass, modern frames that wouldn't look out of place in my condo. I wander farther in, confused, until I find the decal introducing me to the space. It is simple, nondescript, and contains far less information than I'd hoped for: *From the personal collections of Robert E. J. Conrad, William A. Harrison & the Conrad Estate.* I can understand why this floor isn't yet open to the public; compared to the well-manicured, well-organized setup of Margaret's exhibit, it almost feels like a glorified storage space.

Matt's assessment of Harrison & Conrad's tastes was spot-on: they like scene and story, mythos and high drama. I recognize an exhausted Sisyphus pushing a boulder up his hill as spectators watch below, Sirens luring a ship of sailors to their demise against rocks, a room of medical students peering over a corpse, a family of peasants gathered around a cluttered dining table as their pig noses its way through the front door.

I'm so engrossed in the new works that I run into the piece I'm looking for by chance.

The Recurring Nightmare has been framed—no longer a naked canvas on the wall but bordered by thick, ornate gold carving that gives it the impression of antiquity. In real life, the artistry is even more impressive: the crouching man's skin is luminous, like he's made of moonlight, and the brushstrokes give him a dimension that makes me feel like I'm the direct subject of his gaze. I stare back, at first because it snares my attention as it did when I first saw it at Margaret's exhibition, but soon because, well, he looks familiar. It's something about his features: the long, jet-black hair, delicate features, his one visible eye dark irised and monolidded—

Forgive me.

Julian had come to me young, with cherubic curls and lanky limbs and pleading puppy-dog eyes. I'd only recognized him because I'd seen him that way before, in the painting in his apartment. The one entitled *Together*. There was another man in that painting, just as pretty, but in a different, haunting way. The friend that Julian lost.

I suck in a breath.

It's Alphonse. There's no doubt in my mind.

There are logical reasons behind this, of course. Julian and Margaret are old friends too; maybe she knew Alphonse as well. His features are striking; it wouldn't surprise me if he modeled. But why would Margaret choose to depict him like this? As an *incubus* of all things?

Maybe, a voice in the back of my mind says, *because that's what he was.*

A chill descends on my body despite the warmth, and I hold my coat to my chest as I circle the room. Suddenly I can see Alphonse everywhere: he is Dionysus on a throne, surrounded by curling grapevines and reveling worshippers. He is lupine and elegant in samurai armor as he slices through an enemy, their blood marked by an arc of red ink. He is a pirate and a priest and a surgeon, appearing over and over again: a muse for an unknown artist—or artists—whose brushstrokes survived centuries.

I try to consider alternate explanations than the one that is pounding at the inside of my skull. Perhaps this dark-haired man is a mythological icon I simply have never heard of, like a golden-haired Achilles or white Jesus. Perhaps Alphonse just happens to resemble him—

In my panic, I've paced around the whole hall. When I look up, I find that I'm back at the first painting: the one of Sisyphus. Its label dates back to the 1700s, and it's painted in the style of the old masters of the Renaissance, with obsessive dedication to the human form and a composition that shows both the agony and futility of his task. I look more closely now at Sisyphus himself. His straining muscles, his twisted expression, the mop of dark curls that stick to the back of his neck.

I know that face. I've examined it from every angle, closed my eyes to find it smiling at me across a blank canvas room.

"Jules," I whisper.

I move through the room anew, like I've just gained sight. There, and there, and there—the man I almost loved stands, sits, lounges, dances, fights in pieces that cross centuries—the 1700s, the 1800s, the 2000s. Sometimes his hair is shorn as I know it to be now, other times long enough to be tied back. His age varies too: here he springs for a ball with youthful delight, there he pores over documents with a quill pen and a full, gray mustache. It's not a pattern anyone who hasn't spent the hours, days, months I have spent poring over his face might notice, but I would recognize him anywhere, and I recognize him now.

But what my eyes are showing me can't be possible. Can't be real. Because if it is, then I have to accept that Julian Conrad has been alive for a very long time.

Too long to be human.

I power walk through the exhibit, taking photos of the evidence I gather so that I can't convince myself that I've imagined this later, talk myself out of this improbable truth that's hit me like a gut punch. It's not just him I find, but Leila, and another woman who must be Rose. The world feels like it's tilting, transforming before my eyes from a place where every phenomenon can be explained to one in which immortality can exist—

"You shouldn't be here, Dr. Sullivan," a voice calls out.

I spin on my heel, lowering my phone. My adrenaline ratchets up so quickly that I'm almost nauseous with it, but it's only a woman. She's prim and well-dressed in a black jumpsuit with a stylish, tousled French bob, and even from the entrance of the hall, I can tell that her expression is sympathetic.

It's Julian's assistant, Ritika. I've only met her once, at Margaret's exhibition, but I've communicated with her a few times to coordinate schedules, and our interactions have always been pleasant.

"Oh. Hey, Ritika," I say, breathless. My muscles still flex with tension as she approaches, the clacking of her heels echoing through the gallery.

"This exhibit is closed to the public," she says. "Sorry. Matt is a bit green. He shouldn't have let you in."

Shoot. I hope I haven't gotten Matt into too much trouble.

"That was my fault," I tell her. "He was great. I bullied him into letting me up . . ."

Ritika's lip quirks. If I didn't know better, I'd think she looks impressed.

"I don't mean to this exhibit," she tells me. "You're not allowed in the gallery at all, I'm afraid."

It takes me a second to understand what she's saying, and when I do, my stomach drops into my pelvis.

"Julian put me on a no-access list?" I say, astounded. "What? Why? I'm not a stalker."

Ritika doesn't offer me any reassurance on that point, just inclines her head.

"Unfortunately, I do need you to leave," she says. "Or I'll have to call security."

One thing Julian will always be sure to serve me, it seems, is a platter full of humiliation. It was bad enough to not be good enough to fuck, but to be deemed unworthy of setting foot on any of his properties is a new low.

"Don't bother. I'll see myself out." I shove my arms back through my coat and storm past her.

Ritika follows me all the way down. Her heels clack smartly behind me down the three flights of stairs, across the lobby where Matt sheepishly avoids my gaze, and even beyond the swinging glass doors and down the sidewalk to the street.

Annoyed, I spin to face her.

"You planning to escort me to my car?" I snarl.

Something shifts on Ritika's face: a clenching of her teeth, a furrowing of her brow. Determination. She peers left, right, behind her, and just as I'm about to ask her if she's good, wraps her arms around me in a *hug.*

"W-What—" I stammer. My arms are suspended in the air, but she squeezes me closer.

"From Rose," she whispers.

I'm too petrified to process what she's said, let alone respond, when she relinquishes me. She steps back, then lifts her chin haughtily as if I'm the one who just ambushed her with an embrace.

"Have a good day, Dr. Sullivan," she says.

Then she turns on her heel and marches briskly back into the gallery, leaving me there at the side of the road to make sense of what just happened.

Something falls from my pocket onto the ground, glossy and the size of a postcard. I bend to pick it up, then suck in a breath.

Ritika has given me a clue.

Twenty-Four

I sit in my car in the parking lot, shell-shocked, as I stare down at the weighty, lacquered card in my hand, decorated with an embossed image of a single metallic red rose.

Around it, in stylish, curling letters, it reads:

> Transmogrification
>
> by Rose Callahan
>
> February 2, 7PM
>
> Ulrich Art Corridor
>
> Dress Code: Black Tie Formal
>
> Use this invitation for entry.

That's tomorrow night, I realize. There's a note on the back, handwritten in hasty black ballpoint ink.

He loves you. Come to him.

The knot in my throat pulls tight, and I squeeze my eyes shut, because the weight of my discoveries is all at once crushing. My ex-boyfriend is (probably) an incubus. His best friend, who is married to my best friend's ex, is likely his female counterpart. Judging by the fact that they keep appearing in paintings and photographs across centuries, they have been alive a very long time, hiding in plain sight, planting evidence of their existence like serial killers leaving calling cards for paying patrons to see.

And most importantly, they're draining the life out of us.

"Jesus," I murmur, reading over the card again.

Rose was the fourth figure in the painting by Julian's artist, the mysterious artist whose identity he'd refused to reveal. I can only assume she's a succubus herself, and her decision to lure me to her both exhilarates and frightens me. Clearly she and Julian have discussed me, or she wouldn't have included that personalized note, the implications of which I am too frazzled to contemplate right now. Did they decide that I knew too much, and are planning to finish me off? Where does Ritika fit into all this? She seems so distinctly human—

My phone buzzes, and I jolt as I fish it out of my pocket.

Bizarrely, it's a text from *Brandon*.

You around? I could use a little company.

My world comes back into sharp focus. As I sit considering the probability of supernatural creatures, my colleague is alone, contemplating his mortality in a hospital bed. There was a time when we were close enough that a plea like this wouldn't come as a surprise, and I wonder whether he's calling on that old bond now in his time of need. But I don't question it. Right now, impossibly, talking to Brandon feels like it could be a comfort. He is, after all, the only person who feels what I have felt, who might be able to hold my discovery without complete incredulity. My sole co-survivor.

Sure, I type back. Be there in fifteen.

His response is swift. Thank you, he says, and then a few seconds later, I'm so sorry to ask.

I assure him that it's fine, I'm happy to visit, then peel out of the parking lot and to the hospital. Through some stroke of luck and laziness, I've left my badge in the passenger seat, and when I arrive, I throw the lanyard over my head and march inside. I look far from professional in my black leggings, beanie, and puffer jacket, but when I pass the security guard at the entrance, one flash of my ID gets me through.

The oncology floor is eerily silent when I arrive. It's quiet time, past visitors' hours, and the only family allowed are those whose loved ones are imminently dying. The nurse's stations are unmanned, the staff scattering to finally get through their tasks unencumbered by demands. I look for Brandon's room number on the telemetry screens as I try to rehearse how to reveal my theories to him. *Hey, so I'm pretty sure that your wife is a succubus, and she's the reason why you're sick. Don't worry, I think my boyfriend is too. That's why my hair looks like this now!*

Christ. He's going to think I'm nuts. He's going to call Alan and demand I be declared unfit for the lab too.

When I get to his room, the door is slightly ajar.

I register the sound first: wet, smacking, slurping. It takes me a moment to realize that Brandon isn't alone. A woman is with him, clutching his hospital gown in two small, tight fists and dragging his limp body up until her face is level with his. Her eyes are squeezed closed with rapture, and in between sucks she makes small, indulgent moans. Her golden hair shrouds them like a halo, or maybe a funeral shroud.

She lifts her head. Her lips are smeared crimson, and from the door, it looks like blood.

"Sean," Leila whispers. She drops Brandon back down onto the bed. He lands hard, limp as a rag doll. "You came to visit."

I open my mouth to speak, but no sound escapes. When I look down at my hand on the doorknob, it's shaking. *Shit.* I didn't expect her to be here, so sure that she'd already cut and run. I'm remembering that moment in the stairwell, her voice harsh to the point of shrill: *You're eating out of my bowl.* Back then, I'd managed to convince myself that she hadn't been talking about me. But by the way she's looking at me, sizing me up like she's trying to figure out whether she can swallow me in one bite or two, it's clear my initial instinct had been correct.

Pull yourself together. I'm not sure exactly what Leila is capable of, but there's no reason for her to suspect that I know anything. And I'm not about to give her one.

I shake myself off, step inside, and affect a wry smile.

"I was in the area, and Brandon texted asking if I could stop by. He didn't mention that you were on your way," I say. "Sorry, didn't realize I would be walking into a conjugal visit."

Leila blinks once, then wipes her mouth with the back of her hand.

"Oh. Ha. Sorry," she says. Her lower lip, still streaked with what I realize now is lipstick, trembles. "I surprised him. Just got here a few minutes ago. But you know. It's been hard."

To my relief, Brandon opens his eyes. He turns to Leila, utterly enraptured. He doesn't even seem to notice that I'm here.

"Don't apologize, kitty," he says. His voice is paper thin and fragile, like a gust of wind could carry it away. "I'm just glad you're here with me."

My heart sinks. It's one of the first lessons I learned as a physician:

you can give someone all the information they need about their condition, show them the relevant evidence, but you can't force them to give their consent. No matter what I say, I cannot drag the devotion out of this man. Leila has him completely in her thrall, and she knows it.

As if to demonstrate, she brushes gentle knuckles over his forehead.

"Go to sleep, honey," she says, and as if she's waved a wand, he obliges, his eyelids flitting closed. I watch him with trepidation. He's breathing; I can see the subtle rise and fall of his chest. The monitor above his head shows that his heart is beating, that his blood pressure is fine. Despite his stable vitals, he looks awful, worse than he did yesterday.

"He's gotten a ton of pain meds today. He's exhausted," Leila explains, as if she can read my thoughts.

"It's horrible news," I say. "You handling it okay?"

Leila shrugs.

"As best as I can be, all things considered," she says. She tilts her head to the side, circling the bed until she's standing in front of me. The curtain of her hair falls down her shoulder, and I'm distracted by its luster, how it shines like spun gold. She looks even better than usual, her skin luminescent and healthy, a round, youthful rosiness to her cheeks that I don't remember noting before. It's only been a day since Brandon's diagnosis, and his ex-wife looks more wrecked than his current one.

"It was really lovely of Winny to bring me over yesterday," she continues. "She didn't have to do that."

No, she didn't, I want to say, but I dare not.

"She is one of the sweetest people I've ever met," I say. "She and Sophie. That little girl doesn't deserve this." *Doesn't deserve what you're doing to them.*

Leila's gaze sharpens, and a smile tugs at the corner of her lips.

"Life is funny like that, isn't it," Leila says. "Good people rarely get the karma that they deserve. It's the wicked who tend to persist."

I don't respond to that, because I'm not sure what to say. It is as close to an admission of her intentions as I'm going to get. Whatever Leila has started here, she intends to finish it.

"They think he's not going to last too much longer," she finally says. Her eyes are wide, flitting across my face as if in search of a reaction.

My heart thrums in my chest, and I get the eerie sensation that she can hear it, that she's listening to my blood sloshing through my temples and knows exactly how terrified I am.

"Who is 'they'?" I ask, trying to keep my voice even. "The neurosurgeon? His oncologist?" *Or just you?*

Leila circumvents my question like I didn't ask it. Instead, she smooths a hand down Brandon's sheets.

"I heard about you and Julian," she says.

His name pierces like a javelin through my chest.

"Oh?" I manage. My hands are shaking again; I shove them into my pockets. "Well. Yeah. Breakups. They happen."

"I was going to offer my condolences," she continues. The smile she gives me is eerily cheerful, out of place in the dreary space. "Don't take it personally. I've known Julian a long time; he likes to get lost in his little fantasies, but when he comes crashing back to Earth, and he always does . . ." She places a hand on my shoulder. "Well, let's just say that it was only ever going to end badly."

I stiffen. Hatred isn't a feeling I have much experience with, but right now, I hate Leila. I hate her for descending into our lives and blowing us into pieces. I hate her for stealing Winona's husband, and Sophie's father, and my friend, when she could have anyone else.

Leila isn't smiling anymore. She squints at me, and I'm not so addled as to not see that she can sense my hostility.

"Thank you for coming by, Sean," she says. "But I'd like some time alone with my husband."

I want to refuse her. To stand guard at Brandon's side for the rest of the night, protect him from whatever else she has in store for him.

But I don't. I can't. There's too much I don't know, no way to weigh the potential consequences of defying her against the benefits. What I do know: I'm alone, Leila is a predator, and right now she is baring her teeth.

"Of course," I say, walking backward to the door.

She gives me an indulgent smile.

"Goodbye, Sean. Be well."

She sounds like someone who thinks they'll never see me again. But I decide, in that moment, that she will, and soon.

Because something tells me that she'll be attending Rose's event. And trap or not, I'll be there as well. To see this through to its end.

Twenty-Five

I take Onix to doggy daycare and board him for three days. It's a precautionary measure, probably overkill, but I feel like I am going to war and I need to make sure that he won't be left stranded in case I don't make it back. I pack too much food, pay for him to get an extra walk and a peanut butter Kong every day, double-check that Winona's still listed at his emergency contact, and smother his gigantic block head with kisses before I say goodbye. Onix seems to understand that this is no ordinary drop-off, because he whines and resists his favorite trainer when they come to take him to the back. When he's safely stowed away, I get ready for the exhibit.

It may be my last night on Earth, and so I dress to kill. The black floor-length dress I find last minute at the nearby Saks skims down my body from the top of its mock neck down to the floor, the monotony broken by a mesh-covered slit that snakes scandalously up my thigh and across my chest. I brush my hair into glistening silver finger waves, follow a tutorial for makeup that transforms me into an almost unrecognizably glamorous version of myself.

I should be going crazy, but I'm strangely calm. The missing puzzle pieces are turning up, and I'm starting to make a picture out of this strange, macabre chaos. The dreams that have afflicted me since Julian first sat down next to me at the Edison Mansion? Well, that's because he's a creature who infiltrates dreams to seduce unsuspecting victims. My series of unexplained ailments? Withdrawal, from the intoxicating effect of his presence.

Julian breaking my heart in the most efficient, devastating way possible, erasing himself as thoroughly as he could from my life, then reappearing in my dreams to beg me for forgiveness?

I did it for you. To protect you.

He is the thing that makes the least sense here. An immortal spirit who listens to Tyler, the Creator and tries to convince me to ditch my iPhone for a Huawei, who tumbles around my living room with my dog and brings me coffee in bed. The one who kisses me like I'm the first gulp of oxygen after a deep dive, who refused to touch me for three months because the one time he did, he took a part of me with him.

He loves you, Rose's note says, and I read the words over and over, as mystified by them as I am by their writer. I ignore the pang in my chest and focus on logic—and logically, they make sense. If Julian had meant to deceive me in order to siphon away my life, he would have ravished me nightly, not held me at a proverbial arm's length. His hesitance, his hunger, the helplessness in his voice on our last night together . . . that had all been him holding back.

Because he loves me. Julian Conrad *loves me.*

Maybe that love is worth enough that he'd be willing to stop Leila and save Brandon's life.

That's what I tell myself as I drive to Rose Callahan's gallery opening. I am going to him for answers. I am going to him because Sophie loves her father and shouldn't grow up without him, because Winona needs her coparent.

Not because I miss him. Not because I want to nuzzle my head into his chest again and try to guess the notes in his cologne or play him a song that he already knows by heart.

The Ulrich Art Corridor is a little-known gallery in the western suburbs. For as high-profile an artist as probable-succubus Rose Callahan, the fourth friend in Julian's painting, is, it's a small, unassuming venue. But of course, if I'm right, Rose is elusive for a reason, and a bigger, more accessible space might have placed her identity at risk. The organizers seem to take her confidentiality seriously; I have to sign a waiver at the door promising that I will not take photographs or video of any kind.

The gallery hall is separated from the lobby by a wall of glass. Inside, a harpist in an emerald-green dress strums at her instrument as guests mill amongst strange sculptures and large, looming canvases. I push through the double doors, taking a glass of champagne from a passing waiter before I go inside. I down it in one gulp, readying myself. Any moment now, I will see Julian again. It may be across the room, or while examining a piece, but our eyes will meet. I'll tell him that *we need to talk*, and he'll say yes or deny me or delve into my brain. Or maybe I'm wrong about him loving me, and he'll kill me here, he and his succubus sisters feeding from me like a pack of ravenous hyenas instead—

"I'm not sure I've ever seen anyone knock back champagne like a shot," a man's voice says behind me. "Nervous?"

I turn to find a white man in a brown tweed suit smiling down at me. He's somewhere north of sixty and has a harmless, fatherly aura that lowers my hackles some.

"I've had a long day," I answer and he falls into step beside me.

"I'm Harold," he says cheerfully. "You?"

"Sean."

Harold beams.

"What a lovely name. I'm partial to gender-neutral names myself. We named our eldest daughter Ryan," he says. He doesn't wait for me to respond before barreling ahead with another question. "You a fan of Callahan's?"

"Not really," I confess, distracted by a tall man who could have been Julian until he turns to reveal a flat-nosed profile.

"Well, you're in for a treat," Harold says. "She's been one of my favorite creators for years. This tour is her first time showing her face—and she opens every one with a performance."

This gives me pause.

"I didn't hear anything about a performance," I say.

"You wouldn't. You signed the waiver, right? She has a pretty intense team. Her lawyers crack down hard on anyone who tries to spoil her show." He grins conspiratorially. "I only know because I've been to a few of her openings myself. Each one is different, and they've all been *magical*. Benefits of retirement: you get to follow your favorite artist around the country like a rock star!"

I smile despite myself. Harold is sunshine in human form, one of those rare people who can lift even the lowest of spirits.

"It sounds like I have a lot to look forward to."

"You do," Harold assures me. The lights in the hall dim, the harpist stops, and he shimmies his shoulders in excitement.

"It's starting!" he exclaims. He raises his full glass to my empty one. "I'm going to try and get a closer look. Enjoy the show, Sean!"

"Enjoy!" I say, bemused, as he rushes to the center of the room. Other guests follow suit, and I scan the crowd, my frustration mounting. The card had been so clear: *Come to him*. Julian has to be here. I expect Leila is too, taking a night off from haunting her current husband to search for her next one. But even as the room fills, they are nowhere to be found.

The harpist begins to play again, thrumming her chords so softly that I hear the collective intake of breath as the show begins. I wander closer to the center of the room, where everyone has gathered around a sculpture: a thin, oblong, egglike structure that has begun to crack.

"It's hatching," someone whispers.

They are right. My vantage point is not ideal, but even from where I stand, I can see thin arcs of porcelain-like material fall to the ground. The harpist times her strums to each of the strikes, punctuating the captive's escape with a chord that turns the process from a violent emerging to a magical one. Excited murmurs run through the crowd, guesses on what will emerge from the shell, comparisons of this entrance to her last. A fist punches through and hangs in the air in victory, and the crowd cheers like their team has just scored.

The final crack sounds like the Earth is splitting, and the egg collapses, falling to the floor with the tinkling of fallen glass. Dust or smoke or steam emanates from the inside, and a wave of heat passes over the room, so quickly that I would've assumed I had imagined it if the men in front of me hadn't nervously chuckled and fanned themselves.

The room goes quiet. The music cuts out.

A crouched figure emerges from the fog. It is naked, with sagging, liver-spotted skin that folds in on itself in strange, unnatural ways along its abdomen. Its long-clawed hand nearly drags against the floor, and its tubular breasts are peaked with thick, fingerlike nipples that sway over its folded stomach. Its face is broad and strange, mouth set too wide, nonexistent lips going straight to blocky, too-big teeth. Gray tufts of hair sprout in patches across its scalp and on its upper lip. Its bulbous eyes spin, searching the room.

Humanoid, but not human. We regard it in silent revulsion, and it regards us back. Uncertainty ripples through the room; we aren't sure if the creature in front of us is real or part of the performance, if what we have witnessed is the birth of a monster. In front of me, someone claps their hands together and stage-whispers, "Wow, her special effects makeup is always so incredible!"

Then, suddenly, the music resumes. It is frenzied now, and the monster's head swivels, as if searching for its source. It steps forward, and all of a sudden the heat that we felt upon its hatching intensifies, and the creature is engulfed in smoke. It screams, high, human, like a child, as the lights flicker red. Even obscured, I can tell that it is *melting*.

Muck drips from its elevated stage, a blood-curdling, bubbly mixture of flesh tones and crimson. The guests who'd been standing the closest jump back as it oozes near their feet.

Finally, the music quiets again. The harpist plays a soft, sweet melody, and the smoke clears.

Where the monster once stood, there is now a woman. Her short black hair is gelled in wet swirls around her forehead and neck, and her sharp, vulpine features contrast with her shapely, Rubenesque body. She looks like a tawny Botticelli's Venus, arising from the water in her seashell, except she is dressed in a skin-tone tattered dress, and her body is streaked in soot.

The people around me are cheering, but I am frozen. Because I know this face too, and not just from the paintings.

Rose Callahan is none other than Margaret West.

Or perhaps more accurately, Margaret is Rose. Forty years younger, yes, but just as alluring. Her eyes catch mine. It shouldn't be possible across the room, but they hold for a beat, and I could swear that her lips quirk into a smile.

Someone hands her a microphone.

"Welcome," Rose says, "to *Transmogrification*."

The crowd bursts into applause as she comes down from her platform. A crew sweeps behind her to clean the mess of destroyed porcelain and goop from the gallery floor while she glides through the crowd. Her existence, the fact that she is walking around, gesticulating with Margaret's mannerisms, smiling her knowing smile, is greater than any evidence I could have gathered in Harrison & Conrad Galleries. Even knowing the truth, my brain still tries to reject it: maybe she's Margaret's kid, or a lookalike niece—

She stops in front of me.

"Don't you look stunning," she says, with a teasing smile. "*Love* the hair."

I clutch my bag in front of me like a shield. There's something regal and controlled about her that inspires wonder alongside fear. I'd wanted to run away screaming from Leila, but I want to prostrate myself before her.

"Hello, Margaret," I whisper.

Her smile shines with genuine delight, and she lifts a finger to her lips, leaning in close.

"It's Rose now, remember?" She rests a gentle hand on my shoulder and adds with warmth I do not expect, "So you've figured us out, have you?" When I flinch, she chuckles. "It's okay. I'm glad. It's nice to not have to pretend."

My throat feels parched, like the champagne I drank a few minutes before has sucked out all its moisture.

"Pretend . . ." I start, then swallow down my fear, "to be human?"

Rose pulls back just enough that I can see that her eyes are shining.

"If you asked Julian, he'd say that's precisely what we are," she whispers. "Just different. *Enhanced*, so to speak. If you asked Leila, she would say that we are so clearly in a different realm. Gods. My perspective . . .

well. I accept myself as exactly what I am, and I think there's already a name for us. Ritika tells me you went to visit *The Recurring Nightmare*. I'm hazarding a guess that you might know what that is."

The harpist is still playing, but I can't hear the music over the rush of blood in my ears. I have so many questions, but it feels like I might run out of time at any moment, and so I ask the one that has plagued me the most.

"You gave Ritika the note," I say. "Why?"

If her newfound youth hadn't just been siphoned from another living being—likely the bulldog-faced husband she'd carted around at *PERPETUITY*, I realize with a chill—I would almost think of her smile as kind.

"Because, my dear, I'm meddling," she says. "I haven't seen Julian quite so happy as he was with you, or quite so miserable as he's been without. Not for a long, long time. I assumed you'd feel similarly. I'm trying to arrange a reconciliation."

I suck in a shuddering breath, fighting against an assault of conflicting emotions.

"I'm not sure Leila feels the same way," I manage on the exhale, and Rose chuckles.

"I'll work on that one," she says, beaming. "Truly, Sean. I'm so glad that he found you—"

Her voice cuts out mid-sentence, and she sucks in a pained breath. The hand on my shoulder tightens into a vise grip.

"Rose?" I say, concerned, just as a blossom of red begins to spread along the sides of her dress.

The next few seconds stretch, suspended, before me.

There is a man behind her, just one of the many guests clustering around the woman of the hour waiting for their turn, but when he jerks back his hand, I realize that he's holding a knife, and that the knife is covered in blood. I watch him raise it high, watch his crazed lips curl, watch the reflection of Rose's terrified face in his dilated pupils as she twists to avoid the assault.

In the space that his raised arm makes, I see Leila standing frozen across the room, her face pale with horror.

Screams slice through the air in unison, and I learn what is meant by true terror.

Twenty-Six

Sophie was eight years old when she first taught us about the protocol her school gave her for their "armed intruder" drill; old enough to recognize it as disconcerting, but young enough to find it exciting too.

"It's called the ALICE protocol," she recalled for us. "A for alert. L for lockdown. I for inform, C for counter, and E for evacuate. And they said counter means fight back, which doesn't make sense. They have a gun, and I'm just a kid."

It took Winona a herculean effort not to burst into tears. The news, as usual, had been full of stories of mass shootings; just the previous week, three students had died in an incident at a middle school, and she'd been struggling to send her baby in knowing this fate could await her.

"You're not just *any* kid," she told her. "You're my Spectacular Sophie. And if you ever have to use ALICE, you should absolutely run and hide . . . but if you have to fight, baby, fight *dirty*, and fight hard."

People are streaming past me in slow motion, racing for the exit, but I can't move, let alone fight. I'm on the ground, uncertain of how I got there, and when I try to stand, I find that my body has turned to lead. There are others still in the room, some laughing and watching with curiosity like this is just act 2 of Rose's show and they are witnessing more spectacle instead of an attempted murder.

"*Witch,*" the man shouts. "Get out of my head! *Get out of my head!*"

His knife arcs through the air again. It comes down slowly, enough that I can track its intended path for Rose's heart, that I can see the wildness in the man's ice-blue eyes.

A streak of blood, still warm, splashes onto my cheek.

I make people bleed as my job, drive needles into vessels. I know that blood dries down tacky, that it jets out of arteries and oozes out of veins, and that I can use hydrogen peroxide to get it out of my scrubs. It doesn't scare me. Rose's cries of pain, destroyed and ragged, could be the wails of family members when I walk into their room and tell them that their loved one didn't make it through the procedure to save their life.

None of this, I realize, is unfamiliar. It's just the scale, the setting: a formal event instead of a catheterization lab, an artist instead of a patient. I am rooted by this macabre, familiar sight, by the calming certainty that I'm probably not going to make it out of here alive.

But then something changes, and the world speeds back up to real time. Across the room, I hear Leila shout something in a different language, and Rose, her face twisted in agony, grabs the man by the wrist. Her scream is different this time, a warrior cry that I can feel rattling in my own chest. I find my limbs again, scrambling to my feet, and my heels slip in the blood.

The man goes still. I watch, in horror that turns quickly to understanding, as his hand goes limp and his knife clatters to the floor. Wrinkles form and fold in his forehead, at the corners of his eyes; jowls make his cheeks fall. He begins to stoop, his brown hair receding first, at the corners of his widow's peak, then graying, then falling out altogether. His skin pales, then yellows, turning that horrible neon color that I know is synonymous with liver failure.

Rose's hair lengthens, then explodes into a cloud around her head. The pitch of her scream increases to a playground whistle note, piercing, childlike, and she shrinks too, her arms and legs shortening, her dress sagging around her.

She turns to look at me with round, frightened eyes that remind me of Sophie's.

Then, suddenly, my view is obscured. Before I can process what I'm seeing—a man, sliding into a crouch, terrified brown eyes, arms outstretched—I'm lofted into the air. I flail in my captor's hold, my body regaining its survival instincts, but he's strong and firm and pitches me over his shoulder with ease. Up close, he smells smoky and sweet, like chocolate melting over a bonfire, and instantly I know.

I and everyone in this room are in mortal danger, I am living in a waking nightmare, one I may not survive—and yet, for one mystifying millisecond, I'm awash with an almost euphoric relief. *He came for me.*

"You shouldn't be here," Julian hisses, just as Leila's voice projects: "Lock the doors."

Julian breaks into a full sprint. From over his shoulder, I survey what I can of the room: ten or so remaining guests, looking on with confused amusement. The assailant's bloated, yellow corpse on the floor as Child Rose weeps at his feet in a pool of her own blood.

And Leila. Her beautiful face is contorted in fury, a vengeful goddess. She rushes toward us, her gaze locked on to me.

"JULIAN, YOU ASSHOLE!" she screams. "YOU KNOW WHAT WE HAVE TO DO!"

Julian doesn't slow, just kicks the glass doors open and sends us barreling through. We have just crossed the threshold when they slam shut and I hear the crank of a mechanical lock.

"Don't look," he says as we race through the emptied lobby.

The words have hardly left his lips before the horror starts. The lights go out, and suddenly I hear screaming, chaos. A group of men throw themselves at the locked door behind us. One of them is Harold, the man who had been so kind to me when I first arrived. His eyes are wide with terror. He is shouting. I can't hear him, but I see the words form on his lips: "Help me."

A litany of gunshots bursts through the air. Blood splatters onto the glass.

I gulp down air to keep from screaming, and the winter cold cuts my throat like shards of ice. Julian slows, throws open a car door, and deposits me inside. He's in the driver's seat and peeling out of the lot in seconds, flooring it down the road and onto the highway.

Shakes wrack my body, the iron taste of blood lingering on the back of my tongue. I look down at my hands and realize that blood is flaking in the crevices of my palms.

The world is whipping too fast around us. A wave of nausea overcomes me, and I lurch forward over my knees, letting my head hang between them in the hopes that it will abate.

"I need to throw up."

They're the first words I've spoken directly to him in weeks.

"There should be plastic grocery bags in the back seat," Julian says.

I turn, grab them, hold them in my lap, and wait for the heaves to start. They don't. I feel like a ghost, like I'm gliding alongside this car at ninety miles an hour. If I didn't have the evidence of what I witnessed still drying on my palms, I could almost convince myself that tonight wasn't real, that I just watched an excessively realistic movie or woke up from a particularly twisted nightmare. Most bizarre, my ex-boyfriend might have taken part in the killings—if he hadn't opted to kidnap me instead.

"Where are we going?" I ask. I don't expect a real answer, and Julian doesn't surprise me with one.

"Somewhere far away," he says. "Do you have your phone?"

Somehow I do. I'd been wearing my clutch across my body when Julian swept me up, and it hangs off my back. I pull it out.

Julian snatches it out of my hands, lowers his window, and throws it out onto the highway.

"What the fuck is wrong with you?" I shout, watching as my eight-hundred-dollar iPhone gets crushed under the wheels of a semi.

"Leila wants to kill you," Julian says plainly. "She's wanted to kill you for weeks now, but after today, after what you *saw* . . . I think it will be especially difficult to dissuade her." He looks away from the road for just long enough to affix me with a hard stare. "There's a possibility she's had your phone bugged. We shouldn't take any chances with it."

It's the first time I've gotten to look at him, *really* look at him, since I realized what he is. He has bags under his eyes, and he's missed a spot shaving his chin. I assumed I would be able to see the supernatural in him, like I'd just been ignoring it all this time. But I was wrong. This is still the Julian I know: absurdly good-looking, yes, but so very human all the same.

"When the hell would she get a chance to steal my phone to bug it?" I snap. "That is the most ridiculous thing I've ever heard—"

"You're not surprised that she wants to kill you," he observes. Then, more urgently, "You're not asking about Rose." His eyes leave the road to turn, wide, to mine. "You *know*."

The pressure that builds up in my head feels explosive.

"That you're a life-sucking dream demon?" I hiss. "Of course I fucking know. What's your *plan*, Julian? To lock me up in a tower until your succubus sister decides to give up on the hunt?"

Julian doesn't respond, just weaves around a driver who is crawling along in the sixties in the fast lane. The longer his silence stretches, the more apparent it becomes that I might have actually hit the nail on the head.

"You're joking." I'm sans coat, sans phone, and, apparently, sans the rest of my life. "You're *kidding me.*"

"I didn't know you would be there tonight," he says in hushed tones. "This is exactly what I was trying to avoid, Sean."

"Avoid?" I point to my hair, the silver-white curls that I'm getting accustomed to but still occasionally shock me when I catch my reflection in a mirror. "Did you start feeling that way before or after you snatched up my life?"

Julian's body sags with abject misery.

"Look, Sean. You have to understand. I didn't mean to . . ." He fumbles on his words, tries again. "I thought, maybe, we got away with it when we—"

My laughter cuts him off.

"Oh my god. You think I'm an idiot," I accuse between snickers that pulse out of me in waves, my body's twisted interpretation of the depths of betrayal and hurt that I've been tamping down for weeks. "You *didn't mean to*? Be honest. That's why we're here right now. That's why Brandon is in a fucking hospital bed. Because you fully intended for me to end up in the room next to him, so that you could keep on gallivanting around this Earth for who knows how much longer. That was the plan, right, you greedy piece of shit—"

"No. Never," Julian pleads, shaking his head. "Please, Sean, I never—"

"But you did!" The tears that I thought I would never find again come flowing down my cheeks now, and I can't stop laughing, because what kind of monster am *I*? I have escaped sure death when many others were less fortunate, and the thing that makes me cry is the realization that my ex might have sought me out to take advantage of me. "So how much time did you end up taking, huh? Two years? Three?"

"I don't know." Julian grips the steering wheel tight, and he stares, unblinking, at the road. "I wasn't supposed to take any. It was an accident."

"An accident that cost me years off my life," I spit. Important moments that I might no longer be there for. Sophie graduating college. Caring for my ailing parents. All those milestones that I'd assumed I would make, potentially cut short to feed this man's—this *thing's*—centuries-long avarice.

Julian's contrition is already turning to irritation.

"Yes, well," he growls, "at least you'll be living to see tomorrow. You can thank me for that."

I ball my hands into fists. My nails bite into my skin.

"I wish I'd never met you. I wish you'd left me alone."

I mean for it to hurt, and it thrills me when he flinches. It feels like the last claim to power I have left.

Julian doesn't speak for a moment. When he does, it is in a whisper that sounds like he's breaking.

"You and me both."

Julian drives through much of the night. He stops to get gas, takes my order at a quiet roadside fast food restaurant, but otherwise is behind the wheel uninterrupted for the next seven hours straight. I don't have a coat, and so he lends me his, shoving a too-big winter hat over my head before I leave the car to go to the bathroom, because *everyone will remember the young-looking Black woman with white hair if they're asked.* He doesn't use a GPS and refuses to tell me where we're going, but he doesn't prevent me from looking outside, so I know from the road signs that we're headed south.

I consider running. I think if I tried he wouldn't give chase. But as much as I don't want to admit it, the thought of straying from Julian's side terrifies me. At Ulrich Corridor, I'd walked amongst multiple guests and never once thought that one would have a knife, a gun, but now every person I pass is a potential threat that I know I can't face on my own. When I go into bathrooms alone, I imagine Leila materializing in the mirror behind me as I wash my hands. If there be monsters afoot, at least I have one as an ally.

Sometime around three in the morning, we stop at a Holiday Inn Express, and I realize that sleep is something he needs and doesn't just pretend to do. I make a list of his other needs too. Supernatural creature or not, he too requires food for sustenance and water for thirst. When we check into our hotel room and he goes to the bathroom, I can hear the trickle of him peeing and realize that was never an act either.

"What?" he says wearily when he emerges from the bathroom, freshly showered and fully dressed in a black T-shirt and gray sweatpants from the gym bag he keeps in his back seat, because apparently his physique is earned, not just magically bestowed.

"What do you mean, what?" I ask.

Julian sighs. He asked for one room with two beds, and I'm both relieved by his lack of presumption and annoyed, though I currently lack the capacity to properly investigate why.

"You've been watching me like a hawk all night," he says.

"Oh, you know, you're sort of the most dangerous entity in a five-hundred-mile radius, so . . ." When he doesn't laugh, I hug my knees to my chest. My skin still feels hot from my forty-minute scalding shower, and my palms are raw from scrubbing. "You're an incubus, right? I'm just trying to figure out how you . . . work."

A muscle in Julian's jaw twitches. He sits across from me on his bed and rests his elbows on his knees to regard me.

"An incubus," he says, turning the word over in his mouth like it's alien to him. His blink is slow and sensual, a subtle seduction. Then he shrugs. "Well, if the shoe fits."

His eyes tick to my neck, and I wonder, for one delirious second, if I've gotten it wrong and he's a vampire instead.

"It does, right?" I say, hesitantly. "I mean. There's the dreams thing. And. You know."

Julian's lip curls into the closest thing I've seen to a smile on him tonight.

"I know what?" he teases.

My cheeks warm. "Your . . . *prowess*," I manage. My gaze drops down to the space between his legs. Damned gray sweatpants. "Also, you're immortal."

Julian's smile drops.

"I'm not," he says. "Immortal, I mean."

My eyebrows screw up in confusion. The recurring character in the paintings *is* him. I've burned countless hours poring over the photographs I took at his gallery to know that.

"But the paintings, at your gallery—" I start.

Something like admiration crosses his face.

"You've seen the private collection, then." He raises his eyebrows, impressed. "I had that exhibit closed. How did you get in?"

Under better, easier circumstances, I might have told him about poor, sweet Matt the art historian. Instead I stare back until he sighs.

"The paintings do depict me, yes, and were made over the course of many years, yes," he admits. "But I can age, and I can die. Unassisted, I will."

It takes me a minute to understand what he means: Rose, flat-chested and thin-limbed, standing over the aged, jaundiced corpse of the man whose life she had just taken.

"You steal it," I whisper. Chills wrack my body, and I draw the hotel robe—the only thing I have to wear—tighter around myself. In order to be sitting here in front of me now, Julian has expedited the demise of countless people. He might not have ordered the shooting, but he's a killer too, and if the paintings are any indication, his death toll is certainly higher than the one in Ulrich Art Corridor.

"I've never referred to it as *stealing*, but yes," he says.

I tilt my head up to face the aged popcorn ceiling. I feel disembodied, the turbulent rage I'd burned through yesterday puttering out and giving way to nihilistic detachment. It doesn't matter what I say next, because nothing matters anyway, because soon enough I will be nothing. Just like Harold. Just like the man who lies bloated on the Ulrich gallery floor.

"Well," I mutter. "What else do you call taking what isn't yours?"

Julian doesn't respond right away. I hear him shift, the creak of his bed, the gentle pats of his footsteps, first one, then the other. Despite myself, I think of how easy it would be to reach for him now. If I put my hand out, it would hit torso, maybe chest, and he would hold it to him, press it against his heart like he once had.

"I meant it when I said it was an accident, with you," he says raggedly. "If I could take it back. Go back in time and never speak to you at that wedding. Keep you out of this. I would. You have to know that."

The edge in his voice squeezes me around the middle, and I grit my teeth against the pang of longing that courses through me. Implicit in his pleading is another truth: *I would've taken from someone else.*

"Why do you do it?" I ask. It's an impossible question, but it's the first that comes to mind, bypassing the *how*s and *what*s and the other metaphysical *maybe*s for the thing that I want to understand about Julian most. The reason he has subjected me to the agony of denying him.

"It's simple, really," he says. "I'm afraid of dying, same as most everyone else."

His answer strikes me still with its simplicity, and its veracity too. I finally lower my chin to look at him. Kneeling for me, like he is prone to do, his hand over his heart like he's pledging himself to me. A part of me wonders if it's his way of lessening the power differential between us, of average-sized woman and large man, of fragile human and eternal being.

"How long have you been alive, Julian?" I say, my voice shaking. The paintings go back four hundred years, maybe even longer, and the more I stare at him, the larger that number seems to loom. "Is . . . is Julian even your name?"

"It's what I've been called, or at least something close, for as long as I can remember," he says truthfully. "We're not as different as you think. You don't remember how you came to be either. Just one day, you woke up and just . . . were. You were a child, with a name not of your choosing, a family, a context. It's the same for me. I had no parents, but I did have a family—three others, just as desperate, just as hungry to survive. And so we did."

Three others.

"Alphonse. Rose." I swallow. "And Leila."

Julian nods solemnly.

"And what happened last night," I say. "Has it happened before?"

Julian doesn't answer for a long time. When he does, he speaks so softly that I almost don't hear him over the hum of the hotel mini fridge.

"You live as long as I have, and everything repeats itself eventually," he says cryptically. He stands, reaches over me, turns off the light. "Try to get some sleep. We have an early morning tomorrow."

The next morning, Julian leaves the hotel room early. I hear him get up, rummage around, and shock myself by drifting back to sleep before he returns. When he does, it's with a duffel bag full of clothing and toiletries for me.

"I found the body butter you like," he says soberly. "And I'm not sure what you use for your hair these days, but YouTube told me that this brand would probably work for your texture."

He's also managed to pick out comfortable clothing, sneakers in my correct size, and a coat that is both functional and nips at the waist. It's striking how he seems no different from the man I thought I knew: still so attentive, so considerate, if a little more murderous than previously thought. And still so irritatingly delightful to look at. I'm starting to understand why characters in postapocalyptic TV shows are constantly sleeping together in dire situations; knowing the truth about Julian doesn't stop my urge to trace a finger down the tense muscle in his neck.

We eat breakfast in the room because Julian's too worried about being recognized outside it, a mélange of fruit, yogurt, and plasticky croissants from the hotel lobby's free continental offerings.

"So what's your plan for today?" I ask. The *since I know I have no say in it* is silent, but Julian is smart enough to pick it up.

"We have a long trip ahead still," he says after a large swig of his burnt coffee. "I have a lot of safe houses scattered around the States. A few that Leila won't know about. We're heading to one of them."

"And then what?" I ask. "I live out the rest of my life in the middle of nowhere? Take up homesteading?"

Julian's expression darkens. He doesn't know what comes next, and my pointing it out clearly frustrates him.

"And then we figure it out," he says. "I try to talk Leila down—"

I let out a bark of laughter. I see Harold's face again, his wide-eyed terror. He'd gone to the gallery to see his favorite artist and paid for that indulgence with his life. The staccato of my heartbeat reminds me of gunshots.

"Onix is in daycare for two more days," I tell him. "When the staff realizes they can't get hold of me for pickup, they're going to call Winona. She's going to call my job, realize that I didn't show there either, and then she's going to figure out that I'm missing." I pretend to examine my nails, French-tipped press-ons that I'm surprised survived last night's ordeal. "All I'm saying is that it won't just be Leila who's out there searching for me."

By the look on Julian's face, he hasn't yet considered that my absence will be noted.

"We'll cross that bridge when we get there," he says.

"We get there in under forty-eight hours," I remind him.

Julian scowls, then snatches the remote from the desk and turns on the television. He flips through channels—Hallmark, Cartoon Network—before settling on the weather. A man in glasses announces that it's going to be a balmy twelve degrees out today and advises us to bundle up. Then a bar falls across the screen: *Breaking News.*

"A mass shooting occurred last night in Chicago's Riverside suburb at Ulrich Art Corridor, resulting in the deaths of twelve people," the severe-looking newscaster says.

The scene shifts to fluttering police tape and flashing lights outside the venue, then a presentation showcasing some of Rose's works that were displayed.

"Elusive visual and performance artist Rose Callahan's tour for her new exhibition, *Transmogrification*, ends in a bloody scene. The shooter was found to be Peter Clements, a Riverside native and mechanic who has been described by family members as having become increasingly obsessed with an unknown woman over the last several months."

A white man flashes on the screen. He isn't the one who attacked Rose, but his features—brown hair, ice-blue eyes, a plain, oval face—are equally unremarkable, and I can understand how the people who escaped the gallery could have mistaken him for Rose's attacker. The anchor confirms my suspicion seconds after it occurs to me: "Several attendees who escaped stated that Clements attacked the artist with a knife before opening fire on the remaining guests and ultimately taking his own life."

They interview a detective. They believe Clements had an accomplice, someone who whisked an injured Rose, who has still not been found, off the scene and locked the doors behind him, trapping potential witnesses inside.

"We believe this attack was premeditated," the detective declares, "and that the unknown accomplice is likely at large."

They start the typical mass shooting talking points: thoughts and prayers, a press conference called by the mayor decrying this "enormous tragedy," arguments about gun control and the availability of semi-automatic weapons, interviews with sobbing family members. A pretty brunette, probably about my age, appears on-screen, tears streaming down her face as she tells the interviewer that her dad had been excited about the show.

"It was his retirement gift to himself," she says. Her name flashes on the screen, Ryan Fischer, and my vision blurs until I see Harold's face—his genial smile as he greeted me in the gallery, followed by the gasping horror of his final moments. I hear the gunshots again. They come fast, nary a thought of mercy between them. Indiscriminate. I never really knew Harold, but I can imagine him as a good man who was beloved by his family. And now he's gone, all because he had seen *their* secret.

Julian cuts off the segment and stands.

"We've stayed here long enough," he says. "We should get going."

"What's the point?" I whisper. I'm as good as dead as it is. My best-case scenario is a life on the run from a forever-young pursuer, one in which I grow old far from the people I love, the career that inspires and energizes me.

Julian doesn't say anything. I can feel him standing, looming over me, searching for something to say.

"We have to get to our next destination before two," he finally manages. His voice is low, mollifying, like he's afraid that I'll startle at its sound. "Someone will be meeting us there."

I look up to see Julian looking down at me, sorrowful. His hand twitches toward me, then falls back to his side. I'm glad he doesn't try to comfort me. I'm not sure I could withstand it without screaming.

Twenty-Seven

I've often wondered about the first person to find a dinosaur fossil. When they discovered the giant stony jaws, the teeth as long as their arms, how did it change their concept of what could be possible on Earth? How did it feel to be caught in the midst of a paradigm shift, to realize that the world you thought you understood contained secrets beyond your imagination quite literally beneath its surface? It must have been similar to how I feel now: deeply unsettled, disturbed even, but fascinated too. Because if dinosaurs and incubi exist, why can't dragons, chimeras, minotaurs, *magic*?

"Can you control minds?" I ask Julian an hour into the day's drive.

This leg of the journey is less silent and solemn than the first, mostly because Julian has put on Afrobeats. It's almost amusing to think that an ancient being listens to Rema, but Julian mumbles along to every word.

At my question, he cuts off the volume but doesn't take his eyes off the road.

"It's not quite that simple," he says. I wait for him to explain, and he sighs. "We cultivate devotion. We make people . . ." He searches for the word. "*Suggestible.*"

I shudder, thinking of how *suggestible* a person has to become to willingly murder a room full of people at another's request. It reminds me of cult leaders, capable of convincing droves of people to give their lives in service of them. I say as much, and Julian shrugs one shoulder.

"Honestly? Yes," he says. "It is like that. And some people are more susceptible than others."

I remember Melody at the conference after-party. All Julian'd had to do was touch her, and she'd folded to his command.

"What about the weird addiction thing," I say. "I felt sick every time we were apart. How does that one work? Do you have poison in your skin or something?"

This makes him snort.

"What am I, a frog?" he says. "No poison. Not as far as I know. Besides, the dependence goes both ways. When we have regular contact with someone, time apart affects us too."

A revelation lands on me like an anvil.

"Is that why you were so sick?" I ask. "The night we first . . ."

A new kind of image crosses my mind, this time of Julian on his knees, his eyes fixed determinedly on mine as his tongue delved deep into the space between my legs. My thighs clench, and I inhale, shocked by how much the memory still titillates even under these circumstances. Julian goes silent for a moment, and I wonder if he's thinking of that night too.

"Yes." He inhales deep, exhales slow. "That's why I was sick too."

There's something more that he wants to say. I can see it, stuck on the tip of his tongue, a confession that he considers sharing and then swallows down.

"Why get close to people then?" I ask. "If you get sick too. It seems like you'd benefit most from being more promiscuous, no?"

"Yes, well, that was the strategy for a bit," he confesses, and I realize that while I've long assumed that Julian had a body count a mile long, the reminder that he's also had five hundred years to build it and a life-extending incentive makes me feel squeamish. Legions have felt what I've felt with him. To me, sleeping with him was monumental, life-changing, but for him I was as routine as a decent lunch. I'm still grappling with this realization when Julian adds, "But the transfer is much more efficient when there's some level of intimacy."

"Transfer?" I ask, trying to keep my tone even and curious.

"It's what we call it," Julian says. "The process."

I laugh, dropping my head backward against the rest. *Process. Transfer. Unassisted.* Such passive terms for such violence.

"What a sanitized way to refer to draining years off someone's life," I mutter. "Okay. So what about the intimacy. Is it physical? Emotional?"

I don't turn to look at Julian's expression, but I imagine he looks glum.

"Both," Julian supplies. "We need . . . consent, in a way. The other person has to give of themselves willingly."

Give yourself to me, he used to tell me in my dreams. *Say that you're mine.*

"But they don't know what they're consenting to," I argue. "They don't know what you're taking."

"And that's the thing," Julian counters. "Most of the time, they're too enamored with us to care."

I swivel to look at him, horrified. "That's *fucked*," I tell Julian.

Julian sucks in his cheeks in something like frustration but doesn't look away from the road.

"You think I don't know that?" he says coolly. "You think I've lived this long and haven't questioned the morality of my extended existence?" When I don't answer, he continues. "We all deal with it in our own ways. It's been a very long time since I've killed anyone outright. I take in small increments, and I tell myself that I do the same damage as a year of smoking cigarettes or a month inhaling polluted air. That I give it back to the world with my money and my service. I don't do strong attachments, though it would feel better if I did. Rose? She knows this world has never fully punished violent men, so she seeks them out, keeps them under control until they reach late middle age. Whatever life they have left, she transfers, and she considers it a mercy—like putting down a vicious animal."

It's twisted, but I have to confess that I can see their logic. Armed with similar abilities, I can't say with any certainty that I wouldn't have tried to justify evading my own demise.

"And Leila?" I ask. "The one who wants to kill me?" The one, Rose had said, who considers herself a god?

Julian doesn't turn from the road.

"Leila doesn't concern herself as much with such things," he says.

"What about Alphonse?" I ask. "What happened to him?"

A muscle in Julian's jaw twitches.

"You already know what happened to Alphonse."

He turns up the music, as good a conversation ender as any. Petulantly, I slouch in my seat and stare out the window. The road is curveless, the terrain flat, cornfields hidden under a blanket of fresh snow. It feels endless. I cross my arms and watch this world that is so unlike the one I know whip past me, and think of Brandon, who fell victim to the least human of Julian's kind.

We don't speak again for a long time. Julian's playlists are legendarily erratic, and so I'm not surprised when the genre shifts to classical piano, and my fingers thrum against the door, muscle memory playing along with the track. I fidget like a child: lower the car's sun visor, snap open the glove compartment. Something within catches my eye. It's small, postcard sized, and I can see Julian's looping cursive at the bottom. I squint into the darkness, make out the words: *Do you, Sean Sullivan, want to be my, Julian Conrad's, girlfriend?*

Blood rushes to my face, and I slam it shut.

To my relief, Julian doesn't give any indication that he's noticed my discovery. His focus remains locked on the road, and I take note of the five o'clock shadow that has emerged on his face. He often shaved at my apartment before leaving to meet his clients. After he left me, I'd kept his accoutrements in their assigned drawer, unable to throw them out: the straight razor he favored but never returned for, the whetstone he used to sharpen it, his brush, his aftershave. I used to lean against the bathroom door and watch him work, seduced by how easily his deft hands handled the blade. Praying he'd use them to handle me instead.

"Is that how it worked with me?"

The question bursts from me before I can stop it, but it gets his attention.

"What do you mean?" he asks gently.

"Was this all just"—my voice is more raw than I'd like, feeble—"suggestion?"

Julian closes his eyes on his inhale. When he finally responds, his voice sounds waterlogged with sorrow.

"Be honest with yourself, Sean," he says. "When has anyone ever been able to tell you what to do?"

Several hours later, I startle awake to the crunch of gravel under our tires; we are in the middle of the woods, heading up an unpaved road. I'd tried to stay up to keep some idea of where we were, but last night's sleep had been less than restful, and after two hundred miles of flat cornfields and barnyards, I must have dozed off.

"Are we there?" I ask.

"Soon," Julian says. We bounce up a hill, then pull into a clearing.

There's another car waiting for us. It's a silver SUV, totally unremarkable except for its tinted windows. We haven't finished parking before both the driver and front passenger car doors open, and two people in black hop out.

I freeze in trepidation as they approach, not even daring to breathe. It occurs to me that I'm alone with three people in an unknown location in the middle of the woods, and I've come here somewhat voluntarily, like the women in the beginning of every true crime documentary.

"Trust me," Julian says softly. "Please."

He doesn't know the enormity of what he asks, because then he wouldn't ask it. Doesn't know how stupid I feel, that the only two men I have developed strong feelings for have both put my life at risk. That I seem to have a thing for monsters, even if they are of different varieties. That even now, when I face him like this, I have to fight back the urge to smooth the tortured crease between his brows.

There's a simultaneous tap at our windows, and I swing to mine to find a face smiling down at me.

A familiar one, though I've never seen it smile.

"Ritika?" I say, stunned. Julian unlocks the doors with a click, then steps out on his side. I swallow a gulp of air, then do the same.

"Long time no see," Ritika says when I step out. "You've had quite the last few days."

"That's an understatement," I say a little awkwardly. I turn questioningly to the other stranger, a reedy young man who has Ritika's nose and thick eyebrows.

"Aditya. Ritika's younger brother," Julian provides, as if he's in my head. "He'll be taking our car. Ritika will be accompanying us to the safe house."

"I'll guess I should add 'mind reading' to your list of abilities," I grumble.

"Julian can do a lot of strange shit, but he can't read minds," Aditya says in a voice with a bit more bass than I expect. He swings to him, suspicious. "Wait. Can you?"

"No," Julian confirms. He tosses Aditya the keys to his Audi, and he catches them, grinning like he's just won the lottery.

I stand, bewildered, as I try to process what I've just observed.

"Hold on," I say. "They *know*?"

Aditya shrugs, leaning against the door of the Audi and swinging the keys around his finger.

"What, that your immortal boyfriend has weird dream powers?" he says. "Yeah. It's sort of a family secret."

I'm gaping as Julian sighs, grabbing my bag from the passenger seat.

"The Ghoshals have been working with me for generations," he supplies, throwing our duffel bags over his shoulders and heading for the other car.

"He actually scooped our great-grandparents out of India during the Bengal famine and helped them resettle in the UK. When he decided to move to the States, our parents decided to follow," Ritika explains. She barely lets me process the fact that Julian was present during a historic atrocity that I last heard about in my high school world history class when she adds, "Working for him is tradition, at this point."

"First you have to go through that creepy-ass initiation, though," Aditya groans.

If I had questions before, I have a thousand more now.

"Initiation?" I ask, stuffing my hands into my pockets to keep warm.

"Not my idea!" Julian yells from the other car.

"He's right. Our dadu came up with it. He's very dramatic," Aditya says with a snort. "Two lucky Ghoshals are chosen, through some mysterious selection process that definitely has something to do with our SAT scores and how many times we've visited him for tea over the years, to *adventure* with this one. On our eighteenth birthday, they show us this weird old tapestry with that guy on it"—he gestures to Julian—"then give us an offer we'd be dumb to refuse."

It's cold as sin out here, but I hunker down.

"And what is that?"

Aditya and Ritika simultaneously turn to look at Julian. It's a subtle, coordinated movement, reflexive, like moths looking to the moon. Julian shrugs, his permission granted.

"We give six months each of our lives," Ritika supplies. "And five years of paid service managing Julian's estate. In exchange, we get access to a familial trust. But also, if we reveal his identity, our entire family has license to take us out."

"Unless you're crazy like my sis and actually *like* to work. She's on year eight," Aditya says, rolling his eyes. "Or an overachiever like our

Uncle Sanjay. Had to show all of us up by going and becoming a big-shot attorney after his service just 'cause."

The siblings are joking around, but my stomach has seized with horror. The ritual occurs when the Ghoshals are freshly eighteen, and Julian is an *incubus.* I am intimately familiar with his methods, and my reaction comes from not only the realization that he would do *that* with an entire family, but to what amounts to children—

"It's not what you're thinking," Julian, back at my side, says hurriedly. His entire face flushes bronze. "I'll explain. Um. Later."

"Explain *now,*" I demand. "I'm not just going to get in the car with a . . . a . . . supernatural pedophile!"

Ritika and Aditya exchange alarmed glances, then turn, grinning, to Julian.

"Whoa, Julian, has your taste changed since we last talked?" Aditya says.

Julian doesn't look the least bit amused. Instead, he looks like he wants to melt into the earth.

"No, it has not," he says, opening the trunk of the SUV. "Sean has decided that I'm an incubus. That's why she's saying that."

Aditya gives his sister a confused look, but Ritika looks thoughtful.

"Well, if the shoe fits," she says, repeating Julian's earlier words. Then she turns to me and gives me a pitying look. "We don't have to sleep with him, if that's what you're worried about."

I cross my arms, annoyed that my extremely serious concern seems to have been reduced to jealousy. Julian catches me pouting and bites his cheek, grabbing the last of our belongings from the back seat.

"We just have to be in physical contact for the transfer. It doesn't have to be sexual, though as I told you, intimacy and some level of consent makes the process significantly more efficient." He lowers his gaze. "You know this. You saw what happened at the Corridor."

The reminder of why exactly we are on the run mollifies me.

"Also, I am obviously not taking advantage of these two assholes, judging by how they're just *standing around* right now." Julian's irritation is so palpable that the assholes in question jolt to attention. "Ritika, can you, at the very least, open the door for Dr. Sullivan?"

Ritika nods, not at all cowed, and I observe the interaction curiously. From the brief description of the Ghoshals' deal with Julian, I would have assumed that Julian would be akin to a minor god or at the very least a patron spirit to this family, but they treat him like an older cousin they enjoy riling up. After smacking her brother on the back in farewell, Ritika saunters up to the SUV and opens the back passenger door for me.

It's a large car, with a row of seats in the back that have been collapsed to make room for an ungodly amount of *stuff*. Canned foods, gallons of water, space heaters, soap: a doomsday prepper's jackpot. These aren't supplies for one week, or even two, and they aren't a haul a person who expects to have regular access to a grocery store collects.

It's a stark reminder: wherever our destination is, I may be there for a very long time. A princess in her castle, guarded by a dragon whose very touch can send me to my demise. The realization sobers me. I think about my patients, who will show up for their procedures on Monday to find that the physician who promised to relieve their chest pain or replace their valve has disappeared without notice. About Onix, already abandoned once by a family who didn't want him, and who won't know that his second momma misses him desperately. About Sophie and Winona, who don't need anyone else to worry about right now, and my parents, cozy in distant North Carolina, who might hear the news first from police. About Brandon, who may or may not still be alive.

Ritika is chattier than I expected during the drive, though her tone remains deadpan and her wit dry. She apologizes for the unexpected embrace outside Harrison & Conrad ("If I'm honest, I feel like you needed it, and it was a great excuse to slip you the card"), rags on Julian ("He's kind of a dork when he's not doing the whole suave, charming act to lure unsuspecting victims, but I guess you like that"), and ribs me about my piano fetish ("I can't believe he found a woman who cares about a Fingeldoffer or whatever they're called").

She doesn't seem at all perturbed by our predicament. The one time she brings up the Ulrich Corridor shooting, it's to cluck her tongue and say, "Leila, doing the most as per usual," express concern for Rose, and go on a tirade about how Julian has successfully managed to keep his affiliation with her family a secret from his more paranoid sister for generations.

I find Ritika, and her family, utterly befuddling. But there's a comfort in her presence too. It's evidence that there are regular, mortal people Julian cares about who care about him too, and for whom the improbability of his existence is banal. I must be staring a hole into the back of her head, because she catches it in the rearview mirror and smiles.

"You have questions," Ritika observes.

"Oh, you have no idea," I confirm. I glance sidelong at Julian, who has largely been silent during this leg of the drive, his arms crossed and body turned toward his window. I want to ask Ritika about the past generations of Ghoshals, what happens when their service is over, if she grew up with a preternaturally ageless adult occasionally visiting her home or if Julian materialized out of the tapestry on the day of her ritual. I want to understand how she could put a price tag on six months of her life, if she resents her parents for demanding she make such an incomprehensible choice before she could fully understand its consequences. I want to ask her what she and Julian intend for me, if their plan to whisk me off to safety includes preserving the life I've lovingly built.

But I don't, because my head hurts, and my exhaustion is something not even sleep can fix. And so instead I drift, and eventually Ritika turns on an oldies station, and our journey continues to the soft murmurs of the Cranberries and Fleetwood Mac.

Hours later our car is careening off the smooth asphalt of the interstate and onto a wooded gravel road. A few small houses peek out through the trees, all fairly recently built from the size and style, but they are all at least a quarter mile apart. It's daytime, so I can still see, but I notice no signage indicating a neighborhood, no street lights, no evidence that we have entered a community. Finally, Ritika makes another sharp left, and we are bouncing up an uneven driveway and to a large cottage.

"Home sweet home," Ritika mutters.

Under different circumstances, I might have found my new "home" quite charming. It sits atop a picturesque hill, and we're far enough south that when I step out of the car I realize we've exchanged Chicago's bone-deep winter sting for a brisk but survivable Southern chill. Leaves cover the entirety of the expansive grounds, and I spot a veranda with a swing, a basketball hoop, and, to my amusement, an assortment of sun-bleached garden gnomes.

Onix would have loved to run these grounds. When I first adopted him, before his arthritis got bad, he'd take off in zoomies around the dog park, galloping in circles before flopping joyfully at my feet.

"It's just for a while," Julian says from behind me. He hasn't spoken in so long that hearing his voice jolts me out of my thoughts.

I snort. "Oh yeah? You swear?"

He doesn't respond, because *of course he can't.* I shake my head. Then, because I am powerless to do any different, I walk up to the door. "So. Who wants to give me a tour of my jailhouse?"

Twenty-Eight

The cottage where I will be held indefinitely has three bedrooms, two bathrooms, and a beautiful sunroom. The walls in the entryway are painted a soft canary yellow, and the "Welcome" rug is faded in the middle, as if feet have been stamping out mud and snow upon it for years.

"It's . . ." I say, surprised as I whirl around the living room, gaping up at the admittedly pretty high beamed ceilings, "homey."

Julian looks down at me, and I can see the hopefulness in his gaze.

"Ritika and I will unload the car," he says. "You should look around. Pick a room."

I give him a rueful look. He sounds like a dad who's moved his family across the country and is trying to convince his despondent kids to feel less horrible about it.

Which, to my surprise, I do. For some reason, I expected Julian's safe house to be a cold concrete bunker, but this home feels lived-in. There are cat posters on the walls, a plush sectional that I can sink into, a huge, slightly outdated television hooked up to a DVD player. Everything is a little worn and well loved, and I can see signs of a life once lived: a feather wand toy once used to entertain a long-gone cat, a chest of blankets once cuddled under, a lacquered wood coffee table with overlapping water stains.

Next to the kitchen, I find a sliding door that I assume leads to a formal dining room and shove it open. When I see what's inside, I snap it shut again.

"Tell me the truth," I say, when Julian and Ritika return with their boxes of supplies. "Has the Steinway always been here, or did you have it brought in?"

It's a baby grand. It gleams in the dining room, the keys unyellowed by the passage of time. Not just that, but there's an entire shelf of books and sheet music.

"Of course you'd find it immediately," Ritika says with a long-suffering sigh. She places her box down, gives Julian a knowing look, and marches back out into the cold.

We're alone. It feels strange to be, after a whole day with Ritika, even though it used to be the most natural thing in the world. Compared to his assistant, Julian seems so large suddenly, and the breadth of his shoulders and height as he leans against the kitchen counter bestow him a potent, primordial power.

"I had it brought in," he says, softly.

"For me?" I ask.

"For you," he confirms.

It takes time to source, buy, and ship pianos. I know, because before I realized a baby grand wouldn't fit in my apartment, I'd inquired after one myself. Nearly a year to build if buying one custom, but still a hassle to ship a premade one from a showroom to a little house in the middle of nowhere.

It confirms what I've suspected since the second I could think after Julian whisked me off that bloody gallery floor—Julian has been planning this for some time, and he's been planning it for me. His plan B, just in case things go to shit.

I walk past him and into the dining room and plop myself on the bench. I run my fingers along the keys. The seat faces a large French window that has a direct view of the backyard, and I imagine sitting here on a spring day, watching hummingbirds flit by, spotting deer gather at the salt lick, and feeling at peace.

Julian watches me from the doorway. I can feel his gaze on the side of my face like sunshine pouring from a window.

"You were right, you know," he says. "About when we first met."

I hum in acknowledgment. My fingers have chosen to play "Für Elise," the first "hard" song they learned by heart, and I decide to follow their lead.

"I *did* target you," he continues. "You were single. Childless. Not particularly close to your family. By my accounts, a person who very few people would miss. You kept company with Brandon, who was so clearly simple, and I assumed you would be simple too. And Leila was fine with it, because it was supposed to be quick. Wasn't going to get in her way. I take you out, show you a good time, skim a few years off the top, and then leave you a little confused, a bit disappointed, but not too worse for wear."

Hearing Julian talk plainly like this—as the hunter he is—is oddly relieving, even as it sets off a thunder drum against my sternum. Like he's been wearing an unconvincing disguise and has just torn it away to reveal the wolf I've always known was peering out underneath his wool.

"So I was disposable," I say quietly, thinking back to those early days, the moments when I'd turn away from him and feel like I'd just made a narrow escape. "But I'm not anymore. So what changed?"

"I heard you play in that room," Julian confesses. "Saw how you cared for your goddaughter. Watched you live by your own terms. You intrigued me, at first. Then inspired me. And I . . . I don't know. I just realized one day that I enjoyed you. That I wanted to be around you, then be with you, then be yours."

My vision blurs with a whirlwind of emotions: rage, because of the many times I'd chosen to believe his words over my intuition. Hurt, because he'd still initially seen me the way the world so often did: as a woman of a certain age who, having eschewed the positions of wife and mother, was inherently less valuable. Sorrow, because the enormity of his betrayal aside, he sees me in a way that no one ever has.

"What do you want from me, Julian?" I whisper.

I can see his reflection in the window. His arms are crossed, but his gaze doesn't lift from mine.

"Right now?" he says. "To keep you safe."

"And after?" I ask.

Julian doesn't move, but the air in the music room thickens, crackles.

"It's just like you said, Sean. I'm a greedy piece of shit. I want all that you're willing to give me, and even more after that." Before I can ask him what he means by that, he launches himself off the doorframe and turns back into the kitchen. "I'm going to finish helping Ritika unload the car. You should pick a room."

The bedroom I choose is on the first floor. It's the smallest of the bedrooms but has the biggest bathroom and a sizable closet—and most importantly, a window big enough for me to climb through. It means both an easy escape for me and easier entry for someone else, but I can't imagine anything worse than negotiating a leap from the second floor, and so I take my chances. There are more paintings here, old, worn paperbacks in dusty bookshelves, but there are also signs of life: a pastel-pink corded phone next to a Tweety Bird alarm clock, bits of tape left on the walls from posters that have been torn down and not replaced. I wasn't a teenager in the nineties, but the nostalgia still hits me like a ton of bricks, not least of all because, just like then, we have no internet.

Someone lived here, I'm sure of it. This place isn't just one of Julian's many safe houses. It was a home.

"So, did you kill the previous owners?" I ask after I've finished unpacking my meager belongings and sauntered back into the kitchen.

It's dark out. Ritika and Julian have made quick work of the supplies, and the bags and boxes of household essentials that had piled the kitchen counters are now neatly tucked away. Ritika's dead to the world, collapsed on the couch, and Julian sits, cross-legged, at the dining table. He's sipping from a bright-red mug and reading an aged green book; on closer inspection, it's an old Danielle Steel novel. At my question, he lowers it.

"You harbor a very uncharitable view of me nowadays," he says sardonically. "No, I did not kill the previous owners. They were actually great friends. Do you want some tea? There's hot water in the kettle on the stove."

I've been so out of it that I didn't hear it whistle. I open up cabinets, pick out a caffeine-free peppermint variety, and make myself a cup. The only source of light is a standing lamp in the living room and a flickering candle that makes the room smell like lavender, and I catch myself about to fuss at him about straining his eyes. He looks so *normal* right now, in his black hoodie and sweats, his knuckles chapped from carrying boxes in and out in the cold. We've had nights like this before, reading in silence next to each other at dining tables or on couches or in each other's beds. Rolling over to turn off the lights then into each other's embrace, swapping thoughts on what we've just absorbed before drifting off to sleep. The contentment I'd felt in his arms, in feeling desired and understood. How sure I'd felt that this wasn't just a honeymoon phase, emphasized more by the fact that we weren't having the sex that I desperately wanted to have.

When I sit back down with my tea, he wordlessly pushes a book on the table in my direction. It's a photo album, the old kind with plastic sleeves. I open it and am greeted by a two-by-two grid of photographs of a family: a middle-aged man and woman, and a little girl. All three of them are wearing Mickey Mouse ears, and the little girl is dressed as Minnie. In the first photo, they beam at the camera, the picture of a normal, happy family on a trip to Disney World. The woman is white, with a shock of strawberry-blond hair and freckles that dust her entire face and down her arms. The man is racially ambiguous, with hair that is more salt than pepper, a straight nose, skin that looks more prone to burning than tanning, and monolid eyes that hint at Asian or Native American ancestry. Between them, their adorable daughter, with her chestnut-brown hair in pigtails and a giant, dripping ice cream cone clutched in her hand.

"Are these the previous owners?" I ask, flipping through pages of backyard barbecues, pony rides, science fair volcanoes, and Christmases, watching the little girl grow across the pages from a toothy-grinned child to an elegant, if serious-looking, young adult as her parents age alongside her.

"Yes," Julian says.

"How did you know them?"

Julian gives me a brief and disappointed glance.

"I'm surprised you haven't figured it out yet," he says. "You're usually more observant than that."

I frown, flipping through the pages as I sip my tea, scouring the photographs for the secret I am meant to unveil.

The moment I see it, I'm shocked I couldn't before.

"Is that . . ." I say, stunned, "*Alphonse*?"

Julian nods, turning a page in his novel.

"One and the same," he says.

The photograph I'm on now was taken at least a decade after the first. Alphonse's hairline has receded some, and he leans into the shot from the passenger seat of a car, laughing as his daughter gives a thumbs-up from the driver's side. He's still very much a handsome man, but he's got a little paunch and he's wearing a polo shirt and is teaching his daughter how to drive, looking like the dadliest dad I've ever seen. I scan the table, see that Julian has laid out three more albums, and I flip through them voraciously, absorbing the life of this incomprehensible person. Pets—Alphonse and his family seem partial to cats and bunnies—come and go, as do friends and seasons. They have a family garden; there are countless pictures of their handsome yields, images of a tomato canning process that must have become tradition and a blue ribbon awarded at a county fair for the largest cabbage. At some point, a young man joins them in their photos, and a few holiday seasons later there is his daughter again, wearing a hospital gown and holding a small pink baby. By the last album, Alphonse is old, white-haired, and kyphotic, and by the last page, he is gone altogether.

When Julian told me his friend had died, I assumed he meant that he met an early and unfortunate demise. But Alphonse went the way most of us want to, at a ripe old age, surrounded by loved ones.

"Was he human?" I ask. I feel both immensely moved and intensely unsettled, like I'm sitting among ghosts. So much of the house has remained unchanged, from the furnishings in what must have been Alphonse's daughter's room to the soft yellow of the walls. "Or was he . . . like you?"

Julian finally looks up from his book. I realize that the bleariness in his eyes isn't fatigue, but emotion. He'd probably brought the albums out for himself, to remember his friend.

"Is it an either-or?" he asks. When I don't answer, he closes his book. "He was like me. Only braver."

The swirl of my thoughts begins to congeal. I point to the woman, Alphonse's lover. In her later years, she took to dyeing her hair lavender, and her smile is shallow with the chronic sorrow of a person who must navigate the rest of her life as one half of a former whole.

"Did she know?" I ask.

"Mary?" Julian says. "Yes. She did."

I become hyperaware of my breath, the inhale and exhale that is supposed to be automatic now requiring an intention it didn't before. Outside, the wind rustles through naked trees, and the old bones of the house shift and groan.

I'm so glad that he found you, Rose had said. I hear the rest of her words now, the ones left unspoken because of the man who drove a knife into her back.

Someone worth dying for.

Twenty-Nine

I am back in the Ulrich Art Corridor again, except this time I'm alone. I stand in front of Rose's egg, and every crack against the shell rings like a gunshot. When it finally shatters and the imp hobbles out, its eyes are intelligent. They fix on me, wet and wide with what seems like hope. I understand, implicitly, that what it desires is acceptance. It holds out a gnarled hand for me to take.

I reach for it back.

The instant we touch, I'm struck by a feeling like an electric shock: hot, piercing, then painful beyond measure. I reach for my side; my fingers come away sticky.

Eric stands behind me. He looks the same as he did when we first met years ago, but he's somehow less handsome than I remember. I wonder, deliriously, if his nose has always been slightly off-center, if the hazel eyes I'd once found enchanting had always been so lacking in light and dimension. He drives the knife deeper, and I gasp against the spike of pain. When I look back up again, he's gone, and Leila stands in his place. When she smiles, her teeth are stained with blood.

"Found you," she sings.

A hand encloses mine, then and yanks me backward, and I fall into a firm chest. Instantly the howling in my ears quiets, and the pain eases. The air shifts, no longer clinical and cold but warm and laden with lavender.

"Shhh," Julian whispers, squeezing me close. "You're okay. I got you, okay? No one will ever hurt you again as long as I'm here."

I wake up sobbing and alone. Outside the wind is howling: a blizzard blowing through. I push aside my tear-stained pillow, and my hand jumps to my side, but there is no wound and no pain.

It was only a dream, although I'm not sure if this was one of my own making or a warning projected to me. What I do know, without a doubt, is that Julian pulled me out of it.

I don't think. I tear off my bonnet, whip the sheets off, and step out into the cool air. Ritika is sleeping in the room upstairs, but Julian took the master, and I plod across the cottage, through the living room, and knock on his door.

As expected, he's awake.

"Sean?" he calls out.

I shove open his bedroom door as he rolls to turn on his bedside lamp. I know I must be a sight, tear tracks staining my cheeks, one strap of my nightgown hanging off my shoulder.

Julian, on the other hand, is a marvel. He always has been, even now, with exhaustion weighing his features. I've seen the signs of what he wants with me. The grays that have begun to speckle his temples again, the subtle chiseling of his already sculptural features. They'd disappeared after our first night together, but in just a few short months, they're back. They make him so much more beautiful, and I'm tired of pretending not to notice.

I walk purposefully to him and sit down on his bed close to him. His hands curl into fists around his blankets, and I wonder if he's resisting the urge to hold me as he did in my dream.

"I have more questions," I tell him. "And I want the truth, Jules. Will you give that to me? Please?"

It's the first time I've called him that since he left me, and he leans toward me, giving me his undivided attention.

"Yes, of course," he whispers. "Always."

I take a deep breath, willing myself not to falter.

"I dreamt of you, the day you left." I hold his gaze, not wanting to miss even the smallest tell. "Were you really there? Or did I just make you up?"

In the dim bedroom light, his eyes shine.

"I was there," he says.

His confirmation makes my chest tight.

"Everything you said," I manage, fighting for air. "Did you mean it?"

I'm trembling. Julian swallows, and then he's cradling my face with a hand. Aside from when he hauled me out of the Corridor, it's the first time we've touched in weeks, and I almost startle at his warmth.

"Every word," he whispers.

I clasp his wrist. His hand is dry, newly calloused, and large, and I can feel his pulse pounding under my fingers. It's racing, and it gives me a thrill that I make this ancient man who has seen the world, watched empires rise and fall, *nervous.*

"What did you say, then?" I ask.

Julian tips my face up. An errant tear has crawled down my cheek and settles on the inner corner of my mouth, and he wipes it away with a caress of his thumb. In the dim room, his eyes should be dark, but they glint like obsidian shards. He looks, in this moment, like the magic he is.

"I've lived at least half a millennia," he begins. "And what I know is this: people are fundamentally the same across time, regardless of where and when they exist. They want the same things: to dominate, to amass wealth, to have indiscriminate sexual access. And to those ends, they fight, they kill one another, they adopt nonsensical ideologies and then disavow them a generation later, and they learn nothing from their forefathers' mistakes. I found them tiresome most of the time."

It's not the answer I sought, but I hang on to every word, fascinated. I am speaking, I realize, to a living, breathing fragment of history. Whose continued existence defies all reason.

"The interesting things," he continues, "those take time. Technological advancements, the birth and fostering of genius—that is multigenerational work. And for so long, I wished I could rush through time. Just get to the good parts, the things that last. Good music. Compelling art. Radio. Land lines, then cellular phones. *Internet.* Trains, then airplanes. All of it, a different sort of magic, and incredible to behold.

"And yet, I was so rarely intrigued. Even less often inspired. I used to wonder, well, what is the point of still living, of amassing wealth that always regenerates, having the same conversations day in and day out. But the interesting bits, the discovery, kept me going. I could invest in the right people and spur it along, use those few brilliant minds to help create a world worth living in. And death? Well I, like many, find it terrifying. And, like many, was willing to deny the humanity of others to my own ends." He inhales, closes his eyes. "And then Alphonse met Mary, and I met Claire."

The other woman's name makes my heart stammer.

"She was special too," I say.

"She was," Julian confirms. "I . . . didn't really understand love before her. I of course had lovers, but in the grand scheme of things, they were so short-lived, and their devotion to me was so unquestioning that we could never be on anything close to equal footing. And besides, my intentions weren't altogether pure." He gives a small, bashful grimace, as if pursuing his past lovers to feed off their lifespan was an embarrassing past lapse in judgment. "But Claire was like you, I think. So stable in her personhood that I couldn't shake it. So unrelentingly compassionate. She believed, with real conviction, that people were fundamentally good, just in need, just hurting from undressed wounds. I'd lived much too long to agree, but traversing the world with her perspective made it kinder, gentler, softer.

"I would have lived a life with her," he confesses. "It seemed like fate, that Alphonse, one of the few people on this Earth who could understand me, could find the same thing at the same time. It felt like this . . . *revelation.* That the thing we'd missed for so long, that so many of those we'd looked down on could attain so easily, was this overpowering love we could have for another being. We discovered more about ourselves in those few short years than we had in the hundreds that preceded them. That our hearts could be mortal, even if we weren't quite. And so we both decided that this was it. He'd grow old with Mary. I'd grow old with Claire. We would die, and it would be our most beautiful life yet." He takes a breath, like what he wants to say next might cost him.

"And then I lost her."

His voice cracks, his grief a wound split open.

I roll my lips into my mouth, fighting back tears as I see them form in Julian's eyes.

"What happened?" I ask.

Julian swallows, trails a hand down my arm, and twines our fingers together.

"I was attacked," he says. "It was by a group of men who lived close to her place. Her neighbors. Claire gave some of their kids free music lessons, but I looked like I had money, and they thought I'd be an easy target. I got shot. Drained one of them on reflex to survive, took care of two others, but one of them got away and got backup. But they'd seen what I was capable of, saw what I *was*. So they went after my girl instead."

I suck in a horrified breath.

"I should've gone straight to her afterward," Julian continues. "But I panicked. I'd taken so much that I looked like a teenager. And then there were the bodies; I had to figure out what to do with them. And all while I was trying to figure out how to save myself, they were . . ." He shakes his head, turning away from me. "I was lost for a long time after that. You couldn't convince me that any other human on Earth was worth a singular damn. Claire was so good. Kindhearted. She'd helped some of those guys, fed their kids during her lessons. And still. The things they did to her . . ."

The tears spill out, drip down my cheeks.

"Jules, I'm so sorry," I start, but Julian shakes his head. He is looking down at me like I am made of gold, like he has journeyed a thousand miles to find me, and when he drops his forehead to mine, our tears comingle.

"I didn't think it was possible for me to feel that way again," he says. "No. I *knew* it wasn't possible. But then I found you. Impossible Sean Sullivan. Utterly resistant to my charms. Stubborn, self-righteous—"

I snort. "Oh yes, you sound like you really like me—"

"Ferocious, vulnerable, nurturing, brilliant, and unlike anyone I've ever met in this long and fruitless life," he finishes. "You once said that I made the world a better place just by being in it. It couldn't be true. Not with the way I am. Not with the things I've done. But I want it to be, so badly, just to prove you right."

To this, I have no smart retort. Just an ache that is spreading across my chest.

"I've lied to you, and I'm not proud of that," he says. "But that night? When I told you I loved you? I meant it. Every word. Life at your side would feel meaningful enough to end."

Even expecting them, the words hit like an arrow to my heart. I don't know how to react, and so I close my eyes and nod in acceptance, run my hands over the planes of his face, down his neck and his shoulders, too delirious to do anything more than feel. Julian loves me. Our reality right now might seem unfathomable, but there is something grounding and stabilizing and *normal* about this knowledge. It's a tale as old as time, a feat both improbable and mundane: the man I love loves me back.

"Is it safe to kiss you?" I ask.

Julian lets out a breathless laugh, and then he's lifting me onto his lap like I'm a rag doll.

"Depends on what you mean by safe," he rasps. His gaze drops, very much not subtly, to the nipples poking through my thin nightgown, and I roll my eyes. *Still a man, after all.*

"I mean, am I going to die an undisclosed period of time earlier than I'm supposed to if I do," I say wryly.

Julian's expression mellows, and I smile, lifting his chin so he looks at me.

"I'm kidding," I say. "I'd probably take the risk, to be honest. Everyone in my family lives to, like, a hundred anyway. I'm sure I have some years to spare."

Julian doesn't laugh like he's supposed to.

"You don't have to 'take the risk' for a kiss," he says. "I can exercise some restraint there. But I'll be honest. I don't know if I ever slipped up with Claire. She didn't have grays and wouldn't have shown it as obviously as you did, and we didn't have enough time together for me to notice any long-term effects. This is rare, uncharted territory for me."

"Hmm," I say, tracing the edges of his full bottom lip. "How so?"

"The version of me who exists in liminal spaces? He's still *me*, just . . . less inhibited. More likely to lean into my base instincts." Julian's eyelids flutter, and he grabs my wrist to still my touch, then steels me with a look that demands me to *pay attention*. "I wasn't lying when I said I didn't mean to take from you. I didn't even realize that I had. A transfer with the connection we have, with the anticipation we've built"—he holds my hand to his chest—"it's *euphoric*. There's no other way to describe it. And when I'm in that space, it's hard to resist taking what I shouldn't."

I absorb the information with uncharacteristic calm. This, I think, is just like learning any new partner, figuring out their dos, their don'ts, the things that make them tick.

"Hard," I ponder, "but not impossible."

"It'll take trial and error," Julian says. "You'll have to resist him too. If he—*I*—asks you to give yourself to me, you have to say no."

"I say no?" I ask, leaning forward to kiss Julian on his brow, his left cheek, his right. "Even if I really, *really* want to say yes?"

Julian pulls me more firmly into his lap.

"Especially if you want to say yes," he says.

And then he kisses me, and all my remaining thoughts fall away.

I imagined our second first kiss as tentative, and it is at its start, a cautious brush of his lips against mine, as if he's not so sure about his control after all. But we've been holding back too long, have sacrificed too much, to deny ourselves this. I grab his face and drag him closer, crashing into him like a wave against a shore, and he makes a small sound of surprise before wrapping his arms around me and answering my fervor with his own. We kiss for a long time, and I marvel at how he feels both the same and so different now that I truly know him. He's no longer the oddly put together twenty-seven-year-old whom I felt just a little guilty dating, but a being who has lived lifetimes and chosen me among them. The effect he has on me—this overwhelming, drunken pleasure—isn't terrifying anymore now that I know it for what it is, a result of his ability to read me throughout layers of my subconscious. I feel like the luckiest girl in the world. I tell him so, and he lowers his head to the crook of my neck to muffle his laughter.

"You're currently in mortal danger because of me," he reminds me, incredulous.

"Yes, but I'm *also* guaranteed at least one earth-shattering orgasm a day," I counter. "It's not the world's best deal, but you won't catch me complaining."

Julian nuzzles into me, pulling my skin between his teeth.

"Just one?" he teases. "I'm quite sure I did better than that last time."

I roll my eyes and wind my arms around his neck, savoring being held, and he squeezes me so tight that I have to fight for air. We stay like this a while, until, without preamble, the mood shifts. I adjust myself on his lap, he rocks his hips up, and suddenly I'm hyperaware of the hardness underneath me, the way our breaths begin to heighten. I reach between us, close my hand around him, and he stills.

"Are you sure?" he whispers. "We don't have to try this right now."

"I want to," I say.

"I don't want to hurt you again," he whispers.

"You won't." Now that I understand the mechanics, I feel oddly confident. I pull my nightgown over my shoulders and watch his Adam's apple bob in his throat. "I trust you."

Julian exhales slowly, his eyes roving over my body like a starving man presented with a feast. He smooths his hands down my sides, starting high at my rib cage before settling at my hips. His expression is inscrutable: desire, sure, but something akin to sorrow too, like I've just handed him a gift he doesn't think he deserves.

"Thank you," he murmurs, before kissing me again.

We start slow, an unhurried rediscovery of each other's bodies. Julian's concentration is evident in the serious set of his jaw, and when I joke that he looks like he's taking an exam he pays me back by sliding down my body to take me into his mouth. My head drops back, eyes squeeze shut; I don't think I will ever get used to the rapture this man makes me feel. I run my hand adoringly along the back of his head, and in the darkness of my closed lids, I feel *him* emerge.

"You sought me out," his voice says, echoing all around me. "Even after everything."

We're still on the bed, layered upon ourselves like afterimages, except I am back in this Julian's lap, looking him in his shining eyes. I've been thinking of Julian as two entities, the one that walks with me in flesh, the other that haunts my dreams, but this one stares at me with the other's wondrous adoration. It's true that this is the Julian who stole away a piece of me, but he is also the one who cried for my forgiveness on his hands and knees, who tore me out of a nightmare just minutes before.

"I did," I whisper.

He clutches my face, searches it with an openness that turns him young.

"You love me too, right?" he asks. "It isn't just me?"

I haven't realized until he asks that I haven't said it back, and that this Julian is not too proud to seek reassurance.

"I love you too," I tell him truthfully. "But I'm scared."

"Of me," he says, knowing.

"Yes," I confess.

He gathers me into his arms and I gasp; his counterpart has pushed into mine, and I can feel the sensation like a distant, blissful fullness. The Julian before me tenses, squeezes his eyes shut, and I know that he's feeling what I'm feeling, fighting the base instincts that tell him to augment his gratification the way he knows best, the way he always has.

"Your life is yours, and mine too," he says. "Just. Stay here with me like this?"

We hold each other close, breathing in tandem, hands curled together as the versions of us made of flesh tangle, and this Julian of my dreams does not once demand his sacrifice.

We wake up the next morning in a mess of sheets and limbs. White light streams in through between the crack of Julian's curtains, and I roll in his arms, knowing that I'll meet his gaze when I turn. He's watching me carefully, like I'm a skittish cat he's worried he'll scare away. I sense, implicitly, that what he's searching for in my face is regret.

I rub a thumb into the furrow of his brow, feel his whole body relax under one touch. The morning light outlines him in white like a fallen angel. He takes my hand, kisses my palm, my fingers, the ridge of my knuckles.

"You need to tell me what your plan is," I say softly. "How you intend to get me back home. Because I'm not staying here forever."

I don't know what kind of life Mary led before she met Alphonse, but as idyllic as the quiet, secluded life that was laid out in their photo albums appeared, it is not one I aspire to. I want to savor every last minute that I have left with my aging dog. I want my stressful, fulfilling, bloody job, cock-blocking pager and all. I want to take my goddaughter for ice cream to talk about her crushes and check off more countries on the travel list with Winona. And I want Brandon to survive long enough to see his daughter go to prom.

I want Julian too. Every inch of my soul swiveled in his direction when he left, every thought either engineered to avoid thinking of him or consumed by questions of "what if," "where," "why" that I couldn't let go until I ended up at his side again. I want to be with him more than I've wanted anyone, and I've stopped caring whether it's because of some supernatural hold he has over me or because he sees me so completely.

But not at the expense of the life I've worked so hard to build. Not at the expense of *me*.

"I'm working something out with Ritika," Julian says, pensive. "Leila doesn't have the assets I do. Her income has mostly consisted of funds she's inherited from her victims. She never really held an interest in investing like I did, and she doesn't have Rose's art to funnel funds into. Because she avoids aging, she can't easily pretend to be her own descendant, and her protectiveness over her identity has meant that she doesn't have a clear agent for an estate. Given that she'll need to relocate soon, I—" He clams up abruptly, and I sit up, alarmed by his sudden reticence when we have been so open.

"Relocate?" I ask. "Why would she need to relocate?"

Julian doesn't respond. He's squinting into the distance, his lips curled against his teeth as if to keep his words from escaping.

We steep in an uncomfortable silence, stuck at an impasse until I finally step boldly over the line. I surprise myself by not being angry, only resolute. I have nothing to lose here anymore.

"I have spent the last six months thinking that I was losing my mind because of secrets you withheld," I remind him. "If you and I are going to work, you can't hide anything from me. Not anymore."

The old home's radiators groan awake, adding a howling gravity to my words. *And if I find out you have,* I hope he hears, *I will leave you.*

I can see him processing—or perhaps more accurately, stewing on—my words. He doesn't want to tell me this part, but I take the gamble that he wants to lose me less, and win. Julian rolls, with a sigh, onto his back.

"Brandon's dying quicker than Leila thought he would," he admits. "His diagnosis threw her for a loop. I don't know whether he's still alive or not right now, but I imagine that it's not long before she finishes with him and prepares to move on."

Leila, he explains, has the fewest moral qualms about her lifestyle. She prefers to stay young, perpetually living in her twenties, and amasses her fortune like a black widow: by targeting working rich men, well respected in their professions but not particularly well-known, marrying them, draining them of their means over a period of ten to fifteen years, and moving to a new place to start over with a new identity. She keeps a few other extramarital partners in her thrall as well for protection, finding highly susceptible targets who are content with getting rare attention from a beautiful woman in exchange for managing her more unsavory tasks—"like the shooter," Julian explains. It's a gambit that has gotten more difficult in the last few years with the advent of digital databases and anti-counterfeit technology, but it's one she intends to continue.

"I have resources that can make the transition easier for her," Julian continues. "If I offer them to her, help her cover her bases and forge a new identity . . . there's a good chance she'll let us be."

There are too many *ifs* in Julian's solution for my comfort.

"I watched Leila slaughter a room full of people for the crime of being in the wrong place at the wrong time, and I'm guessing that wasn't her first rodeo," I say. "Do you really think *negotiating* with her is the answer?"

"Leila is my sister," Julian tells me. "And we have been through so much together. At the end of the day, even if she grumbles, she wants me to be happy."

I'm not so sure. I think of the painting in Julian's living room, hundreds of miles away. *Together.* Leila, grinning into the sun as Alphonse looks down at them with bemusement. If they are truly like siblings, she has already lost one brother to his human lover. Will she be so willing to lose a second? Or would she think the way I quietly do—*You found someone to love once. You will find another.*

"And what about Brandon?" I ask.

Julian gives me a glum look.

"To be honest, I don't give a damn about Brandon," he says.

A chill goes down my spine. Watching Julian interact with the Ghoshals, hearing him proclaim his love for me—all of that led me to briefly forget that he's not a man who holds human life in high regard. That my life is far from the first he's taken pieces of. If I hadn't meant something to him, he might have left me on the floor of Ulrich Corridor, watched Leila carry out her atrocity, and done little more than cluck his tongue and offer his *services* to make her sins disappear.

"She's already taken so much from him. She can let him at least have a fighting chance with whatever time he has left," I insist. A lucid moment with Sophie. A final few steps on his own. "He didn't deserve this, Julian. If you plan to talk to her anyway, can you at least ask about him?" *If,* I wonder, *he's still alive?*

I can feel Julian's stare burning the side of my face.

"I don't understand why you care so much," he says. "He wasn't a good friend to you. He was a terrible partner to your best friend. He might have been a good doctor, but there'll be another one in his position in three months. What does it matter if he's dead? He's already served his purpose."

His last sentence flash freezes the blood in my veins. It's been a long time since I've felt this primordial fear around Julian, like I'm a common mouse who was meant to be dinner dropped into his snake pen, waiting to be consumed by the glittering, gorgeous creature that curls lovingly into my warmth but still opens his jaws wide every night for my brethren. I want to ask what Julian thought Brandon's "purpose" was. Caring for patients? Fathering Sophie? Or feeding his praying mantis of a sister?

Suddenly, putting my life in Julian's hands feels reckless. I've done this before, I think, trusted someone I loved long after they showed me who they were, and I already know how that turned out for me. Bleeding, alone, my world fading in and out of existence, *I wonder how long it'll take for someone to find me—*

"Sean," Julian interrupts, and I jolt back into reality. He reaches for my hand, and when I twine our fingers together, I realize that he's trembling. "Please. I'm sorry. That was insensitive. Of course I'll ask about Brandon."

His panic grounds me. Julian might not care about most human life, but he does care about mine, and for now, that may have to be enough. I trace the paths of the veins curling in the back of his hand, drop my head to his shoulder.

"I'm the one whose life is in danger, so why are you stressed out?" I murmur.

"Because you're a smart woman, and we both know you should be running far away from me," Julian says. "And I think I'm waiting for you to wise up and do just that."

I sigh. It is agonizing, what I feel for this man. Sometimes I wonder if he's wrong, if I'm at least partially in his thrall, because I need him to the point of distraction. To the point of destruction.

"Love is reckless at baseline," I murmur. "I would just prefer if it didn't regularly put me in mortal danger."

"I'm sorry—" Julian starts again, but I cut him off.

"Don't tell me you're sorry," I say. "Involve me. Reassure me. Tell me that there's no stone you'll leave unturned to make this right."

"Of course," Julian says. "I'm willing to do anything—*everything*—to keep you safe."

I lift my head to look into the face of my beloved. His features are darkened with conviction. He means it, and I know that.

"Would you kill her?" I ask. "If it came to that? Would you kill your sister to save me?"

Julian's jaw tightens, but he doesn't hesitate with his answer.

"She's lived a long time," he whispers. "You haven't."

It's exactly what I need to hear.

Thirty

Ritika is already awake when we emerge from the bedroom, tapping away at her laptop and sipping from a comically large coffee mug.

"I see you've made up," she deadpans.

Julian rolls his eyes.

"Have you sent it?" he asks dryly, then drops into the chair next to her.

I can tell that they've been working together for a long time by the way Ritika only has to look to Julian to get the answer to her silent question of *Is it okay if she hears?* She drags one of the kitchen chairs closer with her foot, and beckons for me to join.

"I was waiting for you to give me the go-ahead," she says. "Take a look."

What we are looking at is a series of spreadsheets and documents that make up the detailed proposals that Ritika and Julian intend to present to Leila. I've spent most of my life gaining increasingly more specialized knowledge of the human body, and so my financial literacy is garbage, but what I do know is that the sums of money being thrown around are dizzyingly immense. It is stunning to see firsthand in dollars and cents what Julian thinks a life with me is worth.

"This is insane," I say, panicked. "It's too much, Julian."

Ritika gives me a sympathetic smile.

"He thought you'd say that," she says.

"Because it's true!" I turn to Julian. "Jules, you can't do this."

Julian reaches for my hand.

"I *am* doing it," he says. "It's just money. It'll come back. And I'll have more than enough left over for us to be comfortable."

"What about you?" I ask Ritika. "What about your family?"

Ritika leans back in her chair and stretches.

"My family has been waiting for Julian to die for generations," she says plainly. I gasp, but Julian doesn't blink. "It's a curse, living the way he does. And not just because of how he stays alive, but how he's forced to live, like a bystander. We're all thrilled that he's chosen you. And besides, he's got a separate trust for us that can only be accessed when the 'Conrads' die out."

I swallow back tears. There's a weight on my chest; I've never experienced love so overpowering that it makes me feel like a burden. What if Julian realizes that I'm not worth this investment? What if the fulfillment he seeks isn't in me after all?

I sit quietly as Ritika and Julian talk through logistics. It's hard not to be impressed by the level of detail they've put into their plan: overseas accounts, secret trusts, LLCs, properties spread out across the world that Julian intends to offer up. They've already sent a brief proposal to Leila, who was evidently intrigued enough to agree to meet in person in Chicago, meaning he'll have to leave us behind in the safe house for a couple of days while he travels there and back.

"Ritika's tough," Julian says. "You'll be in good hands."

The first time we'd met, I'd noticed Ritika's build: like she lives in the gym and never skips upper body. She catches me looking, winks, and flexes an impressive bicep.

"I've got good aim too," she says. When I raise an eyebrow, she lifts her oversized tank to reveal a handgun tucked into a holster at her waistband.

I stare at it, aghast, as my ears ring with memories of gunfire, splatters of blood against glass.

"Hopefully we won't need that," I say in a small voice.

"It's just a precaution," Julian says. He stands. "Speaking of."

He hustles back into the bedroom, then emerges later with a small tote bag. When I see the contents, I laugh out loud.

"Do I have to be cute for house arrest?" I say, turning over the package of nude-colored short press-on nails, not unlike the ones I'd popped off my fingers over the last couple of days.

"They're a tracking device," Julian says. Prototypes, he goes on to explain, from a woman-owned company based out of South Africa that's been working on developing GPS navigation microtechnology with the idea of making it easier to locate people who have been kidnapped, trafficked, or killed. The chips, he explains, are embedded in the thumbs.

"Morbid," I say with a whistle as Julian pulls out a second box, the "decoy": a yellow gold necklace with a heart-shaped pendant the size of a small button.

"The nails are less noticeable, but they're buggy," he explains as he fastens it around my neck. "They go dark every now and then. The necklace is more likely to work, but also much more likely to be taken off you. Ritika and Aditya will have your location at all times. If something happens and we get separated, they'll help me track you."

I look down to where the pendant nestles against my chest. Julian's been thorough; that much is undeniable. But that also tells me that he's scared. He knows his sister. The depths she'll go to guard their secret.

Leila's face pops into my mind. Teeth stained red. Blood dripping down her chin.

"It'll be okay," I say out loud, a prayer.

"It'll be okay," Julian repeats.

Julian leaves the next morning and takes my resolve with him.

"Ritika will handle meals and any logistics. There's another truck in the garage if you guys need to leave, but otherwise try to stay on the property," he says, standing at the threshold of the cottage with his carry-on bag in one hand and my waist in the other. "We're both going to feel like shit for a bit. Tylenol. Hydration. Rest. You know the drill."

"Ah, to be literally addicted to my hot supernatural boyfriend," I deadpan. Julian rolls his eyes affectionately.

"We have to celebrate, once we're back home," he says, "Find a restaurant that'll let us bring Onix and buy him a steak."

"I'll put him in his Sunday best for the occasion." I'm trying to stay strong, but watching Julian leave reinforces the gravity of our situation: he's returning to our home to negotiate for my life. He's also agreed to inquire after Brandon, but when I requested he give Winona an update on my whereabouts, he hesitated. *You don't want Leila to suspect that Winona knows anything about us*, he insisted. *It's best if we remain a bit distant for now.* And he's going alone. No Ritika to watch his back, no Aditya because that might put the Ghoshals at risk. Just my Jules, walking willingly into a lion's den.

"Stay safe," I tell him. Dread is building in the pit of my belly, the harrowing feeling that this goodbye might be our last. He leans down at the same time that I boost myself up, and even though I know he doesn't have time to spare, I hook my hands under his jaw to bind him to me. Tears I've been holding back trickle between my fingers, and he puts his bag aside to return my fervor. I can feel the warmth of his other self hovering just above us, see him behind my closed eyes like a prism.

"I love you," Dream Julian says as his counterpart kisses me. "More than life itself. I hope you know."

"I do," I say out loud, against his lips. "And I love you too. So make sure to come back to me."

"I always seem to manage that," my Julian says, pulling back, and against all odds, we both grin.

Then he lets me go, gives Ritika a nod, piles into the SUV, and drives off.

The first twenty-four hours without Julian are the worst. Physically, I'm almost instantly sick as shit, with pounding headaches and a stomach that refuses to settle. Mentally, I'm worse. I knew, rationally, that I would have to reckon with the trauma of what happened in Ulrich Corridor and what is currently happening now, but I didn't realize how much I'd been distracting myself with my anger with Julian to avoid confronting the horror of the last few days. Ritika tries to help, baking us a sumptuous cardamom pear upside-down cake that leaves the house smelling like the inside of a patisserie and asking me strategically safe questions about my past to avoid triggering a meltdown. We stay up late watching *Dirty Dancing* on VHS, laugh when she asks whether Baby's dad accurately represents most cardiologists. She doesn't ask questions when I start crying during the famous lift scene, just pauses the movie to bring me a mug of chamomile.

By the next day, I'm feeling as well as I can be, under the circumstances. I wake up early to a steely gray sky and light streaming through my window, change into one of the tracksuits that Julian bought for me. I grab the Walkman I dug out from Alphonse's daughter's dresser alongside an old Enya cassette, then step out into the living area. It's eerily quiet; Ritika is still asleep upstairs.

It'll be a short jog, I tell myself as I step out into the cool, fresh air. Just around the perimeter of the cottage's two-acre property. Close enough that I can run back for help if I need it. Movement after so many days of cramped car rides and heavy meals feels like a luxury, and I sigh with relief as my muscles stretch and contract. Out here, it's so peaceful that I can almost believe that I'm living in a snow globe, my world starting and ending at the rim that I circle over and over before calling it quits and heading back inside.

The moment I reach the door I sense that something is amiss. I almost certainly locked it before I left, but when I reach for the knob, it turns. I step back, study the grounds. There are no other footsteps in the snow, no cars idling at the base of the driveway. I've circled the property multiple times; I would have seen someone come in.

"You're being paranoid," I tell myself out loud, even as my stomach twists itself into knots. "No one is here."

A familiar scent assaults my nostrils as I enter the cottage. It's sharp, metallic, so overpowering that trepidation freezes me in place before my mind can label it for what it is.

Ritika.

I force myself to take one step, then another. And then I see her. Her body sprawled brokenly on the floor. Blood pooling under an unseen wound. It's coming from her head. Her expression isn't twisted in pain, but slack, oh god—

"Hi, Sean," a saccharine, sweet voice calls from the kitchen. "How was your run?"

Thirty-One

Leila is sitting, legs crossed, at the dining room table. She sips from a large, hand-painted pink mug that says "#1 Mom" in chicken-scratch lettering and flips idly through one of Alphonse's photo albums. Dressed in a chunky baby-blue oversized sweater and leggings, with her tawny hair secured in a ponytail by a large cream scrunchie, she looks every bit the picture of the kind-hearted girl next door who hand-delivers her neighbors tins of gingerbread for the holidays. It's this air of innocence, I think, that makes her most terrifying. When she looks up from the album to smile at me, I can almost convince myself that she's happy to see an old friend. I watch as she slides a photograph from its sleeve: one of my favorites, of an elderly Alphonse and Mary holding hands across the space of their corresponding rocking chairs on the back veranda.

"Can you imagine giving up immortality for *this*?" she says, disgusted. "He used to be so beautiful. I don't get it."

I spring to Ritika's body. I feel for her pulse. Weak, slow, but still there. She's alive.

"Relax, she isn't dead," Leila confirms, annoyed. She beckons to the table. "Sit."

It's a command that might be followed by a consequence if I don't obey. I collapse bonelessly into the chair across from her, my heart leaping into my throat.

"Ritika doesn't know anything," I say quickly. "There's no need to finish her off."

Leila sneers.

"Please don't insult my intelligence," she snips. "And don't worry. She's too useful for me to kill right now. I'd love to learn a bit more about her, when she wakes up."

I focus on my breathing. Keep it steady to keep my panic at bay.

"How did you find us?" I ask.

Leila's smile is self-satisfied, like she's been waiting for me to ask.

"Julian's smart, but he's so sentimental," she says. "He's got all these properties, but he just *had* to take you to this one. Like I wouldn't know about it? Guess he didn't think Alphonse's wife would send me an invitation to his funeral." Rage flashes across her features, there and gone between blinks. "He hid himself from me, you know, when he chose this human life. Cut me out entirely. Didn't even let me say goodbye. It was very kind of her to try to correct my brother's cruelty posthumously. I didn't go, of course, but it came in useful."

I swallow. My whole body shudders with existential fear as Leila appraises me, her gaze sliding from the top of my head down to my trembling hands.

"Are you going to kill me?" I ask.

"Of course," Leila says, matter-of-fact. "I have to. Bad things happen when humans find out about us. I know the boys have been very casual about it, but that's because the consequences look really different for them. They slip up, they're considered gods. Rose and I? Well, you saw. We get the whole 'Witches, burn them at the stake' treatment." She taps her nails against the table, and they clack, one by one, like a metronome. “I promise I’ll put you down easy. For what it’s worth, I really liked you. You’re very interesting. I get why Julian lost his sense over you.”

The compliment flies over my head; I’m focused instead on how to get out of this. As far as I know, Julian has no other supernatural powers, no preternatural strength or offensive abilities aside from the ones he’s built for himself over the years. Leila can drain me, sure, but she’s already quite young as it is—too much and she’ll turn herself into a child like Rose did. As it stands, she’s shorter and slighter than I am. If this comes down to a battle of brute force, I could take her.

Leila’s grin widens, and she claps her hands together in amusement.

“Oh my god, are you sizing me up right now?” she says. Her giggle is high, shrill, and sends chills down my spine. “Ugh, you’re so cute.” She twists in her chair. “Robbie? Can you come in, baby?”

The back door opens, and a hulking man steps through. He is broad chested and bald, and the skin on the back of his head folds over itself. His face is obscured behind a mask.

Strapped across his chest: a gun.

Blood splashing against the glass. Harold’s wide-open grimace, his mouth still forming around his cries for help. Eyes lifeless and dead.

My body moves before I can stop it, because I can’t just sit here waiting to die, can’t just let her snuff me out—

I hear a click. “Robbie” has lifted his gun, and the barrel is trained on me.

“I wouldn’t run if I were you,” Leila says. “Robbie here’s a former Navy SEAL; he’ll catch you pretty quick. And I don’t want that, because I have the most fabulous end planned for you!”

She pulls out her phone, makes a call, and I hear the tone of a video call being answered.

“Hey, Leila,” a sweet, sullen voice responds.

Time slows. I feel like a giant has grabbed me by the middle and is crushing me in his grasp.

Because it's Sophie.

Oh my god, *she has Sophie.*

"Hi, sweetheart," Leila says. Her expression has changed completely, glee making way for a pitying pout and watery eyes so quickly that it gives me whiplash. "How are you hanging in there?"

"I'm okay," Sophie says. "We've been coloring. Mom hasn't woken up yet though."

Leila's eyes flicker up to me as if to ascertain that I've captured that bit of information, and of course I have: Winona is with them too.

"I know things are hard right now but you've been a very brave girl," Leila is saying, and I hear her as if from a distance, her voice slowed and stretched out. "But anyway! I called because I have a surprise for you!"

"What is it?" she asks unenthusiastically.

Without warning, Leila turns the camera to me, and I have to fight the terror off my face. It's Sophie all right, sitting on a plush teal carpet and surrounded by markers. In the distance, another young girl draws swirls on a piece of paper while she swings her legs. She glances up, eyes catching mine, then ducks away almost sheepishly as Sophie gapes at the screen, and I suddenly understand why Sophie said "we."

Rose.

"Auntie Sean?" Sophie says in disbelief, then the phone rises until her face fills the screen. She looks tired, wan, her normally riotous curls hanging limply around her face. "Auntie Sean! Oh my gosh, you're okay!"

"Y-yes, nugget," I say weakly.

"Mom got called by the doggy daycare that you didn't come back for Onix, and you weren't answering your phone, and we thought something happened," she cries. "We went and got him, don't worry, but you were missing, and nobody knew where you'd gone, and we were so scared—"

"Sean just went on a little vacation without telling you," Leila supplies for me. "Blizzard took out some cell towers and made the drive back unsafe, but I finally got in touch with Julian this morning and came straight down to check on her!" Her gaze catches mine, as if to seek praise for her decent alibi. "But she's safe, and she'll actually be coming with us."

Tears drip down Sophie's chin, and she gets to her feet, heading toward the door.

"I have to go tell Mom," she declares.

Across from me and out of sight of her stepdaughter, Leila rolls her eyes, then turns the camera back to herself.

"We'll call her when we're on the way, okay?" she says. "My battery's about to die."

"O-okay," Sophie says uncertainly, and Leila waves, hangs up, and puts her phone face down on the table.

My world feels like it's tilted on its axis, like it's been flattened into a disc and I'm about to fall off the edge. The people I love the most: Winona, Sophie, even Onix, gathered in one place. And Brandon . . . well. Sophie's state told me everything I needed to know.

"Is he dead?" I ask.

Leila takes a sip of her tea and nods.

"Two days ago," she supplies. "Don't worry. We're planning a good send-off."

I keep waiting for a miracle. For me to gain the ability to travel backward in time to the day a cheerful Leila first appeared in our cath lab, call up her boss, and demand she be sent elsewhere to terrorize someone else. Or, if this was meant to be our fate all along, for Julian to burst through these doors, finish Robbie off John Wick style, and force Leila to deliver my family back to me.

But instead I'm here, hopeless as a gecko in a sticky trap, and Brandon is dead, and I hardly have the space to mourn because his ex-wife and kid might be next.

"They don't know anything." No amount of strength can keep my voice from trembling, and for once, I don't care that Leila can see that I'm scared. "Winona and Sophie. I haven't told them a thing."

"I know that. They're obviously just bait," Leila says, bemused. "Look, I'll keep this simple for you. Winona and Sophie don't have to die. They're sweethearts, as you know, and they think that I've rented a cute little cabin out of town to bond over shared loss. So let's make this easy. You get in the car with Robbie, and we do a nice little exchange. Your bestie and her daughter get to go free. And you . . . ?" A tear drifts down my cheek, and Leila reaches across the table to catch it on her thumb. She looks down at the liquid as if it fascinates her, then sucks it into her mouth. "Well, you know."

I die. For some reason, this knowledge doesn't strike the fear it had minutes before. After all, I should be dead already. These few extra days were simply borrowed time.

"I'll come with you," I gasp. "I'll come, so please—"

"Wonderful," Leila interrupts. She springs to her feet. "Let's get you ready to go."

The first thing Leila has me do is strip naked. In the name of my dignity, she makes Robbie wait outside the door but checks me over with the clinical attention of a devoted dermatologist searching for a cancerous spot. My necklace is the first thing to go, flung carelessly onto my bed, but she doesn't think to comment on my nails, and I have to school my face to keep my triumph from being seen.

The change of clothes she brings for me is a size too big. I've lost weight since we've last seen each other, a consequence of my bouts of Julian-induced withdrawals. The material of the pullover she's given me is luxuriously soft; a peek at the label reveals it to be 100 percent cashmere. It goes on like a prison jumpsuit.

They lead me wordlessly away from Ritika's supine body, through the kitchen door, onto the veranda, and to the edge of the woods, Leila skipping in front, Robbie lugging menacingly behind. I follow her like a ghost, because I will be one soon. I know what comes next, after allowing myself to be moved to a secondary location. I've read *The Gift of Fear* cover to cover, watched enough true crime documentaries to recognize that I am walking into my casket.

I wonder how long it will take for Julian to come looking for me. If he'll realize he's been fooled and will make it home fast enough to get Ritika help. If he'll ever forgive me for going willingly.

We get to a clearing, where a small hatchback is waiting, and Robbie steps in close behind me.

"Hey, so," Leila says, producing a strip of fabric from her pocket. "We can't have you know where we're going. And I'll be having some conversations that I'm not sure you should be privy to."

Numb, I bend to let Leila tie my blindfold. She winds it over my eyes, then squeezes the knot tight.

I suspect what happens next and close my eyes to steel myself against the accelerated whoosh of my heartbeat. They won't kill me here. Leila wouldn't go through all the trouble of putting on these theatrics just to off me on the edge of the woods.

"You're going to knock me out, right?" I say to the darkness. "Go ahead. Do it. But if I may, go for under my chin, or temple. I'll actually lose consciousness that way."

Robbie doesn't respond. I haven't heard him speak once, but his breath rattles behind me. I'm about to suggest they invest in chloroform like old-timey cartoon villains when suddenly a dizzying, smarting pain echoes between my ears.

Robbie has chosen temple after all.

Thirty-Two

Sean.

Sean. What happened? Where are you?

I'm standing in our white room again. My head throbs something fierce. I've been hit, I remember. By what, I'm not sure, except that it was heavy and metal and left my ears ringing like a struck bell. An aluminum baseball bat? A shovel? The butt of a gun? I can hear Julian, but when I look out into the distance all I see is endless nothing.

She hurt you, his voice echoes.

"Julian?" I call out. My teeth chatter; I'm so scared. "Jules, I'm sorry. You have to go back. Ritika's hurt. And I left her. I had no choice; I had to go with them. She has Winona and Sophie, and I couldn't . . . she's going to kill me, but it's the only way—"

Listen to me, Julian interrupts. Even in my head, he sounds fierce. *I will not let that happen. Okay? You will die someday, Sean Sullivan, but it will not be today, tomorrow, or the day after that. I will find you. So keep fighting.*

Tears streak my face. It feels so bleak, but I nod anyway, and when I open my eyes again it is to an incomplete darkness. I know

I'm awake by the way the distant pain in my temple becomes panging and acute, by the iron taste of my breath. My arms are tied tightly behind my back; when I try to spread my legs, I realize those are bound too. I'm in motion; wheels are bumping underneath me, but the vehicle is otherwise quiet. My kidnappers are not chatty.

I don't know how much longer we drive, just that the sky is dark when we finally stop. I need to pee something terrible, but I'm too scared to speak.

Leila does it for me.

"We're here," she says. "Will you promise to behave?"

I swallow against a gravel throat. Wherever we are, Sophie and Winona are too, and they've been fed a story that I have come willingly. Any sign that I've been coerced might put them in danger.

"Yes," I say hoarsely.

I hear the hum of a powered car seat being pushed backward, the metallic twang of a knife slicing through air. There is a tug, then a release. My arms are free. The relief is instant; I have been so distracted by my fear that I barely noticed that my shoulders have locked. I roll them as my captors loosen my blindfold, and then my passenger door is being opened, and I am being escorted out.

I blink, scrunch my face to bring back its feeling, and examine my surroundings.

We're nestled in the forest in front of a charming log cabin. A large pile of chopped logs leans against the side of the home, and there's a wood picnic bench out front, but it is otherwise nondescript, the kind of place that may or may not have running water. There are no street signs, precious few lights, and no evidence of civilization beyond the clearing in which we stand. It hasn't snowed here, and the weather is even warmer than at Alphonse and Mary's cottage; we must be farther south. I glance up at the night sky and suck in a breath: it's alight with an explosion of stars, clusters of galaxies that the light pollution of the city would snuff out.

"Isn't it adorable?" Leila says, beaming. "Brandon bought it for me."

She's goading me, and if there wasn't a hulking armed man standing next to her, I might have fallen for it. And then I freeze, because I hear something in the distance: a series of rhythmic thumps, growing faster and closer, a heavy, inhuman pant. Then, a sound so familiar that my body recognizes it before my mind does: a clatter of claws skittering against wood.

"Onix?" I say, disbelieving, just as a hefty gray body lunges for mine. Onix is one wiggling, whining muscle, leaping for my face to lick, bringing me down to my knees with his enthusiasm. I'm still overwhelmed with conflicting feelings of joy and despair when another body slams into mine.

"Auntie Sean!"

Sophie's eyes are red rimmed from crying and her nose is crusted with dried snot, and she's still the most beautiful child I've ever seen. I heft both my babies into my arms, crushing them to me as if to prove what I see with touch. They're alive, warm, whole.

Then I hear another voice call out to me, and the crunch of her feet against the mulch as Winona turns the corner and races toward us, feel the impact as she collides into us.

Sobs wrack my body, ripping out of me with such violence that they ache on the way out. In truth, I have been so stupid. Winona and Sophie, who have nothing to do with this, are in danger right now due to my own selfish desire for *answers*. By going to Rose's show to seek Julian out, I'd bartered their safety for my own chance at a happily ever after.

And worse, they don't know. They didn't consent to the peril I've placed them in. They're happy to see me, when they should be the ones to put the gun to my head and pull the trigger.

"You scared us, Sean," Winona says. Her hug is the tightest, a brief breath-stealing squeeze. "You really, really scared us."

"I'm sorry," I say, gathering my wits about me. *You don't know how much.*

Winona pulls back to search my face, and I search hers too. She looks exhausted, but intact.

"I'm glad to see you safe, but we need to talk," she says stonily. "Did Leila already tell you about Brandon?"

I look over my shoulder at Leila. She's watching us with an appropriately sorrowful expression, and loathing rises like acid in my throat.

"Yes," I manage through gritted teeth. "I can't believe he's gone. I'm sorry I wasn't there for it."

Winona doesn't respond, just fixes me with a gaze that is one part worried and another wry. Then she straightens, puffs out her chest. "You've had a long journey. Let's get you inside. Robbie said he's cooking something good for us tonight."

"I've got braised short ribs and cornbread going," Robbie says. It's the first time I've heard him speak, and I'm surprised to hear a thick Southern drawl. He lowers his mask to reveal a thick brown beard and gives me a toothy grin. "I hear it's your favorite."

I have to fight to hold back a sardonic laugh, because I'm not quite sure how Leila knew that it's precisely what I'd choose for a last meal.

Sophie grabs my hand and leads me inside the cabin. It's quaint and larger than it looks from the outside, with a cowhide rug draped across the floor, an old wooden console piano that probably needs tuning, and rustic but chic decorations—paintings that I now recognize as Margaret West's but not Rose Callahan's style, cute knickknacks in the shapes of small animals. As I get my tour, I learn several things: that Sophie and Winona believe they are on a grief retreat, that Robbie, the Navy SEAL who pointed an assault weapon at my head earlier today, is posing as Leila's hired cook and housekeeper, and that "Rosie," the thirteen-year-old girl who looks balefully up at me from the living room recliner, is Leila's young adopted cousin.

"Nice to meet you," Rose says. In this form, her foxlike features are more pronounced; it feels strange to know for a fact that she will someday grow into her too-big ears and pointed chin. She struggles to hold my gaze when I take her hand. I recognize her expression for what it is: guilt. "Sophie was really worried about you."

I squeeze her hand hard, and to her credit, she doesn't flinch away from my hold.

"She's a good kid," I tell her.

Rose bites her bottom lip, swinging her gaze to look out through the window into an endless night. Then she propels herself out of the chair.

"I'll show you your room," she says. "Me and Soph got it ready for you when we heard you were coming."

"We just made the bed, nothing special," Sophie insists, falling into step with Rose. I watch them, tense, but Rose is gentle with Sophie, accepting her hand when she reaches for it as they take me down the hall, Onix padding behind us.

My room is small, but well furnished, with a large vanity, a queen-sized bed—"I switched the comforter with mine, because I know you like green," Sophie declares proudly—and a trunk at its foot that I open to find dog food and toys. Sophie sticks to me like a burr, and I observe how she's changed in the short time that I've been away, regressing back to the days when she would cling to her trusted adults so closely that we'd trip over her. Even though she's yapping away, telling me all about her talented new friend, the cabin's extensive collection of art supplies, and the mirrored closet doors that make it easier for her to practice her dance moves, there is a desperation in her cadence that confirms to me that her world has been upended. There was a time when Sophie was a daddy's girl. When her favorite time of day was when her dad, who worked longer, less flexible hours than her mom, came home and launched her into the air. Now she has to live in a world in which he is only a memory, the once unquestionable certainty of his existence now broken.

"Let her rest, Sophie," Winona says. When I turn, she's leaning against the doorframe, watching us with her arms crossed. "She's probably had a hard time the last few days, and it was a long drive. She'll come back out for dinner."

Her gaze flickers reflexively to my hands. I look at them, then hurriedly tug down my sleeves: dark bruises have blossomed around my wrists. Our eyes meet, and her brow raises in a subtle but grave question, and I recognize, with horror, that what I've been seeing in my best friend's face isn't just grief, but unease. *Shit.* Those sharp instincts that can pick up on her clients' subtle emotional shifts are going to get us in trouble.

Luckily, Sophie doesn't seem to notice.

"Oh," she says, walking to the door. "Sorry."

"Don't worry, nugget," I say. "I'll be out soon."

Winona ushers Sophie to the kitchen, but Rose lingers, watching me like a ghoul from the door. When they are out of sight, she closes it behind her, and I exhale, relieved to be able to end my performance.

To my surprise, Onix walks over to her and nudges Rose's hand with his nose. I watch as she scratches behind his ears.

"He's very sweet," she observes. "We don't keep pets. Their lifespans are so short that losing them doesn't seem worth it."

I don't want to think about Onix's eventual demise, especially with mine so imminent.

"Alphonse had cats," I say. "Bunnies too, at some point."

"Alphonse had a lot of things the rest of us haven't," she says. Her mouth thins into a line. "I'm sorry. I tried to convince her not to do this."

It's Margaret West's confident cadence, coming from a spindly thirteen-year-old girl's mouth.

"So you don't think I should die," I say blithely.

"No," Rose confirms. "Julian has offered everything to keep you. He's always been willing to help us, you know, but his wealth has never been *ours*. We're women. We've only been able to keep our own property reliably in the last fifty years or so. He's got a head start centuries long, but he was willing to give it up for you, and that more than anything made me see that he was serious about this. I don't mean the money—it's never been about wealth, for him. It's about what it enabled him to do. He's always struggled the most with the question of his existence, you know. By being able to promote innovation, he gives himself meaning."

I know this, but hearing Rose reiterate it so plainly still sends me reeling. That Julian is willing to throw his entire life's work down the drain for a few meager decades by my side leaves me with an indescribable feeling. It's not joy, exactly, but something stickier, messier, drenched in sorrow. What had he said, when he told me he loved me again? *Life at your side would feel meaningful enough to end.*

"She won't take the deal, though," I say.

"She won't," Rose says. She sighs, crosses her arms. "I'm not stupid enough to come to you demanding you have empathy for her. But you can't imagine what it's like. To be so powerful, yet so powerless, for years on end. To be almost destroyed multiple times over for existing. You might think that what she did at Ulrich Corridor was overkill, but she did it to protect us. She had no choice."

Help me. Harold's final grimace, his unheard death rattle.

"She murdered a room full of people in cold blood," I say, disgusted.

"Because someone first tried to murder me," Rose insists. "It's a mass shooting in America. We're a minor calamity. The news cycle is probably already on to the next one."

I swing my feet against my bed's footboard, and the impact booms through the room like a firework.

"Is that how you justify it to yourself?" I muse.

Rose doesn't respond for a moment, but I can tell I've struck a nerve.

"You're mortal," she says eventually. "You have a desire to live, but also the knowledge that you can't live forever. For us, it's a choice, and a hard one. I miss Alphonse every day, but I envy him too. He was tired of living just for the sake of it. The life he chose for himself . . . it was full of possibilities. Leila saw it as betrayal, but I understood why he chose it. I understand why Julian is choosing it now. And if I'm honest, I'd love to choose it too. Having to start again from childhood is exhausting."

"What's stopping you?" I ask.

"My sister," Rose says plainly. "After all she's done for us? I can't leave her to be alone."

"Of course," I say, despondent. In Ulrich Corridor, I'd thought for a brief moment that I might have an ally in Rose. But she has made her loyalties clear.

"Like it or not, Leila's the only one of us who is willing to accept herself fully," Rose says, as if it's an explanation. "To do the dirty work of crisis management. For all of us. Julian's told you about Claire. Did he tell you that while he was wallowing in grief, Leila was the one to track down and eliminate the men who killed her? And that's far from the only time we've been exposed. Hunted." She folds her thin arms over a chest that had once been full and plush and is now prepubescent. "The work of enrapturing multiple targets is dangerous. There's a window in the process during which the bond is at times tenuous, when our infiltration of the subconscious inspires as much alarm as lust. Our targets . . . they can become obsessive. Violent. You saw what happened to me."

A memory comes to me in a flash: the security guard in our hospital who'd taken to following Leila into the parking garage. I'd written him off as a creep. But the way he'd looked at her hadn't been simply amorous, it had been desperate.

"Are you hoping that I'll be understanding?" I say. "That I'll tell you it's totally fine that she's putting me and my family in danger, because she's trying to protect yours?"

"No," Rose sighs. "I wasn't lying when I told you that I was happy for you and Julian. I want to help you get out of this. I'll do what I can to protect your family. Especially this one," she adds, scratching behind Onix's ear. Then she looks back up at me. "But not at her expense, Sean. I can't."

What can I do but nod? My head feels heavy as a corpse.

She nods back. From the living room, I hear Sophie call for her. Rose gives me one last lingering look, then throws open the door and runs to her.

Finally, I'm alone. I crumple to the floor. Onix trots to me and collapses into my lap, his tail thumping happily on the floor. I lift his head and press it to mine.

"I missed you, baby," I tell him, and he groans his agreement.

I begin to inspect my new space, pulling the drawers open to find all my potential necessities: satin pillowcases for my hair, clean towels, socks and underwear, pajamas, a single change of clothing. The adjoining bathroom is clean, and fresh eucalyptus hangs from the showerhead. I search for cameras and find none, but that doesn't settle my nerves; if Leila is paranoid enough to strip me to search for tracking devices, there's no guarantee that I'm not being watched.

It doesn't escape my notice that the room is completely bereft of any objects I could use for self-defense. The lamps are glued to the tables, and the furniture is too heavy to use as a barricade. I have a window, but it's bolted shut. For all its niceties, I am still in a prison.

There's a clock on the wall. My exploration has taken ten minutes, and I fold onto the floor, trying not to dwell on how many I have left. In the cath lab, we learn to prepare for the unexpected, for a worst-case scenario. We work based on inference with limited information, using injected contrast and X-rays to get the closest we can to the lay of the land in which we work, but we don't have the full picture that a surgeon might. When shit hits the fan, we have to be ready for a bailout, and that requires preparation, but also creativity and quick thinking. And when that doesn't work, the humility to call for backup.

I'm trapped in a cabin in the middle of nowhere with an armed man who has most certainly killed before and who is magically devoted to the mastermind of my kidnapping, with my entire found family unknowingly held hostage. Right now, I can't find a bailout, and my backup is currently halfway across the country.

Frustrated, I flop backward onto the floor. Onix is on my chest immediately, lavishing my chin with kisses, and I'm squirming at his loving assault when I turn my head and a metallic glint catches my eye.

A floorboard under the bed, one of the nails just barely sticking out from the wood.

Leila is right that I probably won't be able to overpower Robbie. But I have an excellent grasp on anatomy, and she's also correct that I can find a vein, or an artery, in record time. Enough force, and I'll have her. And while Robbie will almost assuredly kill me for it, it might buy Winona and Sophie some time to run.

Suddenly I don't care if there's a camera trained on me. I turn off the lights, wedge my hand as far under the bed as I can manage. I can feel the ridge of the loose nail, but can't quite get my fingers underneath the head. Frenzied, I try the thin edge of my press-ons, avoiding the thumb because if I lose that, I lose my backup too—

Someone opens the door, and the light flickers on. I sit up so quickly that I bang my head hard on the bed frame.

"Dinner's ready," Winona says, looking down at me with consternation. "Why are you rolling around on the floor in the dark?"

"Winny," I breathe, so relieved that I have to fight back laughter.

Winona slips inside my room and shuts the door.

"Something's off," she whispers. "I'm not wrong, am I? Leila wouldn't tell us exactly where she was bringing us, and I still don't understand how she was able to find you. She said she talked to Julian, but I know for a fact that you two broke up in the worst way and that you'd rather lose your big toe than let him back in, and you've literally never gone on a trip without telling me, and I don't care what she says, there's no way you'd do that while everything was going on with Brandon. Plus, the vibes between Leila and this cook are weird, like they're *together* or something, and *what* happened to your wrists—"

I suck in a breath, not quite expecting this confrontation so soon. *To be known is to be loved*, I think. This is my best friend; she can read me like an open book, and my split second of silence is answer enough.

"What is going *on*, Sulley?" she says.

I don't think, just hug her close, force her head down so that her lips are obscured by my shoulder, mine by her hair.

"I'm so happy to see you," I say out loud.

Winona stiffens, but to my relief, she doesn't pull away.

"Should I be worried?" she whispers. When I don't respond, "Sean?"

I'm torn. On one hand, if I tell her that she's in danger, she'll want to know more, and her survival is contingent on her ignorance. On the other, she and Sophie are the only people in this cabin who don't understand that they're in a death trap.

"Try to trust me. And act as normal as you can," I say, knowing I have no right to ask this of her, knowing that I don't have a plan beyond a rusty nail, hope beyond a distant knight in shining armor and the finnicky technology on my left thumb. Then, because I don't know how much time we have before Leila decides that I've compromised one of her hostages, I let her go and shove the door open. "It smells so good out here!"

It isn't a lie. Robbie's prowess in the kitchen is not feigned, but despite his efforts I can barely eat. Next to me, Winona tries her best to join in the conversation, but she's clearly muted, only chiming in to respond to Sophie's endless questions and tell her to close her mouth when she chews.

And then, across the table, our warden. Leila is quiet as she eats, observing us with rapt fascination and only tearing her eyes away to give Robbie suspiciously syrupy smiles that Winona catches with a scowl. Robbie doles out a meal for me from a large pot onto my plate, then sits to eat himself, as if to reassure me that the food isn't poisoned. But I am conscious of every bite I take, of the rim of the glass that contains my water, of the hungry stare from across the table. The knife in my hand is dull, unlikely to cut through skin. The fork wouldn't make it deep enough, even with force. There's a large kitchen knife sticking out of a dish rack on the counter, but that would almost be impossible to steal away—

"Do you not like the food?" Robbie asks. "I can whip up something else, if you wait a bit."

He sounds genuinely concerned, and part of me wonders if this concern is a reflection of his true personality, the one Leila has flattened and remolded to turn him into her henchman. If my stomach wasn't already churning, it is now.

I push my plate away.

"No, no, it's delicious, thanks," I say, fighting the irony of expressing gratitude to my soon-to-be murderer. I stand, make my way to the sink. Fury flashes across Leila's face; I know it would look too strange for her to try to stop me. Robbie cleans up after himself; there are no small paring knives left behind, just a couple of plates and a small teaspoon that I hurriedly slip into my sleeve. I'm placing my plate into the sink when suddenly there's a crash behind me.

"*Sophia*," Winona says sternly, then, "Sorry, Leila. We can go into town and get a new set for you before we leave."

Sophie has broken a glass. The remnants have skittered across the floor, one jagged piece landing by my heel. I can see the dull reflection of my face on its surface. Robbie's left the room to get a broom, but Leila is still here, and though she's facing away from me, I can see the tension in her shoulders, I only have a split second, there isn't enough time—

A chair creaks backward, small footfalls.

Rose throws herself into Leila's arms.

"Don't be mad at her, cousin," Rose says, and I startle at how well she plays at being an actual child. I don't have the luxury to ponder whether she's bought me time on purpose, and so I duck down, grab the shard, tuck it into my other sleeve, and feign a yawn as I walk back to the table.

"You guys need help cleaning up?" I ask.

Leila whips to face me, her glower contrasting with Rose's conviction.

"You had a long day today, Dr. Sullivan," Rose says. "Don't worry. We'll handle it."

It's the smallest olive branch, offered to me from the precocious girl who carries an aura too ancient for her small shoulders, and I would be foolish not to take it. Before I can be called back, I trudge down the hall to my room, pacing my steps. Onix follows me.

As soon as the door is closed, I drop to my knees and empty my sleeves of their spoils. The metal of the spoon is thick; I have neither the time nor the tools to sharpen it. The glass—well. It's wide, arced, and would be difficult to wield, but it's certainly sharp enough to slice. I try it in different holds, imagining myself driving it into Leila's neck—

Someone knocks, and I jolt.

"Be up at six in the morning tomorrow." Robbie's gruff twang rings into my room. "Leila wants you to watch the sunrise with her."

I hear his implication like a death knoll. *Possibly the last one of your life.*

There is a jangle of keys, then a click as my door is locked from the outside.

I spend the next hour under the bed, leveraging the spoon under the nail to try to drive it out. It budges less than half an inch, and my arms cramp. I give up and take a shower, use too much bodywash, run the hot water until my fingers prune. I weep, then wash away the tears.

The people I love try to visit.

"Auntie Sean?" Sophie says through the door. My doorknob jangles, then jams. To someone else, "It's locked."

"Let her sleep, Sophie," Winona tells her, wearily. "Today was a hard day for her."

"She just found out about Dad, right?" Sophie says quietly. "They used to be friends."

"That's right," Winona says. "So give her a little time."

I hold my breath until they walk away, then roll back onto the floor.

I wish I could reach Julian, but I find it impossible to surrender to sleep. It's like my body wants to savor every last second it has left. I wonder how Winona and Sophie will react when they realize I'm gone, what Leila will give them as an excuse. If Leila intends for them to live at all, or if I'm simply assuring myself that she will to hold on to my last shred of sanity. Whether I should have told Winona to take her daughter and run earlier this evening, or if that would have put them even more at risk. My mind skips back to my childhood: remembering my failed attempts at playing soccer, the day I got my college acceptance letter, the trip to our family vet to put down my childhood dog. When it thinks of Julian, it remembers the way his lips curl with amusement when I've said something that's gotten under his skin, or how his fingers tap when he's listening to music or his large hands stretch as they course over keys, and instead of reaching him I gasp against the keening despondency in my chest.

I watch the second hand tick and run my hands over my dog's silken fur and think, *Well, it was a short ride, but not a bad one.*

Based alone on the number of patients who have lain on my

catheterization lab table, my net contribution to the world has likely been positive. I've taken care of others. I've furthered my knowledge. I've made art. I've protected the people who mattered the most to me. I've fallen in love.

I want more of this life. Deserve it. But what I have now will have to be enough.

Thirty-Three

The clock above my head reads 5:52 when my door clicks open the next morning.

I'm dressed, my shard and only saving grace tucked securely into my sleeve. The outfit I will be dying in is not exactly to my tastes: a lavender athleisure set and cream fleece that would better suit Leila. But it's comfortable and flattering and as I look at myself in the mirror, I think, *I am too damn fine to die,* and earn myself a laugh.

Robbie is waiting outside the door for me. Without our audience, he returns to the taciturn, menacing presence he was when we first met, not the friendly Southern gentleman that Winona and Sophie know. I make Onix stay behind, and he whines and fusses at the door but eventually obeys. Robbie escorts me out to the back porch, and I only exhale when I realize that neither Winona nor Sophie is awake. The air outside is crisp and cool.

Last night, the darkness was so dense that I didn't realize that we are nestled in the mountains. The cabin sits on a crag of rock that juts out over the forest, looking over rolling hills. When I tilt my head to the sky, it's the violet blue of dawn, the moon still luminescent and high.

A woman I don't recognize is waiting for us on the picnic bench: petite, with deep, dark brown hair. She turns around and gives me a sweet smile.

"Do you like it?" Leila asks, standing.

I stare at her, unsure of what to say. The Leila I know has always been "girl next door" pretty. Gorgeous, sure, but accessible. The kind of woman who blushes and simpers when you called her beautiful, as if it's her first time hearing it.

This Leila, however, is someone else. I've always considered her a white woman, but her newly dark eyebrows and hair emphasize her olive undertones, turn her green eyes mesmerizingly bright, and make her much harder to place. Intellectually, I understand that her features themselves haven't changed, but the woman standing in front of me could walk past me in a crowd and I would be none the wiser.

Julian had done this in the beginning, I realize. His eyes shifting color. His skin tone darkening and lightening ever so slightly, as if trying to decide what version of him I would like best.

"You look like one of the Hadid sisters," I say. It's only half a compliment.

"A useful aesthetic," she says plainly. "I'm going to go for someone older and richer next time, who wants to spend his twilight years with the 'exotic bombshell' of his dreams instead of another all-American girl next door. But life is definitely easier when I'm blond, you know? It's hard to let that go." She stuffs her hands in her pockets and surveys me like she expects me to empathize. When I don't, she shrugs, sits, and taps the seat next to her.

I'm surprised by how easily my body carries me to her side. Dread has deadened my fear, and I tilt my head up to absorb my surroundings: the treetops, stripped bare by wind and chill, the morning calls of birds overdue for the migrations farther south. I know Julian can't hear me, but I whisper to him anyway: *Dawn is pretty here. I had a good dinner last night. Leila actually looks good as a brunette.*

"You're able to manipulate your appearance so that you can fit in more places." It's why they all seem so racially ambiguous, even if in different ways.

Leila throws her head back to laugh.

"You're *quick*, Sean," she says. "And, like, *impossible* to influence. It used to get on my nerves so bad, how Julian couldn't just get you to heel. But now I definitely see why he couldn't leave you alone. It's refreshing." She steeples her fingers, investigating me like she might a bug under a microscope. "Why do you think you're so resistant to him? Speaking from experience, it's definitely not because you're book smart."

"I've had to fight for the right to my reality," I answer cryptically, and Leila grins with all her teeth like I've just given her the correct answer.

"You know, I think you're under the impression that I'm going to kill you because you found out about us," she says. "But that's not it. I actually trust that you won't expose us. You love Julian too much to endanger him. And you're more loyal than most."

A breeze blows by and leaches heat from my bones.

"Then . . . why?" I whisper. *Why do I have to die?*

"Because if I let you live, I lose my brother," Leila continues. She props her chin on the heel of her hand. "You've noticed, haven't you. That Julian ages faster than you when he's not feeding."

I shudder. First at her choice of words—*feed*, so much more visceral than Julian's *transfer*. But also because I *have* noticed. Smatterings of grays. Subtle shifts in his facial structure.

Leila puts a hand over mine and it takes everything in me not to flinch away.

"You'll outlive him," she says. "There's not a clear math to it, but he'll have thirty-five, maybe forty years if he chooses this. No time at all, by our standards. From my perspective, you might as well be planning to drive a knife into his heart tomorrow." She watches me, a soft smile playing at her lips, and adds, "Have you ever lost someone you loved to suicide, Sean?"

I sputter, still processing the information I've received.

"N-no," I say.

Leila nods sagely.

"Then you won't understand," she says. "Losing Alphonse was the worst kind of grief. I kept wondering: Why didn't he think we were enough? What could I have done to make him choose differently? Our lifestyles mean that we move around a lot, me even more than the others, and so we'd spent maybe the last century apart—but I'd sent letters, made phone calls. Maybe I should have visited more. Reminded him that he had us as family, so he didn't have to go chasing connection elsewhere. But by the time I'd realized it, he was already gone."

Her eyes are glassy with tears, and for a brief moment, I feel something close to sympathy for her.

"I don't want you to lose Julian too," I say slowly. "But it isn't suicide, it's a different life. And it's his choice. We should let him make it."

Leila's eyes flash.

"It's a stupid choice," she hisses. "That's why he needs me. To remind him to be proud of what he is."

Her features don't change, but something shifts, turns the quiet terror I feel in her presence loud. *A god*, Julian had said Leila thought herself. But a wretched one, broken, always on the run.

"It's easy for Julian to forget that he's not human," Leila continues. "He lives among you, and quite easily. He's a man, after all, and a handsome, rich one at that; practically as close to a god as he can get. Except for when he feeds—and he does so sparingly, like it's wrong to do, as if it's wrong for a lion to hunt—he can pretend he's one of you. He can even"—she shudders—"convince himself that he *loves* you.

"But Rose and I were born in these bodies—as receptacles for violence. And so we can't forget. We survive, and to do so we can't shy from what we are. And that is different from you. Better than you. The men who aim to take from us, who pursue us to drain us of our beauty, our labor, who want to lord over us, hurt us, *kill us* . . . they become dust at our feet, just because we will it. You saw what they tried to do to Rose, at her show. Saw what she can do to them. How can you pretend that we're the same?"

She's leaning in close. For as much as she may disavow humans, she shares our anatomy, and I can see the subtle flutter of her carotid artery exactly where it should be, and imagine the pliancy of her flesh. Behind us, Robbie shifts on the porch, arms crossed around an apron that probably conceals a gun, and my racing heart sinks. If I attack her now, I won't be able to warn Winona and Sophie.

"Brandon didn't try to hurt you though, did he?" I ask, almost scared to hear the answer.

"He was a forty-year-old man who left his wife and kid for a twenty-two-year-old girl who worked under him," she says drolly. "Are you trying to suggest he was somehow different from the rest?"

"Well, wasn't that your fault?" I mutter. "Supernatural allure and all."

Leila gives me a wry look, the intensity I felt earlier dissipating.

"Oh honey, don't give me that much credit. I barely had to do anything. That one came *easy.*" She stands, and I immediately despair. "I'm glad we got to spend a little time together. And I know it was a small effort, but I really do want to give you a good exit. Your favorite people, eating your favorite meal. And now this glorious sunrise. A befitting end for a woman of your stature, I think."

I huff out my laughter.

"My stature, huh?" I say, dragging myself to my feet. "What, so I'm not quite as inconsequential as the other people you murder?"

"Not even close. I always thought it was cool, seeing you in the cath lab," Leila says. "Most of my life, women couldn't do much to make a way for themselves without a man, no matter where you lived. And here you are, a Black woman in America, not even a full generation after Jim Crow, working as an interventional cardiologist and living independently with no husband in sight." She gestures for me to follow, then walks me to the edge of the cliff, Robbie's heavy footfalls crunching behind us. "It's admirable, really. I thought about doing it myself, at some point."

My curiosity feels morbid, but I indulge it anyway, because why the hell not.

"Why didn't you?" I ask.

Leila shrugs, twirling her hair into a ponytail.

"Because the registration process is just so intense," she explains. "My name and pictures plastered everywhere on the internet. Medical boards, fingerprinting, the whole shebang. Not exactly compatible with my . . . lifestyle." She shudders, remembering something else. "Also, I'd probably have to get old."

"Getting old isn't that bad," I say.

"Yes it is," Leila insists. "I won't deny that Rose makes for a very handsome older woman, but the joint pain? *Menopause?*" She pulls a face. "And on top of that, you become invisible. I wouldn't wish that fate on anyone."

It occurs to me that I'll never experience my mother's hot flashes or complain of my grandmother's back pain, all things I had once looked to with dread and suddenly wish for myself, more than anything.

"I think Alphonse understood something that you don't," I say softly. "Your view of life is myopic. Entirely driven by fear of what is, for us, inevitable. But I've seen enough people die young to know the truth. That even with all its inconveniences, growing old is a blessing."

The look Leila gives me is indecipherable, some part contempt, and something else I don't quite understand. Longing? Then I see her eyes shift to something behind me, soften.

"Look," she says.

I turn. The sun crests the horizon, painting the sky in streaks of pink and lilac and blinding orange. The distant hills are shrouded in fog that glows golden as it is touched by the light, and a breeze blows by that carries the heavy, heady smell of pine. For a moment, I'm so awestruck that I forget that Robbie is still looming behind me. That this glorious view might be the last thing I will see before I die. Instead, I think, *I wish Jules could see this too.*

I hear him, suddenly, in my head. I know it's not really Julian—just the comforting encouragement of a memory, the last words he said to me. I imagine him next to me, shrouded in this morning's angelic light. It hugs close to his high cheekbones, runs the line of his proud nose, and traces the curves of his lip, turns his brown eyes clear as maple syrup. I've seen this sight before, woken up to it in Alphonse and Mary's cottage, the day I finally accepted him as mine.

Fight, Sean, he says. *I know you know how.*

I don't think after that. I let my shard slide into my palm, yanking Leila's shoulder down at the same time as I drive it into her neck. The glass slices open my skin—as suspected, it's too wide to easily grip—but I can feel it diving into hers as well, the bright, blooming scent of fresh blood cutting through the wintry, clean air—

Pain explodes in my jaw, my brain ricocheting in my skull, and I'm launched into the air with such force that it knocks the breath out of my lungs. I land hard on the twiggy forest floor, my vision coming together just in time to take in the heaving, colossal creature in front of me. I try to stand, but Robbie is faster, yanking me up by my fleece and hoisting me into the air like I'm a sack of potatoes.

His face barely looks human. It's contorted with rage, his pupils so dilated that they turn his already beady eyes black. I scrabble against his hold, my core tight and legs flailing over the abyss below. To my despair, Leila hobbles next to him. Her eyes are wild with rage and wet with agony, one hand holding on to her neck as blood pulses out of her wound. She yanks his shirt up, places a hand on his bare side. Robbie's mouth contorts, and the breath whooshes out of my throat as his brown whiskers begin to gray.

She's *healing. Shit.*

I never had a chance after all.

"You fucking bitch," Leila hisses, regaining her voice.

I've failed, I realize. Robbie is going to toss me over, and I will plummet to my death, leaving Winona, Sophie, and Onix to Leila's nonexistent mercy.

"Not like this," Leila suddenly barks. Robbie stills and then pivots and suddenly the world is spinning and I land back hard on solid ground. I almost rejoice until I hear a decisive click: Robbie's gun, trained on me.

I'm a rabbit caught in a trap. From my vantage point, all I can see are Robbie's scuffed boots until dainty sneakers come into view, then knees as Leila squats beside me. She grabs my chin with a hand still tacky with blood and yanks it to her. Her blond hair is back, her green eyes electric with wrath.

"I was going to make this relatively painless for you, but now you've pissed me off," she spits. "So here's what's going to happen instead. I'm going to go inside and get everyone up. We'll bring you in so they can have last one look at you. Then I'm going to kill your goddaughter while her mother watches. I'll tell her why—that they're gathered here because you couldn't just disappear, that you put them at risk to protect your own pitiful little life. I'll wait for Winona to understand, for her last words to be a curse upon your name, and then I'll kill her too. I'll save your stupid little mutt for last. Let him whine and cry, and then get him right between the eyes. And you? Well, I'll give you a little time to steep in their blood, before I kill you too."

I'm in a hell of my own making. Whatever scenarios I'd dreamt up last night pale in comparison to this.

Robbie presses one gun to my temple and then pulls another one off a hidden holster at his hip and hands it to his master. I watch, sick, as Leila skips back into the cabin. She yells loud enough that I can hear her call out their names, telling them to come to the living room, *There's a deer outside, come look.* I know when they see me, when Leila must pull out her gun and train it on them, by Sophie's bloodcurdling scream.

"Come on in," Leila sings.

Robbie yanks me to my feet and drags me, limp, to the back door. Onix runs up to meet me, and he kicks him aside with a steel-toed boot. My gasp of horror is eclipsed by his pained yelp, and in the living room, I can hear Winona sob.

Julian, I try, knowing that he won't hear me. Knowing that I have never been the sort of damsel whose calls for distress are answered. *Julian, where are you?*

The night I met Julian feels like a dream of the best kind. The golden light of the sunset cast a natural spotlight over the piano, and the distant thudding of the bass from the live band pounded an alien beat under my feet. And then there was the man. So beautiful that I had to blink away. So alluring that I couldn't help but follow him to the end.

The scene before me, however, is a nightmare.

Leila is holding Sophie in a tight embrace, her chin resting in her dark curls, her gun pressed to her temple. Winona is on her knees, bulbous eyes too wide with shock to cry, frozen in place. Lingering behind them, lips tucked with shock but making no effort to save my family like she claimed she would, is Rose.

"Sean," Winona whimpers. "What's going on?"

"Yes, Sean, tell her what's going on!" Leila sneers.

I open my mouth, but I can't find my voice. *This is my fault*, I want to say. *Please, forgive me—*

"You know what, I'm bored already," Leila says. "Let's do you first instead. Robbie, the honors?"

There's a sound of ruffling, a metallic clink of his gun being raised. Another scream: Sophie's, maybe Winona's, not mine, because I'm too terrified to make a sound.

My skull feels pressurized. Suddenly, I can hear everything in my body, my stomach churning, air whistling through my lungs, the eighty-eight drum of my heartbeat. *This is it*, I think. The result of my meager efforts. I've saved countless lives on my cath lab table, but I can't save my own, can't save the people I love.

"Winny," I say hurriedly, my final words, coming to me at last. "I'm so sorry—"

I hear the gunshot before I feel it. A deafening boom, heat, wet, the smoldering stench of smelt iron.

I fall and hit the ground and my world goes dark.

Thirty-Four

The first thing I realize when I come to is that I am not dead. It takes a moment to convince myself of this, because for all intents and purposes, I should be. There's the blood, for one, soaking through my fleece, on my palms, running down my nose. Then there's the fact that I'm unable to get up, burdened by an oppressive weight and a jagged, painful javelin poking into my back.

"Sean!"

Julian. My body floods with relief, like I've been wandering through a desert and come across a pool that is not a mirage.

Then clarity hits me like a cast-iron skillet, and I force myself up onto my hands. Robbie is lying on top of me, all three hundred something pounds of dead weight, because that is what he is—dead. The blood that soaks me from midback down is from his body, though I must have hit my nose hard when I fell. Horrified, I try to roll out from under him, but find that I've been pinned.

Someone grunts, then rolls him away. I flop onto my back, use the last of my energy to boost myself up onto my elbows, and find myself looking up at my savior.

"Jules," I say through a cracked, hoarse throat. "You're here."

"I was almost too late." He sounds, and looks, as haunted as I feel. There are dark circles under his eyes and his lips are chapped like he hasn't paused to drink in hours. He has just killed a man. Not by draining his life, but the way most men do—with his hands and steel. It feels wrong to be grateful for his violence, but I am, and so entranced by his beauty too that I almost forget that we are not alone.

I look up and see Ritika who, thank god in heaven, is very much alive, though with a bandage wrapped around her head—her gun trained on Leila, who has put her own aside to curl Sophie in a spider-tight grip.

I suck in a breath, swivel around the room to find Winona struggling and weeping in Aditya's grasp as Onix stands guard next to him, looking between me and Winona for the signal to attack.

"Let me go," Winona sobs.

"It's not safe to touch her, Winny," I say, my head swimming. I'm probably three concussions deep now, and I have to fight to stay conscious. I reach between my legs for Robbie's fallen handgun. It's heavy and alien in my ripped hands, but it feels like armor when I crawl to Winona's side. She looks down at me with a tear-streaked face.

"What is going on, Sean?" she shouts, at the same time that Leila spits, "Stay back! Or I send our little darling on a fast track through puberty."

Her clutch on Sophie tightens just enough to prove that *she can and she will*, and Winona gasps, both understanding and not.

Julian uncurls to his full height. His steps toward Leila are cautious; a lion tamer approaching a feral juvenile.

"Enough, Leila."

Leila shuffles back, squeezing Sophie tighter. Sophie sniffles but doesn't speak, and her lower lip trembles. Immediately I am ravenous with bloodthirst. *How many shots would it take to put you down*? I wonder. *Where do I have to aim?*

Julian's voice, though, is so gentle that I wonder if it is laced with his suggestion.

"I thought we didn't bring children into this," he says.

To my shock, tears sprout in Leila's eyes.

"Since when did you become so self-righteous," she hisses. "I'm doing this for *us*."

"But I don't want this," Julian says. He bends, slowly, until he's on one knee in front of them, then turns to Rose, who has turned bodily away from the scene. "Rose doesn't. And Alphonse didn't either."

"You and Alphonse are the same," Leila seethes. "You don't even *think* about our family. You're all just rushing to leave me behind, all for these no-name bitches who you swear are *so special* even though you'll meet another one just like her in fifty years! Even Rose is going crazy these days, saying she wants this to end too. But you don't understand. You're denying your true nature. You're spitting in the face of our *gift*—"

"Is it really a gift?" Julian asks. "Because I don't see you enjoying it, Leila. I don't see you living. All you do, all the time, is run. From coast to coast, town to town, host to host. All I've watched you do is try to survive. You're alive, Leila, but you have no clue who you are, what your life really could be, if you let yourself be more than this." His gaze flits to me, and I swallow against a hard throat; I'm not sure I will ever get tired of how this man looks at me, like I'm his world shrunk down to person size. "If you let yourself *feel,* for once."

When Leila doesn't respond, Julian places a gentle hand on hers. They overlap, his bronze against her warm tan against Sophie's sandalwood. Despite everything, Leila transforms before my eyes. I understand now why Julian felt so sure that he could convince Leila to give up the hunt without harming her. The Leila Pendersen I'd gotten to know in the cath lab, who was sweet as apple pie and helpful and committed to her job, the one I couldn't help but like, isn't entirely a fabrication. She is the person who existed behind her fear and uncertainty. The mortal, huddled in a god's cloak.

"The world is different than the one we were born into. You know that," Julian implores. "I'll help you start over. Do this right. You've always been the smartest of us; you could do incredible things. And yes, you might grow old, and eventually die, but it can be a beautiful life. One you can look back on with joy and without regret."

Leila's chest is heaving now, tears dripping down her face, messy and uninhibited, and I find myself stunned by how the ugliness of her sobs can only make her more beautiful.

"Like Alphonse did?" she says.

Julian squeezes her hand.

"Yes," he says.

I hold my breath. Wait for Leila to let Sophie go. But Leila is shaking her head, and my heart drops to my stomach.

"No," Leila says. "I don't want that. I want you to *choose me*, Julian. Stay with *me*. We're all we have."

Her words shatter me, and I would fall to the floor if not for Winny, who needs me. Winny, whose hand I grasp as she begins anew to struggle and sob. Julian starts to speak again, frantically now, this time in a language we can't understand, but Leila is still shaking her head, her entire body trembling, and Sophie, knowing she's in danger but not understanding why, begins to weep.

There's a creak, almost missed in the noise.

Rose.

"Stop, Julian," she says.

Julian startles back. He hasn't seen Rose since the Ulrich Corridor, and he takes in her appearance grimly as she glides into the room. She surveys the scene coolly, looks from Ritika to Aditya, to a horrified Winona, to me, before settling on Leila.

"Rose," Julian begs. "Please. Please, I can't do this again—"

She holds up a hand to silence him.

"You've been selfish," she says, her high-pitched voice somehow echoing with command. "You and Alphonse both. You don't even understand what it is you're asking of her. You want her to decide to die, just because you have? To live like you have? You're making light of her just suggesting it. I would've expected better of you."

Leila's eyes brighten with hope just as Julian's collapse in despair.

"Thank you, Rose," Leila says, relieved. "I knew you would understand."

"Of course I understand," Rose says soothingly. "It's different for you and me. It's always been. The boys have gotten to play with their fun adventures, their property and land, and all this time, we've been running, haven't we? Always hiding, when we should be able to stand tall in who we are."

"Yes!" Leila's voice carries high, and Sophie winces against the sound. "See, yes, you get it, Rose, I knew you would! I don't want to do 'incredible things.' I *am* incredible. I've always been!"

"You have, my beautiful sister," Rose coos. She steps in close, cups Leila's cheek in a soft caress, moving around Sophie as if she isn't there. "Let the child and her mother go. They have nothing to do with this, and they shouldn't suffer for that stupid man's foolishness. We'll get rid of *that woman*, get our brother back to his senses, and do things *right* this time. As a family."

"As a family," Leila repeats.

And then, miraculously, her grip loosens, and Sophie slips out of her grasp. Aditya and Ritika mobilize immediately, collecting my exhausted best friend and her daughter into their arms and ushering them out the back door to safety. In the space made by Sophie's absence, Rose slips in and squeezes her sister tight. A sound like a croak comes from Leila's throat, and then they are sobbing in each other's embrace.

I almost faint with relief. I could run too, but then Rose and Leila might give chase, and I'm satisfied with this ending. After all, Rose has kept her promise to me. There's a nudge against my arm: Onix, my sweet boy, deciding to stay. I stumble forward, ready to face the music, when Julian grabs my arm.

"No," he growls. His eyes are wild, manic, and in his other hand, he's holding his gun. "I won't let them touch you. Rose—" But Rose doesn't pay him any mind. She folds herself into Leila, wraps her spindly arms around her waist and holds on tight. They rock back and forth together, tears trailing down their cheeks, making such a picture of familial love that it takes me a heartbeat to realize what is happening.

Because Rose is . . . *growing.*

It happens slowly, then all at once; her arms thickening, legs lengthening across the bloodied floor.

"No," Leila gasps. She struggles, pushes against her sister's hold, which only seems to strengthen by the second. I watch, dumbstruck, as Rose's tiny body overtakes her sister's, first growing taller, then broader, her hips widening and arms lengthening until she eclipses Leila altogether. Their cries change too, heighten then abate, Rose's deepening and lengthening while Leila's disappear altogether. Next to me, Julian looks on in astonishment.

"Rose," he says, bewildered. "What did you just do?"

Rose turns to face us. She looks not unlike how she did when we first met, stately, with fine, chiseled features and eyes sharp enough to cut but now softened by tears. There are subtle lines in her forehead, around her lips, but her hair is still thick and jet-black.

In her arms lies an infant. It stares up at Rose with adoring green eyes, like she is the only thing she has ever known.

This is why Julian calls it a transfer, I think. But I never considered their exchange of life could go both ways.

"She's been suffering too long," Rose says. "This way, she gets to start over with us. Unburdened by her memories. A true blank slate." She looks at me, her mouth set in a line, then back at the babbling baby in her arms. "Motherhood isn't something I've had the chance to experience. Maybe I can raise her right. Will you help, Julian?"

Julian doesn't answer immediately, but he does stagger to his feet. His jaw is tight, every muscle of his back tensed, but when he stands the first thing he does is gather them into his arms. The baby coos, and I see her tiny, chubby hand reach for his face.

"How?" he says, his voice full of wonder. "How did you know you could do that? How did you give it back?"

Rose shrugs.

"I didn't know," she says. "I just knew that I wanted to, more than I wanted anything else. And so I did."

Thirty-Five

I linger, awkwardly, in the room where I was supposed to die. Adrenaline eases out of my system like a leaky pressure valve, and I feel my mind settle back into my body and take note of the damage. My ankle aches from my awkward fall, and my head pounds from the welt left by the butt of Robbie's gun, his punch to my jaw. My back is soaked, for the second time in less than a week, in somebody else's blood and possibly brain matter. I'm starving, having barely eaten in the last twenty-four hours. And I am so very, deeply, ancestrally tired.

My stare has drifted down at the lump of Robbie's corpse when a hand closes over my shoulder and makes me jump.

"You okay?" Julian asks, turning me to face him. The look I give him must be withering, because he tugs me into his arms. "I know. Stupid question."

I burrow into his chest, searching for the comfort of his many elusive fragrances. But there are no notes of pink pepper or sandalwood or ylang-ylang today, only the smell of laundry detergent and the subtle sharpness of his sweat, and instead of comfort I'm taken by unease. Julian is warm and firm and his heart is racing and he has just killed a man in cold blood for me. A man who might have lived many more years, cooking venison stew in a big pot to share with his neighbors, if he'd never happened upon Julian's now infant sister.

"We'll wait outside," Rose says quietly.

Julian doesn't let go of me, just digs into his pocket for keys that he hands over to his sister.

"Not the RV," he says cryptically, but she seems to understand, because she takes the keys, nods, and heads out the door.

Just like that, we are alone.

"You're hurt," Julian says, in the creaking quiet of the cabin. He trails gentle fingers over the welt on my head, the split in my lip, the bruise I know is blossoming on my chin. "I'm sorry I didn't get here sooner."

I hum and lean into his palm. It smells bitter and metallic, like burnt chocolate. Like gunfire. My chest throbs as I study his face and remember the first time I saw it. How my jaw quite literally dropped. And to think I had hardly known him then, hadn't explored the depths of his endless mind, hadn't felt the fervor of his love. My favorite thing about him, I realize, is his honesty—ironic, since his lies are what led us here. But his *actions*, they have never failed to tell the truth. I believe that he loves me. I believe that he would fight for me. I believe that he would give himself up for me, for Claire.

There, I realize, lies the problem.

"Sean." His voice deepens with worry. "Talk to me."

Instead I pull him into a kiss. It tastes like iron and salt, like an hours-long drive around a mountain at twenty miles per hour above the speed limit and a panicked sprint to an unlocked back door. It feels like longing and desperation and a hundred nights we should have had together that we spent apart because he'd hoped to scrub me off his skin. Julian's arm around my waist is tight, the press of his chest into mine so firm that it feels like he's trying to lock us together. I wind my arms around his neck, kiss him hard, kiss him mad. A last supper, so much more sumptuous than Leila could have planned.

When we break apart, we're both panting, and Julian's eyes shine with veneration, like I am his redemption descending from the skies, and it's that look that tells me that I'm about to do the right thing.

"I can't be with you," I tell him gently. "Not now, at least."

It is a terrible thing, to watch a person's heart break. I can see the moment when Julian's daze becomes alertness, when he goes from hearing my words to processing them to understanding their repercussions. There is a future he's created in his mind, one where he carries me bridal style into a world we build together, that I've just dashed away.

"What do you mean?" he says, his voice jagged.

I gesture to the dead man on the ground, in the direction of the door where the other halves of my heart escaped with the Ghoshal siblings.

"This," I say. "I've dedicated my life to giving people as much life as they can grasp. I can't be okay with taking it away."

He holds my hands tight between his.

"But I'll stop," he pleads. "I *have* stopped, Sean, for you—"

"I don't just mean other people's, Jules," I say. "I mean yours. I can't have you sacrifice your life for *me*. It needs to be for *you*."

Julian gapes. I watch as tears spring to his eyes, and he whips his head away to keep them from my view.

"I don't understand," he says.

I nudge him back, make his eyes meet mine so that he can see the truth in what I say next.

"I love you," I tell him definitively. "I'll probably never stop loving you. But I can't be your source of meaning. You can't decide to live this way because you want to be by my side. Because I'm not like you, Julian. I'm fully, totally mortal. I'm fragile, and fickle, and totally fallible. What if I have a heart attack one day and die? What if I fall out of love and leave you? What if you slip up, or Rose slips up, or Leila accidentally enchants someone because she is young now and uninhibited and neither of you has ever raised a child before, and someone comes after my family again to get to yours?" I imagine Claire, who was apparently so much like me. How would she have felt, knowing how much wreckage the love of her life had wrought in the wake of her demise? How many lives were lost or shortened in her name? "Tell me the truth. If you were too late. If I was already gone. Would you have still abstained? Or would you have been lost again?"

"But I wasn't too late," Julian says stubbornly. "We don't have to deal with hypotheticals. We can do this like you said. Choose each other every day and go from there."

But I'm shaking my head.

"You don't know what you're choosing, Jules. Pain, suffering, loss . . . those come in the package. You get in a car accident tomorrow? You'll have to spend months, maybe years, healing. Maybe live the rest of your life with a back that never stops aching and a neck that's always tight. You catch the flu? You tough it out. You can't heal your wounds with a kiss in the dark with a stranger who won't miss what they've lost. It has to all be worth it for you, whether I'm with you or not."

It's a life that Julian has never known and one he can't promise to me without experiencing it first. One I won't force upon him out of my own principles, because I will not have this stunning, powerful being be anyone other than who he truly wants to be. If I didn't want to sob, I might laugh out loud, because the logic is eerily similar to why I didn't want to date him when I thought the biggest barrier was his comparative youth.

Under my hand, Julian's jaw wobbles. A tear creeps from the corner of his right eye, drips down, and settles into the crevice of my palm.

"This . . . hurts," he manages. He grips his own shirt, like he's about to tear his heart out.

"That's being human for you," I say. "It has its definite downsides."

We let out a shaky, simultaneous breath, and I swell with affection for him. Julian doesn't push back against my assessment of his readiness, doesn't try to claim that I'm wrong and that he's sure, and his self-awareness only intensifies my love for him. I gather him close, draw myself to the tips of my toes to engulf myself in him more completely. It feels so unfair, to have to let him go. To finally feel the fireworks, blockbuster movie kind of love, to finally be seen and cherished and adored, only to have to say, *Not yet.*

We hold each other for a long time, memorizing the other's shape.

Julian is the first to pull away. He swallows, pushes his tongue into his cheek, but his gaze is hard with conviction. He holds me at an arm's length, bending until we are at eye level.

"You're right," he says. My favorite words, coming to bite me in the ass. "I have to want this for myself. I have to choose it for me. So I'll do as you say. I'll do it without you. And I won't be so selfish as to tell you to wait for me. But what I will say is that if I do decide that I want to continue living this way, I'll be back for you. And I don't care if someone else is already in the picture. They'll have to find some way to make room."

I nod. I feel drenched in anguish.

We kiss again, a brief, definitive, hard press of our lips, our unspoken goodbye.

Julian stays behind at the cabin as I hobble back outside. There are two vehicles waiting outside: a glistening black RV and a small Honda Civic. The door to the RV opens, and Winona appears on the stairs, a blanket gathered around her shoulders. Aditya stands uncertainly a few paces from the door, sending her furtive, anxious glances.

"Why the hell are you still here?" I shout, limping toward her. I shoot an accusatory glare at Aditya, who throws his hands up helplessly.

"Don't look at me," he says. "*I* wanted to dip fifteen minutes ago. She refused to leave without you."

Winona is a cyclone, her thick, dense curls flying around her like a thundercloud, her face twisted in determination. She takes one step, two, then breaks out into a full sprint and launches herself into my arms. I stagger backward with the force of her embrace.

"I fucking hate you," she says into my ear. "What the fuck happened in there? Why didn't you come out? I thought you might have died in there. Where did that woman come from, and why does she look exactly like Rosie? What the fuck happened to Leila? A fucking *baby*?"

Winona has just dropped more f-bombs in the last five seconds than she has for the duration of Sophie's life, and I loop my arm through hers, rest my head on her shoulder. She's alive enough to be indignant with me, and this I consider a blessing.

"I'll explain," I promise.

"You better," she warns.

We leave first. Ritika and Aditya swap turns manning the RV with Winona, Sophie, Onix, and me in tow. Julian, Rose, and Leila stay behind. I try to ask what they plan to do with Robbie's body, and Aditya assures me not to worry, *we're dealing with experts here*, and that response reminds me never to ask questions I don't want to hear the answers to.

I wait until Sophie has drifted off to sleep, her arms and legs wound tight around my dog, then tell Winona everything. She doesn't interrupt me, just listens intently to a story that sounds so fantastical to my own ears that I almost stop halfway.

When I'm done, she has one question for me: "Are you going to keep seeing him?"

My chest aches, my heartbreak an open wound.

"No," I say simply.

Winona's relief is obvious. She drops her elbows onto her knees, drags both hands down her face, then looks up at me again.

"Are you okay?" she asks.

I laugh.

"No," I say. "But I will be eventually."

I dream of Julian one last time that night.

We get home eleven hours later, and the city is uncharacteristically still, as if holding vigil for all the things it has lost. My apartment doesn't feel like it belongs to me, my bed chosen and made by a woman I don't think exists anymore. I fold beneath the comforter and close my eyes and there Julian is, of course he is, because in the hours since I decided to leave him, he has had complete hold of my thoughts.

"Don't forget me," he says. He sits at the foot of my bed, too far for me to reach, and his distance only adds to the torment.

"How could I ever," I whisper.

And then, as soon as he comes, he is gone, and I don't dream of him again.

Five Years Later

It smells awesome in here, Auntie Sean," Sophie says, blasting through my kitchen to investigate the source. Her backpack hangs off one shoulder; she's just gotten off the school bus, and as is rapidly becoming tradition, decided to stop at my place instead of carrying her scrawny behind home. She lifts the lids on the pots on my stovetop to take a peek at the gumbo bubbling inside and makes a show of drawing a deep breath, and I cluck at her from the sink, where I'm washing my dishes.

"Does your momma know you're here?" I ask, wiping my hands off on a kitchen towel.

Sophie rolls her eyes. It still stuns me how much she's grown in the last few years, shooting up from being a skinny preteen I could hoist in my arms to a tall young woman who has to tilt her chin down to look at me.

"Duh," she says. "Where else would I be?" She pulls out her phone, sending a text to what I assume is her family group chat. "I'm telling Mom you're making gumbo, and that there's enough for all of us." She pauses. "Mom is asking if Steve can come too."

I sigh, as if I hadn't made an entire lobster pot's worth anticipating an impromptu dinner party.

"Sure," I say, "Steve can come too."

Five years ago, when I made it back home to Chicago after escaping imprisonment and multiple near-death experiences, it became apparent that I couldn't continue my life as if nothing had changed. As if I hadn't almost lost my life and didn't lose my greatest love. I'd needed a change of scenery and change of pace. A quick search for interventional cardiology jobs landed me at a practice on the North Shore of Massachusetts. Within a month, I'd put in my notice, signed on a fixer-upper, and made the move.

I shouldn't have been surprised when Winona and Sophie followed three months later. Winona finally sold her house and met her boyfriend almost immediately upon touching New England soil. Steve is a salt-of-the-earth kind of guy, owns a successful construction company, and he's been obsessed with my girl since helping her take her carry-on out of the overhead compartment after landing at Boston Logan.

Our little, strange family, spread out amongst three homes, all less than a quarter mile apart: Winona and Sophie in their cozy duplex, Steve in the apartment complex a few streets down, and me, myself, and my three-year-old hound mix, Copper.

The pace is slow and easy here. The town is just big enough to not be smothering, just small enough that I run into my patients in the grocery store. The air tastes fresh, like the sea, and before he passed, I could take Onix on car rides to the beach.

Sophie sneaks a sip of my gumbo, then exclaims when she burns her tongue. We laugh, and she heads out my door.

"I'll be back in . . . two hours?" she says.

"You'll be back whenever you feel like it and we both know it," I tease.

Sophie flashes me a gap-toothed, million-wat smile.

"We sure do!" she says. She swings the door shut, and I am back in my silence. I check the stove, then wander to my living room.

There's a baby grand here. It's not a brand-new Steinway like the one in Alphonse and Mary's home, or a vintage Bösendorfer like Julian's, but a used Yamaha with a crisp sound that echoes along my walls. I lift my fallboard and play a song from memory, and when I close my eyes, I can almost feel him there, the warm press of his arm wedged against mine, his left hand playing bass, my right covering treble. I start off humming the melody, and then the hums turn to words. Copper plods to my feet and joins in, howling along, and I laugh out loud and ache in a way that most of the time I've been able to ignore.

The thing about grief is that you can't quiet it. It lives in the corners of your mind, looming, jumps out when you least expect it to remind you of your loss. And the person I lost is still living. I *chose* to push him away.

My doorbell rings. It chimes through the house, and I sniffle and wipe the tears from the corners of my eyes. It's probably Sophie again, coming to ask whether she can do her homework at mine just to maximize her chance at a meal.

"That was quick," I call out. "Seriously, nugget, at some point I'm going to start charging you rent—"

The person behind the door is not my seventeen-year-old goddaughter. He's tall and well hewn, with broad shoulders and long legs. His hair is shorn, and his beard is trimmed and neat. His features are a clash of masculine and feminine: a strong jaw, chiseled cheekbones paired with doelike lashes, full lips that I know are plush to the touch. He smiles down at me, and slight crow's feet form at the corners of his eyes.

"Hello again, Sean," Julian says. "Is now an okay time?"

My heart thunders. I don't know what to do with my hands, and so they curl together. I want to tell him that there has never not been an okay time. That I've tried to forget him, to scrub him from my mind, but that he sits somewhere in a layer I can't reach under my skin, marking me like a tattoo. That I hate that he disappeared from my life, but also that I'm glad he was gone, because the one I've made in his absence is so peaceful and calm and I would trade nothing else for it. That even still, I've waited, and hoped, that he'd disrupt it. That I didn't even try to meet anyone else, because I knew that there could be no one else.

"Hello again, Julian."

We smile at each other, and it feels like home.

He steps in close. "May I?"

I nod, and he cups my cheek. My skin burns at his touch, and I shudder, see him tremble too. All this time, and he's still the only person to make me feel this way.

Suddenly there's a sensation. Brisk, cool, like a sea breeze. The ache in my right knee from a torn meniscus last year disappears. The tension in the back of my neck eases.

"Oh," I whisper, clutching his wrist to hold him to me. "Oh. Julian . . . how did you . . . when . . . ?"

"It's like Rose said." He smiles. "I had to want to. More than anything else in the world."

For a moment we're silent; all I can do is take him in. He folds his bottom lip into his mouth, nervous under my appraisal.

"I know I just showed up out of nowhere. Is there . . . do you have . . ."

I know what he's asking, and I duck my head, just a bit shy.

"No, I'm not with anyone," I confess. "You?"

"Five years sober over here," he says, and we beam at each other, unspoken words passing between us. *I still love you. I never stopped. I've thought about you every day since.*

"So . . ." I say. "What's the plan? You just dropping by?"

"No, actually." He looks down at me intently, his expression tender and beseeching all at once. "I was hoping to stay a while. See whether New England is more my speed."

I turn my head until my nose nuzzles into his palm. He's favoring herbal scents these days; I inhale notes of rosemary and sage, pine and freshly tilled soil, like the earth after a rainstorm.

"The gang is coming over for dinner tonight, if you want to join," I say.

"The same folks?" he asks.

"Plus one, minus another," I inform him. "Winona's bringing her boyfriend, and Onix passed a few years ago. You'll meet Copper in a second."

Julian nods, looks around. His eyes shine, and he opens his mouth to say something, then closes it again. When he finally speaks, it's around a voice thick with emotion.

"It's been a long time," he confesses. "I . . . don't know where to start."

I laugh, even as my heart swells in my chest.

"You can start by not letting all my heat out," I say, and at the invitation, he bites back a smile.

I step aside, open the door wide to let him in, and without another word between us, I know that the goodbye we shared so many years ago in that cabin was our last. That this moment has marked the beginning of Julian's new, beautiful, wonderfully finite life, and mine too.

Acknowledgments

Die for Me was written during a time of great transition. It wouldn't be an exaggeration to say that writing this book transformed me; the woman who wrote its first words would be unrecognizable to the one who wrote its last.

First, thank you to my readers, old and new. That you choose to spend your precious time with my work will always be a gift that I don't take for granted. Special shout-out to Shirlygang, old and new! Some of you have been around since the days when I only shared my comics and never showed my face, others tuned in for my medical education videos, and even more have stuck around for my feminist/womanist rants . . . and I am so grateful for you all!

Thank you to my agent, Jess Regel, for championing my vision as always, and to my editor, Nidhi Pugalia, for helping me mold this novel into a version that I can be proud of. Thank you to my sales, marketing, publicity, and social media teams—particularly Emily Fishman, Chantal Canales, Kristina Fazzalaro, Mary Stone, and Paige Touse—for making sure this book gets onto shelves and into the hands of those who might find solace in her pages. Thank you especially for gracing me with not one, not two, but three dozen red roses—you are a team I could only dream of!

I have been blessed with so many incredible friends and supporters who have held my hand through some truly trying times and celebrated me through great ones. First: my beloved Eunhye. My very own Winona. I am so grateful to have grown up alongside you and for the home that we have made within each other. Kemi Doll: thank you for being the big sister that I never had, imbuing me with confidence and wisdom, and reminding me that I actually can have everything that I want. By the time this book comes out, *A Terrible Strength* will already be out in the world, and I cannot wait to see the splash it makes. Chris D: for listening to my many meandering voice notes and helping me iron out plot points. Riss: for helping me conceive of this crazy novel and for our many days and nights drafting alongside one another. Ali, Lo, and Grace: thank you for reading a messy first draft and supporting this not quite vampy story! Lauren: thank you for being the best therapist a girl could ask for. You've taken me through it, chile!

Finally, for those of you stuck in a trauma bond, who have suffered from or are suffering from interpersonal violence, you're not crazy, you aren't stupid, and you can reclaim your life. I did.

Dear Reader,

We'd love your attention for one more page to tell you about the crisis in children's reading, and what we can all do.

Studies have shown that reading for fun is the **single biggest predictor of a child's future life chances** – more than family circumstance, parents' educational background or income. It improves academic results, mental health, wealth, communication skills, ambition and happiness.[1]

The number of children reading for fun is in rapid decline. Young people have a lot of competition for their time. In 2024, 1 in 10 children and young people in the UK aged 5 to 18 did not own a single book at home.[2]

Hachette works extensively with schools, libraries and literacy charities, but here are some ways we can all raise more readers:

- Reading to children for just 10 minutes a day makes a difference
- Don't give up if children aren't regular readers – there will be books for them!
- Visit bookshops and libraries to get recommendations
- Encourage them to listen to audiobooks
- Support school libraries
- Give books as gifts

There's a lot more information about how to encourage children to read on our website: **www.RaisingReaders.co.uk**

Thank you for reading.

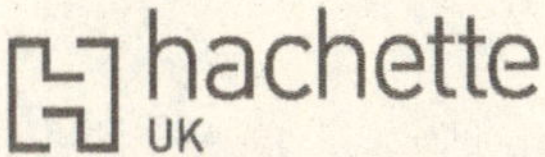

---

[1] OECD, '21st-Century Readers: Developing Literacy Skills in a Digital World', 2021, https://www.oecd.org/en/publications/21st-century-readers_a83d84cb-en.html

[2] National Literacy Trust, 'Book Ownership in 2024', November 2024, https://literacytrust.org.uk/research-services/research-reports/book-ownership-in-2024